STATIC!

Borgo Press Books by MICHAEL R. COLLINGS

STATIC!

A NOVEL OF HORROR

MICHAEL R. COLLINGS

THE BORGO PRESS

MMXI

STATIC!

STATIC!

CONTENTS

PROLOGUE

So she is dead.

The young man sat silently, hidden in deep shadow, sheltered by thick masses of star jasmine heavy with blossoms. The air lay still, cloying with the scent of the flowers, sweltering from the persistent heat. Fourth straight day of triple-digit temperature, and now, well past midnight, it was probably still in the high nineties.

No break from an off-shore breeze tonight. Again.

He tapped one finger nervously on the newspaper lying on the cheap wooden patio table next to him. The pages were folded to highlight the obituaries. The rough paper felt slightly damp.

She is dead.

It said so right there in grainy black and white, hardly more than a sentence outlining birth and death dates. No mention of family or survivors.

What will this mean for me, he thought, leaning his lanky frame against the creaking chaise and crossing his bare feet at the ankles. He brushed at his longish hair, still damp from a shower that had done little to cool him down, clearing his eyes.

He glanced toward his left, toward *her* house, knowing even as he did so that he would see nothing. The jasmine was too thick. That was why he was out here, after all, wearing nothing more than a bath towel loosely cinched at his waist, nearly naked. It was the coolest place he could think of, and there was no chance of anyone seeing him, even if he chose to loosen the towel to the hot night air.

He rolled a cold beer can back and forth against his forehead, thankful for the condensation that helped cool his skin. He felt sticky and slick with sweat, even after the shower. His eyes ached. He'd spent too much time reading freshman essays by a dim lamp, trying to keep the heat down. Should have stopped hours ago but….

He shut his eyes and tried to draw a deep, relaxing breath. The air felt thick and tasted stale from car exhaust drifting up against the mountains from the freeway that wound sinuously through the valley.

It was just too hot.

His mind drifted back to the obituary.

She was dead.

He sighed. The sound seemed oddly loud, disruptive against the heavy air.

Abruptly he sat straight up.

Had he heard something in the dense bank of river willows that bordered the back yard? Rustling, maybe?

He strained to hear but there was nothing now. He must have imagined it, or perhaps picked up on the movement of a squirrel or neighborhood cat. The willow branches hung in a thick veil to the ground, effectively hiding the broken-down slat fence between his place and the one behind him. The ground was so overgrown with weeds that in the months he had rented this place he had never even tried to penetrate them. He just pushed the antique reel mower that had come with the house to the edge of the willows and stopped there, usually streaming with sweat from the effort. No one seemed to mind the jungle-like growth. She certainly hadn't. Or at least she'd never said anything about it.

Or about much of anything else.

He took a long pull on the beer. It felt cool all the way down.

When he sat the can down on the old table, his hand shook slightly, as if he were nervous. Or frightened.

About what?

But now that the thought had passed through his mind, he

couldn't block it. He felt nervous. The sweat beading his brow seemed heavier than the heat could account for. His heart was beating slightly faster than usual.

Thrumm-thrumm-thrumm.

There. There was the sound again. Not so much a rustling as a faint, staticky buzz, almost below the level of hearing. If there had been any breeze that night, if the willows had been moving with even faint, ghostly fingers of wind, he probably could not have heard it.

But there it was.

He sat still, barely breathing.

It was gone.

He sat for a long while, not moving. Finally he reached for the beer again. The can was nearly empty. Maybe he had drunk too much too fast. Maybe he just *thought* he heard the sound.

He glanced over at the willows, their thin branches as insubstantial in the darkness as tendrils of smoke. The leaves seemed to shimmer slightly, just the faintest suggestion of silver as the leaves moved, stirred by...what?

Not a wind.

Maybe a cat. Or a squirrel. A fruit rat.

Maybe.

Finally the young man stood and stretched. He stepped to the edge of the patio, where he could see beyond the jasmine, and stared at the hedge that lined the left hand side of the yard. If it were daylight, he would be able to see the weathered gables of her house, barely jutting above the thicket.

At night, nothing was visible.

He waited there. Listening.

When he heard nothing more, he turned and entered the house, letting the wood-frame screen door slam lightly behind him.

In the yard, nothing moved. Except the willows, dragging slightly across the ragged grass.

CHAPTER ONE

The Greer had been dead for almost two weeks, but Nick Wheeler still shuddered inwardly at the thought of her. *Don't be a jerk,* he reminded himself furiously again and again during those two endless weeks. But whenever memories of the old woman surfaced like a bleached and bloated corpse rising without warning from the dark depths of a stagnant pond, he couldn't help it. He shuddered.

It was not as if he were a kid frightened spitless by a ghost story masterfully recounted over the embers of a dying campfire or anything like that. After all, for three interminable years he had been enrolled at least part-time in a Ph.D. program at UCLA—one class a quarter, that sort of thing. He only had a couple more years to finish the course work or the department would kick him out on his sorry ass, but by the time The Greer died he was not sure he still wanted to try to finish. Even with just a Masters he could usually pick up the odd class or two to teach at local community colleges. The slave wages they offered adjunct faculty was enough to make a few bucks, enough to keep alive.

There was a lot wrong with Los Angeles, Nick knew, but at least he could keep going, nickel-and-diming it semester after semester. With over a dozen small colleges within easy driving range of his place—coupled with a portfolio of excellent recommendations—he had a solid pool of part-time possibilities.

Within easy driving range of his place.

The idea was laughable in its own way, since that was how he had met The Greer in the first place.

Soon after arriving in Los Angeles, fresh from the hinter-lands of Montana, Nick Wheeler realized that he desperately needed a permanent place to live that would let him tap into the pool of part-time jobs while staying close enough for his course work at UCLA. Back then he still dreamed of writing a brilliant dissertation on some obscure Renaissance writer and winning fame and fortune—or at least a respected tenured position—preferably at one of the Ivy League schools. That would mean devoting as much time as he could to his research. And that, in turn, meant that he had to find a close, convenient place.

There was one additional requirement, even more critical given the state of his finances: the place had to be dirt cheap.

Rents were impossibly steep near UCLA. On his first day of apartment hunting, he had looked at a two-room cesspool with peeling hospital-green paint, visibly sagging walls, an exposed water heater in a screened-in back porch that the owner had advertised (with an absolutely straight face) as the "second bedroom," and a blown-out bare-wire bulb dangling from the living room ceiling, its worn extension cord twisted like a strangled idea. One straggling, black-branched apricot tree half his height, stuck like an anorexic tombstone in the middle of a weed-choked back yard, had been highlighted in the ad as a "flourishing fruit tree."

Hah!

The place had listed with the rental agency at more than twice Nick's total monthly income just because it was within five miles of the campus.

I can't live in a dump like this, he had thought as he shuf-fled his feet through littered newspapers and magazines strewn around the postage-stamp living room/kitchen combo. Trying to envision himself settling into that place gave him a chill down his spine, and he had beaten a hasty retreat back to his car where he sat for an hour studying the rental listings he had purchased at an off-campus housing center for $25.00. Nothing else nearby came even this close top fitting his strapped budget, and he wouldn't force his worst enemy to spend an hour in the place, so he ranged outward.

He began by drawing concentric circles on a map, focused on Westwood, and spending Saturdays scouring "For Rent" ads in Green-shoppers, all the while living out of a suitcase in the spare room at the house of a third-cousin-once-removed, his wife, and his three kids. The kids weren't so bad.

At first, in fact, the arrangement with Chuck seemed more than passable. Chuck had tried his damnedest to make Nick feel at home and cut through some of the inevitable Southern California culture shock, even though Nick had parted from Montana—and his folks—on rather less than cordial terms some months before. Terri, whom Nick had not seen since Chuck's wedding almost six years before, was both pretty and nice. Even the kids were fun, especially when, their breath smelling lightly of popcorn or of Oreo®s, the two older ones cuddled on his lap late in the evenings and fell asleep, their rhythmical breathing calming his nerves. It relaxed him, often putting him to sleep before the kids.

But there were problems.

His bedroom was originally intended as Terri's all-purpose room, so he had to live around an ironing board that seemed permanently rooted to faded gray Solarian® tiles, Kmart® bracket shelves littered with Niagara™ spray starch and dead bottles of Spray 'n Wash®, and, on every horizontal surface (sometimes including his bed) heaps of dirty and stacks of clean laundry. There was a touch of his own home about her lacka-daisical housekeeping, so Nick wasn't particularly bothered by the mess.

The baby's changing table was in there too, which, since Nick was the oldest of seven children, didn't bother him either...until the fifth or sixth night.

He was fast asleep that night, exhausted by the first day of graduate-school registration, when Terri shuffled in at three a.m. to change Esther. She was quiet enough, and Nick never did quite know why he woke up. But there she was, standing in her nightgown not six feet away, her figure outlined by the dim light from the hall—dim, but bright enough to glow through the silkily translucent material and give Nick a silhouette view that surely she couldn't have intended.

Staring through sleep-drugged eyes, focusing gradually on her hips and thighs and milk-heavy breasts, Nick suddenly became aware of coolness on his thigh and groin where he must have kicked the sheet away in the stifling heat of LA in August. He didn't wear pajamas or underwear to bed, hadn't since he was twelve and started sleeping away hot summer nights in the tree house he and his buddies built in the crotch of an oak tree in the far corner of the Wheeler's back yard. Now he wished desperately that he had gotten back into the habit. He didn't dare move for fear any sound would remind her that he was sleeping in the same room. If she turned just an inch or so, she would see him

He lay there, silent and still, but intensely, frustratingly aware of her nearness. His body registered that nearness with a rush of heat that made his temples break out in a sticky sweat. He tried not to breath, not to move, not even to slip his leg beneath the sheet and bend it away from where the hall-light glare cast a telltale shadow across his middle. His blood pounded so loudly that surely she must hear it and run.

Terri handled the baby with skill and dispatch—but then she had had enough practice with the older two. It couldn't have been more than four or five minutes before she finished, wrapped the baby receiving blanket, cradled Esther in the crook of her arm, and slipped out the door.

Nick felt stale pent-up air slip silently through lips suddenly desert dry. That was close. Too close. The tension had locked muscles until he could barely move. Instead, he closed his eyes and listened to his heart-blood throbbing in his temples and throat and thought *never again never again never again*. It was over. He was safe. He opened his eyes and glanced toward the doorway. She was standing there as if waiting for him—*daring* him—to look.

"Night, Nick," Terri whispered over her shoulder just before she disappeared down the hall. The light silhouetted her buttocks and legs where they shifted beneath the silken nightgown.

"Won't hear of it," Chuck said boisterously the next morning at breakfast when Nick suggested that it might be better for him to room with a student he knew vaguely from his undergraduate days and who was looking for someone to split rent on an apartment. "Won't hear of it. Nick. Waste of money. We got plenty of room here, don't we, honey."

Terri glanced up at Nick from an oatmeally mess plastered around the chipped edges of Esther's Care-Bear cereal bowl and smiled.

"Sure. You know we're glad to have you."

"That's settled, then," Chuck said, thumping his hand palm-down on the vinyl tablecloth as if making his decision as irrevocable as God blasting His commandments into the stone tablets on Mount Sinai. "You're staying here till you get something permanent. We sure as hell don't mind."

Terri looked up again and smiled. Nick looked down at his half-empty plate.

The next night he broke with habit and wore undershorts to bed. They felt strange after sleeping for so long without anything on, constraining and tight when he felt that he most needed at least the illusion of freedom. The elastic chafed at his waist and legs but even so it was better that way than without.

Terri never gave him any overt evidence of sexual interest but he felt uncomfortable the next night, and the next, when he woke at three a.m. to her soft movements less than an arm's length away. Both nights, she had exchanged her silky nightgown for shorty-short pajamas that barely covered her hips and buttocks. Even when, after the second week and at Nick's quiet insistence, Chuck moved the changing table into their cramped master bedroom, Nick felt uneasy.

For the moment, though, it seemed that the problem with Terri was marginally under control.

There was another problem, however, more personal and

more enduring and if possible more humiliating, largely because of the unpleasant memories it triggered. About two weeks into his stay, Nick began waking up every other night or so to find one of the older kids cuddled against either his belly or his back. Generally that made no difference to how Nick slept.

Unfortunately, little Billy—lovable as he might be—was still not quite housebroken, and Nick had an understandable aversion to rolling over in the middle of the night onto a damp spot and startling awake to a sickening wet squish and the too-familiar pungency of urine. The first time it happened, even before he was fully awake he grabbed himself to make sure his shorts were dry—then realized what he had assumed, even after all the years since he had finally conquered his own extended bout of childhood bedwetting. Stirring those memories made the experience even worse.

The worst, though, was that wetting the bed didn't seem to faze Billy. The damned kid could be spouting like Moby Dick—*thar she blows, sperm whale dead ahead, thar she blows*—and still be sleeping the sleep of the dead. The first time it happened, Terri calmly changed the sheets sometime the next day, neither apologizing nor explaining. Nick had said nothing to her about it, but that night when he slipped between the crisp sheets, he heard the telltale rustle of a plastic pad and within moments felt a sticky clinging of sweaty flesh against impermeable plastic.

It was hours before he finally dropped off into a restless sleep.

All in all, the arrangement at Chuck's was not conducive either to sleep or to study.

After a few weeks of frustration, bad nights, and constantly wearing jeans and T-shirts that were beginning to take on the distinctive odor of baby powder and stale urine, Nick grew desperate to find a place of his own.

As he ranged farther out from UCLA, he discovered with relief that housing established an inverse mathematical ratio: apartments got larger and rents smaller. But for a couple of weeks, the proportion still wasn't good enough.

Finally, he reached the outer circle of the area he had marked, the farthest he could go and not spend more on gas and oil for his car than he would save on rent. The most likely place for a last-ditch search seemed to be a tiny area among the inland foothills of the Coastal Range, in older bedroom communities mostly made up of forty-year-old frame houses on huge lots fronting wide, shrub-hedged streets. The area was not quite ripe for urban renewal, not central enough to sprout multi-level condos overnight. The houses sported sway-backed roof lines and erratically replaced shingle tiles, more than one cracked pane in side doors, and roaches scuttling for cover when kitchen doors creaked open. But the rents were lower. That was the key.

There, finally, he found what he was looking for.

Or rather, what, at the time, he *thought* he was looking for.

The address read 1475 Greensward Lane, Tamarind Valley, California.

CHAPTER TWO

The place wasn't much to look at, but for once the price was right. More than right, in fact. It was perfect.

The house was snug, in better repair than some he had looked at, true, and it was small but adequate. It sat well back from the street, half hidden by trees and over-grown brush years past their prime.

The rental agent, ludicrously if innocuously named Mr. Cleveland Brown and sporting a personality to match, seemed nervous. He hemmed and hawed (as Nick's grandmother would have said) as he slipped his key into the security lock, turned it effortlessly, and pushed the front door open. Even after the two of them entered the living room and Nick looked around at the emptiness, mentally furnishing it with his hand-me-down sofa and nicked end tables (currently in a rent-by-the-month storage unit), Brown kept glancing furtively from one corner to the another, as if there were something desperately wrong at 1475 Greensward. As if there were armies of termites hiding just out of view and waiting for a chance to carry Nick away bodily to some blood-stained subterranean torture chambers; or as if the walls might someday sigh as one and fall into a pile of rubble the first time a prospective tenant sneezed.

But Brown didn't say anything and Nick's poking around in corners didn't lead to anything tangible. Finally Nick just chalked up the agent's tension to a hot day and a frustrating job.

"You got a deal," he said after a long, slow tour of the house, its two bedrooms, cramped kitchen, laughably small bathroom (but then who wants to entertain there), and back to the living room.

Pressing the pen boldly into the paper, he signed the rental agreement.

That's when Nick first saw her name.

Emilia Greer.

Nick knew his Faulkner. He didn't care for much of it—anyway, Faulkner was four hundred years too late, as far as Nick's interests were concerned—but "Greer" was close enough to "Grierson" to trigger his memory. The name clicked the instant he saw it scrawled on the line marked "owner." When he got to her address, he looked up at the agent.

Brown's eyes had been following Nick's. He obviously knew where Nick was on the contract, and he read the address along with Nick: 1477 Greensward Lane.

He smiled—*a forced smile if ever I saw one,* Nick thought grimly—and gestured with one thumb over his shoulder, out the spotted dining-room window toward the house next door. It was some years older than the rental, larger at first sight but more ramshackle, shaded with vines twining through the shadows of the eaves so thickly that it seemed as if they—rather than any internal skeleton of studs and plaster—were holding the entire thing up. From a distance, it looked dark and…God help him, but Nick actually thought the word *foreboding*, like he was the faint-hearted heroine of some bad nineteenth-century pseudo-Gothic horror-pulp. He shivered and inadvertently wrinkled his nose, as if testing the air for the telltale odors of quicklime, decay, death, and, just possibly, a single disintegrating rose.

He looked across the room to see Brown staring at him. "Convenient, eh?" the agent said quickly—too quickly. The forced smile broadened, even though it still didn't quite reach Brown's eyes. "Yep, the landlady lives right next door. Sweet old thing, she is. A bit crippled, won't bother you a minute. Doesn't even want to check out the new tenants, left that all up to me."

Nick stared at Brown, holding his face as impassive as possible.

"It's handy for repairs," the agent continued, as if struggling to make up for some ineluctable deficit in his presentation. "Just call across the fence. Real handy. Whadda ya think?"

His voice sounded odd, tight. He also didn't look at the neighboring house—just pointed over his shoulder.

"Yeah," Nick said after a longish pause, sounding oddly reluctant even to himself, "real handy."

Brown waited without speaking, his eyes focused on Nick. A bead of sweat started just below the man's hairline—*were those hair-plugs,* Nick thought wildly—slipped down his rough skin, paused at the eyebrow, then slipped further along the cheekbone through an impenetrable five o'clock shadow and disappeared into his faintly stained collar like an insect burrowing its way into the living heart of a tree.

"Convenient," Nick finally murmured.

There was another long silence. No chatter about the paneling or the tiles or the handy location—no "just a couple a' blocks from stores 'n' schools 'n' such." The omissions should have set warning bells clanging in Nick's mind—*"the jangling and the wrangling"*—but they didn't. Nick was too relieved to find something—*anything*—to keep his budget from looking like a fatally wounded survivor from a war zone.

So he signed.

A quick flourish of the pen. That quickly, and it was over.

At first he noticed nothing unusual at the house next to his on Greensward...except that he never once saw, really *saw* Emilia Greer. The only time he came close was on the first day of each month, at 6:00 p.m. on the dot, rain or shine, smog or fog, when—plain white legal-sized envelope gripped firmly in hand—he trudged up the stress-fractured concrete walk to her house.

The first time, he clumped up half a dozen steps, crossed her wide, vine-choked porch, and pressed an old-fashioned round buzzer hanging lopsidedly on the door jamb. One buzz—more electrical crackle than musical tone. Before he could jab the button again, the door opened. Startled, he jumped back a step, then caught himself before overbalancing and recovered his poise. There had been no *creeeeeak* like there used to be on the only-in-the-boondocks reruns of that ancient radio show—*Inner Sanctum*, but Nick had called it *Inter Sanctum* when he was a kid wishing he could stay up and listen it instead of just hearing snatches it from his bedroom where he was safely hidden with his pocket flashlight beneath the sheet, wishing It, whatever It was for that week, would go away.

No, no creak or anything so melodramatic. Just a thin line of darkness opening on deeper darkness, but Nick's skin crawled and for a moment, a mad instant, he wanted to run back to his rental, pack whatever he could cram into his one scratched suitcase, and head like living blazes for home. His *real* home way up north.

In that instant, a thin, arthritically gnarled hand thrust out, claw-like, to grasp the envelope containing the rent check and an itemized receipt for minor repairs. Fifty dollars for the Roto-Rooter® man, $26.50 to replace a broken pane in the bathroom window.

That was it.

Before Nick could speak, could move, could do more than draw a single shaky breath, the hand withdrew, the door whispered closed, the dark slit sealed itself seamlessly with the ease of a Hollywood special effect, and the door became as one with the jamb.

Stunned, Nick backed down the step and across the lawn, unwilling to let his eyes shift from the old house, with its single, cyclopean window hanging above the porch line.

Not until he was safely inside his own place, listening to the water hiss as it boiled for a cup of herb tea, did he gradually realize how silly he was being. After all, he reminded himself curtly, it's not as if this were the Bates Motel or anything. It's only a sick old woman next door who likes her privacy.

Nothing to worry about.

The agent was right about repairs, though, as Nick quickly discovered. He only had to phone and explain the problem and her raspy voice would answer "yes" or "no, not this month." Once he tried to go over and talk to her about something—an odd and nerve-wracking *gurgle-swish-gurgle* occasionally erupting from the bathroom drains—but she wouldn't answer the bell. Only at six p.m. on the first day of the month. Otherwise, telephone only.

Each month, when Nick rang the bell, her hand would slither out, grab the envelope, and disappear inside. A few times he glimpsed an eye, a nose, once a whiff of white hair, but never anything more. The experience—repeated month after month—became increasingly unsettling. After a while, it seemed to Nick as if the house breathed a dank sense, not quite an odor, more a feeling than anything else.

There was, however, definitely no lingering scent of Miss Emily's desiccated rose. For that at least he was thankful.

Still, it was odd never to see her. Or rather, never to see her clearly. Sometimes he would catch a glimpse of her after dark, muffled in dark material that seemed more impenetrable bulk and blackness than clothing. Sitting at his desk by the open bedroom window, struggling through yet another set of stereotypic freshman-comp answers to such earth-shattering topics as 'Discuss the United Nations" or "Discuss the role of television in shaping American society" (assigned by the departments, not the instructors...certainly not by lowly part-timers), he would hear a muffled click as the door closed, then the light scuff of feet shuffling across the porch. He would see nothing until she was well onto the lawn. Then there would be nothing but an outline against the dim glow of antique street lights perched on concrete pillars like incandescent cormorants peering into paradise. Even then she was only an amorphous form, not quite human, a lump of darkness lumbering down the street.

Thirty minutes or so later she would return—her lumpishness altered not the least by her now facing in Nick's general direction. Against the streetlights at the intersection a couple of blocks away, she was still nothing more than silhouette. With another shuffle across the porch, she would disappear into her house.

Sometime during the third month of this, she ceased to be Miss Emilia Greer to Nick. She became simply *The Greer.*

Greensward was, as Nick quickly discovered, a sleepy street, inhabited primarily by retirees waiting (with varying degrees of impatience, it seemed to him) for death. Still, he would occasionally see someone walking an asthmatic dog, clipping a forlorn hedge, dragging a half-filled plastic garbage can down to the front sidewalk in anticipation of the Sanitation Department's weekly visit. Subtle though they were, there were signs of life around him. Everywhere, that is, except at the house next door. The only signs of life from The Greer's place, other than her phantom appearances, were the sounds and the lights.

The sounds came late at night, very late, after everyone else on Greensward Lane had doused their lights and gone to sleep. The first time, Nick was asleep, too. It was on a scorching night in late September, when he had his windows open to catch the few remnant snatches of breeze that had started earlier, fresher, at the beaches northward in Oxnard and Port Hueneme and somehow managed to make their way through low passes in the Coastal Range and into the valleys beyond. He struggled out of an uneasy sleep punctured with dreams that fled with waking, leaving only a bitter memory. His sheets were drenched with sweat and stuck like hot glue to his chest and stomach and thighs and feet. There was a moment of searing panic, of heart thumping and chest heaving. Then he heard the sound, really *heard* it, and knew with a rush of relief and gratitude that he was awake.

That first time, he couldn't place the sound. It was just an irritating *screeee*, back and forth, that rubbed against his ears like a child's fingernail against a classroom chalkboard. He sat up, hunched over almost protectively, and closed his eyes, concentrating on the sound and struggling to match it with an image, something visual to explain it away and let him get back to sleep. Finally he remembered the old swing half-hidden on the far end of The Greer's porch. He lay back on his bed, imagining her bulky form moving back and forth, back and forth, her weight forcing an eerie squeal from the rusting chain where it hung from a splintered beam. The image caught him and held him until, without knowing it, he slipped into sleep.

One night, perhaps a month later, he again woke fevered and panting, his skin sticky with sweat and his body exuding the thick stench of fear. He lay on his bed, forcing himself into an unnatural calm, and heard the sound. He sat up and, without turning on the light, tiptoed over to the window—tiptoed, in his own bedroom!—but he couldn't see anything. It was too dark. He slipped through the house, banging his toe on a kitchen chair and cursing softly, as if afraid of waking an invalid aunt... or something worse. He stepped outside into the back yard. Remembering it later, it seemed to him as if he must have been in a trance; he didn't notice anything, not even the coolness of damp grass against his bare feet assuaging the pain in his toe, or the cool night air brushing against his body—naked, the way he always slept now that he was safely away from Terri and Billy.

He followed the sound as far as the hedge between the properties. Squinting just right, he could see a dim shape swinging back and forth on the porch.

Screeee. Screeee. Screeee.

He watched it slip back and forth, back and forth, hyopnotically precise, until his head began swinging slowly in rhythm with the shadowy movement.

Screeee. Screeee. Screeeeee.

He watched and listened for what seemed hours but might have only been minutes. It was long enough to chill, at any rate. He shivered, a long tremulous quiver that started deep inside and rode his spine upward, down, out. Suddenly he became aware that he was standing buck-naked in his back yard, barely screened by a dense pyracantha hedge, playing peeping-tom on an old woman swinging on her porch.

Only the porch was empty and the sound had stopped.

A car turned the corner. Its headlights flickered over the hedge, bright enough to be a spotlight. He broke and ran like a frightened stag into the house, slamming the back door and leaning against it, breathing hard, the long muscles along his thighs quivering and hot.

Cops! For an insane instant he expected the police to come pounding against the door to arrest him for indecent exposure.

When they didn't, he somehow made it back to his bed without knocking over every lamp, table, and bookcase in the house. The room was insufferably hot, even hotter than earlier, and the sheets were damp and clammy. They smelled stale and acrid.

Even so, he slammed the window down and pulled on pajamas and cinched a full-length robe (a not-so-subtle Christmas gift from his mother three years before) around his waist and lay on top of his sheets, panting and sweating for hours before finally drifting into unpleasant, unhappy dreams.

The next time he heard the sound, the waking was less traumatic, the panic diminished. It was only a crippled old woman, after all, hoping for a cooling breeze on a hot night, sitting alone on an old porch swing.

The lights were more difficult to explain. He only saw them occasionally—maybe a dozen times in three years. The first time was late, about two a.m. He didn't stay out that late as a rule, but that day a friend from grad school had landed a job—a real job...full-time, tenure-track, benefits, and everything—and treated Nick to a blow-out dinner at the fanciest restaurant they could think of, that place along Balboa harbor made up to look like an old-time paddle-wheeler. The prices were outrageous but the food was almost worth it. In fact, watching Perry sitting there, white plastic bib hanging ridiculously around his neck, as he struggled with the assortment of forks, pliers, and corkscrews the waitress gave him to attack his bouillabaisse came close to being worth the price. Perry was more the TV-dinner type—with or without a TV.

What with drinks and everything, and then talking, and finally the interminable drive back to Tamarind Valley, it was at least two when Perry's antiquated Volkswagen rolled up in front of Nick's place. They talked a while longer, Nick got out, and they talked through the open window a few moments more before Nick finally waved goodbye and the VW stuttered down the deserted street, taillights bobbing at every rut and crack like apples in a barrel at a kid's Halloween party.

Nick watched until the car turned the corner and disappeared. He listened to the half-silence of early morning. There were stars shining, a rarity for Southern California, and he could see some favorite constellations from when he was a kid—Virgo, the Big Dipper, bits and pieces of the Little Dipper if you squinted just right. He scanned the sky for Orion but couldn't find it. Beyond that, he discovered that somewhere over the intervening years, he'd forgotten the names of most of the other stars and constellations. The discovery seemed unutterably sad.

Finally, he turned and walked toward the house but stopped halfway across the lawn. There was a movement, a ghostly movement more sliver or blue than white, coming from behind The Greer's.

He looked again. The windows facing his house were dead black, as if the faded and streaked muslin-colored draperies he could see from the outside were merely linings for heavier material that swallowed all light from inside. It struck him as odd right then, but he had *never* actually seen a light in her house at night.

Now there was something there, a moonlight shimmer on the leaves along the far side of the house. He almost went inside his place, then abruptly turned around and crossed the lawn to the sidewalk. He slipped through the darkness, trying for nonchalance in case anyone drove by, but in a few seconds he was far enough in front of her house to see the light flickering through a narrow window near the back. All of the other windows were dead black.

He stood there, trying to identify the light. When he finally did so, he had to go back years to when he was a kid in Montana.

The Wheelers lived in a small town. It was fair-sized, compared to others in the state back then, but after living in

LA, Nick realized that Montana-big was generally big fish in a small—no, make that miniscule—pond. The town was culturally backwards as well. One lonely McDonald's®, no Long John Silver's™ Fish and Chips, no Taco Bell®, no four-in-one drive-in theaters (or twelve-screen walk-ins, for that matter). No nothing, it seemed in retrospect.

And only one channel on the television.

More than a decade later, that single fact seemed incredible to Nick as he consciously framed the thought. After all, right that minute he could go home, swivel his chair away from his desk and turn on his portable Sony to pull in thirteen VHF channels and maybe fifteen more on UHF—plus Showtime®, HBO®, Playboy®, sports channels, news channels, rock-video channels, even a Japanese soap opera if he wanted. If The Greer ever let him spring for full cable, he could multiply that number by about twenty. Having only one channel must have meant that he had led an almost criminally deprived childhood or something without even knowing it.

Even worse, no one he knew had a color set. Nick didn't even hear about color sets until he was almost ten or see one for a lot more years. Everyone he knew watched the single offering on black-and-white, nineteen-inch wood-grain cabinet models.

He still remembered walking down the streets in late evening on long summer days, sometimes alone, sometimes with the guys, looking for fun—or maybe a touch of very minor-league trouble. The street would be pretty much deserted, with the little kids inside and the bigger ones heading out in a variety of jalopies and hot-rods for the Rimrocks and a hot night playing at sex. Usually mosquitoes buzzed through the night, but he and his little gang learned to ignore the insects. And all he could see of human life would be weird silver-blue lights from televisions showing black-and-white movies in dark living rooms. From every house, that ghostly flicker, spilling onto lawns and rose bushes and making them look like alien landscapes from another planet. He and his buddies didn't need books by King or Straub or Campbell or Koontz to fill their worlds with horror.

Werewolves and vampires and ghosts slithered through the silvery shadows even as they walked their own haunted streets. The mosquitoes buzzed more loudly.

The memory clicked.

That was what he saw through that tall, narrow window at the back of The Greer's house.

The light leaking out of the blackness of that house reminded him of a suppurating wound.

Distantly, as if an echo's echo, he heard an electronic buzzing.

He shivered and ran to his back door and hurried inside, switching on every light in every room as he went until he reached his bedroom. He never could remember going to sleep but he woke up at 10:30 the next morning, dressed to his shoes, sprawled on a rumpled corduroy bedspread, threadbare and faded, that dated back beyond his undergraduate days. His head pounded and his back felt stiff. Every light in the house was on. For an instant, he couldn't remember why, and when he finally did remember he felt so stupid that he had to laugh. Here he was, grown and a man, and afraid of the glow from a television screen!

After that he only saw the light occasionally. Each time it was late at night, after the normal life on Greensward Lane had gone to sleep. He never mentioned it to anyone and, after a time, he simply ignored it.

His years as tenant to The Greer, though largely uneventful, were thus stranger than they might otherwise have been, what with the lights and the sounds and his irrational reactions to them. Add to that the fact that Nick never once saw her, not fully, not even when they found her dead on the back porch of her house, and anyone could understand why Nick hated even thinking of her and felt unduly nervous about meeting his new landlord: her great-nephew, a fellow with the unlikely name of Payne Gunnison. Nick Wheeler didn't want to meet him at all, not this soon after The Greer's death.

CHAPTER THREE

Yeah, The Greer died.

Her death was as odd as everything else about the old woman.

For the last month or so, maybe twice a week a delivery boy wearing a uniform shirt from the pharmacy a mile away would bicycle up to her front walk and hop off, letting the bike wobble on under its own power until it thudded down on the straggly grass, front wheel still slowly turning, looking for all the world like something dying…or just dead. He would take the porch steps two at a time and hammer on her door. Nick could hear him clear across the lawn, so he could imagine what it must have sounded like to her. Apparently she never complained because the kid did the same thing each time and Nick never heard her yell at him. There would be the hammering, then silence, then the delivery boy clumping down the stairs to retrieve his bike and pedal off. The last few times he took the steps with less energy than usual but rode off faster. The kid never looked back.

On the last day, a thunderstorm built up in the northwest late in the afternoon, something unusual for Tamarind Valley in the early summer. The air was stifling, heavy; it had topped ninety degrees by eight a.m. and for most of the day it seemed like nothing was moving—no clouds, no insects, no birds, no breath of wind. Nick was working his way through a particularly wearisome stack of freshman papers, typing intermittently on a short story when the reading got too tedious to bear. In the background, his little portable Sony® TV chattered quietly—a creature-feature on Channel 9, full of moans and groans and creaking doors punctuated by shrieks. Just the right thing for the batch of papers that he really *had* to finish by the next day.

The temperature climbed steadily. The portable fan he had picked up on sale at Builder's Best® for $19.95 stirred barely more than a breath; when it did the hot air was almost worse than no circulation at all. He was stripped to his shorts, and already even they were uncomfortably clammy and sweat-damp around the elastic. His back stuck to the imitation leather of the chair. He thought about going to the bathroom for a towel to throw over the chair but the imagined benefits didn't seem worth the exertion required. Sweat beaded on his lips and forehead and neck; the saltiness stung where he had nicked himself shaving that morning. He could smell himself and the idea of a shower—or better yet a long, cool bath with a favorite book propped on the cracked porcelain tub—sounded better and better.

"One more paper," he promised himself, muttering into the silence. "Just one more."

At that moment, as suddenly as if the house had heard his resolve and decided to thwart him, the lights blinked out. The fan blades stuttered to a standstill. With a final shriek that tapered into static, then silence, the TV died.

Nick looked up. "What the hell!"

In the first moments of a power failure, things don't always register right. Whenever it happened to Nick, he habitually toggled the nearest light switch even though it would be obvious from the darkness everywhere in the house around him that it wasn't a problem with just one fixture.

This time was no exception. He jumped up, almost upsetting his chair, and slapped the light switch by the door. Up. Down. Up. Down. Pause.

Up-Down. Up-Down. Pause again.

UpDownUpDownUpDown.

Nothing.

He glanced out the window again to see if anyone else was having problems. It was difficult to tell in the daylight, but old habits die hard and Nick always checked at night when the power went off. His eyes weren't adjusted to the brightness outside; he blinked a couple of times but even so he thought he saw sparks and blue fingers of current dancing on the leads to The Greer's.

He crossed the room and leaned across the cluttered desk for a closer look.

Nothing.

He rubbed his eyes. They burned when the sweat touched them. The sticky heat was worse without the fan.

The sparks were just imagination, he finally decided. Imagination and fatigue—or boredom.

He heard a jingling whir and looked out again in time to see the delivery boy plow across the lawn, a packet tucked in the back pocket of his worn jeans so the white end of the pharmacy envelope stuck out like a surrender flag. The kid jumped onto the porch and began pounding on and off for three or four minutes. Nick was just about to yell out the window for him to be quiet when the boy stopped, jumped down the steps, and jogged to the back, cutting between Nick's place and The Greer's. Nick could see that the kid's forehead glistened with sweat. Dark patches crept from under his arms, along the back of his neck, and around his waist. He disappeared around the back corner.

Seconds later, before Nick had time to settle into his chair, the kid was back, running along the side of the house. He grabbed his bike and peddled up the road like the Creature from the Black Lagoon was just around the corner. Still wearing only his shorts, Nick ran through the house and onto his front porch, staying hidden in the deep shadow of the porch. The boy raced past two or three houses, stopped, turned, and pedaled slowly toward The Greer's. He stopped one house beyond hers—the place belonged to the Harrisons, an elderly couple who smiled and nodded to Nick whenever they saw him. The boy raced up to their door. He knocked, the door opened, and after a second he disappeared inside.

Everything's all right, Nick thought. The kid just forgot a delivery for the Harrisons.

But there had only been one packet, and when the kid entered the Harrisons' house, he wasn't carrying anything in his hands.

Nick shrugged and went inside. The fan was running again. The TV cut to an iced-tea commercial with some has-been football player falling backwards into a swimming pool. At least *he* would be cool. Nick's mind kept trying to argue that the boy had just forgotten that second delivery, that he had a message from the pharmacist for the Harrisons that he had remembered at the last second. Something like that.

But later, remembering that afternoon—the heat, the almost tangible sense of oppression, the chill that invaded his spine as he sat down and glimpsed the corner of The Greer's house and the electrical wires shimmering in the heat-waves—Nick realized that even then, even before he saw the white-shrouded corpse, something deep inside was telling him that he didn't want to go over to that house…ever.

He wasn't surprised when the siren wound up Greensward and died to a whine outside his window. He pulled on a pair of ragged cut-offs and went outside. Two men in blue shirts jumped out of a paramedic truck, grabbed bags and satchels, and ran up the walk. By the time they disappeared around the back corner, a police car had arrived as well, its bubble-gum lights flashing, siren wailing. Two or three minutes later, the ambulance pulled up.

Nick waited, watching the house, watching the knots of curious people that clustered here and there along the block. Not a soul ventured closer than the edge of The Greer's property. Most of the people were old and acted as if they were slightly more than curious about seeing death close up. Dress rehearsal for the real thing, Nick thought. Couples leaned against each other. One old woman, so thin that even from his porch Nick could see blue veins on her hands and arms, plucked nervously at a seam on her husband's shirt as if to ward off this implicit threat of his (or her) approaching mortality. The Harrisons stood near their front door next to the delivery boy. Nick could see that the kid was white and shaken. Cops were talking to the three of them.

Mr. Harrison looked up and, across the expanse of The Greer's lawn, caught Nick's eye. For a moment, Nick intuited panic…relief…fear—a complex of emotions captured in those eyes. The Harrisons walked every night in good weather, out their door, then right, up the sidewalk and away from The Greer's. They returned the same way: He never saw them walk in *front* of her house.

He started off the porch, intending to cross The Greer's lawn and speak to them. Mr. Harrison whispered something to his wife. She looked up, shot a single glance at Nick, and shook her head violently, then grabbed Mr. Harrison's arm. They said something quick to the cop and hurried inside the shadows of their own home.

Later, Nick grew increasingly convinced that he should have kept going and talked with them. He might have saved their lives.

Or maybe lost his own.

But he didn't go. Instead he retreated into the shade, sweating in the growing heat but unable to go inside…yet.

Fifteen minutes passed before the stretcher reappeared. He expected the paramedics to come through the front door of the house but they didn't. It was as if no one really wanted to stay inside. Instead, the two paramedics pulled the clumsy apparatus over the uneven grass from the back yard around the corner of the house and across the lawn toward the waiting ambulance. They moved slowly, as if speed wasn't a priority any more. The body was covered with a sheet and tied down in three places with black webbing.

The Greer was dead.

Nick had never once seen her.

Several days later, he received formal notice from Mr. Cleveland Brown that her heir, one Payne Gunnison, would take possession of the house at 1477 Greensward Lane. All agreements between Mr. Wheeler and the late Emilia Greer would be honored by Mr. Gunnison until the expiration of the lease, at which time they would be re-negotiated as necessary. Rent was due, as always, on the first of the month.

Nick didn't want to meet Payne Gunnison. If he was anything like The Greer, life on Greensward Lane might remain unsettling.

Or—given the right conjunction of nightmares—he could be worse.

CHAPTER FOUR

In spite of a perhaps understandable hesitation about even meeting the new landlord, Nick abruptly did much more than just that. In fact, even though the other man didn't know it, Nick actually saw Payne Gunnison the night he arrived in Tamarind Valley.

Nick was reading late, well past midnight. This time it was for pleasure rather than as part of an assignment. He was immersed in about the tenth reading of a Stephen King novel, *The Shining*—the classic about the haunted hotel up in the Rockies. He was just at the place where the topiary animals begin to move around and, taking his cue from the novel, had almost decided to wander into the kitchen for a cold drink. He leaned back in his chair, stretched, laid his hands on the armrest, and thought seriously about pushing himself up. But instead of getting up, he simply stared. Out the window. At nothing. He sat for five minutes, staring into nothingness and thinking thoughts that never quite found form enough to be remembered. It was just one of those absent lapses that happen to everyone at odd times. They happened to Nick more often than to most, maybe, and he had learned long before not to fight against them. Some of his best ideas came in intuitive flashes during such moments— images and ideas, sometimes whole poems and lines for stories.

When he came back to himself, he leaned forward again to pick up the book, having finally decided against the drink as too much trouble.

That was when he heard the car stop out front.

From the study window, he could barely see the pale yellow trapezoid of light that marked the top of a taxi. *Valley Cab, probably*, he thought, since that was the only company that regularly worked Tamarind Valley. The wan glow filtered through the leaves of a scraggly hibiscus, fragmenting itself into shards that were as much shadow as light.

A dusky cab, outlined by dim porch lights across the street, had stopped at the end of the sidewalk leading like a strip of molten lead beneath a flat-metal moon from The Greer's porch to Greensward. As Nick watched, a man got out, pulled a suitcase out of the back seat, leaned into the window (presumably to pay the cabby), and turned toward the walk.

Payne Gunnison had arrived.

For days, Nick had been trying to visualize him. The best he could come up with was a nightmarishly masculine version of The Greer, with fleshier claws and a bulkier shadow but still hiding like a festering malignancy behind a barely opened door. An unconscious image of some of Faulkner's less savory characters probably had filtered into the composite as well. At any rate, Payne Gunnison was not someone Nick Wheeler believed he would be thrilled at the prospect of meeting...and particularly not this close to the witching hour.

Before Gunnison made it to the sidewalk, Nick's hand flicked to the base of his flexible-neck, bullet-shaded study lamp and twisted. His room was suddenly dark—darker than the moonlit night outside. He sat at the desk without moving.

The cab left before Gunnison was halfway to The Greer's front porch. The man might own the house now...and Nick's, but as far as Nick was concerned both were still The Greer's. The name lay like a shadow over both places in Nick's mind. He wasn't sure he would ever change the way he thought about them.

But The Greer was dead!

Nick couldn't make out any details until Gunnison crossed in front of the window, and then Nick only glimpsed an outline—someone, a man, carrying a suitcase. Tall, possibly quite thin.

Beyond that, nothing.

He waited a little longer. The figure disappeared into the shadows that obscured the porch. Distantly, Nick heard the front door creak and saw a sliver of light—healthy, normal yellow incandescence from a light bulb—before the door creaked shut and darkness swallowed the house. No light showed through the heavily curtained windows facing his place. Nick hadn't expected it to. In his three years living next door, none ever had.

He waited ten minutes longer before he turned the light back on and hunched over the King novel. He read the next chapter. When he turned the last page, he looked up. *Someone was watching him*. He felt it, *knew* it—but all he could see through the window was the dark heap of shadows that was The Greer's house.

Still no light. Nothing but darkness, foreboding, imposing, looming against the distant, star-specked sky. The moon had dropped behind the trees.

He hated that house, he realized suddenly and passionately. Hated it...and *feared* it. It threatened. It intimidated. It seemed self-satisfied, as if, serpentine, it had just gulped down Payne Gunnison whole and was now sated, bloated, settling back to digest him and wait patiently for the next meal.

And that meal—baked, barbecued, or fricasseed—would be Nick Wheeler.

"What am I thinking?" Nick blurted out. He didn't need an answer. The sounds echoing from the walls of his study reassured him. He shook his head violently, once or twice, as if to clear water clogging his ears after a long summer swim. The feeling disappeared. In its place, he merely felt foolish.

He glanced at the pages on his desk, grabbed the book, and tossed it open onto the stack of freshman papers.

It slid off, taking most of the papers with it and scattering them on the floor. One of the books' pages ripped loose from its binding, the cheap paper rough and ragged along the inside edge. He looked at the mess and shrugged.

"Tomorrow," Nick said. Tomorrow he would straighten up

the pile, finish reading the papers, maybe finish the King novel again. Maybe finally buy a new copy to replace that one. It was falling apart. And it wasn't the first book he had literally read to pieces.

Tomorrow.

When haunted houses leave their pages and infiltrate real life, he thought, it is definitely time for a reality check, and then for sleep.

The next day was Friday, usually the one day Nick had no school assignments scheduled, either as student or as teacher. So without even thinking about what he was doing he slept in until well past ten o'clock, batting the alarm off the night stand when it began stuttering a short time after six, and sleeping on until his eyelids slit apart of their own accord. It felt late but he didn't know how late. The electric clock hummed along the baseboard where it had fallen face away from him. He could smell his own stale breath, the slightly acrid scent of his body after a long, hot night. The air touching his face was already stifling. He felt full and needed to relieve himself. But as soon as he pulled himself out of bed, the first thing he did was to glance across the lawn toward The Greer's.

There was no movement, no change, nothing to suggest that the house was now tenanted by anyone—or any*thing*—other than the old woman's shade. The windows were sealed by the usual layers of faded gray-white material. The door was clamped tightly shut. The porch remained an island of dusty shadow in the bright Tamarind Valley morning.

He went to the bathroom, took care of his most immediate problem, then wandered into the kitchen, started to pull out juice and eggs, and glanced at the clock over the sink. There was a note stuck to it with scotch tape. He suddenly remembered writing the note, remembered putting it up there, remembered why, and remembered that this Friday he hadn't planned on sleeping late. He shoved everything back into the refrigerator.

"Shit," he hissed as he strode back into the bedroom and threw on clothes...not the usual cut-offs and T-shirt, but slacks, a polypress shirt, clean socks, oxfords that still bore the remnants of their last polishing. By 10:25 he was out the front door to meet Perry Oppenshaw at UCLA.

Perry was visiting again, half for pleasure, half for business. He hoped to do some research at the University Research Library and to touch bases with his family before returning on Sunday to his teaching job in Missouri.

Nick had planned to meet Perry at noon in the walkways beneath the URL. He pulled into the only empty space in the only parking lot his sticker allowed him to enter—at least there *was* a parking space, he thought. Usually he had to drive around for ten or fifteen minutes before one opened up. He angled the car in, crawled out and locked it, and dashed across campus toward the URL. Panting, he leaned against the concrete supports and looked around. He had only seconds to spare before he saw Perry climbing the steps from the visitors lot.

"Hey," he yelled, waving and pulling himself away from the cool concrete.

"Hey, yourself," Payne answered as they slapped each other on the shoulder and grinned. As Nick has expected, Perry was full of news about his job, his students, his life in Missouri. They talked over lunch, kept talking in whispers that threatened to become too loud for Perry's temporary and cramped carrel on the fifth floor of the library, and found themselves still talking at dinner in Tiny Naylor's Drive-In in Westwood and then on the way back to the campus. Perry finally decided to break up the visit about 10:00.

"Early morning tomorrow," he said half apologetically.

'Come on out with me to Tamarind," Nick said as they stood next to Perry's Honda in the UCLA parking lot. The rest of the lot was almost deserted, only a few cars here and there to remind them of the crush of student life Perry at least had moved beyond. "I've got plenty of room. There's an extra bed just crying out to be used."

"Naw," Perry said. "I've already got a room at the Howard Johnson®'s by the beach in Santa Monica. Greatest view in the world. Chock full of chicks. Anyway," he continued, more serious now, "I don't want to lose any time getting to the URL in the morning. After all, this visit has already cost me more than half a day's work among the dusty tomes."

Nick looked guilty, and Perry grinned at his discomfiture. "No problem, Nick. I've got a lot done, really, but I better stay out here." The irrepressible grin broadened lasciviously as Perry ostentatiously checked his wristwatch. "And there's still time to get lucky."

Nick nodded and grinned back.

They said their good-byes in the parking lot, and Nick left.

He stopped about halfway home for a cola at a 7-Eleven®—something to keep him awake—and cursed himself for maybe the hundredth time for renting so far out. Of course, usually the only time he felt like that was when he stayed out too late, when he was tired and still had half an hour on the freeways to get back to Tamarind Valley. But when the feeling struck, it usually struck hard.

By the time he got home, it was almost midnight. The Greer's place was dark. No silvery light slipped out any unwatched windows to escape into the blackness. Nick slept well that night. No dreams, no nightmares.

He must have been more tired than he thought, because either he didn't hear the alarm when it blasted as usual at six or he forgot to set it when he retrieved it from the baseboard and returned it to the night stand near his bed. He had fully intended to get up early and attack the stack of papers, half still waiting like a silently guilty conscience on the edge of the cluttered desk, the other half spread on the floor and held down by the bulk of the King novel. But when he finally rolled over and squinted at the clock, it said 10:30. For a few moments he just lay there staring incredulously at the thin black hands, the second sweep humming industriously across the plastic face. He wondered how it could be so late, why he had slept so late, why he didn't feel terribly guilty about sleeping late, and why he was unaccountably fully awake.

Sometimes something out there in the waking world wakes you. It might be disguised as part of a dream, even a forgotten dream, but you know that there *was* something. The knowledge makes the transition from dream to reality difficult, at times even frightening. For an instant, you exist simultaneously, impossibly, in *both* worlds. And are not sure which you truly belong to.

This morning, *something* had disturbed Nick.

He sat straight up, breathing shallowly and harshly. He waited a moment, pulled in a lung-full of warm air, then leaned back on his elbows. An unusual sound filtered through the open window, a sound that was at once frustratingly familiar and oddly out-of-place, strange. He got up, stumbled over the clothes still piled where he had dropped them on the floor the night before, and looked out the window.

Or tried to. The bright daylight blinded him. He squinted against the painful light. For a moment, the light stabbed like a knife slipping into his brain and twisting sadistically back and forth, then his eyes adjusted and allowed him to focus.

Someone was out there.

A man, presumably Payne Gunnison, was working on The Greer's front lawn. On *his* front lawn, Nick emended, although he was not surprised that he still thought of the place as *hers*. The man had found an old hand mower, at least as old as the dinosaur Nick occasionally pushed across his own lawn. It had probably been hidden in the piles of rusting tools and moldering papers Nick assumed filled the garage that leaned against the back fence like an old tired warrior, sagging at the ridgeline, its side door canting from a single hinge. As far as Nick knew, that garage had never been entered in the whole time he had lived next door. But now, he noted, the door hung smartly from two shiny new hinges, and an unknown man was wheeling an old mower around the yard.

Perhaps Nick should have noticed more about the man at first, but what grabbed his attention was the yard itself. The Greer never seemed to care about the upkeep of her own place, although she had insisted through Mr. Brown that Nick's rental be at least marginally neat, with a monthly trim of the scrap of yard and an occasional pruning of the shrubs that shaded the sides and back. Though she had never communicated anything directly, he got the impression that The Greer would have insisted on his hiring a gardener had he become so lax as to let the yard go entirely to ruin.

But she apparently had no such qualms about her own place. The shrubs hung straggly and overgrown against the paint peeling in long strips from the ancient siding—in some places, the curled paint was as ragged and long and tenuous as eucalyptus bark. The lawn was heavily cankered, with random dead patches as brown as LA smog interspersed among an uneven dusty green.

Occasionally a neighbor boy, who seemed to be one of the few living souls in the area below the age of incipient senility, would trundle his family mower down the street, past the four intervening houses, and chop away at the excess, never quite finishing the job. The result always looked like a kid's attempt at cutting his own hair, shaggy in the wrong places, with weeds spilling over the cracked sidewalk like out-of-control sideburns. The kid's parents must have told him to do it, or maybe they paid him to, because he never knocked on The Greer's door afterward, never walked away stuffing a couple of tattered bills into a back pocket. He just killed the motor and trundled the mower back-up the street, its metal grass guard clattering irritatingly on the rough asphalt. He did a good enough job to keep anyone from calling the fire department about weed abatement or having the place declared a public nuisance, but he never put more effort into the job than a superficial once-over required. Even after he finished, the place looked shaggy.

But now this man, this stranger, was mowing with all the diligence of a homeowner about to put his place on the market. He was catching edges that hadn't been touched in years, exposing patches of sidewalk black with mildew and studded with snails and pill-bugs curled against the sudden light, and generally disrupting a myriad of other insects that had lived generations of safe, protected lives beneath the fringes of The Greer's lawn. He manhandled the machine back and forth under branches that had escaped from the discipline of being hedges to approach full-fledged jungle status. He had already trimmed the most egregious growth away from the split wooden pillars supporting the porch roof, piling the casualties like corpses neatly along the side of the house. From Nick's perspective, the yard looked like that famous long-distance shot of the Civil War dead in *Gone with the Wind*, the South's glorious dead in this case being represented by slaughtered oleanders and firethorns.

The man had apparently been hard at work since yesterday afternoon, or at least some time after Nick had left for UCLA, since no one could have done so much in only a few hours. Nick had only roused enough to hear the mower a few moments before—that was the *something* that had awakened him.

The yard was trimmed, the shrubs neat, the lawn manicured, even the sidewalks swept, everything more like it should have been in true-blue suburban America, as if Greensward were an archetypally Fifties street straight out of *Leave It to Beaver* or *Father Knows Best*.

Except that there was something wrong with it all. Something so wrong that for a couple of minutes Nick didn't even consciously notice what his new landlord looked like. He was captured, trapped, by the eerie sense that....

That The Greer's house was *naked*.

It was as if an old recluse, an octogenarian dowager wearing an ankle-length paisley dress and an age-stained bit of jet-beaded lace clasped tightly at her withered throat by a cameo-brooch, had been caught on the public streets by a street-gang and stripped, her sagging flesh and wrinkled skin exposed to ridicule. She could try in vain to hide herself with hands deformed by years of arthritis and pain, tears streaming from eyes too dim, too milky white with cataracts to see her attackers clearly. She could try...but her feeble attempts would only accentuate the horror of her nakedness.

At least that was what Nick imagined when he saw the man whacking away at knee-high grass, pushing the mower into dark secret places where no one—no *man*—should ever intrude. It was like he was stripping the house, raping the house.

As soon as Nick's mind defined the image, he laughed. The ravaged dowager vanished, and all Nick saw through his window was a tall young man his own age, dressed in sneakers and cut-offs, cleaning up a yard scarred by years of neglect. And the place was, after all, just an old house, more ravaged by time than many, but that was not so unusual. One couldn't expect an old woman, especially a *crippled* old woman, to climb onto the roof and replace broken shingles, or to straighten a lopsided shutter on the forlorn attic window that made the place look like it had a single eye in its forehead, forever squinting, winking evilly at him when he walked by.

"Enough," Nick said sternly to no one in particular. If every time he started thinking about what Gunnison was doing he began to fantasize that he was living next to Hill House, or the Overlook, or the House Next Door, or the House Beyond the Hill, then he had better get himself put away somewhere.

The thought made him smile.

Anyway, he decided after looking at it objectively for a few minutes, the house certainly did look better this way. The building had some interesting lines in the front design. At one time the place must have been professionally landscaped—the remaining growth attested to that in spite of its exuberance and wildness. Probably twenty or thirty years ago this was one of the neighborhood's showplaces. With a little water to green up the brown spots, maybe a dash of sulfur, and a little more judicious trimming, the place could be presentable. And one certainly couldn't complain about a new owner wanting to make the best of his property.

His property, Nick thought in a conscious attempt at reminding himself of the fundamental change in things. *His* property, not hers.

Nick shook his head, turned away from the window, and

headed to the bathroom. A few moments later, he was in the kitchen for a quick breakfast of juice and toast. Nick was not much for breakfast usually, but he did enjoy sitting at the table and watching the sun ripple through the hibiscus leaves that framed the window and spread into a solid bank punctuated with reds, yellows, pinks, and whites along the far side of his driveway, or listening to the birds or the breeze playing through the branches. Sometimes he read and time disappeared and he came out of his self-created trance about lunchtime…once in a while it would last until dinner. But this time, he didn't have that chance.

He was just treating himself to a helping of Knott's Berry Farm® raspberry jam on whole-wheat toast when the doorbell rang. Still munching, trying to lick away a blob of jam that had dribbled at the corner of his mouth, he padded through the living room and was reaching for the doorknob when he real-ized that he hadn't bothered yet to put on any clothes. His mind registered the fact, but too slowly, too late to do anything about his hand, which was already turning the knob and pulling the door open.

He stepped sideways behind the heavy wood-paneled door and peeped out, toast balanced precariously in one hand, rasp-berry jam still probably smudging his cheek. He decided later that he much have looked like a cross between a street urchin and the way The Greer looked when he had delivered the rent.

At first he couldn't see much. The caller was in shadow with the sun bright behind him. When Nick's eyes adjusted, he was startled, mostly because up close, the man from next door, who could be no one except The Greer's nephew Payne Gunnison, looked so normal. Nick was expecting—well, almost anything out of whatever weird film or novel you wanted to name.

Instead he found himself looking at a pleasant young man, perhaps twenty-five, with curly brown hair, deep-set eyes, and a bright smile. He was flushed from working; Nick could see trails of sweat along his ribs. He was still wearing only tennis shoes and running shorts but somehow that didn't seem inappropriate. He seemed quintessentially the outside type, the California sun-and-fun type, only there was something in the way he had been working that morning, and the way he stood there, half expectant, poised to move, that told Nick there was more to him than just that.

And as Nick had already learned, he was fundamentally wrong anyway—the man wasn't from California The letter from Brown had said something about Gunnison coming from back East. Nick had never been east of the Rockies himself; for all he knew, the man might as well be from Mars.

I must look like an idiot, Nick. thought, *staring out from behind the door like a crazy, sloppy old woman afraid to confront the world outside. Like The Greer.*

CHAPTER FIVE

The stranger shifted his weight from one foot to the other, then cleared his throat.

"Mr. Wheeler? Nick Wheeler?"

"Yeah. Uh, yes. I'm Nick Wheeler."

"I'm Payne Gunnison. Just moved in next door." He could have continued and said that he was the new landlord, that he owned the bedroom Nick slept in and the kitchen he sat in to eat his toast and drink his juice. Gunnison could have been a real shit about things—and, whether justifiably or not, Nick fully expected him to.

Instead he was just a normal guy, sweaty from manhandling a obsolescent mower that should have been retired years ago.

Nick's thought processes finally caught up with himself, and with his visitor.

"Hey, sorry for being so slow," Nick said. "Just got up."

"I didn't wake you with the mower, I hope. I waited until I thought it was late enough."

"No," Nick lied. "It was just time for me to get up. Lots to do today."

Gunnison stood silently for a long moment. Nick started to extend a hand and stopped just before his toast and jam dropped to the floor; then started to invite him in, and remembered for the second time that he was naked, so finally he just stood there too.

After a bit, Gunnison laughed, a light, refreshing sound against the already oppressive heat of the Southern California morning, then began again.

"I know it's pretty early and you don't know me. But I've got this little problem and yours is the only name I know in this town—in this half of the country, in fact. Except for some lawyer downtown, and I don't think he would be interested. I just got in the night before last."

"I know, I saw you."

Gunnison looked at Nick, rather oddly Nick thought. But then Nick's comment had itself been odd; he realized belatedly that, in some sense, he had just pleaded guilty to being nosey before he had been accused.

"Anyway," Gunnison continued, his face bright again and open, "I've run into a snag with the yard and need a little more muscle. Could you come over and give me a hand?"

That was it. He needed something. And yet there wasn't any hint in his voice of a hey-I-own-this-place-help-out-or-get-out tone. Just one neighbor asking another for a hand.

"Sure," Nick heard himself answering. "Give me a minute to dress and I'll be right over."

"Okay."

Gunnison waved and was gone.

Nick closed the door, ran to the bedroom, and pulled on jeans and sneakers, tugging his favorite T-shirt (with "Reality is a Crutch for People Who Can't Handle Science Fiction!" printed in red on the beige cotton—courtesy of Change of Hobbit in Santa Monica) over his head.

Gunnison was around the side of his house, on the far side, hacking away at a huge oleander. Severed branches lay neatly stacked against the wall. Gunnison had already trenched around the roots and was trying to dig the thing out.

The side yard was pretty well cleared; At least you could get from the front yard to the back without fearing sneak attacks by anacondas, elephants, or such like.

"Well, what do you want me to do?" Nick was startled to hear a small edge of anger in his voice.

Gunnison turned and smiled, as if he had either not heard the momentary tone or refused to identify it, and defused the situation with an easy gesture. "Mostly I think I just need leverage. I can't cut and lift at the same time. Lean into the trunk here, would you?"

He pointed. Nick leaned.

Nick was not normally an overtly physical person. In fact, it was all he could do to convince himself to jog a block or swim a couple of laps a week at the UCLA pool. But push he could.

The roots tugged and caught. Gunnison hunkered down, one leg swallowed by the tangled roots, his hand axe flashing in the sun.

The trunk gave an inch or so. Nick heard cracking and tearing underneath, felt the soil shift, jerked forward half an inch as the stump gave slightly.

"One more cut, maybe," Gunnison muttered. Then, louder, "Can you push harder?"

Nick could and did. The roots now hung dangerously over Gunnison's ankle but he didn't seem to notice. If he cut the last root and the trunk shifted the wrong way or if Nick wasn't pushing hard enough….

The axe blade dropped, glinted once in the sunlight before disappearing into shadow. Chips splintered in the dark soil. The trunk cracked, wheezed, and suddenly toppled, pulling Nick forward and carrying him with it. He found himself hands and knees in damp grass, his nose almost against the peeling siding on the house.

Gunnison laughed and reached over, helping Nick to his feet.

Nick brushed off his knees as Gunnison slapped his back.

"Thanks. It would have taken me hours by myself."

"No problem. That's what neighbors are for, Mr. Gunnison."

The other man nodded. Then very slowly, formally, ritualistically almost, he extended his right hand. "Payne."

Nick responded: "Nick."

They shook hands. Neighbors meeting, potential friends exchanging possible vows of commitment. That sort of thing, but without words to mar it. Nick remembered his wild wish not to have to meet the man and smiled.

"Come on in for a drink? Something cool?" Payne asked..

"Sure. Why not."

They walked to the front of the house and started up the steps to the porch. Gunnison took the rickety steps two at a time and had his hand on the knob before Nick had set foot on the first one.

And, in fact, Nick found to his horror that he couldn't take that step.

He stood motionless at the bottom of the steps, one foot firmly on the cracked concrete, the other raised, hovering in mid-air over the splintered wooden riser, frozen. He could not move up onto the step. *Literally.* He couldn't force his foot up. It was like standing self-consciously in the corner at a party, he thought, and having the prettiest girl come out of nowhere and say "Hi" and having your jaws lock so tight that not even a groan could escape and she would look at you like you were a genus-subhuman/species-geek and turn away and waltz coolly and gracefully across the floor to flirt with every other person in pants but you. He knew the feeling—knew it well—and hated it.

But even so, Nick *couldn't* take that small step.

Because of *her.* The Greer.

He had no business being here. It wasn't the first of the month. He didn't have a white, legal-sized envelope tucked in his pocket. She wouldn't approve. She wouldn't even answer if he *did* ring the buzzer.

And worse, she would blame me, he thought wildly, *indict me in the rape of her house, me, standing here idiotically, one foot off the ground, a hot bead of sweat trickling down my ribs and beneath my waistband as I stare at the naked openness of the porch and at her shadowed swing, her private place.*

Part of his mind kicked in, the rational, conscious part.

Don't be ridiculous. Look at Payne. He's an okay guy, maybe even a friend already, and you've only known him a few moments. What's to worry?

But he still couldn't convince his brain to send one simple message through his neurons to his muscles: *Brain to foot— move onto the first step, dummy.*

Already at the front door, Payne turned, looked down and Nick, nodded sympathetically, and said with something resembling a choked chuckle, "I know how you feel. That first night I got here, I almost turned around and ran to the nearest hotel. It wasn't anything specific, just a feeling that…. Anyway, that's why I decided to get the yard cleaned up so fast, to let in some light, get rid of some shadows. This can be a pretty scary place sometimes—and I didn't even know her. But wait till you see the inside!" He grinned like a ten-year-old kid with something secret—harmless, sure, but possibly crawly or slithery or creepy—hidden in his pants pocket.

That did it for Nick: this was a chance to see inside The Greer's cave.

Nick's conscious mind imperiously overruled any subconscious messages and the foot moved. It was hard—like trying to run on a dry sandy beach or to swim through molasses—but he moved. Up the steps, onto the porch, up to the door itself.

Payne had swung it open. The first thing Nick saw was an entry paneled entirely in dark, lightly grained wood that stretched up the walls and continued across the low ceiling. The floor was dark also, almost ebony. A thick curtain closed off the rest of the house; that material, too, was so dark as to suggest black. It looked heavy, stifling, like overstuffed Victorian at its worse—just what Nick would have expected from The Greer.

Payne held the door open, inviting Nick in.

Nick walked into the entry and waited as Gunnison passed and pulled back the curtain, exposing the interior of The Greer's house to light and vision.

For far longer than was strictly polite, Nick stood there, speechless, stunned.

CHAPTER SIX

Even as Payne closed the outside door behind him, Nick still didn't quite know what he expected to see; he had never gotten so far as to envision exactly what the inside of The Greer's place *might* look like.

Certainly nothing like the great haunted houses of folktale and film. After all, this was reality, not fiction. In spite of his wildest midnight imaginings, the old woman had been just that—an old woman, crippled and arthritic to boot, living in a modest house on a quiet street in a genteelly aging neighborhood on the outskirts of one of the world's largest, most cosmopolitan population centers. After all, Tamarind Valley wasn't some Lovecraftian backwoods New England village with its local variant of the monstrous Marsten House perched on a hill above narrow winding streets and randomly rotting eighteenth-century cottages, crouched and decaying on its hill like a revenant vulture waiting for everything within its purview to die and rot and live again in some unholy manifestation.

No, nothing like that. The house would be dark though, Nick was sure of that—dark and stale and creaking, like his earliest memories of his grandparents' farm house, rough-hewn inside and out, rarely aired, heavy with lingering scents of home-cooked meals long past and forgotten; of dust and old bodies that worked too hard and went too long between Saturday-night baths in a tin tub set awkwardly in the middle of the kitchen and replenished with gouts of steaming water from a teapot on the back burner of the cast-iron stove; of patent nostrums for man and beast that smelled heavily of mint and age, and half-filled bottles of rancid petroleum jelly perched on dusty window sills, and mentholated cough drops desiccating in the far back corners of bureau drawers stuffed with forgotten mementos of long-dead relatives.

It would be full of heavily dark Victorian furniture, probably. Massive stuff with carved ball-and-eagle-claw feet grasping at too-thick dusty-rose carpeting or fading embroidered hangings draped over heavy-grained paneling and drooping limply to the floor and swirling in ostentatious display onto the carpet. Perhaps oak plant stands darkened by the breath of years and hidden beneath gray-green sweeping fronds of Boston ferns dragging loads of accumulated dust and decay almost to the polished hardwood floor. Certainly an antique sideboard with a dust-silvered, flyspecked mirror above deep drawers secret with tarnished flatware bundled in flannel and fragile china so thin as to be translucent, patterned in languishing pink roses twined with ivy leaves.

He would have expected things heavy and old and dark. That was what The Greer suggested to him: things heavy and old and musty and dark.

What he saw contradicted anything he could have imagined.

He stared in shock at what lay before him.

Payne laughed, a brightly startling sound.

"Surprised you too, huh?" he said.

Nick nodded and stepped through the shallow entry niche, past heavy white curtains ruffled on one side and fastened with a white cord, and into The Greer's living room, still unable to find the right words.

The living room was white—starkly, literally white.

Everything in it.

Not that there was much. The walls gleamed sterilely, their white expanses unbroken by paintings or bric-a-brac. Heavy white draperies shrouded both windows, and a blank television flat-screen was built into one wall. The floor was carpeted in white; not an inch of bare wood peeped around the edge of the room. A white sofa commanded the center of the room; in the corner opposite the TV screen, hunched an armchair—Danish modern or something equally and stridently contemporary—done in white-enameled metal and white leather. That was it.

Otherwise, the room was as empty as the proverbial tomb.

No, there was one more thing, Nick noticed belatedly. Along the upper moldings, four white video cameras protruded from equally white brackets, one from each corner. He could see his own reflection in the nearest lens-eye—a small, dark, distorted blot against a flat, white background. Turning, Nick saw that the inside lining of the curtain he had just passed through was also white, dead white without any hint of the dark material facing into the entryway.

Payne laughed again.

"It's something, isn't it? The first night, I was so surprised I dropped my suitcase. On my foot. It hurt like hell later, but at the time I hardly noticed." He stepped past Nick into the center of the room.

"But...," Nick began.

"Not what you'd expect of someone like Aunt Emilia—*Great*-Aunt Emilia," Payne repeated, punctuating the first syllable with a mock bow. "But this isn't anything yet. Just the beginning. Wait until you see the rest of the place."

Unaccountably, Nick shivered. *Get out* slipped through his mind so quickly that he actually took a step backward, toward the front door.

Don't be stupid, he thought. It's just a house. Nothing to hurt me here. Just an old house. The floor plan's probably just like mine. I could probably find my way around here in the dark, blindfolded.

By that time, he had started forward to follow Payne.

Payne opened a door thick with matte white enamel that reflected no light; the panel was as depthless and as deep as time. He led the way into a corridor. Here the whiteness was less pronounced, in part because there was barely any light and in part because the carpet ended at the door and the hallway floor was gleaming wood, dark and thickly veined and polished to a mirror gloss.

Nick felt like tiptoeing, afraid that even his sneakers might scuff the finish.

He entered the hallway. The temperature dropped appreciably as soon as he was out of the white living room.

He walked down the cool dimness, staring.

At rigidly, precisely measured intervals along the wall hung over a dozen certificates. Most were framed in modish brushed silver aluminum and covered with unmarked squares of non-glare glass. Each bore the name of *Emilia Kent Greer*. Nick counted three doctorates—engineering, electrical engineering, and physics—and assorted master's degrees surrounded by certificates of merit or achievement from the National Association of This and the International Association of That. He didn't take time to read each of them.

He simply stared.

Payne laughed again, only this time the laughter was tinged with nervousness.

"No one in the family knew anything about *this*," he said, gesturing to the walls. "As far as I know, everyone just thought that she was a slightly dotty old lady who lived out in Hollywood."

Nick touched one of the frames with his finger.

'I mean," Payne continued, "none of us had *any* idea. I barely knew her name, let alone that she had so much education. I don't know how or why she kept it from the family all those years, especially since the best any of us has been able to do is to get an occasional BA. You'd think she would be proud of what she accomplished. I never even finished myself, still have a year or so to go. Everyone in the family I talked to before I came out here figured her for a lonesome old crank who chose to hole up in California. Mom had no inkling of anything like this. As far as the family was concerned, Great-Aunt Emilia was an old weirdo, like the other weirdos out west.

"Obviously none of the family had ever been inside *this*

place, or they would have added levels of weirdness to their descriptions. I'm still trying to figure things out, and I'm right here, staring at all of this." He reached out toward one of the certificates, stopping just as his finger was about to touch the spotless glass.

He laughed again, even more nervously, and pulled his finger away. "Don't want any fingerprints here," he whispered in a mock-conspiratorial tone.

"Come on," he said after a second, this time in a more normal voice. "There's more." He gestured down the hall. Nick followed him, a step behind.

Payne opened the first door. There was no telltale creak, no Inner Sanctum *screee*, just the smooth silence of well-oiled hinges. The room had originally been a bedroom, a few square feet larger than Nick's own next door. Now it was empty except for its white carpeting and draperies, a white cloth-covered sofa, a brass floor lamp with white shade, and a flat-screen built into the wall facing the sofa.

"Come on in," Payne said to Nick. "Look." He pointed to a corner. A camera hung from a swivel bracket in the ceiling, like the spy-eye in the local banks—and like the four in the living room.

"Video camera," Payne explained. "It works. Picks up anything in this room, like it zeroes in on sound or movement. I've tried it. It's eerie."

He backed out of the room and disappeared before Nick had a chance to move. Nick heard the other man's voice from behind him.

"Now try this for weirdness."

Nick left the bedroom, oppressed by the brightness, the unalloyed whiteness that seemed blatantly symbolic without any referents that would help him interpret the symbol.

He didn't like the feeling.

The next room was a bathroom. Again, everything was white, including the heavy curtains hanging stiffly in front of the enameled tub as if femininely, modestly hiding the interior from their prying masculine eyes. And again, there was a silent television screen in the wall across from the tub, making the tub look like an *avant-garde* couch. In the opposite corner, another of the ubiquitous video cameras stared blankly down at the head of the tub, reflected in the gleaming silver fixtures. There wasn't a single water spot or splotch of soap film on any of the metal in the room. Nick did notice, though, that the toilet lid was up; Payne apparently had picked up the same bad habit he had, one that his mother and sisters had screamed at him about for years.

"In the bathroom?" Nick asked finally, looking up at the camera.

Payne shrugged his shoulders and grinned. "Great-Aunt Emilia must have had some interesting personal habits."

Something about Payne's voice—an almost little-boy sense that they were sharing intimate not-to-be-spoken lightly secrets about adult mysteries—caught Nick unaware, and suddenly he was grinning back at Payne as if the two of them had been pals since kindergarten and could communicate without words as well as with. The chill of the gleaming bathroom warmed slightly, and Nick felt the muscles along the back of his neck and shoulders loosen, even before he had become aware of how tight they had been since he had entered The Greer's sanctuary.

"Come on," Payne said, interrupting Nick's reverie. "There's more and merrier."

Opposite the bathroom was another bedroom. This one had a single-width bed with a white-painted pine bedstead and thick white comforter tucked beneath a plump pillow. Except for its by-now typical monochromatic effect, the bed seemed out of place, too soft, too fluffy, too feminine for the crisply mechanistic atmosphere of the rest of the house.

In addition to the bed, there was only a small matching dresser with neither mirror nor tangle of personal effects on the glossy white top...and a television screen in the opposite wall and a video camera on the ceiling.

At the foot of the bed, a pair of worn blue jeans rumpled on the floor jarred with the pristine clarity of the room. The twisted elastic band of a pair of undershorts peeked out from the waist-band of the jeans, and the soiled toe of a white sock from one of the pant legs.

Payne strode into the room and swept up the jeans with a smooth movement; there was a faintly dark spot, no more than the shadow of the shadow of dirt, where one scuffed knee of the jeans had rested overnight against the soft, white pile. Payne pulled open the closet door and tossed the clothing into the waiting darkness.

Nick had an image of a mouth opening, swallowing, closing again.

"Sorry," Payne said, "I try to keep the place up better than that. I don't want to get into any bad habits, living alone. Tends to make one sloppy."

Nick remembered his own bedroom.

"Hey," he began, intending to move into some such cliché as "it's your house," or "you should see my place," but the words refused to come. In fact, Payne's action seemed eerily—perfectly—appropriate and necessary. Instead of speaking, Nick nodded.

The kitchen was at the back of the house. The windows seemed grimy but were so only from the outside. Nick realized that these were the first windows he'd seen that actually revealed the outside world, and even they were so thick with dust that the elms along the back fence were little more than monstrous black shadows against a backdrop of gray. All of the other windows in the house had been tightly draped or curtained. It took him a moment to realize that all of the dust and caked-on dirt was on the outside; the inside surfaces glistened spotless and smooth.

Other than the outsides of the windows, though, the room was as immaculate as the rest of the house. Dead-white refrigerator, dead-white stove, dead-white enameled cupboards tightly—virginally—closed, dead-white linoleum tiles without a mark or scratch. And a television screen in one corner, video camera hanging in the opposite corner.

By this time, Payne had simply ceased commenting. He

leaned against the white Formica® counter and waited for Nick to speak.

Nick was beyond words.

CHAPTER SEVEN

"Come on," Payne said finally, tugging at Nick's elbow with a familiarity that Nick—by nature reserved and isolate—found at once surprising and engaging. "One more room to go. The best."

The last room should have been the back corner bedroom on the side farthest from Nick's place. Payne paused before pushing the heavy door open. "Behold...."

Nick was ready for white walls, vast emptiness.

The walls were covered, floor to ceiling, with dozens of shelves sagging beneath the weight of books, machinery, files, boxes, tapes, with garishly colored plastic sleeves and bright paper dust jackets and glittering metallic knobs and dials vying for attention. After the starkness of the other rooms, it seemed a mad flurry, a frenetic kaleidoscope, a riotously proliferating insanity of shapes and textures and patterns and colors that baffled and offended.

It was larger than the other rooms, Nick noted slowly, apparently originally intended as the master bedroom.

They stepped silently into the room. One wall was devoted to equipment: two flat-screens, three DVD consoles, half a dozen recorders and players of various sorts, amplifiers and speakers and knots of wires leading from and to like overgrown vines in a tropical jungle. Nick recognized some of the consoles; others looked strange, alien. But then, he reminded himself, he wasn't exactly a triple-Ph.D. in electrical engineering and physics.

In the center of the room—and Nick would have been willing

to bet his next month's salary that it was the mathematically *exact* center of the room—rested a black high-backed swivel chair, soft and heavily padded, more substantial than any of the other furniture he had seen. The windows opposite the chair were tall and narrow, inset with frosted glass so that they looked like the stained windows in a church where the curtains were pulled back to admit thin, twin shafts of light. This, Nick realized, was where the monster oleander had been growing—and where the silver-blue flickering had come from late at night.

"The master control room," Payne stage-whispered.

"What?" The sound startled Nick. His voice sounded sharp and strained, even to him.

"The master control room. The MCR. That's what I call it. I haven't had time to try much of this stuff yet, but I think that this bank of panels controls all of the screens and cameras in the rest of the house. Plus hidden speakers in every room, with state-of-the-art quadraphonic digital sound. They must be plastered over or something. I haven't found any yet, but I wouldn't be surprised if you can hear perfectly from any spot in any room."

Nick nodded mutely.

"These are records and CDs and VHS cassettes and DVDs," Payne said after a brief silence, indicating a long cabinet built into one wall. He continued around the room, point to items as he walked. "Tapes...what look like professional journals and books...I think these are her research notes."

There was an odd emphasis on *her*, Nick noted.

"And this," Payne said, standing back, "this, as far as I can tell, is her library of probably every movie made in the last seventy years." He gestured grandly to the wall along the back of the house and the inner wall that had been initially hidden by the open door. Both were covered with small plastic cases neatly lined in rows, small white dots placed precisely in the middle of each exposed edge.

"What?" Nick was beginning to hate his inability to say anything except that one word.

"Well," Payne said, "maybe not *every* one. But a helluva lot of them. There's a list over there with a name for each of the numbers on the cases. I checked it out the first night —I couldn't sleep in that monk's cell up the hall, especially knowing that was where *she* had slept...and died."

Nick shivered at this, unaccountably and violently.

Payne seemed unaffected by it, however, as he continued. "So I got up and checked the films out. I looked up some of my favorite films. Every one was there. *Every* one. And most of the other movies that I've ever heard of."

"What was she doing with them?"

"No idea. There's nothing in her notes that I can understand, and besides most of them are dated seven or eight years ago. It looks like she just spent the last few years collecting cassettes, polishing the hall floor, and going quietly blotto." He glanced around the room and lowered his voice. "But she was sure as hell brilliant at one time."

Nick crossed the room to look at the shelves of equipment more closely. Payne was right about at least one thing. Most of the stuff looked old, well used. It was cared for but lacked the pristine glimmer of newness. Besides, he hadn't seen anyone carry electronics equipment into the place in the three years he had lived next door. Except for the delivery boy, he hadn't seen *anyone* approach the place. He examined the monitors and consoles for labels and brand names but couldn't see any. Maybe the old lady had hyped up things herself, keeping her hands and mind busy. "The Word Processor of the Gods" and that kind of thing. *Idle hands*, as his grandmother might have said.

He reached out to touch the control panel of a DVD unit. Just to touch it, the way someone does when he can't quite believe that a thing is there, or, perhaps more accurately at the time, the way children do in an antique shop when they're told not to touch anything but the temptation to run a finger along flashing crystal or polished wood surface is just too great to withstand. Nick didn't intend to turn the DVD on. Later, he was sure of that. In fact, he wasn't consciously aware that he was about to make contact with the dark plastic and bright aluminum of the casing.

But he did. Marginally, briefly.

As soon as he touched the cool surface, something crackled viciously and a thin arc of electrical blue sparks curled around his fingertips.

For the instant that the static charge played along his flesh, he felt that time had stopped. And more than that. The blue flickering seemed...more than what it was. It didn't so much burn—not even the tingling burn/not-burn of electricity—as tug at him, pull at something Nick felt instinctively was *essentially* him. A memory flashed through his mind of being seventeen and of a painfully persistent tugging, pulling deep inside that stretched across his abdomen from his gut to his groin and that he had suffered in silence for three months before he got up enough courage to overcome his fear of finding out he had terminal cancer or of having to admit to things he had done late at night in the secrecy of his bed and that he, in his ignorance, half-believed had hurt him horribly inside, there in the focus of his manhood. It took him three months to admit his pain to his parents and finally go to the doctor, only to discover that it was *just* a hydrocele and that *all* the surgeons would have to do would be to cut him open and pull one of his balls from its scrotal sack and remove the fluids and then shove the ball back inside and sew him up *nothing to it, a little soreness for a while, buck up lad*—and *that* had frightened him more than the drawing pain or the threat of cancer or even the fear of discovery. *That* had threatened the core of his self, his masculinity, his new sense of maleness and sexual potency, even though the operation itself had in fact been more anti-climactic than traumatic.

But the memory of that pulling sensation, of the feeling that something was tugging at his core, pulling at his sex itself and trying to pry it loose—that memory was startled back into life by the subtle play of blue electricity that crackled around his fingers and seemed intent on sucking whatever was essentially Nick Wheeler through the blunt ends of his fingertips. The light crackled once, twice, then died.

The memory died as well. The drawing sensation in his abdomen faded with it.

But all of this was the matter of an instant, the time it took for him to draw a single breath and release it in a whoosh of sound.

"Shit!" he yelped, jumping back, wide-eyed and breathing shallowly in counter-rhythm with his accelerated heartbeat. He was not hurt exactly but was so startled that for a minute he was afraid that he might have wet his pants. He shoved his fingers into his mouth and sucked on the tingling tips.

Payne spun to face Nick. "What...?"

Nick jerked his fingers out of his mouth, aware of how silly he would feel if Payne saw him standing there like Jordy Verrill trying to suck meteor-shit off his fingers. He grinned—probably a sickly attempt but at least an attempt—and studied his hand. He could not see anything. Not even redness.

"It shocked me," he said, gesturing with his head toward the glistening machine. "Nothing much, though. No damage," he concluded.

But Payne was already at his side, considerate and solicitous. "You okay?"

"Yeah," Nick said, shaken but recovering. He stared at his fingers. Not even a slight redness. Nothing but lingering heat and tingling that started at the tips and died where they met at the center of his palm. "I'm fine. Just startled."

Payne stared at the DVD player, careful not to come in contact with it. "I'll have to get someone out here to check on that. Can't have guests barbecued in my own place." He leaned over the casing and peered into the darkness behind the unit. "Maybe a faulty plug or something. I'm no expert on electricity. I can't even see a light or anything that shows the thing is plugged in, but I can't tell unless there's a red idiot light on the front or something."

He was talking out of nervousness as much as anything, it seemed to Nick.

"It's okay," Nick said again. "Don't worry."

Payne faced him and stared at him for a moment. Then he

broke out into that infectious grin and nodded toward the open kitchen door just visible through the doorway.

"Drink?"

"Sure."

Payne steered Nick into the kitchen, sat him down at a white bar stool and pulled a couple of cans from the fridge.

Payne poured beer into two tall, clear glasses, talking all the while, as if assuring himself and Nick that Nick wasn't more than just shaken up.

"Not much current in there, I think. Not enough to do any real damage, for sure. Still feeling okay?"

"Just tingling," Nick said absently, rubbing his fingertip along the rough seam of his pants.

"I'll have that looked at next week. Don't know much about it myself, but it shouldn't take much to get it fixed. The stuff looks like good quality, probably just a short that nobody could have expected. Maybe I didn't luck into such a good deal after all. You would have thought, to hear my relatives talk, that I had inherited the Taj Mahal." He slipped into a broken falsetto, apparently intended to suggest the inimitable vocal qualities of an Aunt Matilda or Second-Cousin Harriet. "Two houses in Los Angeles and property downtown, why, you'll be rich Payne dear, rich and then when us poor relatives come out to visit we can see how the filthy rich live out there in California, only we probably won't ever be able to afford the trip and you probably won't want us cluttering up your life once you get to be rich yourself, it's not as if Aunt Emilia couldn't have divided things up a little more evenly, after all I used to write to her every Christmas and on her birthday and...."

Nick tried to listen, but he couldn't.

Payne kept talking about his relatives and Pennsylvania and the flight to LA, pausing only to take deep drinks from the cold glass in his hand. Nick's glass sat untouched on the counter. Payne's voice surrounded him, higher pitched now, almost whining, but Nick didn't hear it. All he seemed to hear was the crackle of electricity as it had entered his body—as it had tried to invade him, to pull and tug within him, then suddenly pulled back and died away.

He heard the crackle again in his imagination, and again, and again, and each time he felt as well the cold wash of night air on his naked body and the prickling of icy blades of grass along the bottom of his naked feet as he crouched in the shadow of a night-black bush months before.

The crackle had sounded like the squeak of The Greer's porch swing, creaking and squealing through the silent darkness of dead night.

CHAPTER EIGHT

Nick didn't blame Payne for the shock, not really. After all, it could have happened to anyone, at any time. It was probably just a short in a piece of well-used equipment.

So he thought at the time, at least.

He did get out of the house pretty quick, though, as soon as he emerged from his trance-like thoughts sufficiently to finish the beer. Payne was still wandering on about people Nick didn't know, would never know, would never want to know.

"Hey, uh, thanks, but I gotta go," Nick said in a brief moment when Payne fell silent.

Payne looked at him and grinned. Damn, Nick thought, it was such an infectious grin. Every time, just when he was ready to mark the guy off as a nothing—or worse, as someone too odd to want to get to know—out would come that smile and everything would change.

"Sorry," Payne said, still smiling but infusing a note of seriousness into his voice. "You know, about the shock and about blithering on. Haven't had a chance to talk to anyone for a while and you just got drenched in the overflow. Must be homesick, I guess. Or something."

"Yeah. Sure," Nick said. "I understand." And the funny thing was that he really *did* understand. Nick was a loner as much by choice as by circumstance, but he still knew just what Payne meant.

Payne stood and opened the kitchen door into the back yard, inviting a welcome breeze into the still air of the house, as well as a brilliant shaft of light into the dimness. That warmed Nick to him as much as anything else the man had said or done—somehow, Nick didn't want to re-negotiate the dark internal corridor through the house and then cross that antiseptically sterile living room again.

They chatted for a minute or two at the back stoop, mostly about what Payne was planning for the yard.

"I'll probably paint the garage this month, pretty soon at least, maybe even re-shingle it before the rainy season—it does rain out here, doesn't it?"

Nick nodded. "Some."

"Yeah," Payne continued, almost more musing than conversing, "before it rains. Then I want to take down that fence and put up a slump-stone wall. It's safer and sturdier. And I've got to figure out what to do between our houses, whether to let that hedge stay or replace it with something more permanent."

He was off and running again, Nick saw.

"Look, Payne," he said, aware that he was interrupting but needing to get away and think. "Thanks again for the beer. But I got a pile of freshman papers higher than your fence waiting for me, and if I don't get to them they may start to mold and then be even worse than they are now. Maybe they'll spawn and multiply." Payne apparently remembered enough about school to crack a grin at that one. "Really," Nick finished, "I've got to get going."

"Sure," Payne said. "Sorry. And thanks for the help."

"Help?"

"You know, the roots, the bushes."

"Yeah. No problem." *The roots.* It had only been an hour or so, but Nick felt as if a lifetime had passed since he had leaned his shoulder into the unyielding flesh of the oleanders and pushed, watching Payne's legs twist as he struggled to slash away the heart of the tree. "I really wish I could stay, but…."

With that he started away from the door.

"Nick."

He turned.

Payne stretched out his hand. "Thanks, neighbor."

Feeling more than a little foolish, Nick shook Payne's hand. The hand was strong, the skin of its palm warm and dry. Nick wasn't used to shaking hands. No one he knew did it much, and he had trouble remembering the last time any of his acquaintances had actually initiated such a ritual. Usually they held back, keeping to their own spheres and not inviting anyone else in. But Payne pumped up and down once, twice, then relaxed and let Nick's hand drop..

"See you around," Payne said, then disappeared into the house.

Nick spent the rest of the day laying down, trying unsuccessfully to read, trying equally unsuccessfully to ignore the tingling in his fingers that recurred, dissipated, recurred at odd intervals throughout the long afternoon.

"Much more of this," he finally said several hours later, "and I'll have to see a doctor." Once he went so far as to pull out his old brown address book and begin looking up his doctor's emergency number, but the sensation died away before he dialed the telephone and for some reason he decided not to after all.

By the time he went to bed just before midnight, he had forgotten the tingling; by morning, it was as if he had never received the shock at all.

* * * * * *

The two men didn't see much of each other over the next week. Payne was busy most of the time, coming and going throughout the day. He was usually dressed in a business suit, so Nick supposed he must be taking care of the legal details relating to The Greer's estate. The two weren't unfriendly or anything; whenever Payne saw Nick he would wave and call out a greeting, and vice versa. They simply didn't have time to get together.

Nick kept pretty much to himself. The one class he was teaching nights at Camarillo College was approaching end-term, which meant additional sets of examinations and research papers to read, usually during the late evening and early night when the unseasonable heat was more bearable. During the long, hot days, he spent as much. time as he could spare at the beach, away from Tamarind Valley and the heat and the smog.

When the next weekend rolled around, Payne seemed to have left town. At least he wasn't visibly in residence in Tamarind Valley. The house next door to Nick's lay dark and still. No shadows moved inside the part-opened draperies, no one puttered in the yard, even though the manicure job on the front lawn remained unfinished and grew more ragged each day. Nick had not seen Payne leave; but then, Nick reminded himself early Saturday morning as he glanced out his bedroom window and noted that the house seemed strangely neglected, he wasn't his brother's keeper—or his landlord's. He wouldn't join the frustrated Soap Opera set and stand by the window watching the latest doings next door.

The Harrisons apparently did, though.

Late Saturday afternoon, Nick was enjoying the quiet on his porch. The remains of a cold beer was balanced on the floor beside him, the last of the current research papers fluttered loosely and mostly unnoticed in his lap. The few people his age that lived in the area had apparently packed up much earlier and were now probably at the beach. They should have been; it was perfect beach weather. But, on the other hand, that also meant that the masses were no doubt jammed shoulder to shoulder on the beaches. Nick had decided to remain at home and take advantage of an unusual cool breeze swirling down from the mountains and freshening the air in Tamarind Valley. So he was lazing on the porch. The street at the end of his walkway was quiet, dead, not a car moving. He dozed for a while, roused when the papers slipped with a quiet, fluttery *thwump* onto the wood planking of the porch, then sat back again, half asleep and half awake and not really caring which of the two states would win.

"Hello, there."

A sprightly, almost strident voice startled him. He jerked awake and simultaneously recognized the voice as Mrs. Harrison's.

As was their habit in the late afternoons, she and her husband were out walking. Mr. Harrison—Nick had never actually heard his first name—was a retired civil servant who was now by all signs virtually deaf and, if Mrs. Harrison's hovering attentions were any indications, equally helpless physically. She clutched his elbow and steered him along the rough concrete, a tugboat guiding a liner through the intricacies of some huge modern harbor; only in this case, the tug was at least half again as heavy and substantially larger than the ship it was supposed to safeguard.

In the past week, the couple had started actually walking in front of Payne's house, as if the change in ownership had lifted an unspoken ban on passing along that particular stretch of sidewalk. Once Nick had seen them exchange greetings with Payne as he was hurrying toward a cab waiting for him at the curb. The three had seemed neighborly enough, almost friendly.

"Afternoon," Nick replied, pitching his voice to carry across the lawn and out to the sidewalk. He sat straighter and waved from the shadows. Mr. Harrison nodded from the walkway but didn't speak. Nick could not remember ever having heard the man speak. The old fellow glanced distractedly this way and that, apparently more intent on the yellow-freckled under-leaves of an ancient Queen Elizabeth rose struggling to bloom in the corner of the yard than on Nick. When Mrs. Harrison released her grip on his elbow and started walking toward Nick, Mr. Harrison shuffled over to the bush, bent over with obvious difficulty, and examined the leaves and canes closely. Nick had tried to prune it a few weeks before but he could tell by the way Harrison fussed and muttered and glanced toward the shadowed porch that Nick had seriously muffed the job and that his inadvertent ravages would not be lightly forgiven.

Mrs. Harrison came up the walkway as Nick went down the steps to meet her in the middle of the yard.

They talked for a few minutes—actually, she talked and Nick listened—about the weather ("wonderful, but fall will probably be far too hot"), illnesses (hers), and other people's odd habits (mostly her husband's). Once she called out to Mr. Harrison to "come over and be polite," but he was too interested in the apparently unique collection of aphids on the Queen Elizabeth's buds to bother with anything as mundane as another human being. Gradually Nick stopped listening and concentrated on nodding and making appropriately positive or negative noises, whichever seemed required, and on keeping from yawning in front of her. He had had plenty of experience at that kind of non-communication with his grandmother before she died four years before at ninety-two. She had wandered when she talked, but his sitting there and holding her hand and making noises had seemed to satisfy her and made her happier for a while. Mrs. Harrison wasn't quite so far gone, Nick decided, but the principle was the same. He began casting around for a polite way to tell her to get lost.

Then he pricked up his ears. She was talking about The Greer—"Miss Emilia," as she called her. By the time he was back to full attention, she was in the middle of an involved story about a scandal from years before, so long ago that only she and Mr. Harrison remained of the original neighbors. And presumably only they remembered the details.

"Everyone else that lived on Greensward then is gone now, of course," she was saying, "and I never speak of it to any of the newcomers."

Apparently she either did not consider Nick a "newcomer" (which he believed instinctively to be highly unlikely), or she was simply unaware of what she was saying, carried away by the quiet and by the opportunity to talk.

What little Nick caught of the story sounded like a bad retelling of "A Rose for Emily"—a haughty young woman, proud of her intellect and her achievements; a wandering suitor who won her over and jilted her; subsequent and lingering rumors of strange happenings at the little house on Greensward Lane.

"Mind you, I'm not saying anything against Miss Emilia," Mrs. Harrison chattered on as if unaware herself of what she was saying, "but *I* looked in that kitchen window, just after the big storm that blew the transformer on the power pole and blacked out the town for miles around—back then, blackouts weren't so common as they are now, and nobody was ever really prepared for one. We didn't even have any candles or flashlights handy, and Mr. Harrison was feeling poorly, poor man, so I had to run over to Miss Emilia's to see if we could borrow something. But now, why it seems like every other day someone hits a power pole or the Arabs decide to charge more for oil or a power plant goes on the blink and the electricity comes and goes whenever it wants to—'brown-outs' hah! This new 'nucular' power isn't any better, either. I don't trust it; atoms running around in the electrical lines, getting into everything, making everything radioactive and all. And it goes out just as much as the old kind. Power failure ruined a whole season's frozen strawberries last summer, you remember, when the power was out for almost two days. And the summer before…."

"What did you see, Mrs. Harrison?" Nick asked.

"What?" she blinked owlishly several times and looked around. When she caught Nick's eye and noticed his curious expression, she flushed as pink as the Queen Elizabeth buds and dropped her eyes, as if she had just awakened and found herself standing naked in front of strangers in a strange room.

"In the window," Nick prompted. "Next door. At The Gre… at Miss Emilia's. What did you see that time?"

The flush washed away to the sickly pallidness of terror. Beneath their two highlights of vivid red rouge, her cheeks drained of blood; from Nick's point of view, they were suddenly the color of death. Her eyes flickered serpent-like from Nick to the house next door. He glanced over his shoulder. The attic window glared down at them from an angle that made it look as if someone were surreptitiously watching beneath canted eyebrows. The missing shrubbery where Payne had trimmed away excess foliage allowed a clear view from the window to

Nick's yard, with the Queen Elizabeth rose bush in the corner and Mr. Harrison, Mrs. Harrison, and Nick frozen where they stood.

Mrs. Harrison let out a little shriek, threw her hands to her lips in a gesture Nick had sincerely thought only happened in grade-B movies, spun around so fast that he was afraid she might over balance and fall, and jolted down the sidewalk. It was probably the fastest she had ever moved—certainly she had to have set a personal record that went back at least fifty years. Mr. Harrison was just snapping off a couple of green rose hips when she swept by, an irresistible force of nature, and grabbed his arm and pulled him along with her. She was halfway home when she seemed to realize that she was walking directly in front of The Greer's place. She turned her head to stare at the empty, silent porch. Her face went even paler, if that were possible. She dropped Mr. Harrison's arm and clutched at her throat as if she were choking. Mr. Harrison still held onto the broken rose hips; they hung stupidly from his hands. He looked around, confused, not sure what was happening or what he was doing.

Mrs. Harrison's choking grew into a deep rasping that might have been a heart attack or something else serious. From pasty white her complexion flooded with color, sufficiently for Nick to see the sudden change from half a house away. He ran down the sidewalk toward her, but she must have heard him coming over the sounds of her own breathing and she whirled to face him and screamed, a harsh, ear-splitting sound that to Nick seemed too loud to have issued from the old woman's throat: "I didn't see it, I didn't see anything!" She wasn't looking at Nick, he realized with a cold shock; she was looking upward, directly into the black window in the attic above The Greer's porch swing where the afternoon sun reflected back at her like a sheet of white fire.

As if awakening from a decade of senility, Mr. Harrison suddenly seemed to gather his senses and take charge. He opened his curled fingers and let the rose hips drop dead to the cracked concrete before he waved Nick violently back, propelled Mrs.

Harrison along the sidewalk and across their lawn until they were on their own porch, then without further words drew her inside their own house. The door slammed with a resounding *thud*. The sound echoed along the empty street. For an instant, nothing else moved, nothing else made even the slightest noise.

A moment later, Nick saw the faded, lace-trimmed living room curtain flutter once, as if someone had twitched it aside to take a furtive look outside. Then, again, there was no visible movement along the whole length of Greensward Lane.

Eerie, Nick thought. If the old woman had crept at him while making the sign of the evil eye or sporting a genuine, certified, satisfaction-guaranteed-or-your-money-back anti-vampire crucifix hanging from a silver necklace or studded with 100% pure garlic imported directly from Transylvania the night before, he wouldn't have been more stunned. Worse, he couldn't forgive himself for not listening to her when he had had the chance. It was probably the first and only time in years that she had opened up about The Greer and talked about why she and her husband refused to cross in front of The Greer's property. Finally, after all this time, The Greer was dead and Mrs. Harrison could tell what she had seen—at least her subconscious had assured her it was all right to tell. Her conscious mind seemed to have strong reservations in the other direction, however, and Nick had spoiled things, first by not listening closely and then by asking questions. Obviously the wrong questions.

Were there any *right* ones, he wondered.

He stood at the sidewalk, staring at the Harrisons' house, until he became painfully aware of the hot sun searing his neck and arms.

"Stupid, stupid, stupid," he repeated aloud as he went inside, not sure quite what he meant by the phrase. But this sudden surge of aggressiveness, this volatile anger—*this* was the right mood, he decided, to attack the next set of mid-term exams.

By evening, any lingering sense that the day had begun as perfect had disappeared. Sudden black clouds piling alone the upper ridges of the mountains threatened a storm, while in the valleys, even the most hesitant breeze had long since given up hope and expired. The clouds grew darker and dropped lower as day slid imperceptibly, irritably into night. The hills above Tamarind Valley echoed with occasional thunder, a rarity in California but for Nick the more enjoyable for that. Nick loved thunder—at least he did now that he was grown up, mostly because it reminded him of summer storms in Montana and Idaho when he was a kid. He could lean back in his chair, close his eyes, hum some tuneless noise, and watch replays of the monstrous black thunderheads stacking up along the edge of the plateau surrounding Billings, crouching as if they were sentient beasts waiting for the signal to attack and *thrumm* the air and terrify every kid under ten in the whole town. When he was a child, thunder brought simply mind- and heart-stopping fright; now, it brought the vaguely nostalgic scent of a pure, long-gone, virginal sort of terror.

By midnight, the thunder had moved over Tamarind Valley. The claps rang out—close, long, and loud, rumbling until the glass shivered in Nick's bedroom window and the vibrations transmitted themselves from the floor to his bed frame. It was warm outside in spite of the storm, so his window was open a few inches—not enough to let any rain seep in but enough for him to smell the sweet fragrance of damp heat on freshly washed leaves. He lay back, allowing his head to sink deeply into his pillow, his eyes closed. All the lights were off but the bullet-lamp arched like a vulture—or maybe like a cormorant—on the edge of the desk. He remembered other stormy evenings from long ago and far away and consciously replayed memories of exquisite moments of fear.

One night, when he could not have been more than eight years old, the thunder had rolled so close to the glass patio doors leading from the family room where he and his brother and sisters had huddled during the storm that he had half believed it would knock the house down. At least he and the other kids did; Mom and Dad seemed demonstrably less worried. Seconds later, a bolt of lightning had struck the power pole in the back yard, arcing electric blue through the night and illuminating the whole neighborhood. Lights flickered and died for an instant; in the darkness, distorted shadows of trees and bushes and shrubs streamed like ghosts into the family room, propelled by the unearthly electric glow. Then the lights blinked on again and abruptly everything seemed normal. Nick's Dad warned the kids not to touch the television set, though, not even to turn it off. Back then, everyone thought that TVs could store up electrical charges.

"If you touch that," Dad had threatened, gesturing with an outstretched thumb over his shoulder toward the static-drowned screen, his voice heavy with sincerity and threat and his broad shoulders shadowing the four children sitting in terror at his feet, "the shock could fry you in your shoes and throw your little charred bodies across the room like so many overdone hot dogs!"

For days after that, Nick had refused to approach the TV, wondering how long it would take for the murderous charge it had accumulated to die away. And for longer than that, he had punched the on/off button with a long, dry stick he had cut expressly for that purpose from the dead willows along the stream.

But that was years ago, and with a shocking transition that startled him and set his heart thumping Nick was suddenly thrust back into Tamarind Valley and the present as lightning and thunder struck almost simultaneously, so close over the nearby hills that he could smell the ozone. Then the rain began, torrential, Southern-California-cloudburst rain. The wind kicked up viciously and drove horizontal sheets of wetness against his window pane, through the crack between window and jamb, and into his room in a fine spray that floated in the air before settling onto his desk and bed. He jumped up, slammed the window closed, swiveled the casement lock, then ran through the house shutting and securing the rest of the windows and doors. He even had the presence of mind (for once—because he still remembered what Mrs. Harrison had said about blackouts) to set half a dozen candles and matches in strategic places throughout the place.

Just in case.

CHAPTER NINE

As events turned out, he didn't have to use them, but he later wished fervently that he had...that a few blown fuses and a few minutes of candle-lit darkness had been the only consequences of that storm.

The lightning struck again, closer. He tried the old counting game, *one-one-thousand, two-one-thousand*, like the father has the kid do in *Poltergeist* just before the dead tree breaks through the window and tries to pull the kid into never-never nightmare-land.

One-one-thousand, two-one....

In the real world outside, lightning crashed again, disturbingly near. Nick hadn't noticed any demonically skeletal trees branching outside his windows, but the sound made him nervous, made the air seem charged with tension and terror.

"To hell with it," he muttered finally, refusing to give in to the panic that lay just beneath his consciousness. Instead, he forced himself to relax enough to go to bed.

He turned out the lights throughout the place, including the one on his desk, and stripped for bed in the darkness. He was caught once, half-naked and vulnerable-seeming, even to himself, when white light exploded nearby and outlined him through the window. In that instant of light, his hands and arms and legs and feet had glowed unearthly pale, dead, moving with a haunting jerkiness that made him shiver. He turned his back to the window, finished undressing, and slid between sheets faintly damp to the touch, clammy, as if the rain had lightly caressed them, but he didn't want to get up and change them. For a long while, he lay unmoving, stiff, staring at the uneven shadows that played across the ceiling. After a while, he began to drift toward sleep.

When it came, the lightning bolt lit up his room as if he hadn't turned any lights off at all, almost as violently blue-white as that time when he was a kid. His eyes flew open at the flash and the instantaneous thunderclap that seemed to deafen him. As if trapped in his childhood nightmare, he saw an outline against the wall opposite the window, a wavering black shape, witch-hands with tree-twig fingers reaching out to him, beckoning, the monstrous, bloated head surrounded by a sickly silvery-white light overlaid with menacing blue.

He stifled a scream and sat bolt upright, the sheets slipping from his chest to pool at his waist. The air was chilly, brittle with rain-swept dampness.

Suddenly there was another sharp crackle, a flash of light closer to the ground than lightning had any right to be, and the blue-white shadow of a shower of sparks. The outline on the wall wavered, sharpened, resolved into the ragged semblance of a human form and, with the suddenness of an over-heated light bulb shattering at the touch of an icy wind, disappeared.

His head jerked toward the window. He jumped out of bed and ran across the room, slipping into his robe as he went, cinching it tightly around his waist with a violent jerk on the velour belt.

Outside, a power line had fallen. It was the one running in front of Payne's place. Its ripped end clicked an insidious tattoo against the damp concrete of the sidewalk, spitting sparks with each sinuous shudder. The houses along the other side of the block were pitch dark, whether from power failure or from the people being asleep, he couldn't tell; but the reassuring hum and glow from his night-stand clock let him know that he at least still had electricity.

The downed line sparked once more on the wet concrete, then lay momentarily quiescent, like a satiated serpent.

He hit the wall switch and felt an inordinate relief when the lights burned steadily and brightly. He grabbed the telephone to call the power company and report the down line.

Something thumped against the window. He whirled toward the sound. Whatever it was, it sounded heavy, sodden, alive.

A figure appeared, disappeared, reappeared through the wet glass.

"Shit! Who's there?" he yelled.

Someone mumbled something—he couldn't understand any of the words over the pelting rain sheeting like thick oil on the window pane.

He edged closer.

Mrs. Harrison, as wet and bedraggled as an overweight hen caught outside the coop, huddled outside, her shoulders wrapped in a thin sweater half concealing what appeared to be an old-fashioned flannel nightgown. She banged again at the pane, her white knuckles twisting against the glass like five pale slugs, her face wrenched out of recognition by the storm-ridden shadows and by her tears. The distortion from the rain-streaked window, coupled with the eerie back-light of electrical sparks and distant lightning flashes that kept the sky shimmering blue-black, made her look more like a walking corpse than a living woman.

Nick stood stock-still, staring.

The apparition motioned jerkily toward the front of the house, then faded into the darkness. He ran down the hall and through the living room, wrenching the front door open before she had a chance to knock again.

The old woman burst into the house, dripping, breathless, her nightgown plastered to her shoulders and hips and thighs. The thin material hung obscenely transparent where, in the glare of his living room overhead light, the faded, sodden flannel molded tight against sagging breasts and withered flesh.

"Mrs. Har—"

"It's Fred," she panted before Nick could say anything more. "He's had...his heart...real bad...I think he's dying...."

"Heart attack?"

She nodded jerkily, her own face unhealthy and pale. Her breathing was deepening but was still shallower than sounded good. Nick motioned to the sofa and reached out to take her arm. She shrugged him away, shaking her head.

"Phone's out," she said. "Call somebody. He's been bad for years, but never like this. *Please call.*"

"Okay," Nick yelled, trying to outshout the wind that swirled around the porch and through the doorway. "Come in and wait here."

"No, I'll get back to him. Hurry!"

"I'll call. Meet you over there in a minute or two. Okay?"

"Okay," she yelled, but she was already moving. The expression on her face was more stunned than animate, but she headed purposefully into the shimmering darkness. She almost stumbled on the porch steps but found her footing and lumbered toward the sidewalk. Nick raced to the bedroom, wishing that he hadn't had his phone installed there instead of in the living room. A few seconds might make the difference for Mr. Harrison, the difference between life and death.

He punched 911, heard one ring, glanced up, and in the glare of a passing headlight saw Mrs. Harrison clear the corner of the house and dash toward the front of The Greer's property line.

Along the horizon, a sheet of lightning-flame split the sky, followed a breath later by the sharp roar of thunder.

Mrs. Harrison passed the Queen Elizabeth rose, its canes whipped almost leafless by the storm. Nick heard the second ring at the police station.

"Hurry up, damn it," he murmured to whoever should have been standing at the desk, hand hovering over the telephone as if waiting for Nick's call.

The third ring.

Another sheet of lightning and instantaneous thunder, so violent that Nick felt it through his naked feet. It must have struck just behind his house.

For an instant, Mrs. Harrison's black form was highlighted

by the lightning, white-sharp and frozen in mid-stride, her leg hitched, outstretched, one toe almost touching the shimmering concrete of the sidewalk directly in front of The Greer's place.

The downed power line whipped out. Mrs. Harrison screamed, threw up her hands as if to protect herself from something hideously unseen, and spun, twisting until she faced directly toward Nick's bedroom window. The sepulchral whiteness of her face floated against the night. She opened her mouth to scream again and the power line slashed her cheeks and curled around her temple and something exploded against her skull in a burst of violent blue light.

The phone rang a fourth time, crackled, and a voice spoke, distantly, coldly, echoing through Nick's numbness.

"Tamarind Valley substation. How can I help you?"

Right then, at that moment, before the paramedics arrived or the ambulance or the squad cars, seeing the old woman's eyes grow distant and cold even as her body struggled to take one step more, Nick knew that Mrs. Harrison was dead.

He knew as well that Mr. Harrison would not survive this night.

He screamed the Harrisons' name and address into the telephone and punctuated it with a shouted "Hurry, for God's sake!" and dropped the receiver onto the table. It lay in a damp spot on the wood, buzzing like a mortally wounded insect. Barefoot, he raced through the house, out onto his porch, onto the drenched lawn, down to the silvery, slippery sidewalk connecting his yard with The Greer's. It was dark again; the lightning had stopped for the moment and clouds hung low and heavy, seeming to almost touch the tops of the trees. Mrs. Harrison's body was a motionless black lump against the glistening dampness of the concrete. The power line lay mute and dark where it twisted beneath her. He stared, afraid to move closer, afraid to come within striking distance of the broken line, yet deeply ashamed not to try to do something to help the old woman.

But she is already dead, part of his mind said.

He backed away as far as the porch and waited until he heard the whine of sirens. He was safely shadowed when red lights flashed around the corner and the ambulance and fire engine squealed to a halt in front of The Greer's. He stood on his porch, his sodden robe heavy on his icy shoulders and clammy against his hips and belly. Water pooled around his naked feet as he watched the activity two houses away. In the back of his mind he saw Mrs. Harrison's face as it had been when she had fled from his yard that afternoon. Whatever she had seen once in the window of The Greer's house had etched fear and terror into her eyes. He had seen that same fear and terror as she died, the power line enfolding her body and spitting death.

He waited in the shadows, unnoticed, while the paramedics covered her body. One of the neighbors across the street hurried over, spoke urgently to the nearest fireman. They scurried across the lawn to the Harrisons and the fireman banged twice, three times, four on the front door.

The man lunged with his shoulder against the jamb and broke in.

A moment later, he reappeared.

"There's another one. Hurry!" he said, his voice etched with strain. Two men disengaged themselves from the crowd and disappeared into the house. Before Mrs. Harrison was two minutes inside the ambulance, her husband had joined her.

Nick watched the ambulance drive away—no sirens this time. No need to hurry.

He didn't go inside for a long while, not until the night wind penetrated his sodden robe and chilled him inside and out. The tie cinched around his waist held the water and cut into his flesh like an icy blade.

Finally, numb with cold and shock, he entered his house, shutting the door against the wind without even noticing that he had done so. He shuffled into the bathroom and dropped the sodden robe into the bathtub. It slapped the porcelain with a heavy *thwump*, then lay black and shapeless against the stained white tub.

For longer than he could remember, Nick stood in the middle

of the bathroom, naked and shivering.

When he did finally return to his bed, it was to lay awake, staring at shapes formed by lightning shadows on the ceiling of his room. He did not sleep for hours, and blessedly, when he did, he did not dream.

Payne Gunnison wasn't seen on Greensward Lane for upwards of five days. By then, the Harrisons were buried and their house already had a bright blue "For Sale" sign staked into the lawn.

CHAPTER TEN

For most of the next week Nick suffered under the expertly Inquisitorial torture of the summer cold that followed his drenching the night of the Harrisons' deaths. It kept him in bed, snuffling and bored, methodically decimating a full-sized package of Kleenex per day and ingesting gallons of cold medicines. It forced him to miss the funeral on Wednesday afternoon.

Why do they always hold those things at one o'clock on Wednesdays, he thought miserably that morning, upset and saddened to realize that his body simply wouldn't allow him to drive far enough or sit long enough for him to pay his last respects. He didn't know the Harrisons that well, of course, they were of different generations and all of that, but they had, after all, been next-door-but-one neighbors for three years.

With the funeral over and Nick's cold on the mend, the next weeks passed uneventfully. The quarter at UCLA stumbled to an apathetic close. His class at Camarillo came to an equally unsatisfying conclusion. The students at both schools saddled him with batches of inept finals that left a bad taste in his mouth. Fear of his own failure as a teacher struggled with frustration with his students. In the end he virtually ignored them to begin serious research on his dissertation topic and study for the comprehensive exams scheduled in the fall.

Finally, though—blessedly—summer break arrived.

He had planned the summer reading schedule carefully: Spenser's *The Faerie Queene,* Chaucer, Milton, Shakespeare. And some work on the moderns—Joyce, Pound, Hemingway—

with some science fiction and fantasy worked in around the edges to keep him from getting stale. It was a heavy list but after all, from the perspective of the first fresh week of summer, all things seemed possible.

Payne had returned shortly after the funeral and resumed work around his house. He began by cleaning up a tangle of branches in the back yard, then refining the landscaping here and there. He hadn't made as much progress as he should have, though, Nick thought more than once as he stared over the piles of books and papers on his desk and through the window. The side hedge and back yard were still visibly overgrown. The lawn looked shaggy again, but so far Payne hadn't hauled the ancient mower out for a repeat performance. In the right light, most often under the elongated shadows of evening, the place still reminded Nick of a memory-haunted old woman, haggard and half-naked.

Still, some days Nick would see Payne outside, dressed in T-shirt and shorts, puttering around the house or the garage, replacing the odd missing shingle, opening and airing the musty garage, making it look less resolutely run-down by re-glazing the shattered pane in the side window.

At other times, however, Payne seemed less sure of himself, starting one project and shifting to another before the first was even part completed. On those days, it seemed to Nick as if Payne was working outside by default, as if he had decided that staying indoors was simply too much for him and outside was the only alternative.

Gradually their acquaintance deepened into friendship in spite of Nick's resolve not to let anything come between himself and his studies. Payne was naturally more aloof than seemed usual for mellow, laid-back Southern California, probably a hold-over of his Eastern upbringing, Nick decided. And there were some oddly awkward moments during the days following the Harrisons' funeral. Payne was to all outward appearances unaffected by their deaths.

"Too bad about the old folks," he said when Nick saw him a

few days after the funeral. Then, "What do you think, should I replant that hedge or pull the whole thing out and start over with roses." It seemed pretty callous to Nick, whose nose and eyes were still painful, puffy reminders of the night the "old folks" had died. But after all, Payne had barely met the Harrisons and could not really be expected to feel anything other than generalized sympathy for their passing—even though Mrs. Harrison had died literally on his front sidewalk. For his part, Nick could not forget the look on her face that afternoon, the terror locked in her dead eyes that night. Somehow, Nick sometimes thought vaguely, Payne seemed...well, not exactly responsible but tangentially involved.

Nick couldn't quite work it out.

CHAPTER ELEVEN

As the days passed they nodded and spoke when they saw each other on the sidewalk. More frequently Payne called out as he left home, his voice carrying through the open windows to where Nick, seated at his desk, slogged through page after page of Renaissance love poetry. A quick wave through the window, a returned greeting from Nick, and Payne would be gone for the day. Nick didn't know where nor did he ask.

After a while, so gradually that neither noticed that a choice had been made, they began meeting once or twice a week at one of the houses for an evening together.

When they were at Nick's, they played chess or just talked. Payne had attended a community college back in Pennsylvania long enough to be able to trade stories about gruesome profs or talk reasonably intellectual shop. These evenings began early and ended early. Nick was sticking to his reading schedule, which surprised him no end, and Payne kept busy around The Greer's place…Nick still had trouble thinking of it in any other terms. Payne wasn't working an outside job, though, Nick discovered, at least not yet. The Greer's estate could carry Payne through a decade or more of absolute indolence if he chose, so he was taking a few months to sort out the contents of her study and catalogue everything the old woman left him, generally getting a sense of the estate and what he might do with it. Certainly there would be some cash value in the film collection and equipment, he mentioned to Nick one day, if he could work out arrangements with the lawyers to liquidate it.

On other nights, the two would meet at Payne's. The first time, a week or so after their first chess match at Nick's, they fully intended to play chess. Payne's first additions to the house's sparse furnishings were a couple of extra chairs, one in the living room and one in the kitchen. That way, Nick could at least sit in comfort. Payne added a small table in the living room as well. Nick noticed it right away.

"Something new?" he said as he stepped through the entryway. Payne kept the heavy curtain tied back with the bit of white braided cord, making the transition from dark entry into brightly lit living room less of a psychical and neurological shock.

"Yeah," Payne said, almost as if he were embarrassed. "I thought it might be helpful if we wanted to play chess over here to have somewhere to play. The kitchen didn't seem right."

Nick glanced around the room. The white curtains at the living-room windows hung three-quarters open, grudgingly allowing the remnant of late afternoon to spill inside. The room seemed alight with a soft golden glow that reflected from every surface as if the walls themselves were incandescent. Intrusive glimpses of leaves and hedges and yards through the spotless windows created a carnival of colors and shapes and textures juxtaposed to the Arctic sameness of white draperies, white carpet, white walls, white furniture.

The new chair was white, too. It didn't match the old one, though Nick, except in color; the style was subtly but definitely wrong for the room. The small table between them was white also. It looked plastic, modernistic, too much like a squat cube. Somehow it was not what Nick would have expected Payne to buy.

"Why did you choose that one?" he asked pointedly, gesturing with his thumb at the chair and allowing Payne to interpret the "that one" to mean either color or style. Both seemed wrong.

"It is pretty awful, isn't it," Payne said with a boyish grin. "But it fits the room. The white. I saw others I liked better, but they would have stood out too much in here."

"Then change the room. Add color. New carpets. Prints on the walls. Repaint if nothing else."

"I can't." There was an odd timbre in Payne's voice when he spoke, as if he were not feeling quite well.

Nick looked at Payne. Standing as he was next to the wall, with the light reflecting onto his face and burnishing away planes and angles, blotting out shadows, Payne didn't look all that well either.

"You don't want to? You *like* this…sterility?" Nick was aware suddenly of what he was saying. Payne could very well take it as an intrusion. Nick wished at once that he hadn't begun this line of conversation. After all, it was Payne's home. And Payne *was* his landlord.

"Hey, I'm sorry for blurting out like that. It's just that…."

Payne didn't take offense. In fact, he nodded his agreement. "You're right, though. It is sterile. I don't like it. I think I dislike it more each day."

"Then change it. Do something to it."

"I can't." This time his voice was low, almost a whisper.

Nick started to say something, but Payne cut him off.

"No, Nick. I mean it." He turned away to stare at the blank white wall. "I really *can't*."

"What do you mean?"

"It's in the will."

"In the…?"

"Yeah. It's really strange. I get the house…both houses plus some property downtown that's worth as much as these pieces and a whole lot more. And a wad of money that the lawyers found a couple of weeks ago in some long-term investment accounts. They think there may be some more property up north, too. All that from an old woman I never met and barely even heard of.

"Funny," he added, looking back to Nick then away again to resume staring at the same blank spot on the same blank wall. "I lost my mother to cancer…."

"I'm sorry," Nick said. "I didn't know. You never said anything."

"It was a long siege, painful for both of us, and a relief in some ways when it was finally over. One week later, I lost my job when the mill shut down. Then another week and POW! I get a letter addressed to my mother from some attorneys in California. In spite of cousins and nephews and nieces all over the place, Mom was named specifically as sole heir to everything Great-Aunt Emilia owned, and I was *her* only heir. Suddenly, out of the blue, I'm rich. I mean, really rich. Filthy rich." He tried to laugh, but the sound strangled.

"And the only restrictions in the will," he continued, "were that Mom…that *I* must live here, in this place. And that I can't remove anything from the house, can't change anything down to the paint on the walls. Would you believe it, there are a dozen cases of white paint stacked up in the garage, along with a formula for making more when that's gone.

"The same goes for the furniture. I had to argue with the lawyer for an hour before he allowed me to bring in these two things. And then he had to pass on the materials—just metal and plastic, no natural woods, etc."

Nick whistled, the sound low and chilling even to his own ears. He looked around the room again with a new eye. "No pictures? No new paint?"

"Nothing. It apparently has something to do with the sound system Aunt Emilia was developing. I think she stopped actual work a year or so ago, but by then it was pretty much in place. Pounding nails or hanging pictures or even using any other kind of paint would foul things up. So I'm stuck with this. Through the whole house."

Nick shivered. *Someone's walking on my grave*, he thought, remembering his grandmother, she of the warmly cluttered cottage with its massive dark oak furniture clustering along each wall, its worn braided rugs made from bits and pieces of her lifetime—even at ninety-two she had been able to tell him where each piece of material had come from, who had worn this suit to Great-Great-Grandma Kerr's funeral during World War I or that dress to a senior prom at the Grange Hall in the fifties or that pair of pajamas the night his youngest died of diphtheria during the depression.

Nick overlaid the richness of those memories onto the emptiness of Payne's house and shivered.

"Come on," Payne said quickly, smiling broadly as if to bridge an uncomfortable moment, "let's forget all that weirdness and get down to some serious chess. Wait here."

He disappeared into the hallway. When he returned a moment later, he had a large, flat cardboard box tucked under his arm.

"Got this yesterday."

He set the box onto the white carpeting. It created an ugly splotch of brown against the whiteness. Payne squatted next to the box and lifted the top. Nick noted that Payne didn't drop the top to the floor; he laid it carefully on the new chair.

White tissue crackled loudly against the silence as Payne folded the edges to the side to expose a chess set as starkly simple as the room itself. The kings were almost featureless columns, their surfaces faintly rippled by swirls that implied rather than defined faces. The other pieces were equally abstract, equally suggestive of forms without actually *being* forms. The pieces gleamed in flawless porcelain, white and black. Payne lifted them out and pulled the board from the bottom of the box and unfolded it. It was made of heavy cardboard overlaid with fine-grained leather, luxurious smelling, obviously expensive, with white and pearl-gray squares.

Payne set the board on the small table, placing each piece painstakingly, precisely in the center of its square. Nick waited to one side, watching. When the game board was ready, Payne straightened and grabbed the empty box. He stuffed the wrinkled tissue to the bottom and slipped the top carefully over each edge.

"Just a minute, huh? Be right back."

He disappeared into the hallway. Nick saw him turn from there into the kitchen. For a few moments, Nick stood next to the new white chair, oddly uncomfortable at the thought of sitting down. He paced, but only a few feet to either side of the small table now crowned with the abstract white and black pieces. He waited for Payne to return but the moments stretched into longer minutes and his patience suddenly wore thin. He hurried down the hallway and looked through the kitchen door, expecting to see the chess box sticking out of the waste can and Payne methodically setting out cheese, crackers, and beer for snacks and drinks.

"Can I give you...?" he began, then stopped. The room was empty. He glanced through the windows, cleaner now than they had been the first time he visited the house with Payne, but even so they were overlaid with an obviously fresh if thin coating of dust that made the back yard slightly hazy.

From the kitchen he could see Payne stuffing the chess box into one of the large, battered garbage cans lined like sentinels between the back fence and the alley. Payne replaced the lid carefully, rattling the can once or twice to make sure it was snug, as if he were deathly afraid that the box would come to life and climb out—or that someone would notice that it was in there to begin with. As Payne straightened and headed toward the house, Nick faded quickly into the hallway. By the time Payne entered the living room, Nick was seated, studying the chess set.

Situation A-OK, everything normal.

Nick heard Payne come in, knew that the man was standing just over his shoulder. He counted ten seconds, fifteen, and still Payne said nothing. Nick relaxed, waiting for the inevitable joke, the gag, the comment about the chess set and their last game at Nick's and how badly Nick was going to get the pants beaten off him tonight.

"Mind if I sit there?" Payne asked quietly. Surprised, Nick looked up. He hadn't consciously thought about where he was sitting; he had simply chosen the closest chair when he hurried back down the hall. As luck would have it, it was the old one. *The Greer's chair.*

"Sure, help yourself," he said, and he stood up and stepped around Payne. He moved to the new chair and sat down. He felt more comfortable there anyway.

Payne dropped into The Greer's chair, literally dropped, as if he were a puppet and someone had savagely cut his strings with a single *snip* from a pair of shears. The springs snapped and groaned with the burden of his sudden weight.

"Okay," he said, grinning as if nothing were unusual at all, "let's get into some serious chess. I feel lucky."

Without asking Nick to choose a color, he slid a black pawn forward two spaces.

"Your turn."

Nick couldn't move. *Couldn't* raise his arm to touch the gleaming white pawn that would counter Payne's opening. It was as if there were a threat emanating from the pieces, the ebony burning like Milton's darkness visible in the brightness of the room. The gray squares almost disappeared from two yards away, blending with the white men. But the black pieces....

The game itself suddenly seemed sterile, the white pieces invisible, the black obscene intrusions. Nick's head ached with a sickening, throbbing ache. His stomach flopped over once, twice. The room suddenly seemed hotter than a concrete sidewalk at noon in July.

"Hey, Nick," Payne said, leaning across the board to rest his hand on Nick's knee. "You okay?"

Nick looked up, his expression dazed. He barely felt the weight of Payne's hand through the heavy material of his jeans. *Someone had said something someone spoke to him he should answer.* "Uh, what?"

"You okay? You've been sitting there for a minute or two, barely breathing. You feel all right?"

"No...yes. No, I guess not. Not for chess, anyway, not today. I'm...I guess I'm just not in the mood." He massaged his temples with his fingertips, swallowing hard against the bile in his throat.

Payne looked at him as if about to say something, then shrugged and settled back into the chair and crossed his legs.

"Okay. Wouldn't want to force anyone to get the pants beat off him. Another time?"

"Yeah. Sure. Tomorrow, huh?"

Payne nodded.

Ten minutes later, Nick was home, lying on his bed with a cold, damp cloth covering his eyes and shutting out the light. He lay quietly, his body barely moving except for the shallow rise and fall of his chest. But still he felt as if the bed were tossing in a gale. His head pounded more fiercely.

CHAPTER TWELVE

In spite of their best intentions, Nick and Payne were wrong. There was no tomorrow for the chess set in Payne's living room. It stood unused on the small table until the end, unmoved, untouched as far as Nick could see. The glossy surfaces seemed never dulled by the slightest haze of dust.

And the black pieces never became part of the room.

Later, when he started visiting Payne more frequently, Nick could not bring himself to touch even one of the pieces.

Neither of them said anything, but after that abortive attempt, it was tacitly agreed that chess was played only at Nick's, using his plastic $4.98 Kmart® special. At Payne's, they watched films.

They watched one the next night, in fact. Nick fully intended to begin the aborted chess game. He felt better, his headache had disappeared sometime during the night and his stomach was quiet by breakfast. He went out to the front porch after eating, in time to see Payne leaving the house.

"How about coming over tonight," Payne called over the hedge.

"Sure. Chess?"

"Only if you want me to beat the pants off of you."

"No way you'll do that," Nick yelled. "Not this time."

"Seven, then," Payne said, taking up the challenge. He waved and went on down the sidewalk.

"Seven," Nick called after him.

Now it was seven o'clock. Seven-five. Seven-ten. They sat

uncomfortably for a few minutes more, their faces and bodies opposed, the chess set stolidly between them, its presence a static obstacle even to speech.

Finally Payne stood.

"Let's forget this for now. Come on into the other room. Let me show you what I've figured out."

Nick rose—not without a good deal of relief—and followed him down the hall to the Master Control Room. There were no obvious changes in here, not even a second chair. But the shelves seemed subtly more orderly. The cabinet doors that had hidden yards of LPs, their cardboard sleeves fading remnants of another age and time, and more up-to-date CDs in gleaming plastic cases were pulled open. The room looked vaguely more human, more lived in—almost livable. Payne crossed to one of the DVD players.

"The video set-up wasn't too difficult to figure out," he said. "I've run it quite a few times now. I'm sure it has functions"— the jargon slipped out smoothly—"that I'm not aware of, but at least I can get us a movie going."

Nick remained motionless in the center of the room. He had stopped dead still when Payne approached the DVD player.

"Don't!" he thought he had yelled, but the sound emerged as a whisper, barely a breath. *Don't touch it.*

Payne turned at the slight sound.

Nick rubbed the tips of his fingers along the rough seam of his jeans, trying to wipe away an irritating tingle that ran from tips to palm.

"Hey, it's okay," Payne said, remembering and flushing slightly at his innocent oversight. "I've been playing this thing for days now and it hasn't sparked me once. Whatever happened was a fluke. Come on."

Nick started over, then stopped, turned, and walked instead to the shelves of DVD cases on the opposite wall.

Payne shrugged and turned his attention back to the player.

"How do you find anything here?" Nick asked a few moments later. "All I can see are numbers and letters. Is it some kind of code?"

"Yeah," Payne said over his shoulder, his back to Nick. "I haven't figured it out entirely, but there is a master list in that binder at the end of the shelf. Everything in it is entered alphabetically by title. Go ahead, pick one out."

Nick pulled the binder down, its thickness mute testimony to The Greer's thoroughness in her collecting.

There must have been a thousand DVD cases along the wall, maybe more.

He thumbed through the lists.

"Here's one," he said finally. "I haven't seen it in years, but it was funny. *Arsenic and Old Lace.*"

"The Cary Grant film?"

"Yeah, that's the one. Dark old house filled with crazy people. Peter Lorrie. Karloff, too, I think."

"What's the number?" Payne asked as he crossed the room.

Nick read off the code—several digits and letters in an apparently random arrangement—and Payne began running his fingers over a section of the shelves.

"No, it wasn't Karloff," he said as he checked coding dots on case after case. "The guy just *looked* like Karloff, I think." He pulled a thin plastic case down. He flipped it over and scanned the small print on the back.

"Right," he said, looking up and grinning, "it was Raymond Massey. He plays the murderous brother."

He held the case up.

"This the one you want, then?"

Nick nodded. Payne slipped the cartridge into the player and punched a series of buttons before he turned to face Nick.

"Okay, we have about five minutes to get settled; there's some kind of delay-relay that lets us go to one of the other rooms to watch. Which do you want, living room or study?"

"What?"

"The films automatically show in every room of the house. We can make ourselves comfortable anywhere, even in the bathroom, and watch the screen. Although the tub is a bit cramped for two, I suspect." Payne laughed. "Or maybe not, if they're the right two." His eyes glinted with little-boy glee.

"That's crazy!" Nick meant the viewing arrangements.

"I know," Payne said, his face still struggling against a smile. "But that's the way it is here. Let's go to the front study. The sofa there is pretty good sitting."

Nick agreed; he didn't want to spend a couple of hours sitting in the living room. Not yet, anyway.

They walked down the hall and into the study. It was the small squarish room on the corner closest to Nick's place. Payne went in first and drew the curtains. White, as usual. The room went black. Not just dark or dim. Totally, abysmally black.

"Whatever this stuff is," Payne said, fingering the heavy drapes, "it really works. Not a bit of light comes in unless I want it to. It's eerie, total darkness in the middle of the day."

"Yeah," Nick agreed. *And even eerier, total darkness from the outside as well. Night after night. Year after year.*

The screen lit up and the credits scrolled across the silvery light. There was no warm-up, no fragmentary static as the disc began. All at once it was Halloween in Brooklyn, with the promise of strange and hilarious occurrences.

They settled on opposite ends of the sofa—it was comfortable, Nick decided, more so than either chair in the living room—and enjoyed the blue-gray flickering on the screen.

Halfway through, Nick and Payne were laughing out loud.

They had forgotten any fleeting cares, worries, and fears.

CHAPTER THIRTEEN

Given that the two men lived next to each other and that, for a time at least, each was perhaps the nearest thing the other had to a close friend, Nick probably should have noted the gradual changes in Payne. Had Payne's faceless cousins and aunts and uncles in Pennsylvania been just a little stronger and able to suppress their envy long enough to visit him, or had they been just a little weaker and willing to succumb to their greed and try to pander to him, they might have seen something, especially after Payne's first two or three months in California had passed. Even then they might have merely chalked the changes up to his normally reserved personality or, if they were feeling especially nasty, to his becoming stuck up and snooty. But Nick saw Payne nearly every day for weeks. To give Nick credit, though, many of the changes were so gradual that he simply didn't notice.

And he *was* busy, keeping up with his reading schedule and preparing for fall exams. But that wasn't a good enough reason for him to close his eyes. He should have seen; in fact, perhaps, he *did* see. Like so many people who are suddenly thrust into unusual and uncomfortable situations, he just didn't *understand* what he saw.

That was that.

During the early weeks of summer, of course, there was no problem—at least nothing evident to Nick.

The two got together increasingly often, as many as three or four times a week to play chess at Nick's or watch films at Payne's. They chose films more or less by consensus, usually things both had missed or that somebody one of them knew had recommended…by an unspoken consensus, they gravitated toward older titles, things they had seen—or wished they could have seen—as teens.

There were plenty in the Greer's collection. Nick had missed most of the later theatrical releases, in part because of the time he spent on studying and the distance from Tamarind Valley to any decent theater, but mostly because of money—$7.50 and more per flick in the better theaters was too steep for his budget.

Payne hadn't seen many because the single theater in the backwoods Pennsylvania town he came from just didn't show them. There was only one movie-house in Brenton.

"Honest to God, it was really called the *Bijou*," Payne said once to Nick.

From what Payne said about it, Nick didn't think the ancient manager of the Brenton Bijou ever showed a film made after 1957—certainly nothing like the old *Herbert West, Reanimator*, or *From Beyond* or any of the more recent *Aliens, Predators*, or *Hellraiser* offerings. At first, the evenings at Payne's were adventures for both of them.

Then things changed, slowly but irrevocably.

The changes were simple at first, non-threatening, almost compellingly logical. For one thing, Payne began selecting more of the films, sometimes by himself. From the beginning, they had enjoyed fingering through the master index and tossing off suggestions for the night's viewing almost as much as they enjoyed watching the final choice. But as the summer progressed, more than once the chosen disc was already nestled in the DVD player when Nick arrived.

The evenings also took on a spooky seriousness for Payne.

For the first while, the two men talked openly during the movies, chatting about town, weather, people, or crunching crackers and popcorn, popping soda or beer cans, and laughing when one or the other got sprayed. Sometimes they ignored the film altogether and drifted into conversations that would last until well past midnight and be totally forgotten by the next dawn.

Then Payne became more attentive to the films, hesitating to answer Nick's questions, responding with something like irritation when Nick spoke.

Finally, one night in mid-June, while they were watching *Gothic*, Nick turned to Payne.

"I don't like this," he said.

"Shhh," Payne hissed without taking his eyes from the screen.

"Hey...," Nick began, but Payne silenced him with another "Shhh." Melodramatically (Nick thought at the time), he pressed his finger against his lips and shook his head. It looked so hokey, so much like something out of a bad soap opera that Nick burst out laughing.

"Shit!" Payne said, jumping up and slapping the palm of his hand against the power knob on the monitor.

The picture died, suddenly and abruptly, without the fading half-light Nick expected.

Payne whirled to face Nick.

"You want to talk, okay, let's talk!"

"Look, man...," Nick began, half-rising from the sofa.

Payne glared at him for a moment, then something died in his eyes and he smiled and motioned Nick to sit back down. He turned the monitor back on.

"Forget it," he said. "I just got too involved in the thing. Sorry."

"No problem," Nick said. But for the rest of the evening, the only sounds in the room came from the monitor.

The kind of films Payne chose changed, too, subtly but definitely. Episodes from *Star Wars* or *Star Trek* and the bloodless high-tech SF clones that followed them soon disappeared. In their places, Payne began concentrating on high-violence, high-blood epics. *Alien* was the first, even though it was one of the older films they watched; it was also one of the last ones they chose by consensus. It was part of the pattern, Nick later realized, but a pattern isn't too easy to spot when there is only one point. How can you have a streak of one?

But it was the first point.

On the day Nick finally understood that there was a problem, that the evenings were no longer what he had expected and come to enjoy, Payne had thumb-tacked a note to Nick's screen door sometime after noon, long after Nick had left for a stint at the Tamarind Valley Community College library.

For the first hour or so, he struggled through a couple of volumes of mandatory criticism that he was surprised to see on the shelves in such a small library. The stuff was frustrating to read, some of it so self-involved with the ingenuity of the critic that it seemed more masturbatory than elucidating. Disgusted, he gave up and instead checked out the local holdings in Renaissance drama.

There wasn't much, so he spent another hour or so skimming through some SF novels on the week-checkout table.

He didn't return home until later than usual—almost 7:30. He almost didn't notice the sheet of lined yellow foolscap paper, but he dropped his key and, kneeling to pick it up without spilling the load of books balanced precariously in the crook of his arm, found himself eye to eye with a thumbtack and a fluttering scrap of paper.

He hurried into the house, dropped the books on the table, and went back outside to retrieve the note.

He recognized Payne's scrawl before he read the words: "Something good today. Film at 8. Don't be late."

"Nuts," he said, as much out of frustration at Payne's marginally peremptory tone as at his own lateness.

He rushed inside and threw some soup onto the stove, taking a quick shower while his Campbell's cream-of-chicken heated, then wolfing down the hot soup as he stood, towel wrapped around his waist, eating over the kitchen sink and staring out the window. Almost before he swallowed the last spoonful, he let the bowl fall clattering onto the stained porcelain.

Thank god for melamine, he thought as he heard bowl and spoon chitter together in the bottom of the pitted sink. By then, he had pulled the towel off and was halfway into his bedroom and his pile of clean shorts, T-shirts, and socks.

It was 7:53.

In spite of everything, by 8:00 sharp, he was dressed and standing on the porch only a few yards from the old glider-swing, half a box of Better Cheddars under one arm and a six-pack under the other. His finger reached out, still shaking from running across the yard, and touched the doorbell button.

The buzzer crackled electrically.

Payne's porch seemed dark even though the sun still had an hour and a half before setting and there was almost two hours until full night. The inside lights were off when Payne opened the front door to greet Nick on the porch and usher him into the study.

"Everything's ready," Payne said as Nick settled into a new chair.

White, but somehow less frigid-seeming than the older pieces of furniture.

"Where'd you get this?" Nick asked, running his fingers over the smooth vinyl armrest.

Payne laughed.

"Had to spend another hour arguing with the lawyers on that one. Apparently I've already made more changes in the place than Aunt Emilia would have liked. According to them."

"It's about time," Nick said, then looked up apologetically. "Look, Payne, I didn't mean that the way...I mean...it's your place and all." His voice trailed off.

"No problem," said Payne, laughing again. "I feel the same way. And anyway, it's sort of a game now: *Payne 3, Lawyers 0.* It helps that I'm a kind of problem, keeps them off balance sometimes."

"Huh?"

"Technically, I suppose, I'm not even supposed to be here. My mother was actually Aunt Emilia's heir, had been for years even though no one back home knew that—or probably would have cared if they had known. It was very specific in the will, though.

Mom got everything. No one else was mentioned beyond being excluded from inheriting anything. It was an idiosyncratic will, but iron-clad.

"Apparently Aunt Emilia never knew Mom was sick—certainly she didn't know how desperately ill Mom really was."

He fell silent.

There was something self-absorbed, grieving about the way he dropped heavily onto the end of the worn white sofa, only an arm's distance from where Nick sat. Nick wasn't sure what to say.

He finally decided not to say anything.

After a couple of moments, Payne continued.

"Mom was...it was pretty bad for the last couple of months. Lots of pain. For both of us."

He looked up and glanced around the white room as if seeking an escape from the prison of his memories. In the flat light, his face looked haunted. Then he relaxed and settled into the soft cushion of the sofa.

"Aunt Emilia died the day after Mom did, even though we didn't find out for a while afterward. And Mom died without saying a word about this to anyone." He gestured absently to indicate the house. "I don't know if she even knew. I didn't. But suddenly, instead of all of this going to Aunt Emilia's niece, it went to her heir, Emilia's great-nephew. Me."

He thumped himself theatrically on the chest.

"The lawyers had a fit when I walked into their office. They had sent letters, papers to sign, even flight information and a ticket, but somehow had never quite caught on that I was me, not my mother. Took a while for that shock to pass.

"But this is probably the last time they'll let me bend the rules of the will," Payne said, grinning, as he leaned across the short gap between sofa and chair and patted the slick surface of the armrest, just missing Nick's outstretched hand by a couple of inches.

Nick didn't care for Danish modern, and the chair was more angular than he enjoyed, but it was passable. In fact, from that moment on it was *de facto* Nick's chair during the films.

Payne seemed satisfied with the old white sofa.

Nick wasn't sure what to say—an increasingly common and frustrating situation that evening—so he glanced up at the monitor. Everything was ready, including the disc, already in the player and set to go since the red idiot light along the bottom of the screen was on, indicating that the machine was warmed up.

He sighed.

There was an oddly stifling sense in the room, an unusual heaviness of air. Another point on a pattern not yet apparent.

"What's on for tonight?" he asked as he settled back into the chair. He swallowed once, trying to calm his stomach. The cream-of-chicken soup was sloshing around inside as if it hadn't had time to settle into the serious business of digestion—which, in fact, it had not.

Payne stood up.

"Something you'll like, I think. *Alien.*"

"Great. I missed that one."

"I know. You mentioned that last time."

"All right, then," Nick said, gesturing magisterially (and, he felt, idiotically) toward the screen. "Home, James. On with the show."

Payne laughed—giggled almost.

Nick started to laugh, too, but the sound didn't make it past his lips. His stomach still churned.

In point of fact, Nick had seen neither *Alien* nor *Aliens* although he had heard and read about both of them. He had fully intended to see them. Once, three years before, just after he had moved into his place, he had even gone so far as to plan to rent a player and the two film, but on the way to the video store, he had run over scrap of wooden shingle from a decaying house nearby and picked up a nail in his rear tire—the only one on the car that was anywhere near worth its weight in rubber.

Since the previous flat had been changed by the pros at the tire shop, the lug nuts were screwed on so tightly that it took him almost an hour and four scraped fingers before he finally made the change. By then he was out of the mood for movies. Instead, he just drove back home, wrenching the steering wheel viciously at the blind corner just off Greensward, and screeched up outside his house.

He had stomped inside, not even stopping to turn on the hall lights or anything, but went right into the cramped bathroom and, under the rippled reflection in the mirror, dribbled merthiolate across his knuckles.

From there he went into the kitchen and pulled out a bottle, got quietly drunk to forget the sting, and passed out fully dressed on the living room couch, mindless of lumps and sprung springs and sagging cushions.

That was it for *Alien* and *Aliens.*

Somehow, after that, he had just never gotten around to renting them. So his enthusiasm was genuine, his interest high. It should have been a great night. But the viewing went subtly wrong.

Oh, the physical arrangements were no different from when they had watched Butch Cassidy and the Sundance Kid grab hold of that belt and leap yelling from the cliff into nothingness. There was still the single sofa, now next to the Danish modern chair Payne seemed to avoid. The curtains still cut the light from outside like it was a physical substance that could be severed with a kitchen knife; on the other hand, the resulting darkness sharpened the clarity of the images on the screen glowing from the monitor that hung from dead-white wall.

On the surface, everything was the same.

But there was a difference nonetheless. Payne seemed ill-at-ease, talking more than usual. He stood again and left the room suddenly, yelling "Be right back" at Nick as he trailed down the hallway to the kitchen.

He returned carrying a hunk of cheese on a wooden cutting board and a bowl for Nick's Better Cheddars. After he sat down, he chattered, almost querulously it seemed. Nick nodded vacantly, looked up at the monitor filled with snowy static, glanced around the sterile study, *hmmmmned* absently at appropriate times—and felt a cold shiver crawl along his spine when he remembered that he had done the same thing to Mrs. Harrison the day she died.

Just before the credits began, Payne let something slip, something that altered the tenor of the evening.

"You'll like this one."

"Yeah," Nick agreed. "I think so. I've heard enough about it."

"I'll have to invest in a copy of *Alien 3* and *Alien Resurrection*," Payne said as he came through the door. "They're the only ones Aunt Emilia apparently didn't have time to collect. They made big enough splashes when they came out."

By this time, Nick was halfway out of his seat, offering to help set up the cheese and crackers.

Payne motioned for him to sit back down.

"I really wanted to see them, too, when they came out," Nick said from the depths of the chair. "But I just didn't have the bucks. Not to mention that my folks wouldn't let me go to see them anyway. I was what, fourteen or fifteen when *Resurrection* finally made it to the theater in our little metropolis in Montana. Figured I'd have to wait until I got a bit older and it showed up in the video places."

"I'll try to pick it up this week," Payne said absently as he made some adjustments to the plates and bowl, studied the final effect, and nodded to himself.

"I saw the original version, though, on TV, when I was a kid," Nick said.

"What?"

"You know, the B-flick from the fifties that they based *Alien* on. I don't remember its name."

"Me either. Must have missed that one, too."

He was still studying the arrangements of cheese board and bowl, his lips pursed and his eyes narrowed.

"But this one is great. When I was watching it this afternoon...."

"You watched it already?" Nick said sharply, looking up.

"Sure...." He pushed the bowl infinitesimally to the left. "Why not?" Payne answered offhandedly—studiously offhandedly, it seemed to Nick. The tone was wrong, so carefully neutral that it sounded practiced.

Yet there was no reason for it to be other than neutral. There was nothing, after all, to say that Payne couldn't watch anything he wanted. It was his house, his film. But they *had* tacitly agreed that on the nights they watched together they would stick to things either definitely old or definitely new.

Payne had suggested it, in fact. That way, he had argued, they would either discover the film at the same time, or both be able to make intelligent comments.

Now Payne had watched *Alien* for the first time just before Nick arrived.

Speaking into a thick silence, Nick finally answered Payne's question. "No reason, I guess."

Payne continued talking, as if the interruption had never happened.

"It's great. Good effects, especially the lighting. I'd like to see it on a big screen, in a real theater. You miss too much, too many details, when everything is television-sized. The sets are strange, though, really strange. Erotic...sexy. I read somewhere that the director or producer or designer or someone had worked penis and vagina imagery all through. Cocks and cunts."

Nick stared. It wasn't simply the sexual references that surprised him. He was used to such things, having survived several courses under Freudians who insisted that every walking-stick or ship's mast in Hawthorne and Melville stood for the author's repressed sexuality—or, according to the more aggressive critics, repressed homosexuality.

Nick had in fact heard similar things said about *Alien*, from literary people as well as from film buffs.

No, the references themselves didn't bother him. But the words did, and even more, that Payne had said them. To begin with, Payne anything but literary-minded. His strength seemed to be business, the pragmatic side of life. According to what he had told Nick over the past weeks, he had already begun working through his aunt's notebooks, trying to interest a number of companies in exploring ideas in them. And he was getting some surprisingly positive responses. But he couldn't get beyond "hello" in any conversation that was based seriously on writers and writing.

Payne was stridently practical. He could repair a garage door and mow a lawn, while Nick often had trouble turning on a light. But Payne never seemed to read—at least Nick never saw a book in the house. In the bedroom, perhaps, he might have installed a small bookcase (if he could get it past the lawyers), but Nick didn't think so. Aunt Emilia had probably covered that particular point quite well in her will. Books would have jarred too violently with the exotically, essentially visual high-tech feeling of the house and its ubiquitous screens. No, Nick was sure The Greer would have argued "Why read a book when you can just turn a screen on."

Nor, in the weeks Nick had known him, did Payne seem interested in sex *per se*. Not that Nick knew much about that part of his life, of course. They shared their quota of mildly blue comments, just two guys kickin' 'round *and by the way did you score last night.*

There was a girl, Nick knew, but he hadn't met her yet. He didn't even know her name.

Generally, though, Payne was even more reserved about matters sexual than Nick was—which meant essentially comatose most of the time.

He wasn't backwoods or ignorant, just reserved. His language was oddly straight-laced for someone of his generation, with few words stronger than an occasional *darn* or *shoot*. And none of the more common sexually-freighted slang at all.

So if the words *penis* and *vagina* might have seemed uncomfortable coming from him, the other two were shocking. Yet he had said them—calmly, coolly, unemotionally.

Nick tried to shrug it off. After all, he had only been around Payne a few weeks; he couldn't really claim to know the other man that well. This was just a new facet, another channel tuning in.

When Nick didn't say anything for a long while, Payne glanced over at him, then stood and left the room.

Nick heard the distant click of a door closing, followed a moment later by a slightly different *click* as it opened again.

Payne reappeared in a few seconds.

"Just turned the player on," he said tonelessly.

He sat down as the credits began.

In the darkness, Nick heard Payne breathing heavily, rapidly, as if winded from running.

Alien was darker than Nick had anticipated, both figuratively and literally. He didn't care for the implications of the plot, with its suggestions of corporate manipulation and the dispensability of humans in the face of profit. Humanity divorced from its essence.

The cinematic manipulations were even worse: strobic lights and pitch-black darkness and cats screeching out of nowhere; everything set up so that the monster could terrify not only the crew of the *Nostromo*, but the viewers as well.

That was the way it had been designed, Nick knew, but he still didn't care for it. The result was exciting, generally thrilling, at times even blood-curdling, but for some reason that he found difficult to identify or define, tonight he didn't like it.

"Hey," Nick whispered to Payne at one point, just after the third crewman died. The room was still essentially a theater, after all, even if it was in Payne's home. Anymore when he wanted to say something, he whispered. He was about to suggest that they watch a different film.

"Shhh."

Nick could see Payne's profile, the planes of his forehead sharpened and angular in the monitor's glare, his cheeks alternately lit and shadowed by its flickering blue-gray light.

Tiny beads of sweat glistened like cheap Christmas glitter on the taut skin of his temples. The shifting light made his lips look twisted, his face taut. But somehow it didn't seem like it was because of the movie, Nick realized, or maybe not *just* because of the movie. Payne was rapt, enthralled, watching with an intensity that chilled the full length of Nick's spine.

For the rest of the film, Nick sat stiffly, surrounded by the angles of the Danish modern chair, ill at ease, more uncomfortable than he could remember ever being at Payne's as he half-watched *Alien*, half-watched Payne.

He noticed little things. The way Payne's hands twisted, knuckle over knuckle, like an old man's crippled with arthritis— but only during the most vividly, visually violent segments. Not during the moments of suspense. Nick noticed the shuddering that wrenched Payne's hands and arms, especially when the left hand gripped the arm of the sofa at the moment the plucky heroine pinioned the creature—Nick caught the sexual overtness of the image and connected it with Payne's earlier comments.

Rape.

Violence.

Inversion.

Female raping male.

Payne's fingertips dug into the thick white upholstery, his knuckles white even in the monitor's glare.

Then it was over. Woman and cat lay curled in their womb-like pod. Asleep. Safe.

Payne's fingers slowly relaxed. The tendons on the back of his hand softened into faint lines and disappeared into the texture of his skin.

From where he sat, Nick could see the sweat on Payne's shirt, at the collar and under the arms. The air in the room suddenly smelled acrid with a musky sweat-odor even though the evening was in fact rather cool and a faint breeze fluttered from some-where—perhaps through the crack between door and jamb— and chilled the room enough that Nick shivered.

Finally, Payne leaned into the sofa and breathed deeply. They didn't talk much. Only a few comments, desultory at best, abrupt at worst. Mostly from Payne.

Then Nick left. At his own suggestion, not Payne's. But Nick thought that Payne was as relieved as he was.

He let himself out.

CHAPTER FOURTEEN

Looking back later, Nick decided that that evening had begun the overt change. Oh, there were a couple more nights of mutually chosen films, of open discussions, of uninhibited enjoyment. But in spite of them, the pattern had begun to form.

Soon Nick began, however unconsciously, to avoid Payne's invitations, fabricating excuses, afraid to tell his landlord flat out "No." And the fact that Nick began thinking of him as *the landlord* stuck him as even more frustrating, at times threatening.

"Tomorrow night, Payne? Hey, I'm sorry, but I've got this book that I have to get back to special collections on Friday, and I'm only half way through. If only...."

Or "Tonight? I wish you'd asked an hour ago. But I've got to go...."

If Payne had pressed, Nick would not have been able to give a single, concrete reason not to come over.

Even so the invitations continued, if anything coming more frequently than before. Payne would drop by Nick's house, three, four times a week, and more often than not, Nick ended up following him across the ragged grass and into Payne's place to watch a film.

One Saturday they watched two films rather than the usual one, putting Nick a couple of hours behind in his own work and reminding him of C. S. Lewis's comment about listening to the same symphony twice in one day.

Even with his hesitance about going over to Payne's too often, the films threatened to eat up more time than he could easily allow. After all, he had to get through *The Faerie Queene* plus relevant criticism in the next few weeks or his whole schedule would be shot to hell.

Then, too, the kinds of films changed. *Alien* was only the beginning. Some of the others Payne mentioned had far less to offer in terms of plot, character, development, or literary or cinematic excellence. Some were merely excuses for decapitations or exploding crania or ripped limbs—in short, for spilling as many gallons of blood as possible on the screen. *Extro* and *Videodrome* and *Silent Night, Bloody Night* and *Slaughter Junction* left Nick with a bad taste in his mouth. Payne's choices seemed to have degenerated into simple, mindless exercises in blood.

The night came, as perhaps it inevitably had to, when Nick simply walked out on one. The next day, he couldn't even remember the name of the film. In the middle of a scene detailing with excruciating, almost lovingly depicted care the dismemberment of a six-year-old boy strangled moments before by his rapist, he stood up.

"Got some papers I have to read tonight," he mumbled, his eyes drawn in spite of his revulsion to the scarlet splashes on the screen. The back of his legs bumped against his chair. "See you tomorrow."

Payne didn't seem to notice. He neither looked away from the screen nor answered. In the eerily-lit study, his face was silhouetted by crimson, the light slicing away at the angles of cheek and forehead, throwing his hair into black shadow. Nick shivered and backed out of the room. He made it through the hallway by the reflected light from the monitor. The crimson glare struck the metal-framed diplomas and glittered back at him. He heard sounds from the other rooms—muted sounds of monitors spieling their visual images into emptiness, spinning horrors for no one to see. He shivered again.

At the hallway door, he stopped. The living room was pitch dark. The screen was dead; the white carpet was a flood of blackness except for the first few feet from the hall. There, the nap was tinged with flickering red and blue and silver. He swallowed and stepped into the darkness.

Consciously deciding to cross that living room just might have been the bravest thing he ever did. The fact that the living-room screen had apparently shorted out and then suddenly flared on as he reached for the door knob didn't help. His fingers were just about to curl around the knob that was visible only as a slight lessening of the darkness, a subtle glow tinged with hints of gold.

Suddenly the antique brass knob burst into flame, faceting light like a thousand shards of fire as it reflected something glowing and red behind him. He whirled, his heart thumping so hard that he could feel the blood pulsing through his temple, his neck. A scream caught behind his teeth and strangled itself on his fear. As he turned, a wave of static distorted the screen on the far wall, throwing the room into silver relief.

Then the static died, as suddenly as it had appeared. In its place, he saw the red-stained corpse, a hand reaching into the open wound, tugging and pulling at something unnamable that brought the scream—or its twin—back into his throat. In the light of the monitor, the white room was tinged with scarlet, all but the black chess pieces glimmering on the board. In them, Nick saw the blood-red and ebony of Poe's *Masque of the Red Death*. Unmask! Unmask!

He almost retched before he could spin on his heel and wrench the door open and run outside to stand beyond the bottom step of the porch for a long moment, bent over, shaking hands braced on shaking knees, drawing deep breaths of clean air and feeling his pulse gradually calming.

The street lights glowed somberly, sedately. Stars winked from behind occasional coverings of clouds. Somewhere at the end of the block the sounds of a car roared, died, roared again and gradually faded away as someone drove away from Greensward and disappeared into the night. Across the street, a light in a side window blinked off. Then the night was silent and still and cool, and Nick turned to go back up the steps, to cross the envelope of night within the porch and swing the heavy front door closed. It was already closed. He couldn't remember closing it but the panel stared back at him like a slab of night, darker than the star-haggard sky.

In spite of his parting comment that night, Nick didn't see Payne for three days. Payne never openly invited Nick over again to watch films. He came to Nick's place occasionally for chess, but the games were taut, their cordiality forced on both sides. Then, suddenly, days might pass without one seeing the other. When their paths did cross, Payne was courteous, polite, friendly—but an essential something had disappeared.

Finally a week went by without Nick seeing Payne, hearing from him, or speaking to him. At the end of that week, working late one night on a difficult passage from Spenser, Nick suddenly froze, one hand halfway to the edge of the page, ready to turn it but stopped in the middle of the intention. For a moment, he couldn't figure out what was wrong. He glanced at his clock.

Two-seventeen.

He listened carefully, at first hearing only the mechanical *hummmmm* of the clock, the faint creaking of the old house settling, sounds that he had grown used to; in fact, now he couldn't sleep unless he *could* hear them. Then he heard the other sound, starting so faintly as to be nearly subliminal but even that subtle hint was enough to chill him.

He strained to hear, afraid to move, afraid even to lean over the haphazardly piled papers cluttering his desk and put his ear closer to the open window facing onto Payne's place. It grew from faint to soft, then became unmistakable and chilling. It was the *squeeeeak* of the glider-swing on the porch as it swung back and forth, ripping squeals of protest from age-rusted links where they hung suspended from an eye-bolt in the splintered beam.

CHAPTER FIFTEEN

Yes, there was a girl. And it was true that Nick hadn't seen her yet or heard her name. Payne had barely mentioned her to Nick. But she existed nonetheless.

Payne had met her purely by accident.

He had pretty much stuck close to the house during the first weeks after his arrival, other than for those occasional trips relating to Great-Aunt Emilia's properties—as on the weekend when the Harrisons died. In fact, he had lived on Greensward Lane for nearly a month when he realized suddenly and inexplicably one bright Saturday morning that he had been living in Southern California all that time and had not yet even seen the ocean, other than a quick glimpse as his plane swept in at Los Angeles International, and then he had been too tired from the cross-country flight to notice much.

At first, it would have been too much trouble for Payne to get out there since he had no transportation for himself, but in the meantime—after finding out just how extensive Great-Aunt Emilia's legacy was—he had bought a car, his first, actually. It was a brand new Toyota that cost him more than he had expected, even after becoming reasonably conditioned to Southern California prices by watching the local TV channels and being deluged with automobile commercials. But the mpg estimates seemed good and the engine ran smoothly and it was the right size for him to feel comfortable in the crush of freeway traffic.

About ten o'clock on the first Saturday after he bought it, he backed it down the driveway and pulled along the sidewalk in front of the house. The motor idled quietly. He had his hands draped over the steering wheel and had relaxed back against the bucket seat, smelling the smell of new car—*Okay, it comes directly out of an aerosol can labeled "New Car Smell,"* he reminded himself, but who cares. *It's a great smell, especially when the car's mine*. He closed his eyes, listening to the soft purr of the motor. The sun was already warm, the sky bright, the air light with the fragrance of flowers and new-mown grass from across the street. He wore a pair of old trunks, a well-worn T-shirt, and an old pair of Adidas runners.

He opened one eye a crack and glanced at his own lawn. Along the crumbling concrete walk, strands of Bermuda grass trailed over the edges, making the whole place look shaggy already, even after the crew-cut he gave it only.... Shit, almost a month ago, he thought. I gotta get on it or it'll be so tall I'll never get that mower through it.

An image of Charles Schulz's claustrophobic Snoopy lost in over-grown grass popped into his mind and he grinned. In fact, he even went so far as to cut the engine, open the car door, and drop one foot to the cracked asphalt before an inner voice sliced through the image, shattering visions of Snoopy and the ragged lawn and any thoughts of work today:

You've never even been to the beach.

Right. Stupid. All this time and never seen the beach.

He pulled his foot back in, slammed the door shut, and, then and there, decided it was time to change that insane state of things.

He didn't know exactly how to get to the beaches, but he did know that the Pacific Ocean was pretty big and lay pretty much to the west of Los Angeles. Since not even he could miss something that big, he began by driving south and east on the 101, back toward the San Fernando Valley, then transitioning (he hated that word, "*I transition, you transition, he/she/it transitions!*" but the radio traffic-reporters insisted on using it, that was what everyone called it out here, shifting from one freeway to the next) to the south-bound lanes of the 405 that would take him toward LA. After all, it wasn't as if he were late for an appointment or anything.

He wandered for an hour or so, enjoying the sights, trying to get used to freeway driving, mentally comparing California drivers with the ones he had known back east. Rather to his surprise, he found that most were usually more courteous and only a few sometimes crazier. Finally he found himself on Highway 10 cutting through mid-town Los Angeles toward Santa Monica, heading straight-arrow west. Santa Monica. He recognized the name from television shows and movies

The magic name!

There was a beach out there somewhere if he just kept driving west.

About the time he spotted the first crescent of sand, the freeway died out, arcing north out of a short tunnel to become Pacific Coast Highway—another name to conjure up images of sun and romance, made familiar by film and television.

He kept driving as the highway turned northward, glancing at the stretches of sand to his left, catching inviting glimpses of bikinis and frisbees and volleyballs, trying to keep one eye on the lanes of traffic and another on the ocean. His radio hummed quietly—two characters interspersing old-time records with comedy routines in oddly androgynous voices.

He drove on. After all the time it had taken him to get out and find the ocean (*as if* it *were lost!*) he didn't particularly want to stop. Just driving along with the windows wide open to the breezes, breathing salty air and listening to the subtle roar of the surf was worth the time.

Fifteen minutes later he passed a sign reading "Malibu." Another Mecca for sun-worshippers, whose fame had penetrated even the heartland of Pennsylvania. *You're really here, Payne old boy, right in the homeland of sun tans and movie stars.* He grinned and slowed down, trying to see the magic for himself. Whatever it was that he had expected, Malibu disappointed him. Most of the way he couldn't even see the ocean for the buildings. The beach side of Pacific Coast Highway was lined with tall, narrow houses—rabbit-hutches, his grandmother would have called them—with garages doors facing PCH like blank faces without mind or soul; the ones that were open revealed dark, raw throats angling back from the pavement.

The fabled golden beaches were hidden, draped, obscured. Further on, he could see where the ocean bowed outward, pulling the houses even farther from the highway and forming The Colony, where the stars really lived. Entry there was obviously by invitation only; Payne passed the formidable guardhouse without slowing.

He headed north over curving hills overgrown with estates and houses surrounded by pools and tennis courts and eroding sandstone abutments cloaked in violet verbena and scarlet ice plant. At a spot called Point Dume, he passed a shopping center that seemed out of place, too normal for Mecca. Just beyond it the highway swung to the left and slid down the ocean side of the hill. At the base, the road split into a Y where a green sign announced "Public Beach" and pointed with a weathered arrow along the left-hand branching.

For no good reason except that the sun was warm and high and the air cool and fresh, he turned left, guiding the Toyota along a two-lane road that threatened to dead-end at the beach. At the last moment, though, the road turned left again, angling south along the base of sandstone cliffs crumbling into rank undergrowth and nascent sand. Lying on his right now, the ocean glittered beyond waves of white sand and tanned flesh. He kept driving.

Halfway along the beach, he shut off the radio. The sounds of kids squealing as they built sand castles and teenagers *thump*ing volleyballs across sand courts billowed through his window.

At the end of the stretch, the road bore left again, this time upward, climbing above the beach toward monstrous homes perched like cormorants above the sand. At least one stuck out a dozen feet or more from the cliff, a foot-thick slab of concrete cantilevered into dizzying space. Payne felt momentarily light-headed just glancing up at it.

Straight ahead, however, a guard booth straddled an adjunct road. Its peeling plywood front supported a hand-lettered sign:

Parking—$4.00 Per Day
NO RETURN ON ENTRY TICKET

On an impulse, Payne pulled alongside the booth and slipped four crumpled bills from his pants pocket. The attendant was a bare-foot, deeply browned kid about eighteen, with bleached hair and faded red trunks fraying at the seams.

He sauntered alongside the car, barely bothering to glance inside, and grabbed the money Payne held out to him. With his other hand, he reached into the Toyota and tucked a yellow ticket along the inside of the window before returning to the shade of an umbrella hitched behind the booth, hiking his feet up onto an overturned plastic bucket, and burrowing into a newsstand-fresh copy of *Playboy*.

The kid hadn't spoken a single word during the entire interchange.

Payne drove through.

On the far side of the booth, the road was rougher than the highway and not as well repaired. At times, it was little better than gravel, with bites of pavement missing on the ocean side, as if storms had washed away more than the county could (or cared to) restore. Undulating dunes alternately hid and framed low waves swirling like frizzled hair against the neck of the beach.

It must be low tide, Payne decided. The air had a decided pungency to it that suggested more than just salt and sand.

Every fifteen yards or so, county maintenance workers had thrown down asphalt speed bumps, so Payne drove the mile and a quarter to the parking lot at between ten and twenty miles an hour, grimacing every time the rear end swayed or the front tires thumped against the sun-bleached humps that straddled the roadway. Several bumps were hidden by miniature dunes;

when his tires crunched against them, they seemed to hit his car harder than the rest. But he didn't try to go any faster.

Finally, the road pulled away from the ocean and widened into a parking lot. The inland side abutted almost vertical cliffs of eroding rock, ferrous-red banded with dingy yellow, cut with frighteningly deep ravines. Every so often, frail wooden stairways led from a back yard above down to the beach, perching their hundreds of worn steps precariously against the crumbling rock face. On the ocean side, Payne saw open beach studded with three lifeguard towers and two cinderblock restrooms.

He drove on to the far end of the lot before parking next to a chain-link fence. He stopped, turned off the engine, and just relaxed. The air was fresher here, tangy with salt but clean-smelling.

He raised his arm as if to punch a dial on the radio, then stopped. This part of the beach was almost silent, save for the muted whisper of the waves a hundred yards distant. There were no children here, no families picnicking. All he could see were the outlines of three or four sunbathers stretched out on oversized towels. He savored the silence.

Finally, though, it grew too hot in the enclosed car, dizzying, headachy hot. He stepped out, rolled up the window, and slammed and locked the door.

A few steps more and there he was, facing the Pacific where it threw itself against the damp sand of the beach. All thoughts of house and property and Aunt Emilia and bone-white walls fled, leaving him standing in the quiet and the calm.

Inside and outside, everything was warmth and sunshine.

He walked straight toward the ocean, stopping just before the waves doused his Adidas®, then looked up and down the beach. Farther northward, where the beach curved out of sight, a few families clustered in knots at the water line, with older kids splashing in the low surf and younger ones dabbling in sand architecture.

Southward, there were almost no people. An odd precipice of rock jutted outward, ending in collapse as its tumbled boulders cut off the beach. Payne turned southward. It took him only a few moments to reach the boulders. The tide was low enough that it looked possible for him to slosh through shallow pools around the rocks, far enough at least for him to see if there was anything on the other side.

He started around but had not even gotten his shoes wet when he glanced up along the fragmented face of the cliff. There seemed to be a pathway over the rocks—through them, really. He began climbing. The boulders felt gritty with sand, slippery where the sun dried them and the sand no longer clung. He climbed slowly, carefully, using both hands more than once to retain a precarious balance. Once his foot slipped and he barely avoided gashing his leg open on the shattered remains of a beer bottle. As the path crested, the rocks became more uneven. The handholds were clammy beneath his fingers, and small pockets of sand caught smelled distantly but distinctly of urine.

At the top of the rock heap, a weather-beaten bench stood guard over the promontory a dozen feet away. He considered climbing to the bench and then abandoned the idea when he got close enough to see that all of the wooden slats had been ripped off, either by vandals or by winter storms. All that remained were the metal supports cemented to the boulder.

Instead of going further that way, he followed the pathway down toward an isolated pocket of beach. The path narrowed, transforming before he noticed into little more than a tiny, slippery ledge on a sandstone cliff. Payne moved more carefully now. Twice he almost fell.

Finally, with a series of short jumps from rock to rock, he thumped onto wet sand, his ankles twinging from the sudden, jarring impact. He looked oceanward to water framed in boulders six-feet high and bearded in seaweed and barnacles. The beach was behind him and to his left as he stared across the breaking waves. Eyes focused on the ebb and swell of the first ocean waves he had ever seen this close, he began walking along the shore.

Someone ran past him from the beach into the water.

A man.

A *naked* man.

Surprised, Payne stopped and stared into the ocean. By the time what he thought he had seen registered in Payne's mind and he could focus on the waves, the man was little more than a knot of head and shoulder jutting out of blue-gray surf. Payne turned away from the water and stared along the beach.

Angular rocks formed pockets of sunlight and shadow, studding the beach with intricately repeating patterns of white and black over gray-brown sand. Hollows around the rocks were filled with bodies, some nude, some barely covered by bikinis tinier than any Payne had ever seen. Closest to him sat a couple of girls, probably no more than thirteen or fourteen. Even though they had little enough as yet to fill them with, they wore scanty two-piecers—one with blue stripes on a yellow background, the other studded with pink dots on pale green.

The girls were studiously pretending *not* to look at a sleeping man of about twenty lying on his stomach not a dozen feet from them. From the tan lines on his waist and thighs, he usually wore Speedos; and from the darkness of his tan where it contrasted with the paler tones of his buttocks, he usually wore them often. Today, he wore nothing.

No matter how hard the girls struggled to look in other directions, Payne noted with a smile, they always lost the battle. They would stare around for a while then, as if on a silent command, shoot a quick glance at the man, then turn away and huddle shoulder to shoulder and head to head, and giggle. A few seconds later, they looked again.

"I'd *die* if Sean knew I was here," blue-stripe said breathlessly between giggles.

Payne could only imagine what Sean would have done if the boy were standing where Payne was standing, watching the entire performance.

"Or Bobby! Gawd!" That came in a stage-whisper from pink-dots. The last sound elongated until it was less a word than an inarticulately strangled response pulled from the center of her pubescent self. They cast another set of darting glances over their shoulders.

"Think your Mom is looking for us yet?" Blue-stripes asked, probably more out of concern for the time than for Mom's worry about their well-being. It wouldn't do for Mom to come searching for the little darlings and find them in the middle of a nude beach.

Pink-dots shook her head. They stared intently at a spot on the cliffs, then chanced another glance over their shoulders.

"He looks like Zac Efron, doesn't he," Blue-stripe breathed.

"Gawd," Pink-dot agreed.

By this point, however, Payne knew full well that the man under scrutiny was not asleep. Each time the girls turned away, his eyes slit open enough for sunlight to glint off dark pupils. Suddenly, while the girls huddled and whispered, the man rolled casually onto his back, his legs stretched out toward the ocean and his hands cupped beneath his head. Although his eyes were closed tight against the glare, he was smiling broadly.

If you've got it, flaunt it, Payne thought almost admiringly.

The man had it, and he certainly knew how to flaunt it.

The girls turned for next their stolen glance…and froze. They went whiter than the sand they were sitting on. Two adolescent jaws dropped with a single snap. Two faces burned a sudden scarlet that spread onto their necks and shoulders. Without speaking another word, they snatched up their towels and ran past Payne toward the path. Payne watched until they disappeared over the crest. By then, the young man had turned onto his stomach again and was, to all appearances, peacefully asleep.

The peace of the beach had been preserved.

Payne took another moment to study the beach. In spite of their nudity, he realized gradually, few of the people seemed consciously exhibitionistic. Most were artfully draped by shadows or curves of sand caught by angled boulders. The only exception was a man curled against the cliff. He must have weighed three hundred pounds, and it was obvious that this was his first foray into sunlight this season. His skin was dead-fish white and his mass had all of the appeal of a dead or dying beached whale. Everyone else looked young —in their thirties or less. In spite of his back-East inhibitions, Payne had to admit that most of them, male as well as female, took good care of their bodies and maybe had a right to show them off. It was, he decided at last, a *conservative* nude beach, if such a thing were possible.

Still—it was a *nude* beach.

Payne unconsciously slipped his thumbs into the waistband of his old trunks—faded, full-cut, and baggy at the legs—and pulled them up tighter around his belly. He angled away from the water and from most of the sunbathers toward an unclaimed outcrop. He settled in the warm sand on the far side, shutting out most of his view left or right but keeping open the lower beach and the expanse of ocean.

This is a nude beach, he repeated unnecessarily to himself. He had heard about them back home through carefully edited clips on the eleven-o'clock news, late enough that impression-able young minds would long since be in bed. He had heard about them, sure, but he hadn't expected to stumble across one, certainly not this accidentally. As he sat there, he realized with a mild shock that in spite of what he might have expected he wasn't necessarily offended by the nudity. In fact, the confron-tation with it was so sudden that he had not yet had time to decide *what*he thought, but the idea was certainly new and took time to assimilate.

From where he was sitting, though, he could see no one, nude or otherwise. Nor could he hear anything except the crash of waves against barnacle-bearded boulders. Once, twice, three times an unusually strong wave sent a veil of misty spray over him, cooling his back and shoulders where the sun struck with mid-day ferocity. For all he cared, though, he was alone, the only person for an infinity of miles.

He pulled his T-shirt off and spread it against the rock behind him. Slipping his feet out of his shoes, he lay back to enjoy the warmth and the breeze and the rhythm of waves meeting rocks and parting again. He slept without even knowing when reverie slipped into dreaming.

His dream was as dark and confused as the beach was bright and orderly. Aunt Emilia was somewhere in it, or at least that part of her he saw as a spectral figure that ebbed and flowed as if hidden behind a veil that parted with the slightest breeze. He never saw her face, never heard her voice, but she overwhelmed the dream, making it more hers than his. Whiteness played a part, and the house, and other things that Payne could never remember except as shadows and shudders.

When he woke he was glistening with sweat, and not entirely from the afternoon sun reflecting off the rocks. His trunks were damp along the elastic waistband, clammy, even in the heat. He lay disoriented for a moment, almost lost.

To his right, beyond the rust-colored boulder that hid him, he heard voices above the thrum of surf. Most of the voices were male, with only one or two women. He couldn't distinguish any words, just sounds like distant murmurs inside sea shells. *The ocean listening to people*, he thought, then shook his head to disrupt the image. For a while he felt unusually depressed, frustrated, and oddly but pointedly fearful. His heart still thumped and he felt winded. When he sat up, his head swirled like he was drunk.

He sat still for a long time. Finally he stood up. The beach was empty except for four or five clusters of people stretched out in the sunlight. The beached whale was gone; so was the sometimes-sleeping young man. Two other men, both nude and sharing a zebra-striped wool blanket, lay on their stomachs where the young man had been. Like him, they seemed to be asleep. Their elbows touched.

Payne's stomach knotted, flooded by the darkness and half-remembered threat from his dream. Images flickered through his mind so rapidly that he could not distinguish one from the other. Yet in their totality, they terrified him. And what frightened him even more was that he did not know why. He swallowed. The sun was searing. His eyes burned; they felt gritty and dehydrated. He was thirsty. When he swallowed, his throat felt rough and raw.

He coughed.

At the sound, one of the men shifted, turning halfway onto his side to face Payne. He smiled. Payne jerked his head away to the softly curving surf, the yielding golden sand, the line of rocks stretching like a barricade between him and the cliffs and the single cormorant perched above a streak of lime-stained stone.

Someone moved.

A figure emerged from the shadows where the cliff cut around, then as quickly disappeared again.

CHAPTER SIXTEEN

He squinted against the sun, concentrating on the flicker of movement, consciously turning his back to the men on the blanket. *Get thee behind me,* he thought. And didn't know why.

The figure shimmered, moved closer. Clots of dream-world distorted his vision; for an instant, the figure seemed only a dark lump against the brightness, a night-swathed, crippled figure lurching from behind the rocks. Then the instant passed and the figure stepped out of the shadows into full light.

It was a girl. She was dressed in almost immodestly short cutoff levis and a T-shirt with something printed on the front. The words were too faded to read; by the time she was sufficiently close for the words to be marginally legible, Payne would have been too embarrassed to stare long enough to read them. She was barefoot.

She picked her way carefully along the damp rocks, leaning into the cliff when the spray threatened to reach her. She made slow progress, as if she had no particular purpose in following the ridge of rocks bursting through the ocean spray. She was too intent on finding and keeping her footing to notice anyone.

Behind Payne, two voices joined the muted undercurrent of sound. The two men were awake and talking, their voices blurred by the pounding waves and by Payne's pounding heart. Payne knew which of the two was speaking and didn't know how he knew it. Part of him wanted to turn around. He swallowed hard, and for a second he saw the blank white wall of his...of *her* room back in Tamarind Valley.

He shook his head violently and the whiteness turned red then disappeared, blending into sandstone cliffs rising cormorant-stained and rain-cut above the girl. She was nearer now, almost ready to drop from the last boulder onto the sand. She crouched down, balanced herself with one hand against a cut in the cliff. As her legs spread wide, he saw a thin ridge of muscle tracing the inside of her thighs. He focused on a deeper shadow.

Static-twisted blue lightning flared through his mind, crashed against his ears. *The dream.* He shivered, passed his palm across his eyes, panting in the delicious coolness of the shadow of his own hand. The fingers on his right hand twinged with a passing pain.

The men's voices rose, fell, rose again in a cadenced counterpoint to the surf. He understood no words but the intonations of intertwined sound grew more intimate, more threatening. He knew that he would turn and instead he looked straight ahead, concentrated again on the smooth line of silken muscle along the girl's inner thigh. A single drop of ocean spray had caught there and glistened in a perfect droplet.

She still had not looked up. She had not seen him standing there. The girl jumped. Her feet thudded against wet sand, leaving shallow prints like fading echoes. She straightened and walked along the beach, her feet just inside the tide line where froth curled around her toes and slid over the arch of her foot, licking away glittering sand.

Payne followed her with his eyes. The men's voices faded again. The dream struggled to the surface once, then faded also.

He followed her with his eyes. She continued down the beach, looking neither left nor right. Payne felt dizzy. The sand between them stretched white and unruffled, studded by rock as black as midnight scattered across the whiteness. The cliffs bleached out, whitening to match the lime streaks of generations of sea-birds.

He swayed, steadying himself with one hand against a rock. The men's voices rose and fell, sparkling like blue-white static against the stillness. About to faint, he half-turned toward them, then twisted back.

"Hey," he whispered to the girl. Then he spoke again, stronger, tossing his voice toward her retreating back. He let his gaze drop from her shoulders to her buttocks, to the clean, neat line of her legs.

"Hey, there."

She paused. For a moment it seemed that she would continue onward, then she glanced over her shoulder. The beach was silent, except for the layering of surf through the air.

"Me?"

"Yeah, wait just a minute. Please." He stooped and retrieved his T-shirt and shoes, then walked down the beach toward her.

The two men did not notice him as he passed; they were lying on their stomachs, apparently asleep. Their elbows touched.

The girl waited for him. Payne thought he saw relief flicker across her face when he emerged from behind the waist-high boulders. He was wearing swim trunks. Had she expected something else?

He caught up with her, smiled, and asked, "What's on the other side?" as he gestured back to the ledge jutting into the ocean.

The sand was gray now, not white. The rocks were reddish-brown, bearded with dying seaweed and locked barnacles. There were no voices at all.

"Back there? Not much. Mostly rocks. No beaches, at least not for a mile or so. I like to walk there. There's never anyone else there, or at least not very many. I can be alone there, to think."

"Oh. I see." He started to turn away.

"Hey," she said with a laugh, "that's okay. I've thought my quota of deep thoughts for today. I'm just leaving."

"Oh."

They walked a few more steps. Payne felt urged to speak but lacked words. He dug his toes into the hot sand.

"Live around here?" he finally managed.

"Down the highway. And you?"

"In the hills. Tamarind Valley."

"I've been almost everywhere in the area, but never there," she said, sounding mildly surprised. "I've heard it's nice."

"Yeah. It is. I like it. I've only lived there a few weeks, though." As if that explained something important.

They reached the end of the beach and began climbing the rocks. Their silence remained unbroken except for an occasional *watch out, there* or *you okay* on the trickier parts, until they both dropped the last foot or so onto the damp sand at Zuma. By then, Payne already knew a lot about her.

Her name was Cathy Litton. She was a student in LA. She had been born in the city and lived her life there, moving from suburb to suburb with her family but always circling like an eternal satellite of Los Angeles. Now she shared an apartment with two girls in the older part of the city south of Santa Monica. She loved walking along the beach...obviously!...and—*what luck!*—she loved watching old films.

That much he learned as they walked from the point to the parking lot. By then he had forgotten his dream, his panic, even his uncharacteristic boldness in calling out to her, although he was certainly pleased that he had done so. She seemed to like him; he certainly liked her.

"How about lunch?" she said as they neared the lot.

"Here?" He glanced at the beach, this part now crowded with families and umbrellas and volleyball nets where an hour or so earlier there had been only sea gulls and silence. "I didn't bring anything." That last came out more apologetic than he liked.

"Neither did I. And not here. Follow me." She slipped into a small car waiting only two down from Payne's and pulled out of the parking space and onto the roadway, gunning her engine impatiently as he fumbled for the key to his Toyota—*shit, the thing looked a wreck next to hers and it wasn't polished and he had left a pile of papers in the back window where she could see what a clod he was and it won't turn over shit what's wrong now the thing better start this time.* It did.

He followed her along PCH, never lagging more than a couple

of car lengths behind, pulling closer when someone threatened to cut between them. Not fifteen minutes later, she turned into the shopping area in Malibu.

John's, a little sandwich place, was almost hidden behind a row of stores. The place was nothing more than a plain wooden counter where you ordered, a pick-up window where the cooks yelled out the numbers of the orders, and some benches and tables outside in the middle of a rose garden.

It was not what Payne expected. The benches were bare wood but aged and weathered, scarred by hundreds, probably thousands, actually, of seam rivets from Levi's back pockets until the wood seemed almost malleable, like some oddly grained upholstery.

They ate lunch together at John's. It was not a date really, he kept telling himself, as if trying not to let his hopes build too high. They were just eating in the same place, at the same table, at the same time.

The sandwiches were great, he decided, but because the alternative would have been to talk with Cathy, he ate more quickly than usual. Then he sat and stared at the orange rind curling along the side of his paper plate. Even though he had enjoyed the lunch, sitting outside and eating next to a beautiful woman who seemed to like him, he felt suddenly self-conscious. There was a long moment of silence.

"Look," he said finally, staring at a single red-and-white rosebud unfurling a yard away. "You don't really know me or anything, but if you'd be interested, I make a great spaghetti dinner and I have hundreds of old films on videocassette. If you'd like to...?"

"Come up and see my etchings, eh?" Cathy said, twirling an invisible mustache and dropping her voice into a creaky *basso* in imitation of a leering, lascivious melodrama villain.

Payne flushed and faced her, his mouth working but no sounds coming.

"No," he finally squeaked, embarrassed by her response as much as by his reaction.

"Hey," she said, recognizing her mistake. "I'm sorry. It's just that sometimes guys...well, sometimes they come on stronger than I want."

He started to stand but she laid her hand on his arm. "No, I'm really sorry," she said. "That crack wasn't called for." She paused a second, looking directly at him. "And I *love* spaghetti." She tugged at his shirt sleeve, using gentle force to pull him back to the bench. She spoke again.

He looked away.

After a moment, "Look, I'm used to guys and lines. I'm not bad-looking, it happens to me often enough. I guess so often that when the real thing happened just now, I didn't recognize it. Seriously, I would love to come over. Do you have *Casablanca*?"

"Sure." He turned toward her.

"It's my favorite."

He brightened. "Okay. Can you come now? You could follow me into Tamarind Valley. I'd only have to stop to pick up a few things at the store." He felt childishly eager and for a moment thought Cathy might agree. Instead she glanced at her watch and shook her head.

"I can't right now. I've got an appointment at three." She saw him begin to retreat again. "Seriously. No line this time. But I can get to Tamarind Valley by five-thirty or six. Okay?"

He nodded.

"Great. It's set." She rested her hand on his arm again. "I've always wanted to see Tamarind Valley. Even the name sounds peaceful and quiet."

He walked her to her car. "Five-thirty or six," he called into her open car window as she backed out of her parking place.

"Right," she called back.

He watched until she pulled out of the parking lot and disappeared between the rows of stores. His car was not far away, glistening in the sunlight. It took him only seconds to cross the black pavement; the heat radiated though his shoes and the asphalt gave softly beneath his feet, as if the summer sun were melting it. The heat increased when he stood next to his car, taking the full reflection of sunlight from its windows.

He reached for the handle. "Shit!" He jerked his hand away from the burning chrome. Swearing softly, he wrapped his shirttail around his fingers, gingerly opened the door, and slid into the car.

It was oven-hot and stuffy inside. He rolled the windows down, grateful for once for the cheap plastic knobs painted to look like metal. Metal would have blistered his fingertips. The steering column was in full sunlight, though, and the wheel was too hot to touch. For a moment he envied the guy who owned the car in the next space; his car had some kind of aluminum fan-like apparatus connected by a suction cup to the base of the window. When the fans were open, the inside of the car was shaded.

The sun reflecting off the hood of Payne's car bleached the metal into a glare of unbroken, searing white. He stared at it, his thoughts trailing into nothingness, into the emptiness of white sand. He stared, and black boulders appeared in the sand. Static rose in his ears, like whispering male voices at first, then more and more like a television tuned to the wrong channel. Sweat beaded from his forehead and dripped to his cheeks, his upper lip, his neck.

He decided to open all of the windows, get out, and wait outside the car in the shade of an arbor of Double Delight roses, just until the wheel was cool enough to touch. He didn't move. The static grew louder and the white vista through his windshield spread. It encompassed John's Sandwich Shoppe, the gardens, the rows of stores, everything, until there was nothing left but white and black and roaring static. Payne stiffened, his muscles tight, his right hand curling into a claw on the hot leather beside him. Without knowing it, he slept.

CHAPTER SEVENTEEN

Nick was busy the night Cathy Litton first came to Payne's. He had been carefully busy for several nights in order to put off Payne's persistent and recurrent invitations to watch films. Still, he considered Nick, a friend, perhaps his closest friend. Nothing had happened to change that.

Certainly Nick would not have been jealous had he known at the time about Cathy. Later, when he knew about her and had time to think about things, he was sure of that.

Nor would he have consciously tried to spy on Payne and Cathy if he had known beforehand that she was coming or if he had seen Payne escorting a girl from her Lexus up the long side-walk to his place. Nick might have noted it, sighed, and turned back to a pile of papers, or to slogging through Spenser, or to whatever else was in the works at the time. He certainly wouldn't have slipped through the hedge and tried to pull a Peeping-Tom at the living room window—or at the bedroom window.

Besides, as he would have discovered by glancing up from his work at the darkened house next door that night, all of the draperies were pulled as tightly closed as they had been when The Greer was alive.

As a matter of fact, though, Nick didn't even hear about her until a couple of days later when Payne was over at Nick's house to play chess. Usually Payne was pretty good and handily beat Nick game after game, but that night his moves were desultory at best, criminal at worst. When he slaughtered his own queen almost without noticing it, Nick came close to calling the game right then. Obviously this wasn't the right time for chess.

"What's up?" Nick asked instead, his hand hovering over an endangered pawn. "Something wrong?"

"What?" Payne looked as startled as if Nick's voice had called him from a deep reverie.

"Your game's sure off tonight," Nick answered. He made his move and quietly set Payne's knight next to the other pieces lined along his side of the game board. "Something wrong?"

"Uh, no," Payne said, "nothing much, I guess." He glanced at the board and slid a piece from one square to the next. Nick could see no sense in the move, especially since it put at least three of Payne's pieces into jeopardy.

Nick reached across the chess board and moved his bishop. Payne seemed hardly to notice the resulting danger to his king. His next move was nothing short of stupid.

"Check," Nick said patiently. "Look, Payne, this game is wasted time tonight." He hesitated—*'tis a far, far better thing I do than I have ever done before*—before coughing to clear his throat and continuing. "Maybe if we, you know, went over to your place and watched...a film or something, at least that way part of the evening might be salvaged."

Payne looked up, his eyes showing interest and life for the first time that night, and nodded slowly. "I got a couple of new cassettes yesterday. They might be fun to watch."

He reached to move his remaining knight.

"Thought you were too busy for films, though," he said as he moved the piece.

The comment came out flatly, neutrally, but it seemed to Nick that there was a hidden edge to Payne's voice. Irritation? Anger? He wasn't sure.

"I...," Nick began.

Payne's hand hovered about six inches above the chess piece.

Then he stopped. Just that—he stopped. For a second Nick wasn't sure if Payne was even breathing. He was eerily still, stone still, as if he were in a trance. Nick started to speak, to call his name and ask him if he felt all right, when he saw Payne's other hand curl over the crease of his trousers just above the knee.

"Payne?" he said finally, as the seconds stretched uncomfortably and Payne still did not move, except for the faint scrabbling of fingernails on the coarse, thick material. In the silence, Nick imagined that he could feel the nails scraping along the woven fibers—*screee, screee, screee.* He shivered. "Payne, are you all right?"

Payne looked up at the sound of Nick's voice. His eyes widened and his breathing increased as if he had been startled. Nick had the feeling that they were no longer sitting in his living room, at least as far as Payne was concerned—that the other man was seeing and hearing something Nick couldn't. Payne's eyes and ears seemed tuned to an entirely different landscape.

Payne's hand moved like an automaton, like one of those waldo hands designed to manipulate things too small or too dangerous for direct human touch. The fingers closed over the chess piece—a black knight, more traditional in design than the pieces in Payne's unused set. The fingers tightened until the knuckles glowed bloodlessly white. It looked like either the plastic knight or his hand would shatter.

"Hey, Payne," Nick said, lightly touching the other man's wrist.

Payne shuddered like someone startled out of sleep, saw Nick's hand on his, and started to smile. His eyes cleared. His other hand straightened, the fingers taut and stiff. He jerked backward. For a moment, before his eyes blinked and Payne—the *real* Payne, Nick thought, as much confused as frightened by the sudden impression—looked out through them, Payne seemed almost ready to lash out at Nick.

Nick pulled away, restoring the neutrality of the chessboard between them. Payne stared at Nick for a moment before he gently returned the knight to the board—to precisely the same place it had been.

"Sorry, Nick. I was thinking of...something."

"That's okay," Nick said automatically. But it wasn't, not

really. There was something ominous in Payne's eyes, or there *had been* something for a second, that frightened him. Now it was gone.

Payne stood and smiled and gestured to the front porch.

"Let's sit out there for a while. Just relax and talk."

"Do you want to watch a...?" Nick began.

"No." Payne stiffened momentarily, then relaxed his tensed shoulders. "No, not tonight. Maybe tomorrow. Let's just sit and talk and drink."

They moved out to the two rickety chairs on the porch. Payne pulled one over by the edge-rail and slouched deep into the fraying cushion, feet hooked over the white railing. Nick sat for a moment in the other—Payne had taken the one Nick usually preferred—before getting up and going into the kitchen to rummage through cupboards and shelves, finally returning with a couple of boxes of crackers, a wedge of cheese about to make the transformation from cheddar to something pungently stronger, and a couple of drinks.

Payne hadn't moved. It was as if he were a statue staring out over the same landscape for centuries, not seeing the changes wrought by time and the recurring seasons, not caring, just a static part of things without knowing how or why.

Nick sliced the cheese, poured a few crackers into a bowl, popped the tab on a beer. Still nothing from Payne.

So Nick settled back.

Maybe five minutes later Payne spoke, his eyes still focused at some point a few feet above the house across the street. The only thing that moved was his mouth, as if some kind of alien were speaking through him, appropriating his physical apparatus but remaining essentially foreign to it.

Nick flashed on that kid's performance in one of the last films the two of them had watched, *The Hidden*. His brow furrowed as he tried to remember. *What was his name, the one who was Paul Atreides in the monstrosity they released as* Dune, *the guy with the high, white cheekbones and jet black hair and whose lips barely moved when he spoke and who was really an alien*

Altairean in disguise? The voice that crossed the silence of the porch was Payne's though. It sounded distant and quiet at first, but it was recognizably Payne's.

"I met a girl the other day."

"Oh." Nick was nonplussed. The comment was miles from anything he had expected. He looked at the man across the porch.

Payne was apparently waiting patiently for him to say something. His body was tensed, his shoulders high and almost hunched. Payne's eyes still strained outward, to the other side of the street.

"Oh," Nick finally repeated, "Where?"

"Some beach." Payne waved vaguely westward with his left hand. The movement looked more as if he were swatting a pesky fly than suggesting a direction. "I don't remember which one."

The voice seemed strained but gradually relaxed as he continued. "We had lunch together. She came over for dinner. Nice."

"Good." Nick wasn't sure what to say next. He didn't know where Payne wanted to go with this conversation, why the other man was unloading this information on him right at this moment.

Suddenly Payne swung his feet down and turned to look at Nick. "Her name is Cathy Litton."

"Linton?" The name rang familiarly In his memory.

"No, *Litton*," Payne said, almost irritated. "Like that company, you know, the one that makes...computers, I think, or ovens. Something like that. There's no connection, though. She didn't mention one. We talked a long time."

He fell silent, as if exhausted by the outburst.

Nick waited. Payne seemed to want to say something but at the same time not to. Nick had been in that situation; sometimes the only thing a listener could do was just wait. Nick ate another bit of cheese and took a long drink.

"We watched *Casablanca*," Payne finally said, "and talked and had a few drinks and...and had a nice time. She's a nice girl, Nick. You'll like her. I'll bring her by the next time she's over."

Nick still didn't know why Payne was going into all of this. But he nodded and said something appropriately innocuous, just to avoid the sense that he was Payne's father and that Payne had to clear his girlfriends with Nick.

For another five minutes, there was silence on the porch again. Finally, though, Payne finished, the words exploding in a rush.

"We watched the Bogart thing. I'd never seen it. Have you, Nick? It's great. A great period piece, full of mood and atmosphere and those tremendous close-up shots of...of...Bergman. Great. Great. We watched it and then talked about it. Then she had to go home. The DVD player had been acting up toward the end—it's never done that before, you know, never. Not too bad, just lines across the screen during the Bergman close-ups, a few breaks, like the tracking was off. Whenever I stood up to fix it, it would clear. And then the sound started to buzz. It gave me a headache...it probably gave Cathy one too, because she looked a little pale when she left. We said good-night and my headache lightened up. I watched her car until the tail light disappeared around the corner and then I went inside and fixed myself a strong drink and tried to sleep. I remembered Cathy on the beach, saw it again so clearly that I could almost smell the salt in the ocean spray and then the headache came back, blindingly, until I couldn't see anything except the static from the DVD player after the disc finished playing. And I had nightmares all night."

He stopped.

In spite of the cool breeze, he was sweating. Nick could see his forehead glistening and dark patches spreading at his armpits. Nick didn't feel at all warm, though. He felt cold, chilled. *Someone is walking over your grave,* his grandmother would have said.

Payne laughed, although the action seemed to suggest as much relief as humor.

"So now I guess I had better get the damned thing fixed. I can't have it sputtering like that every time I try to watch it. I have to leave LA for a couple of days tomorrow, so could I ask you a favor?"

"Sure." Nick wasn't sure but felt that he had to say so.

"If I give you the address of the repairman my aunt used to call, would you go by and give him a note from me and the spare key, and have him come by tomorrow or the next day. I called him this afternoon and he said that was the arrangement he had always had with my aunt. He worked on her stuff for a couple of years, even sold her a lot of it by phone but never once saw her. When he came out here, the house would be empty and quiet. All of the rooms would be closed up except the one he was supposed to work in. She always knew which one. He said he thought she was sitting in the next one, listening with a glass to the thin walls to see if he touched anything other than what he was supposed to. He said he never did, it was too scary to hang around and she paid him too well for him to take any chances at screwing up the arrangements. Anyway, he said it would be fine, that he could come by late tomorrow or the next day."

Again, Nick sensed an explosion behind Payne's words, but he shrugged and said "Sure."

Payne reached into a back pocket and pulled out an envelope and handed it to Nick. One end felt heavy—as it touched his fingertips, Nick recognized the weight and shape of a house key.

Payne stood and stretched and yawned. "Long day tomorrow." His voice was languid now, as if all of the energy had drained out. "I've got to fly home to meet with some more lawyers. Nothing to worry about, they said. Besides, it'll give me a chance to answer all the non-questions I keep getting in letters and phone calls from the folks back there. You know, what's the place like, what was she like. Anyway, it'll be fun to be home for a while."

They talked a few minutes more—trying to say goodbye but somehow the conversation kept going of its own volition for ten or fifteen minutes more. By sundown, Payne was walking across his lawn toward his darkened porch. He must have pushed the glider seat as he passed, because Nick thought he heard that odd squeak just before Payne's front door opened and a thin streak of light spilled out into the night.

Nick sat for a while, picking unconsciously at the cheese and crackers and trying to sort out his thoughts. It had been a strange conversation, more one-sided than anything, and frustratingly irresolute. Just when it seemed as if Payne were about to break open and say something, he would shift directions, then explode in a flurry of words that said nothing but intimated something deeper, almost a fear.

Nick finally gave up and went inside, leaving the envelope with the note and key perched on the tray in the kitchen, next to the empty cracker box and a rapidly drying-out remnant of cheese. It could all wait until morning.

He decided to read since it was too early for sleep and he didn't want to watch TV. He went to his one good bookshelf; the others in the place were brick-and-board makeshift things that held his books without straining his budget too much, but this one was an antique, over a hundred years old and build of solid oak that was darkened by age and use to a burnished, dusky glow. This was where he kept his small collection of special favorites, mostly hardcover and mostly, like the bookshelf itself, more expensive than he could really afford. It was an eclectic collection, including a couple of nineteenth-century editions of Milton and Swift that he picked up for fifteen or twenty bucks apiece at library sales, an autographed *The Stand* that a friend gave him when Nick finished his Master's, things like that. When he was restless, he liked to let his hands hover over the shelves like the pointer on a Ouija board and decide for themselves which one to pullout. His unbreakable rule was that he had to trust his subconscious. Whatever it picked, he read. It always worked.

But that night he broke the rule. He let his hand drop until he touched the heavy gilt binding of an 1890s leather-bound volume that had been his grandmother's favorite: *Wuthering Heights*. Normally he would have enjoyed re-reading it, but not that night. The book felt wrong. He needed something lighter. He settled for his old dog-eared paperback of Peter Beagle's *The Last Unicorn* and sat at his desk to read.

It must have been two hours later. He was most of the way through the novel, about to where the Lady Amalthea enters the clock to become transformed again into the unicorn. A noise filtered through his open window, coming from the direction of Payne's porch. It was a slight sound but enough to draw Nick's attention. He looked up.

A dark figure stepped off the porch. He couldn't see it clearly but it seemed to be wearing a long, dark coat. Maybe black. The figure turned along the sidewalk and headed toward the stop-light three blocks away, where there was an all-night quick-shop and a couple of gas stations. He watched the figure intently.

It wasn't Payne. It couldn't be Payne. Nick was sure of that. Payne was taller and much thinner, even if he were wearing a coat. And who would wear a thick coat on a warm summer night in LA.

Nick thumbed the light switch, casting his study into dark-ness. In a few seconds, he could make out shapes outside, the lurching mass of a hibiscus by the corner, the ghostly thin column supporting the street light whose bulb had burned out weeks before and had never been replaced by the city. He noted the silence, too, the absolute silence that happened only rarely in Tamarind Valley. No birds, no insects, not even the distant hum-roar of cars on the main boulevards. He shivered.

The figure had gone past the far border of The Greer's yard now, a dark shape hunching along in front of the still-darkened, still-empty house where Mr. Harrison had died. Nick's eyes smarted from the strain of peering so intently through the dark-ness. But he couldn't stop. There was...something wrong, some-thing about the shape that bothered him.

He stood and leaned over the desk, his hand sliding on a stack of papers and knocking them out of order. Something wrong.

Something.

With a chill, Nick realized what it was. He swallowed and slumped back into his chair, sitting for a long while in the darkness.

Whoever that was, he (or she...or *it*?) limped.

Just like The Greer had on those rare nights when he had seen her figure, swathed in black like this one, limping down the street.

But of course it *couldn't* be her.

She was dead.

Besides, Nick decided after a moment's reflection, running the image through his mind and measuring height, weight, probable body type against the distance and the darkness, *besides, this person was taller, not as bulky, not as awkward as The Greer seemed to have been.*

But it wasn't Payne, either; he was still sure of that. There was nothing of Payne's easy grace in the movements, nothing of the natural athleticism that came through even though Payne didn't seem interested in athletics themselves.

Nick glanced out the window toward Payne's. There were no lights visible. Not even a blue ripple along the hedges from one of the television screens. By the time Nick looked back to where the sidewalk intersected with the night, half a block away, the figure was gone. Even craning his neck to see as far as possible, he could not spot the dark form against the vague lights further down the street. It had disappeared.

Nick shivered and tried to finish his reading. But Beagle's story didn't have the old magic anymore. He didn't finish the book that night, and he didn't sleep well either.

By the next morning, he was half convinced that he had dreamed the whole episode. There was no mysterious figure, no sinister outline in the darkness, just unpleasant dreams and wild imaginings. At ten o'clock, he had even gone so far as to start across the lawn to Payne's to share a laugh over his mind's attempts to dredge up an "ectoplasmic apparition." Halfway across, he stopped.

"Damn," he muttered. Payne had probably already left. He had said he would be taking off early. Nick went on anyway and rang the bell and waited. He stepped back from the door and ran his fingers through his hair, feeling for all the world as if someone were spying on him and that he should look his best, just in case.

"Don't be an idiot," he said. "There's no one home."

He turned to scan the quiet street.

The sidewalks were deserted. Even the windows of the houses up and down Greensward seemed dark and withdrawn. There was no one on the street or on the lawns, not even any faces gleaming from cracks around the jambs of closed doors. Payne's place was locked and still, too. Nick's ringing the bell raised no more than a memory of an echo.

He walked around to the side. Payne's car was gone. Nick shrugged and started across the lawn.

By the time Nick got back to his own place, he had almost forgotten why he went over to Payne's in the first place. He let himself in through the back door and wandered into the kitchen. The tray from last night was waiting, along with Payne's note and spare key. Nick tucked them both into his shirt pocket, making a mental note to deliver both that afternoon.

For a change, he actually remembered to do it. He had a habit of forgetting obligations and commitments unless they were particularly enjoyable. But the rustling of the envelope every time he bent or turned that morning was enough of a reminder.

About eleven o'clock he jumped into his car. He had a number of other errands to run and had decided to treat himself to lunch somewhere. It turned out that the repair shop was only three or four miles away, well out of the residential part of Tamarind Valley but not quite into the business district either. Nick checked the address on the envelope, found the street with no trouble, and cruised along until he found the right number.

It was a neat little place, hardly what Nick would have expected of a major audio-video outlet. Tasco's Audio-Video Outlet appeared to be a single room, more of a catalogue store than a showroom, that shared the ground floor of an old house that had been spruced up with a new front and a coat of paint. The place next door was a thrift shop that, judging from the display in the front window, specialized in unusable junk.

Nick maneuvered his car into a parking spot that was inches too small for comfort, got out, stretched, and headed toward Tasco's front door.

CHAPTER EIGHTEEN

Ric was a born loser.

Everyone said so.

Old lady. Old man. Guidance counselors at school. Ball-busting skirts that teased but wouldn't put out.

Everyone said so—except Ric.

He knew that he was goin' places. This crummy job was just a stop-over, a chance to bag some small change until the big money started rolling in.

He had lots going. Maybe a drug deal over in the eastside. Maybe not. Ric could afford to wait, to choose just the right thing.

Until then, Old Man Tasco was an easy touch and the job was a snap.

He was stacking boxes along the back wall when the bell rang up front. Someone had walked in. Big shit surprise.

He didn't straighten up, not yet. He was wearing one of those sleeveless T-shirts designed to show off the upper arm—and he had plenty to show off. Whoever was behind him would see the muscles in his back and legs as he knelt to pick up a couple of boxes. Where the shirt rode high and his worn jeans low, a sliver of skin showed.

Sometimes chicks came in—he liked to give them a real show. Just last week one of them, maybe twenty, twenty-five, slipped around the counter and patted him on the ass and whispered "Nice" in his ear before he turned around. He copped a five-buck tip for carrying her stereo out to her car and could probably have gotten more if he'd been in the mood to ask her for a number. She wasn't his type, though. Hang-dog ugly bitch.

Anyway, Ric figured that it never hurt to put on the show. He reached up, stretching, knowing how that would make the muscles shift beneath his shirt and jeans. His movement was fluid, graceful as a panther. Strong.

"Hey," someone called as Ric lifted the last box and set it on the top of a stack. "Can I get some help here?"

"Shit," Ric murmured to himself. A guy.

He turned around suddenly, acting as if he had been startled by the sound. He didn't smile. He took in what he could see of the man in a single glance and decided that there were other games he could play with this one.

"Yeah, man," he said, injecting a street-wise tone into his voice as he studied the guy more closely.

Older, maybe twenty-five. Pale, skinny. Shabby. *Nerdy.*

There was something else, something indefinable that Ric felt more than saw.

"Is Mr., uh, just a minute," the guy stuttered. He pulled an envelope from his shirt pocket and glanced at it, holding the paper up to catch the light that filtered through the dusty show-case window along the front of the store. "Is Mr. Tasco in?"

"Gone to lunch," Ric said. *Let's play this one tough.* He moved to the counter along the wall and sauntered behind it to stand next to a stack of reference books and a small cash register. "What can I do for ya?" It came out more as a challenge than a question.

"I'm here...about a repair job. I'm Nick Wheeler."

Ric nodded noncommittally, hooking his thumbs in the loops of his jeans and leaning back against the wall.

The guy continued. "I have a letter for him from Mr. Gunnison."

"Who?"

"Payne Gunnison. On Greensward Lane."

Pansy address Ric thought, sneering inwardly but keeping his face carefully immobile while the guy talked on.

"I live next door to him," Wheeler said. "He called yesterday about some repairs. Payne Gunnison," he added unnecessarily.

The name sounded familiar. Ric flipped open a thin book and ran his finger along a page, his mouth moving slightly as he read the entries. His finger was long but calloused, rough and dark. He looked up and smiled. It was a startling and not entirely pleasant smile—he had been told so often enough. The guy on the other side of the counter seemed to withdraw, almost flinch back like he'd been hit.

"Oh, yeah," Ric said, carefully pulling the guy back into the conversation. *Don't let him get away yet, play him along, there more fun to be had.* "Payne Gunnison. He lives where old lady...I mean, where Miss Greer lived."

By the time he finished the sentence, Ric was almost polite, had stepped nearer the counter. He was close enough now to see the rough texture of the guy's shirt, close enough for the splintered wood along the counter to nudge into his waist when Ric leaned forward and smiled again. This time the smile invited rather than repelled.

Ric could see the flutter of a shiver in the guy's cheeks. No one else would have seen it, but Ric did.

The smile broadened.

"That's the one," the Wheeler guy said. "Anyway, I have a note about what needs to be done and a key for Mr. Tasco."

Ric glanced toward the open street door and then back to Wheeler. There was a thin line of sweat along the guy's upper lip. The guy's eyes flickered to the door and back, half a beat behind Ric's.

"Here, I'll take care of it," Ric offered, reaching out for the thin envelope Wheeler still held suspended above the scarred counter. "I'll need you to sign a work order and receipt, though. Let me fill one out."

He pulled a pad from beneath a counter and started to write. "Name."

"Nick, uh, better make that Payne Gunnison."

"Address."

"Don't you have...?" Wheeler began.

"It's in the files. I could look it up, it'd take time." He waited.

The guy mumbled out the address. Ric finished the form by filling in the date.

"What's wrong with the stuff?" he asked, looked straight at Wheeler. Even after the guy started to speak, Ric kept staring straight into the guy's eyes. It always unnerved them; Ric could tell. There were enough queers like this one hanging around. They cruised him as much as the chicks did. He shifted his weight behind the counter, thrusting his hips forward a fraction of an inch.

"Uh, the sound breaks up," Wheeler said. "The picture, too, sometimes. I think. That is, that's what Mr. Gunnison says."

Not much help there, Ric figured, for a minute concentrating on his job. *The whatchamacallit rubs against the doohickey and makes this funny sound.* Made as much sense as what this Wheeler guy had said. Most of the guys who came into Tasco's didn't know crap about sound.

The shits.

Wheeler seemed to think for a moment, then added, "And the machine shocked me once."

Ric looked up and smiled again. He had overheard a counselor who said it was a *feral* smile—he had never taken the time to find out what that meant. Sounded like something tough, though.

"Not too badly, though," Wheeler hurriedly added, as if afraid that he was putting too heavy a demand on Ric. "Just a small jolt."

"What make is it?"

"I don't remember," Wheeler answered.

"I've got to have that for the work order. Mind if I check the note?"

Ric was opening the envelope even as he spoke, glancing again toward the door as he slid his finger along the sealed flap. He tugged the paper out. The key fell with a clatter to the counter top. He pretended not to notice.

"Here it is," he said, leaning over the pad and laboriously filling in a space with a serles of numbers and initials. He was left-handed and had only a passing acquaintance with school—they had parted some years before, school and he, on a mutually antagonistic level. His handwriting was large and uneven, more that of a ten-year-old than an adult. It didn't fit too well with the rest of him—his long, roughly styled hair, the way he filled his T-shirt and jeans. Maybe sometime some chick would invite him to come over to her place for some lessons in penmanship—it might be a good scam. Good enough for him to get lucky. Or her.

"That's all," Ric said, straightening up. "Just sign here." He pointed to an X and a line across the bottom of the form. Wheeler wrote his full name, adding underneath "for Payne Gunnison," then slid the pad back. Ric studied the name for a second.

"Thanks...Mr. Wheeler." He looked straight into the guy's eyes when he spoke.

"Nick," the guy said finally. "I live next door to Payne."

There was a pause. The silence in the shop was heavy, thick.

"Yeah," Ric said, really getting into the game. This shit was ripe for stringing along.

Maybe tomorrow when he went over to fix the DVD player, he'd fix something else, too. He'd done that often enough, bashed the freakin' queers that tried to feel him up in alleys and johns.

Ric ripped off the top sheet and handed Nick a copy. He flashed the smile again.

"Sure thing, *Mr. Wheeler.*" He hit the name hard, throwing everything he could into his voice.

The guy almost winced.

Ric slipped the original into a manila folder and stacked it with several others alongside the well-worn cash register.

"The key?" Wheeler said suddenly, shoving the bit of metal across the counter with a fingertip. *Right on cue,* Ric thought, *couldn't have done it better if I had told him when and give him a stopwatch.*

"Oh. Yeah," he said as he picked it up, easily, as if he had completely forgotten that minor detail. His fingers brushed against Wheeler's, curled around the key, and dropped it into the folder. "Thanks."

The front door clattered open. Ric jerked his eyes up and called out over Wheeler's shoulder.

"Hi, Mr. Tasco." He smiled. It was a different smile. Safer.

As he spoke, he slid the ripped envelope out of sight across the counter and dropped it into the wastebasket.

Wheeler turned just as an old man crossed the room, grunted at the two of them, and disappeared through a door hidden behind a stack of packing boxes.

Ric grinned. "He loves pizza but can't eat it without getting gas. He's probably back there chugging down on some white guck right now. Thanks for bringing Mr. Gunnison's stuff by."

He was every inch the conscientious clerk now. Hs could hear old man Tasco rummaging through desk drawers, probably looking for his medicine and burping and farting. He stared into Wheeler's eyes again, noting the almost imperceptible flinch as he did so.

"Come again soon."

"Uh, yeah. Thanks," Wheeler said hurriedly as he left the store.

Ric watched the door swing shut, listened to the clatter as it hit against the worn jamb, even followed Wheeler's silhouette until he slipped into his car and edged it into the lane of traffic and disappeared.

Then he laughed.

It was a high sharp laugh, not at all pleasant.

Tasco yelled from the back room. "Enrique, quiet out there."

Ric swallowed the rest of the laughter, almost choking. He glanced down at the name and address. Then he reached over and touched the side of the folder, touched it right where the key to The Greer's place lay next to the purchase order. Yeah, there could be some fun times ahead. *Gotcha, fag.*

CHAPTER NINETEEN

When Payne returned three days later, he was in an unusually good mood. He felt rested and refreshed in spite of a grueling flight back to LAX—the plane had been detoured twice because of mechanical failures and had spent a total of six hours idling in the hot sun on tarmacs in Houston and Denver. Even so, by the time he climbed out of his car and onto the porch, he felt good. He could breathe more easily here in the coolness, and the scent of the decades old jasmine blooming along the edge of the house smelled like rich perfume. He was happy to be back. To be home.

More to the point, perhaps, things had gone well. He had been able to field most of the questions his relatives, friends, and even a few former neighbors had posed about California, Los Angeles, and Great-Aunt Emilia, and he had had a fruitful meeting with the Pennsylvania lawyers about his mother's estate. He even checked with them on the restrictions in Aunt Emilia's will—the provisions were peculiar, everyone had agreed, but legal. One of the lawyers had pointed out a few possible loopholes. Payne might be able to make a few *necessary* changes around the place to make it more livable.

In addition, he had discovered just where he stood, financially. He had known that he had inherited a fair amount of property from Great-Aunt Emilia, but until the details of both estates had been clarified, he had not known just how obscenely wealthy he was. He glanced into the darkness, toward where the new Toyota sat cooling in the driveway, its engine *plinking* faintly and its new-car polish hidden by a thin coat of airport parking lot dust. *I should get it washed soon*, he thought absently. Somehow, the car didn't seem as horrendously expensive now as it had when he signed his name on the check a few weeks ago and drove away from the dealership nervous and emotionally exhausted. With his inheritance, he had discovered, he could probably afford a new car every month for years if he wanted, even after taxes took their chunk.

In exchange for having that much money, he had decided on the last leg of the flight home, he could put up with a few minor inconveniences like dead-fish white walls and eerily effective draperies and television monitors in every room.

His mood lightened even more when he unlocked the front door and walked in. Tucked beneath the unused chess board on the small table in the living room, he found his key and a bill from Tasco. He glanced at the amount—after the sums the lawyers had been discussing, it seemed ridiculously small. He stuffed the paper and the key into his pocket and dropped his suitcase off in the bedroom. It made a dark splotch against the whiteness, like sweat on a white T-shirt, even in the dimness of the hall light.

He started to change, pulling off his tie and tossing it still half-knotted onto the dresser. It coiled against the mirror, a narrow, conservative blue-and-gray striped serpent staring hypnotically at itself in the glass. He unbuttoned his shirt and tugged at one sleeve before deciding against changing right then. He shrugged back into the shirt and walked out of his room and down the hall into the control room.

He pulled out a DVD and slipped it into the machine without even looking at the title. While the player was warming up, he returned to the bedroom.

It was late. It had been dark for several hours, but Payne's body was still trapped somewhere between California time and Pennsylvania time. This flight had not been as traumatic as the first one—*was it only six weeks ago?*—but here in the real world of Tamarind Valley it was ten o'clock, maybe ten-fifteen.

He crossed to the far side of his room and pulled his shirt off. The soft fabric was damp to the touch as it slid over his back and arms. Without it, his skin felt warm where the night air caressed it.

He wadded the shirt up and tossed it through the doorway into the hall. He would pick it up tomorrow and put it with the rest of the dirty laundry from the last day of his trip.

He sighed, slipped his shoes off and threw himself onto the bed, hot and sticky from travel but suddenly too tired to stir. He heard a static crackle. A bluish tint flickered on the white walls.

The DVD player flickered into life.

Almost too tired to move, he glanced at the monitor. The film looked like a musical or something, fairly old at any rate. It was in black and white. He didn't recognize any of the actors. He listened for a moment, but the tune playing over the credits wasn't familiar either. He turned away and stared at the white wall opposite, noticing the subtle play of shadow from the screen on the smooth plaster only inches from his face.

He was home again.

Home.

He felt tired but comfortable. He had missed the place, missed this bed, *his* bed, missed the films and the sounds and the sights. They all made up for anything else. Even for a night that was hot and sticky. He was hot and sticky. He was tired.

But he was safe.

Safe!

He sat up, his heart thumping. Why had he thought that? After all, what was there to threaten him back home in Pennsylvania. Only his childhood, his youth, his relatives who—slightly greedy and covertly envious, perhaps—nevertheless seemed to enjoy his visit. So why *safe*?

The blue and silver reflections danced across the wall. The sound was pitched low enough that the vaguely forties-style music faded to a solemn hiss, rising and falling with his breathing. Or his breathing with it.

For a few moments he relaxed. He almost fell asleep half-dressed on his bed.

The opening credits finished. There were a few seconds of dialogue, still too soft to be intelligible. He glanced over in time to see a man and a woman standing shoulder to shoulder, studiously ignoring each other against a backdrop of a railroad station.

He sat up again and swung his legs over the side of the bed. He stared at the monitor for a long time before he finally sighed and stood up. He loosened his belt, unzipped his slacks, and let them drop to the floor. Now he wore only dark nylon dress socks and the black bikini briefs he had bought on impulse only the day before in the Sears store across the mall from the lawyers' offices—a puzzling purchase for him, since he always wore conservative, full-cut boxers.

He felt suddenly and unaccountably ill-at-ease standing in the skimpy underwear, half embarrassed at their low-cut waist and high-cut legs. He felt as if he were doing something forbidden and was suddenly and irrationally afraid his mother burst through the door without knocking and seem him standing there and laugh at him and then punish him by taking away his TV privileges for a week.

Cut it out. Don't be stupid.

He felt an instant of embarrassment, not at what he was wearing but at how he had thought about his mother. She had never, would never have burst into his room uninvited. Would never have laughed at him.

He glanced at his image in the mirror, seeing his body cut off at mid-thigh by the coiled tie. What he saw was not bad, he decided. He sucked his stomach in and tensed his abdominal muscles until they stood out taut and firm. Not bad at all. And the briefs did fit nicely. He kicked one leg outward. The high-cut leg openings gave him a sense of freedom.

He stretched, trying to relax the tired muscles in his arms, shoulders, and back.

He would have to see about getting some more briefs. Give the old boxers to Goodwill or something, stuff them into the collection bins that littered supermarket parking lots all over the area.

He crossed the hall to the bathroom and soaked a washcloth in cold water and wrung it out and drew it across his forehead, letting the water drip down his skin and bathe his neck and shoulders. A few drops beaded down his back, rolling until they disappeared beneath the elastic on his briefs.

"Shit," he murmured, wetting the cloth a second time and reaching across the tub to open the window. What breeze filtered through was as hot as the inside of the house.

He thought about a cool shower, even went so far as to pull his socks off and step out of the sweat-damp briefs before deciding against it.

Too much trouble, only get all sweaty again drying off.

He sniffed at one armpit experimentally, then the other. He could almost hear his mother's whine—*Disgusting habit*, she had always insisted, but what the hell, he was alone now. If he could stand himself, who else was there to worry?

Instead of showering, he slapped at his underarms with the damp washcloth, patted dry, then tucked a clean white towel around his waist and walked barefoot into the kitchen.

The linoleum felt hot and sticky. There was barely anything on the shelves, even less in the fridge. He had pretty well cleaned everything out before he left.

He found a couple of slices of hard cheese tucked behind a plastic container of outdated yogurt. He filled a pitcher with tepid water and dropped in a dozen ice cubes from the freezer.

Sipping the water as he walked, he returned to the bedroom and lay down. He breathed deeply. Inhale, exhale, inhale, exhale, force the chest to rise, the belly to press against the spine as the air passed in, out, in, out. The loosely knotted towel loosened even more until it fell onto the bedspread beside him. The terry-cloth rippled whitely, like sun-bleached sands at a beach. He glanced at the screen again, barely half conscious as hero kissed heroine and the credits flickered over the screen.

Can't be over. Not enough time. I've only been home a few

minutes.

He looked at the clock on the nightstand.

Eleven-forty-seven.

He must have drowsed off relaxing on the bed, napped without realizing it. He thought vaguely about checking to see if Nick's study light was on. If it was, he might invite Nick over to watch something. The thought passed.

Anyway, he decided, he was too tired. And it was probably too late. His stomach growled. He could walk down to that all-night place up the street and pick up a couple of cans of Campbell soup, maybe some tuna and bread, but even that seemed more exertion than he wanted. So he just lay there, eyes on the credits, mind miles away.

He thought of Cathy and, silently, thought passed into dream. *Sunlight glistening on her hair, gold on gold, sunlight on her cheeks, sunlight surrounding her like a nimbus as they sat in the fragrance of the rose arbor at John's. Her laughter at dinner, her smile, her sparkling eyes. She was a splash of color against the whiteness of his rooms, a splash of life against the evenness of his life.*

Dream fingered through memory, remembrances shifted and distended, and *she was there again, dressed as she had been at the beach, and he was beside her, lying with their dark flesh on white sand, and feeling the warm sand—no, the* hot *sand where it dug into bare flesh of shoulders and hips and thighs.*

And then she was naked...and he was naked and strong and hard and aching for her as she suddenly sat just beyond his reach where she watched waves slipping onto the sand, consuming the sand, spiraling it away, oblivious to him, to his need. He reached to touch her, tried to pull her down to him and feel her against him, surrounding him....

The heat increased as the sun focused on them. The waves hissed louder, no longer slipping gracefully onto the shore but assaulting it, spitting anger and naked fury at the white sands and black boulders and the naked figures motionless just beyond their reach. Their roar grew until it distorted into white static, the white sands wavered beneath the heat, merged with the black of boulders, striated, elongated, and blurred into visual static. Cathy was still beside him, but now looking directly at him, terror in her eyes.

Run run run run run *she radiated, her throat quivered as she struggled to speak, but her tongue refused to move, her lips refused to form coherent sounds. But Payne knew anyway.*

She wanted to run, run from him, but she could not. For some reason she could not even stand. Instead, she knelt in front of him, hunched over, and tried to hide herself with her hands. The shadows of her arms where they crossed her breasts cut blackly against the whiteness of her breasts.

He was sweating, slipping in sweat that became waves and died into flurries of burning snow. The static intensified. She screamed.

The knife shadows cut deeper and now black blood flowed down the curve of her belly.

She screamed again, a piercing keen that blended with the static.

He reached for her, touched her. As if she were a statue of white snow beneath the shadow of a naked oak, at the heat of his touch she dissolved, flesh steaming away to ghostliness until his hands penetrated her, reached through her to nothingness. Beyond her, superimposed on the ghostly afterimage of her face, images moved jerkily, like characters in a badly filmed movie, black and white figures distorted by too many shadows, too much darkness. He couldn't identify them but they terrified him. One—suddenly dwarfed by Cathy's face—curved around the hollow of her eye; another rested supine beneath her lip. Both were naked, faded to a dismal gray against the white and black flurries of snow.

He tried to stand, to move through her to them, discover who and what they were. He was still hot, his skin slick with sweat. His stiffness throbbed painfully.

The tiny figures swirled, shifting across the landscape of her face, transforming the angles of her cheeks, the roundness of her lips into hills and vales, slipping along the planes of her nose, twining and intertwining at the jointure of her mouth.

He leaned closer.

He could hear his own breathing, his heart racing in the heat.

He could smell her, them, the fetidness of heat and sweat and rotting crabs rejected by the waves at high tide.

He leaned closer.

It was as if he were trying to kiss her, to kiss a ghost.

Cathy disappeared. Gulliver-like, he peered into the minuscule world of the figures, studying them as they intersected and joined, swirled apart, coalesced and separated yet again. The eroticism of their movements penetrated to his core, achingly, burningly.

One settled recumbent into the curve where Cathy's lower lip had been. The other lay rigidly on top of the first.

He leaned even closer now.

The figures shifted again, became denser, fleshier...became recognizable forms.

Human forms.

More than that....

He screamed!

What had been sexual play transmuted into vicious assault and acute physical pain—into torture. The curving figure attacked the recumbent one, plunging fists again and again into unresisting flesh. Pools of darkness flowed from the body across a sandy nothingness until they surrounded the figures and clouded Payne's vision. He jerked backwards, away from them.

Cathy was gone. Never was, had never been, never could be.

All that remained was the wilderness of sand and heat. And the distant twining figures.

And the blood.

He urged himself closer, unwilling to move but unable not to. Walking was painful, the soles of his feet pressed against burning sandpaper. A wave broke upon him from behind, stunningly and savagely, with such ferocity that it spun him forward.

He stumbled across the sand toward the black boulders, his body merging sweat with sea saltiness. The static bellowed, blinding him as the figures exploded in a whirlwind of white and black tinged with red and finally resolving into white as....
He sat bolt upright on the white bed in the white-walled room, panting. His skin was slick with sticky sweat.

The monitor glowered down at him like a blank white face tinged with scarlet. He stared at it, blinked twice, sharply.

There was nothing there.

Nothing but a monitor displaying the staticky gray that always signaled the end of a disc.

Everything was okay.

He was in his room, his own hot and stuffy bedroom, his body exhausted from the day's stress.

Now the screen was blank, not even marred by snow.

That was all.

He pulled the edge of the towel from under himself and rubbed it against his forehead and chest, then lower, discovering with sudden inexplicable shame the wet stickiness on his abdomen.

He dried himself, wadded the towel up and threw it into a corner. It lay coiled like a dusky gray serpent, staring at the thinner, darker one still unmoving on his dresser.

"God," he whispered, "what a nightmare."

He stretched his hand out in front of him. His fingertips trembled. His knuckles were white. He stood and went into the bathroom and turned on the shower.

As he waited for the water to flow, he looked over his shoulder. In its corner, the monitor hissed gently at him, dying as the DVD player automatically turned itself off. The disc—whatever it had been—would be unmoving, still, ready for the next screening.

Payne stepped under the cold needles of water, drenching away the fear and the panic and the shame along with the sweat and the heat. He didn't try to analyze what had happened.

It was a bad dream.

That was all.

Nothing more. In the corner, hidden by the faded shower curtain, the monitor stared blankly, silently.

CHAPTER TWENTY

When the telephone shrilled the first time, Nick's bedroom light was burning but he was asleep. It took him a few seconds to wake and orient dully on the telephone, a few more to stumble over and lift the receiver to his ear. Sixth ring. He squinted at the clock to see what time it was but it was turned away from him.

"Hullo," he mumbled his throat thick with sleep. His teeth felt gritty where his tongue rubbed against them.

"Nick?"

"Yeah." The answer was punctuated by a yawn.

"Payne." This time there was something in the voice—a tone, an edge that startled Nick instantly awake.

"What's wrong?"

"Well...the...nothing, really. You're usually up late. Hope I didn't disturb you. You weren't asleep, were you?"

Nick blinked. He noticed consciously for the first time that the light was still on. The book he had been reading lay face down on the floor, one page crumbled against the braid of the throw rug. He had apparently drifted off and let the book slide. He leaned over and turned the clock on his nightstand around until he could see the face.

Two a.m.

Shit, what does he think I was doing at this time of the night!

"Uh, no," he said. Like so many others, he suffered from an irrational but tenacious hesitance about letting others know that he slept occasionally; here it was, two a.m., and he couldn't admit over the phone that he had been far gone into Night-Night-Land. "I was just reading. Trying to get through Spenser."

Payne laughed. It sounded hollow to Nick.

There was a long pause before Payne spoke again.

"Uh, Nick, want to...look, I know it's late and all, but could you come over? For a while? We can watch a movie or something."

Nick didn't want to. He knew that.

And it went beyond the hour or his sleepiness (which had evaporated at the sound of Payne's voice) or his need to study. He simply didn't want to go over there tonight. But in a sense he really had no choice. Beneath Payne's words swirled icy currents of fear and despair—Nick didn't know why, but he had seen and felt enough about that house to understand Payne's need.

"Okay, yeah," he said finally. "Sure. Give me a couple of minutes."

"Okay."

There was a click, silence, then that irritating, almost subliminal buzzing of a telephone suddenly cut off.

Well, Nick old boy, you're in for it now. That house in the dead of night.

The dead of night.

The phrase chilled his spine as he stood there almost naked, telephone in hand, and stared at the darkness that loomed outside where he knew Payne's house stood but where nothing could be distinguished from the unbroken blackness.

And here you go, traipsing over to The Greer...to Payne's, he corrected himself, wondering why he had slipped. He hadn't thought of her in days (*yes you have don't lie not to yourself not just yet*), and besides Payne probably just had a fight or something with his girl and wanted someone to talk to.

He dressed quickly. The night was warm, so he pulled on worn shorts and a T-shirt, slipped his feet into a pair of old beach thongs that huddled by the bedroom door.

He could feel the coolness of damp grass curling up to brush at his toes and the sides of his feet as he crossed the lawn. In seconds, the soles of the thongs were damp and cold. Outside, the night was considerably cooler than it had been inside; moist fingers caressed his arms and legs. By the time he reached Payne's, he was even slightly chilled.

He started up the steps, walking carefully as the thin rubber soles slipped on worn wood. First step, second *Remember Hill House where something walked but not alone* third *the Marsten House* fourth *The House Beyond the Hill* and he was on the porch itself, stifled in the sudden closeness that cut out stars and sky and hesitant breaths of night air.

He crossed the porch, shivering once.

Screeee.

As he passed the porch glider, the seat dropped back an inch. It's the wind, he thought.

Screeee.

The hinges squeaked miserably a third time, *screeee*, squealing as if the cool dampness had created instant rust and the metal were wearing against itself in an insane attempt to ward away an intrusion. His mind flickered to an odd image— someone, Dame Judith Anderson perhaps, playing Lady Macbeth in an ancient black-and-white film he saw once in class. She was rubbing her hands together, fingers splayed, tendons taut and pulling across the back of her hands like piano wires. She scraped palm against palm, uselessly, anxious to remove bloody stains that only she could see. The movement matched the painful squeak of the porch glider, back and forth, back and forth.

A light flared inside the house and Nick realized that he had been standing on the porch for a long time. He didn't have a watch to check, but an internal monitor warned him that minutes—many minutes—had passed. The swing was silent and still, so massive at the end of its heavy chain that it looked as if it would never, *could* never move.

He shuddered...from the cold he assured himself, and reached for the doorbell. He paused. He didn't want to touch that buzzer. Didn't want to disturb it as it stared at him from its monk's cowl of dark metal—a tiny black knot gleaming in the light. The buzzer startled and intimidated. Without bothering to ask himself why *ask me no questions and I'll tell you no lies* he rapped sharply on the door.

"Payne?" he called out. The question was useless in a sense, since he knew Payne was expecting him, and anyway who else would be there?

"It's Nick!" Again useless. Who else could it be?

Payne opened the door so quickly and quietly that he must have been standing behind it waiting for Nick. His skin was flushed, his face damp and his hair slicked back as if he had just stepped from the shower and pulled a comb through it without waiting to dry it first. The shower image was emphasized by the white towel he had cinched around his waist. He wore nothing else. He had been in the sun a lot during the summer, Nick noted abstractedly. Payne's skin gleamed dark and richly golden against the whiteness of the towel, except for his chest and shoulders and face where the tan was suffused with a blush of red. Payne seemed not to notice or care how he was dressed.

"Uh....," Nick stammered, unaccountably taken aback. He shouldn't have been, perhaps. It was late after all. Maybe Payne and the girl had been...maybe he was so upset that he didn't think about changing. *But the wet hair, the shower, the flush....*

"Come on in," Payne said, rushing the words as if he wanted to close the door against the night.

Nick stopped thinking and reacted. He stepped in.

The house was mercilessly bright. Every light seemed to be burning furiously and the white walls glowed with an inner iridescence more their own than reflected from the bulbs. The TV screen in the living room wall was playing something in grainy black and white but Nick couldn't tell what. In the middle of the room, the chess set gleamed starkly, shadows spilling in distorted shapes across the gray squares. Nick shivered again, even though the house was warm, almost hot.

Payne didn't notice. He motioned for Nick to sit down.

"Not in here, okay?" Nick said suddenly. "How about the

kitchen or the film room?"

Payne looked at Nick curiously, questioning and...and something else.

"It's too bright," Nick said, clutching at an obvious excuse that made more sense than the real reason—he couldn't bring himself to say that he simply did not want to stay in that living room, surrounded by what abruptly seemed like unlimited acres of glowing white.

Payne's eyes flickered and Nick saw an unreadable something (*Payne/pain*) in them. He shivered again and held his arms tightly against his chest.

"Must be a draft in here," he said apologetically.

Payne shook his head, seriously, denying even the possibility of such a thing.

"Not a crack, not a breath," he said.

He led the way into the kitchen anyway. As they passed the bedroom door, Payne disappeared for a moment, then reappeared carrying an old terry-cloth robe.

"Here," he said. "You look cold." He slipped the robe over Nick's shoulders. "Your skin's like ice."

"Thanks," Nick said. The robe felt good. He had gotten more of a chill than he had thought. His toes tingled and the thongs were like thin sheets of snow.

They continued into the kitchen. From the silver bars of light cutting beneath the doors in the hallway, Payne must have had every light in the house on. Nick could imagine the electric meter hanging beside the outside back door, its disc spinning in crazy confusion at having to deliver so much power in the middle of the night. Yet from the outside, the house had seemed unbroken blackness. The drapes again, those eerily effective, unnerving, light-consuming drapes.

The kitchen was preternaturally bright also, maybe because Nick knew that outside only the stars and the focused glow of streetlights perched like vultures on concrete pillars punctuated the night. Inside, it was as if Payne were trying to kill all shadows, pierce their vitals with shards of light until they had bled out their essences and there was nothing left to bleed out but whiteness reflecting whiteness—except Payne's own body, a harsh intrusion of darkness and life and color in the room, itself bisected by the startling white of the bath towel.

Nick felt uncomfortable in his ragged, stained cut-offs and color-spattered shirt, the fading reminder of a weekend art-fair in Summerland, a sleepy place up the coast near Santa Barbara. Even its faded colors seemed to burn against his skin, pressed inward by the overwhelming whiteness.

He pulled the robe closed. It had once been tan—he could see hints of original color preserved in the seams but it had worn to a soft ivory, almost white, that blended better with the room.

They sat down. The monitor in the kitchen was on also, apparently playing the same film, although Nick still had no idea what it was. They sat for a while, occasionally glancing at the TV screen, at the bare walls, at everything except each other.

For a while Nick watched Payne but every time Payne raised his eyes and met Nick's, he turned away as if burned. The flush would creep up his neck again and the room would seem to grow hotter.

"What's wrong?" Nick finally asked.

Payne paused before answering.

In spite of the lateness of the night and Nick's discomfort at being there, he still thought he had a pretty fair idea of what Payne would probably say. *A fight, a spat with his girl. Maybe she had stayed over and in the middle of in the middle of things it had gone wrong and she had stormed out, leaving him...unsatisfied and frustrated.*

Something like that. So Nick figured that he would be ready for whatever Payne finally came out with. It really couldn't be anything else.

But he was wrong. Nick could not have anticipated what Payne would say. Not at past two in the morning, sitting in a kitchen that seemed to have klieg lights screwed into every sixty-watt socket, in a house brighter than midday, not talking with a man draped only in a damp towel as they watched some unnamed film dancing across one of half a dozen screens.

"I've been having some trouble with the televisions," Payne announced flatly.

Nick glanced up at the screen, back at Payne.

Nick started to laugh, then stifled the sound before it was born. The man was serious! Payne was staring intently at Nick, his eyes belying the surface neutrality of his voice. Nick wanted to say something about the inappropriateness of the time and the place, something inane and obvious, but he couldn't.

Payne turned toward the monitor. He was immobile except for the blood pulsing through the veins of his neck and temples and for his right hand as it curled and uncurled along the fraying edge of the towel. His jaws were tensed; bunched muscles stood out against his cheeks like cordwood against a weather-stained wooden wall. This wasn't the time for a joke or a stupid comment, Nick decided. Whatever it was that Payne really wanted to talk about, he certainly wasn't joking.

"What kind of trouble?" Nick finally whispered.

That seemed to break whatever spell Payne was under. Or at least bend it. Payne looked at Nick. Nick could see the stiffness drain from muscles, trouble drain from tired, glazed eyes, to be replaced with self-consciousness and embarrassment.

"Nothing really," Payne said, his old voice infusing the kitchen with warmth and concern. "I guess.... Just...I guess you could call it a double exposure. I thought I saw two...shows"—he stumbled over the word, as if it had not been his first choice—"two shows at once. It was eerie. Would you mind watching to see if you notice anything unusual?"

It was an odd request. Nick understood without further words that there was more to it than Payne had admitted. But he couldn't bring himself to ask, to pry openly into Payne's secrets. Instead he simply nodded.

"Sure," he said softly. "But not in here. It's too bright."

He fidgeted slightly. "And this chair's digging into my back."

Payne laughed, a curiously fresh sound. "Got it. How about

the TV room." As if every room in the place wasn't a TV room.

Nick nodded.

They went down the hall and into the front study—by consensus the official viewing room. Again, all of the lights burned feverishly but Payne dimmed them immediately. Nick dropped into his usual chair, stretching to make himself comfortable. Payne sat on the near end of the couch—an odd choice for him since he almost always sat at the opposite end. He seemed to need to be near someone tonight, Nick thought. Once or twice, coming out of the kitchen, Payne had accidentally rubbed against Nick, shoulder to shoulder, arm against arm, as if to assure himself that Nick (or perhaps *he*) were real.

"Want to watch anything In particular?"

Nick shook his head. "Can't think of anything. Whatever's on. It should be enough to make sure the system's working all right."

Payne settled back into the couch. He seemed more himself although still nervous.

"Say, wasn't someone, that Mr.—what was his name anyway?—supposed to fix the thing?" Nick said suddenly, speaking into the silence.

"Yeah," Payne said, his voice small and absent as he stared at the screen as if afraid that at any moment it would transmogrify into some horrendous Creature from the Black Cutting-Room-Floor.

"Someone was here, left a note. Said they couldn't find anything wrong. But there is. Just watch."

Nick watched, splitting his time and attention between Payne and the screen. Payne seemed not to notice that Nick was watching him. His hand still rubbed occasionally against the selvage on the towel, the fingers stiff and knotted, almost arthritic, although Nick hadn't known that Payne had any trouble like that. He had not mentioned anything, at any rate. Maybe the hand was just stiff from something he had done earlier that day, overextending the fingers and wrist working in the yard perhaps. That happens sometimes, Nick knew...you work so hard at pulling shrubs or heavy weeds that your hands and wrists swell and it hurts even to move them.

Except that Payne had not been home working in the yard earlier that day. He had still been gone, out of town, away on a trip.

Well, Nick decided, it could just be a trick of the light—or the fact that it was closing in on three o'clock. But he couldn't help glancing at that hand moving slowly up and down the nubbed terrycloth as if it had a will of its own (*the monster with five fingers the hand that terrible film with Michael Caine as a cartoonist of all things taken over by his own hand that's not his anymore even the Crawling Eye would be better than that*) occasionally catching the edge of the towel with its nail and tugging it up a bit.

Nick swallowed.

If it weren't Payne sitting over there, he thought, I would be getting the hell out of here, right now. I didn't need this kind of thing. But it is Payne and he needs me.

They sat for over an hour, watching until the end of the film. Nick never did find out its title or plot. He couldn't even recognize the characters, so it must have been a low-budget thing, maybe foreign—the pacing and setting suggested Canadian or Australian, but he couldn't tell for sure.

The screen never flickered once. Nothing unusual happened. Except that Payne finally relaxed. His hand uncurled and rested limply on the arm of the couch, palm up and fingers curved slightly, naturally. He seemed tired, like a marathon runner during the first seconds after a race.

When the closing credits began, he closed his eyes and leaned his head against the back of the couch.

"I guess there wasn't anything wrong, after all," he said after a few moments. The credits finished. The copyright logo flashed by—the film *was* Canadian, Nick noted—and then there was just static and snow. Payne's fingers jerked convulsively once or twice when the static began, then relaxed again.

"I must have been dreaming or imagining," he said at last.

"I'm sorry, Nick. I shouldn't have kept you here all this time. I shouldn't even have called you. I can't think now why I did."

Nick made some slight motion, a wave of the hand to say "Hey, that's okay, I didn't have anything else to do but sleep."

Payne shook his head. "No, I mean it. I'm really sorry for all of this. But I'm glad that you did come. We haven't seen much of each other lately. You know, with me being out of town, and with Cathy and everything. We'll have to get together some-time. I want you to meet her. She's really...well, she's...I think you'll really like her."

He stumbled into silence.

"Yeah, let's do that." Nick couldn't think of anything else to say and hated himself for falling back on that old line—*Fer sure! Let's do lunch sometime*! How California! How disgust-ingly Valley!

He glanced around, as if looking for a clock. It's getting late, his mind kept urging him, restating the obvious.

"Look, I've got to get going now, Payne. But thanks for... the evening." Payne smiled. When he stood, the towel loosened around his waist. Nick's heart flipped, missing a beat. Then Payne cinched it tighter, unconscious even of doing it, and led the way back into the living room.

"Thanks again, Nick."

"It's okay. Call if you need...well, you know."

"Here," Nick said, pulling the robe off. "Thanks for the use of it. I was pretty chilly for a while."

Payne smiled and took the robe. For an instant his fingers touched Nick's and Nick had the most disconcerting sensation that it wasn't Payne smiling at him but someone else. The fingers touched again, and Nick pulled his hand away *is he trying to come on to me or something?—No, don't be stupid, it's only Payne just like always, only Payne, relax already*—and stepped outside onto the porch.

He turned to say goodbye. His glance drifted over Payne's shoulder, down the long central hallway. It was dark. Payne smiled again and nodded.

"Thanks," he said quietly.

There was no sound as Payne swung the heavy door closed.

Nick didn't realize until he was halfway across the lawn that even the thin strips of light that had oozed from beneath the closed doors that faced the hall had disappeared. The hall was dark. The rooms on each side, including the kitchen, were dark. Everything was dark but the living room and the entry hall. But Payne had never left his side all night. He had never touched a light switch.

CHAPTER TWENTY-ONE

Payne woke late the next morning. It was almost the next afternoon, in fact, it was so late. He had an odd half-memory of having made a fool of himself somehow, like the after-image of some ridiculously stereotypic lampshade-over-the-head stunt at a party that had suddenly grown wilder than anyone expected. He felt hung-over without having been drunk. For a moment after waking, he couldn't place the problem.

Then he remembered.

Nick.

He had called Nick for assurance, cried out for help, for all the world like a child imagining some monster lurking in the shadows outside his window and calling to Mommy and Daddy for help. *Please Nick save me from the bogeyman from the nasty television that shows things I don't want to see.*

For a second, Payne felt like he had as a child when he had vacationed every summer on his grandfather Gunnison's farm in the mid-west. Grandpa had lived in a place so small it would probably have fit into the Tamarind Valley shopping mall with room left over for a respectable football field. The old man had been about the last person in the county to invest in indoor plumbing, so even Payne, young as he was, could remember a nightly run to the outhouse. It wasn't far, maybe a hundred yards, but it seemed a hundred miles through weeping box-elders, past the haunted relic of an antique sleigh long since a rustic (and rusted) condominium for generations of spiders and mice, its runners so heavily oxidized that they had virtually become part of the soil. The dirt path to the outhouse skirted the granary and disappeared between two rows of trees overhung with deadwood that drooped skeletally above the walkway even in summer when the rest of the branches were in full leaf. Farther along, maybe a mile or so, the trail crossed into the apple orchard and intersected the path the cows took on their stately progress morning and evening to the milking shed.

But the outhouse wasn't that far down the trail. It hunched like a dead thing, directly beneath the heavy-hanging shadows of the trees.

At night, trailing with a couple of the other half-dozen or so grandchildren at Grandpa's during the summer, Payne *knew* the trip had to be at least five miles long. One night, at the end of the line heading back to the house, relieved of the growing bladder pressure but if possible even more skittery and frightened than on the way out, Payne saw something.

Even before he glanced over his shoulder, he had known *it* was there, had felt *its* presence. With a prickle up his spine that filled his bladder again, he sensed breath hot and heavy against the small hairs of his neck. He almost smelled the stench of the unnamable thing. In another instant the heavy cloying coppery smell would assault his nostrils; they flared wide with fright and anticipation. In another instant....

He shivered, shuddered, waited for the touch of teeth, of claws....

Screwing up his courage, he slowed, his feet kicking tiny whorls in the dust. The toes of his summer-scuffed Keds trudged through dirt suddenly as thick as the dried-up library paste they used in his Sunday School class in the old rock church on the hill. *In the church above the shadows and the trees. Where it was safe.*

He stopped, his heart thudding. He could break and run, or he could turn to face the monster. It was simple: him, or the thing back there. He couldn't ignore it any longer. He closed his eyes and strained to hear any small signs of its approach. A leaf crackled. A twig snapped where there shouldn't have been any sound.

He took a deep breath and held it.

He turned his head.

He screamed.

His feet churning through the dust like furious pinwheels as he ran for the safety of his grandfather's outstretched arms. The other kids laughed, but Grandpa just scooped Payne up into his arms and cuddled him against the rough denim bib overalls he always wore. Payne remembered the cold embossed metal buttons—"Oshkosh" or "Pennys"—against his cheeks as he sobbed out his terror.

That night, he slept between Grandma and Grandpa, listening anxiously to their deep, regular breathing, smelling the stale smells of their bedroom: Grandma's lavender potpourri bags in the drawers, Grandpa's liniment pungent and minty on the window sill, age-browned lace cinnamon sachets hanging in the cedar-lined closet. The smells muted and mixed into something uniquely Grandma and Grandpa, echoed by the faint ticking of the antique Seth Thomas clock on the dresser. He didn't remember sleeping at all, but somehow it was suddenly full morning light and Grandma and Grandpa were gone and he was alone in the old room filled with shadows and memories. From outside, he could hear the other kids yelling and playing.

That morning, after breakfast, Grandpa led Payne by the hand back down the trail. Payne pointed out the place behind the third willow on the left where the monster had crouched. Grandpa circled the trunk. Payne's heart kept counterpoint to the old man's movements as Grandpa solemnly examined layers of dirt and decaying leaves, prying at decaying bark with fingers stick-thin and gnarled with arthritis and age. Finally he straightened.

"Payne."

Slowly, like a condemned man marching to his doom, Payne approached, unable to look into Grandpa's face, terrified of whatever Grandpa must have found; without seeing, he knew what the marks would look like, deeply cut prints of long claws, curving, slicing into the hard-packed ground.

He looked down.

There was nothing.

Only Grandpa's mud-caked boots amid wind-whirled piles of disintegrating leaves. A black beetle crawled from beneath the skeleton of a box-elder leaf, then scuttled back when Grandpa shifted his weight and his boot crunched against the leaf. The leaf quavered, then everything was still. The beetle was gone. When Payne looked up, Grandpa smiled, gently and quietly.

But the other kids had followed and now hooted their laughter. They spent the rest of the day weaving in and out of the willows playing monster. Payne hid in the attic among the shadows and the dust and the old forgotten boxes and the blue-bottle flies rapping incessantly at the window in the western gable. When the pressure in his bladder built beyond what he could stand, he still couldn't face the cousins so he slipped out the kitchen door and, ignoring for the moment his fear of snakes and other creepy things, crept through Grandma's raspberry patch and into the apple orchard on the other side. He finally found a gooseberry bush along the fence, one large enough to blot out most of the world, and pushed back the branches and peed against an old, brittle fence post the bush had long before hidden away while he prayed *please god don't let anyone see me here don't let grandma see me doing this* here!

Even as an adult, Payne blushed at the memory of the terror and the humiliation he had felt that night.

Now he had done the same thing again—panicked over imaginary monsters and gone running to the nearest person for help. At least, he thought, he hadn't told Nick everything. He hadn't blithered on to Nick about the images. Be grateful for small favors.

He swallowed. His throat hurt and his hand ached clear up to the elbow as if he had bruised it or over-worked it and the muscles had tightened. He massaged it with his other hand. He wasn't hungry, which was just as well since there wasn't much to eat in the house. He would have to do some major shopping soon or content himself with living like old Mother Hubbard's dog.

(Later, he decided that that final thought had been the last piece in a complex of images: night, fright, day, shame, hiding in an attic, Old Mother Hubbard, like Grandma still wearing those old-fashioned aprons regardless of what she had on underneath. To the end of her life, she wore polyester pantsuits with nylon blouses and flour-sack printed cotton Mother Hubbard aprons, some of them twenty or thirty years old from the looks of them.)

Still in bed, half way to resuming sleep in spite of the lateness, he was startled fully awake by a knock on the front door.

"Minute," he yelled, his voice echoing down the hallway to bounce off the white walls in the living room. "Minute."

He struggled into his jeans, pulling a T-shirt over his head as he half-ran barefoot down the hallway and across the living room. He jerked the door open.

"Mr., uh...Mr. Gunnison?"

"Yeah." Payne searched his memory for some hook, some name to put to the kid standing in the shadows, thumb hitched through a fraying belt loop, a slip of grimy paper in his other hand. The kid looked sixteen, maybe seventeen on a good day. He could use a bath and a clean shirt, Payne thought, maybe even a haircut.

Payne glanced at the slip of paper and saw his name and address scrawled in smudged pencil. He glanced over the kid's shoulder. A Ford mini-van canted on the pavement, its front passenger wheel settling into the grass just over the curb. "Crusade for the Blind" shouted in red block letters on the white side of the van.

"Yeah," Payne repeated, shaking his head to remove the last traces of wake-up fog and finally remembering.

"Pick up." The way the kid said it, the phrase was as much statement as question. He was chewing gum; his jaw muscles moved rhythmically as he chewed.

"Out back," Payne said.

The kid started into the house but Payne stepped outside and shut the door behind him.

"This way."

"Sure," the kid said, eyeing Payne as if to ask *whaccha got in there, a crack factory 'r' somethin'?* The chewing speeded up; the jaw muscles bulged and deflated, bulged and deflated.

Payne ignored him.

On the back porch stood the three large cardboard boxes that held most of Great-Aunt Emilia's cast-offs, the things she directed should be donated to a deserving charity. The boxes had already been packed when Payne arrived, in fact, as if Great-Aunt Emilia had left a list of disposables and some obsequious lesser clerk from the lawyer's office had spent the day (or maybe several of them) collecting the oddments: tattered books, half-empty notebooks with the used pages neatly severed at the bindings and filed elsewhere, the occasional duplicate VCR cassette or DVD (Payne had checked them carefully; all of those in the boxes were worn, ready to be tossed). Nothing much of value. But the will had directed that they boxes go to a good cause, and who was he to argue.

"These," he said curtly, pointing to the collection.

The kid said nothing but shouldered the first box and tucked the second, smaller box under his other arm. Payne watched him struggle around the side of the house, the smaller box threatening to slip at any moment and scatter its contents on the ragged grass.

That one had some old catalogues, he remembered. It was heavier than it looked. He glanced at the third one. He hadn't opened it, hadn't gotten around to it or had decided that he really didn't care—he wasn't quite sure which. The top flaps were folded over but not fastened. Idly he pulled one flap back.

Clothing.

A lot of Great-Aunt Emilia's things still hung in the closet in the front study, ghostly reminders of mortality sealed behind a two-inch-thick panel door. He would have to pack them up and get rid of them too, but he hadn't gotten around to that either.

The clothes were obviously cast-offs. A torn apron with scorch marks around the hem as if someone had tried to take a hot pan out of the oven using the apron as a hot-pot-holder, and held it too long. Three white bath towels so worn that any design was now more problematical than obvious.

He picked up the towels to see what was underneath.

Underwear.

Payne was not unsophisticated, but for some inexplicable reason, he flushed at seeing the clothing. *Unmentionables,* he thought, unconsciously using his grandmother's phrasing: bras so worn that the elastic in the back had begun to flake through the material; slips translucently thin; panties much briefer than he would have expected for someone of Great-Aunt Emilia's age; half a dozen pair of nylons balled together in the corner of the box.

"That it?"

The kid's voice startled Payne. He slapped the cardboard flaps closed and nudged the box with the side of his foot.

"One more."

"Sure." The kid reached down for the box. "Want a receipt?"

"Huh."

"Receipt. For the stuff. Tax deduction come April."

"No, no, I don't think so."

"Okay. Thanks."

Then the kid was gone. The screen door slammed behind him, leaving Payne alone on the porch. Payne followed him with his eyes until the kid disappeared around the corner. A few moments later, he heard the roar of the van and a flash of white reflected in a dusty pane in a back window at Nick's place. For an instant, the red block letters—backward and cruelly distorted by the aging glass—rippled and flowed, and then the kid and the van and the boxes were gone.

Payne went inside and leaned against the cool kitchen wall, dead-white inside where it was clean and safe but rusty gray outside and streaked with weather and dirt and fading paint that had suffered decades of abusive sunlight. His shoulders sloped back until they touched smooth plaster. He closed his eyes and enjoyed the coolness.

He must have drifted off *what kind of an idiot would fall asleep standing up against a wall like that stupid horse in Cat Ballou* because gradually he felt the whiteness grow and deepen until it began to seep through his thin T-shirt and twist along the curve of his spine, even in those places where the flesh did not touch the wall at all. The whiteness grabbed his flesh and grew there, knotting him to the wall. Tendrils of terror penetrated deeper and deeper until it seemed as if the whiteness would reach his center and obliterate it. And now along his spine he felt fingers, hands sticky-hot with sweat and sexual fever, reaching through the whiteness to grasp hold of him and twist him into something different, something only partly, perhaps not at all Payne Gunnison. Something he couldn't understand. The hands pressed slimily against his sides, then penetrated to caress his organs—kidney, heart, intestines—and draw from them their life-bearing heat. His tissues froze at the touch of the probing fingers until Payne was a cold whiteness, a frozen barrenness with heat and life and color diminishing until it survived only at the core.

As the hands reached toward that single point of color to extinguish it until all became whiteness, his head dropped forward with enough force to startle him fully awake.

"Shit," he breathed. "Don't you go all crazy on me, Payne-me-boy!"

He straightened away from the wall, which was now warm and damp with his sweat, and crossed the room in three strides. He pulled a glass from the shelf and filled it with tepid water straight from the faucet. He gulped the water down in one breath, refilled the glass, gulped again, and refilled until his stomach burned with the indefinable burn of tepid tap water confronting emptiness. He was sweating. He thought about pouring a bowl of cereal but decided against it and chewed absently on a rock-hard bagel instead, then went into the bathroom and relieved himself of at least one and a half glasses of water that was as tepid coming out as it had been going in.

By the time he returned to the kitchen, he felt better. Marginally. His head ached slightly. His ears buzzed. Not much, not a frantic mosquito's *BZZZZZ*, not even a distant bee's more ethereal *bzzzz*, but something less defined, more irritating because most of the time it remained subliminal. He shook his head and yawned widely to pop his ears. That helped a little.

What the hell's going on.

He avoided speaking out loud.

First there was the utter stupidity of his panic last night, then that equally stupid memory of Grandpa and the outhouse monster, and now some half-assed daytime nightmare about the kitchen walls and ghostly hands sticky with sweat at handling worn-out undies left behind by a woman weeks in her grave.

"Shit," he said again, but this time there was an undercurrent of humor in the word. He was going dotty or something.

Maybe it was something in the paint. Yeah, that was it. Some secret formula Great-Aunt Emilia concocted in a secret lab behind a secret door in the ramshackle garage. White paint to white-out the mind.

He grinned.

He wouldn't put something like that past her, given what little he knew about her, but to give the old bitch her due there really wasn't any room in the garage for a secret lab.

So—*the whole thing is jitters and the best cure for that is to do something. Get off your ass and get something done.*

But what?

He seriously considered washing the car. It was still coated with a layer of dust from its days in the LAX parking lot. He glanced through the window to where the car sat in the drive. The sun glinted sharply from the hood and top, glaring into the kitchen.

Nope, he decided without much hesitation. Too hot. And his eyes hurt when he stared too long at the glistening chrome. The car needed a wash but it would have to wait. Maybe tonight, more toward dusk.

Or he could check out the attic. It would be dark up there, easier on his eyes. The crawl hole was easily accessible, too, a cut-out in the ceiling at the far end of the hallway. He had noticed it before and thought that he should climb up some day and see what was there, what shape the place was in. And, after all, there was that single window beneath the eaves out front, the one that sometimes glowed in the sunset like a cyclopean eye, so there must be some sort of room overhead.

He went to the garage and returned a few moments later with a small, rickety stepladder copiously spattered with white paint. He set it up at the end of the hall. He tested the lowest rung with one foot.

It wobbled but felt like it would probably hold.

You should wait until tomorrow and check on a new ladder at Lumber City a mile or so down the main street, part of him argued. That would be the safe thing, the wise thing, the careful thing. After all, who knew how long this ladder had been sitting around, warping and decaying, its hinges rusting, its rungs loosening in their corroded steel grommets, its wood gradually turning to mush. One wrong step and....

But by the time he had reached that stage in his thinking, he had pushed the ceiling cover back and was boosting himself up onto the joists of the attic.

It was warm up there. He was glad that he was wearing cut-offs and no shirt. The air smelled stale—like at Grandma's in some ways but essentially different. It was a generic staleness, blue-banded and plain-wrapped. He conjured an image of air trapped in a white bag, the sides rhythmically expanding and contracting like lungs, and blue letters marching boldly across the front reading "AIR: For Attic Use Only." Probably stocked on the shelf next to "GRANDMA SMELLS" and "GRANDPA SMELLS."

He sat on the edge of the opening and pulled his legs through. Someone had done some work up here long ago. Thick dust carpeted everything, but the spaces between most of the ceiling joists had been covered with half-inch unfinished plywood paneling to make a rough floor. At the far end, the window diffused light through dust and layers of flyspecks. He walked toward it.

He knelt in the thick dust. It puffed out beneath his knee, then settled down to cake on the upper surface of his thighs. Kneeling in the hot, stale air made his ears buzz again, louder this time and more insistently. He peered through the rippled glass. He could see nothing. He looked around. Behind him was thin stack of old newspapers. He grabbed the top one and rubbed a clean circle in the middle of the window. Through it, he could make out the sidewalk, a portion of the street, most of the house across the way. He hadn't met the people who lived there, but Nick said they were an old couple.

He looked down at the sill, heavily layered with dust as if all of the dryness in the house were funneled up here to lie undisturbed as a motionless record of passing years. Embedded in it, like fossils stratified in gray opaque amber, lay bluebottle flies, small black kernels of death. In an upper corner of the window, one live fly buzzed an unending monotone—a "blue uncertain buzz," he remembered from somewhere. It matched the buzzing in his ears and for a moment there was only one sound; then his ears kicked up to a higher pitch and *hummm*ed an irritating duet with the fly.

Aunt Emilia's attic was smaller and darker and dustier, he decided, but it still could have been Grandma's. The papers at his feet were yellowed and torn. He picked one up and squinted at it in the dim light. The date was unreadable. He tried a second sheet: March 28, 1953. Over fifty-five years old.

He duck-walked through the dust to three cardboard boxes huddled like frightened orphans where the roof angled down to touch the rafters. One by one, he pulled back the flaps on the boxes. There was nothing in any of them except a couple of inches of excelsior. He pushed his hand through the stuff but found nothing. Only after he finished with the third box did he stop to think what might have been there instead of old artifacts: spiders, rats, mice, maybe nests of vermin, their droppings at the least.

He glanced around. There was no sign of rodents. Not right here where he was kneeling and apparently not anywhere in the attic. The dust was undisturbed except for where he had walked and for occasional indentations of nearly obscured footprints that might have been months or years old. There was no sign of scurrying little things hiding in the darkness.

He moved to another pile of boxes a few feet away. These too were empty. That left only the last cluster, half a dozen stacked on the other side of the drop-way into the hall, near the back of the attic.

He went to the opening and sat on the edge, dangling his legs through the drop-way until his toes just missed the last rung on the ladder.

The light was paradoxically dimmer and harsher back here, well away from the dusty window at the front of the house. The light from the hallway cast heavy shadows upward that made it difficult to see inside the boxes, but they were close enough for him to tip them back and look. As with the others, most were empty except for occasional bits of packing materials. It was as if something had been delivered, then the boxes were simply tucked out of sight. Waste not, want not. He peered at the nearest label. It was stamped *electronics* but he couldn't make out anything more.

He lifted each of the remaining boxes and tossed them to the center of the attic, enjoying the swirls of dust that rose as each thudded onto the plywood floor. Finally he tugged at the last one to slide it closer. The cardboard ripped noisily, tearing from top to base.

The box was heavy, obviously not empty.

Curious, he pulled with both hands, trying to slide the box without ripping it further.

The box refused to slide.

He drew his legs up and moved over to the box, pushing back the remaining three flaps.

It was apparently full of magazines. He couldn't read parts

of the top title because the fine print in typewriter font was obscured by dust and age, but he thought that it had something to do with electronics. What else would one expect from Aunt Emilia, he asked himself, rather more disappointed than he quite understood.

His ears were buzzing again. Or at least he noticed again that they were still buzzing. He felt a little flushed, too. Time to get out of here and back into the fresh air. He decided to climb down and finish up here another day, pick a cool cloudy fall day when there was a crispness in the air and attic would be chilly rather than stuffy and his ears would settle down and let him hear.

He shoved the box to the opening, climbed down the ladder several steps, and started pulling the box out. For one bad moment he almost lost his balance. The ladder swayed beneath him, threatening to pitch him off backward, but then he was back in control and his right foot touched the floor. A minute later, he dropped the box onto the kitchen table.

Dust billowed from it, thick and acrid. He waved his hand to dissipate the cloud. His hands were caked with dust. He looked down. His chest and shorts and legs were gray, more like antique, decaying flesh than glowing with Southern California health. He clapped his hands against his thighs, intrigued as the dust clouded in tiny spurts. The attic had been far dirtier than he had thought.

So—a shower first. He walked toward the bathroom, kicking off his shoes and stepping out of his pants as he went. But inside, just as his hand reached to pull back the shower curtain and turn on the old-fashioned faucets, he stopped.

He yawned to pop his ears and shook his head again. He hooked his fingers in the waistband of his underwear, then paused once more.

Why would Aunt Emilia stuff magazines into the attic when everything else relating to electronics was neatly catalogue and stored in the Master Control Room? What was so unimportant about the stuff that she would store it up in the attic but so important that she would not have it boxed up with the other junk and sent on to charities?

Still dirty, he walked out of the bathroom. What was a little dust, anyway? The shower could wait.

He returned to the kitchen. He leaned against the doorjamb to study the box on the table across the room from him. It seemed definitely out of place, the only blot of dust and filth in the pristine kitchen. He scanned it for labels. It was plain. No packing label. No name stenciled on the side. Just a plain brown box. The magazine on top was frosted with dust that made it look like the fading ghost of a magazine. He padded to the table and picked up the magazine, leaning over to blow away the coating of dust.

And froze.

The buzzing In his ears spiraled into a scream. He screamed. High-pitched and thin, like a woman in final terror.

A second magazine, lying neatly underneath the first one, glowed clean, fresh, vividly colored, without a speck of dust.

It showed a fully, frontally nude male.

Payne dropped the electronics magazine. It fluttered to the floor and lay half open, squashed on the tile like a wounded bird whose fragile wings had failed.

He stared, his mouth dry and aching, his right arm throbbing.

He saw a naked man erect and grinning up at him.

With a shaking hand, Payne lifted the magazine out of the box, handling it as gingerly as if it were a poisonous snake. The picture on the cover of the magazine beneath was like the first—worse even, if that was possible, with two men twined around each other like perverted summer vines. And the next, and the next. To the bottom of the box.

By the time he had finished, male nudes littered the tabletop. Payne was sweating, the drops mixing with dust and streaking his arms and sides and chest.

When the box was empty, he picked up one of the magazines and flipped through it. More of the same as on the covers, but worse and worse. More graphic. More explicit.

He licked his lips. Aunt Emilia apparently had strange taste in art. All of the magazines dated after 1998. No one else he knew of could have put them in the attic. He glanced over the scattered pile, noting the general sequentiality of the things, oldest on top of the table, most recent hidden or half-hidden. The reverse order from the way they had been inside the box.

Probably she put them up in that box, one by one, month after month.

He picked up one and thumbed through it, the pages rippling past like images from nightmares. Suddenly he stopped turning pages and stared at one of the photographs.

"My god," he whispered barely above a breath, as if afraid someone might overhear and come into the kitchen to investigate.

The photograph had been defaced. It was scratched and gouged and scored exactly over the model's genitals.

Payne shuddered.

The next page was the same. He flipped toward the front of the magazine. He hadn't noticed it before, but almost every photograph was mutilated. Only the genitals, but with a precise violence that left him shattered.

His hand trembled, his arm ached. He dropped the magazine and massaged his sore muscles.

Aunt Emilia, he thought wildly. *These are hers. She liked this kind of thing. She liked looking at pictures of naked men.*

But it was worse than that, he knew intuitively. Far worse.

For one thing, these were not just pictures of naked men engaged in activities Aunt Emilia probably should not have even known about.

There were the gouges. He ran one finger over the roughened paper.

She had loved *and* hated. *Lusted,* perhaps, *and* felt repulsed.

Lifting his hand, he saw a dark smudge across the glossy finish of the photograph. He looked at his finger, at the back of his hand where the dust was damp and caking, then at his stomach, bare and streaked with dirt, the only clean skin a narrow band between where his shorts had been and the crisp blue elastic of his underwear. He was filthy, standing almost naked in the kitchen, filthy and dusty and dirty.

He went to the bathroom and stripped, staring for a long moment at the solid line of dust at his waist.

What the hell was going on here?

Payne stepped into the shower, welcoming the cold water that gradually warmed then grew almost uncomfortably hot before he adjusted the faucets. The heat washed away layers of grime and dust and tiredness and fear. White lather from his shampoo spilled over his face, stinging his eyes but cleansing cheeks and neck and shoulders.

He stood under the spray for what seemed hours. When he was finished, toweled and dried, hair combed, dressed in jeans and jogging shoes and a long-sleeved chambray shirt buttoned tightly at the cuffs, he returned to the kitchen and stacked the magazines carefully into the box, oldest on the bottom, newest on the top.

He set the electronics magazine over that one, centering it to make sure nothing showed of the magazine underneath it. He taped the torn side with silver duct tape from the utility drawer, folded down the flaps and tucked them inside each other to keep them folded, then taped over each of them.

There was an old metal drum In the back yard. He would take them right out and burn them. Right now. This minute. He might have to live with a dirty attic, but that kind of dust you could get rid of if you wanted to. This kind of filth was something different.

He slid a hand under the box to lift it. There was a sharp *bzzzz* like a wasp about to attack. He flinched, just as the kitchen light blew with a flash of light and a shattering *ping!* A splinter of glass sliced across his knuckles, drawing a bead of blood.

Damn, he thought, *now I'll have to change the bulb.*

Lucky thing the ladder was handy. He shoved the table to one side and pulled the ladder into the middle of the room, then rummaged through a corner cabinet for the replacement bulbs he had seen there several days before. It only took a couple of minutes to replace the bulb. The wires inside had disintegrated; the bulb had cracked from the metal base to the imprinted wattage statement at the top.

When he finished tightening the last screw on the milky globe covering the bulb, he rinsed the blood off his hand, deciding against applying a bandage. He left the kitchen and walked through the front of the house and out the door and onto the porch. He did not slide the table back beneath the light fixture. He did not touch the box that day or the next or the next.

Finally, nearly a week later, he simply shoved the box back up into the attic, not particularly thinking about what he was doing, just getting it out of the way. It sat near the opening, just as Aunt Emilia had done. He left.

He never consciously noted that on the day the light bulb blew, he had not turned the kitchen light on.

CHAPTER TWENTY-TWO

Two days after he returned the box to the attic, Payne called Cathy for a date. She arrived at six and stayed until a little after midnight. They ate, talked, did the dishes, watched a film Cathy had missed never heard of, *Somewhere in Time*, a box-office bomb that the critics had hated, but Cathy fell in love with Christopher Reeve and the hotel and the nostalgia and the sense of loss. Afterward she cried. They talked and had a drink or two and she left. She kissed Payne goodnight and then she left.

The next night, he went to her apartment. She shared a couple of rooms in a decaying part of town with another girl who was fortunately on vacation for two weeks and currently camping out somewhere between Ogallala, Nebraska and the Mississippi River. They had the place to themselves.

After a dinner of thick steak and fresh salad, they listened to quiet music on Cathy's CD player and talked some more. It was silent except for the music, something subdued and harmonious and romantic, especially in dimmed lighting, especially in an apartment with a beautiful woman who curls on a couch and watches you move across the room to pour another drink, her eyes misty, her smile tender. Whose breasts press invitingly against the fragile linen of her blouse. Whose smile is invitation.

Payne had drunk more than usual that night. He wasn't drunk—not quite. He had carefully stayed on the sober side of that thin line. Instead of feeling pleasantly relaxed, however, he felt oddly tense, nervous. The feeling increased as the evening wore on, transforming from a light and wholly accountable first-date sort of jumpiness when he raised his hand to knock on her door, to an intense, discomforting sense of something desperately wrong when she leaned against him where they sat together on the couch and he smelled her perfume and the light lingering fragrance of the shampoo in her hair and felt the warmth of her breath against his neck. She laid her hand on his leg and scratched her fingernail lightly against the taut fabric.

The room flooded with heat. Payne was not naive. He was not sexually innocent; certainly he was not a virgin. And Cathy was attractive in every way he could imagine. She was beautiful— and he wanted her. He wanted to draw her even closer, wanted to touch and whisper and love.

Instead he stood suddenly and strode to the door. A clock on the wall chimed midnight as he reached for the knob. The witching hour.

In a fluid movement, Cathy rose and was beside him.

"Payne," she said. Her voice rose barely above a whisper. She tilted her head up and kissed him on the lips, a kiss warm with affection yet tinged with disappointment. He reached for her. One arm held her tightly against him. He felt her hips against his. His other arm hung stiffly at his side. The fingers clenched and unclenched along the seam of his jeans.

Payne felt suddenly and inexplicably fatigued, as if half of him had just won an exhausting endurance race but the other half—the darker half—was about to break away and begin running again. He broke away.

"Thanks," he said. "For the dinner. I wish I could stay but I...I've got to leave."

"Don't...," Cathy began. He placed his finger against her lips, feeling their warmth and moistness. He wanted to feel them again pressed against his own. He almost kissed her. Something flickered behind his eyes—a fleeting image too evanescent for him to consciously absorb. Inside of him, the pull away from her intensified.

"I know," he said. "But I have to. Okay?"

"Okay," she answered, her voice dropping.

He nodded and moved toward the elevator at the end of the hall. The elevator doors slid open just as he reached them, as if they had been waiting for him. She watched him. He hesitated before stepping in.

For a moment, he almost turned back to her, then he entered the shadowy interior of the elevator. He seemed to favor one leg.

In that final moment of hesitation, though, he looked over his shoulder and smiled at her and raised a hand in a twist that seemed a wave. Or a gesture of dismissal.

"Call me, okay?" She waved back. The elevator doors slid shut with a quiet whoosh and Payne was gone.

When Payne arrived home and pulled his car into the drive and killed the engine just outside the garage still crammed with Aunt Emilia's trash, Nick's windows were dark. Wheeler was either out or asleep, Payne decided. He walked slowly around the house to the front door, enjoying the coolness of the evening, wishing that Nick would stick his head out a window and invite him over for a talk.

He wanted to talk.

He needed to talk about the evening even though nothing had happened. Especially, perhaps, because nothing had happened. He climbed the steps to the front porch carefully, wondering why he was coming in through the front door when he usually used the kitchen door. He glanced to the side and fought off an impulse to sit in the glider and swing, swing, swing through the darkness and the coolness.

His leg still pained him. It had started as he got into the elevator, a knife-sharp hitch in his hip that now made his foot scuff the worn planks of the porch. It had made the trip home a minor version of hell, pumping up and down on the accelerator to change speed with the erratic night-time traffic, and now it made him limp noticeably. His hand curled tightly against his leg for balance.

He stared at the glider as if daring it to creak its way through the night, propelled by a ghost or the wind or whatever. It remained still. He forced his curled fingers open and pressed his palm flat against his thigh and planted his feet flat against the porch and shifted his weight from his good leg to his bad until both bore him equally. The hitch disappeared. He unlocked the door, reaching awkwardly across his body with his right hand and pulling the key from his pocket, as if to prove his control over his muscles. When he stepped into the house, it was with his right foot first, his hip swinging smoothly now and without pain.

He hurried through the living room and down the hall to the kitchen, switching lights on as he passed. The house was still; it seemed to be waiting. The planking in the hallway creaked when he stepped onto it from the living room rug. *Creeeeeak— like something out of The Fall of the House of Usher.*

"Shut up," he said. No reason to spook himself by thinking stupid things like that.

In the kitchen, he poured himself a glass of ice water from the refrigerator and pulled a chair over to the telephone. He lifted the receiver and, without hesitating an instant, he dialed Cathy's number. He sat back, tapping a finger against the headset as it rang once, twice, three times, four.

"Hello." Her voice sounded tired, sleepy. He sat up straight and pushed his glass away, sliding it smoothly across the white counter.

"It's me."

There was a pause.

"Yes." Her voice was cautious, but he thought he detected a hint of something more—hope, forgiveness, maybe more?

"Look," he said in a burst, "I'm really sorry about tonight. I guess I just didn't feel like myself. Headachy, tired. You know how it is sometimes." *Lame lame lame dumb dumb dumb* his internal censor chanted as he spoke.

He was gushing, he knew, the words spilling out of his mouth before he heard them in his mind. He hated doing that. He hated people who did it. His hand tightened on the receiver, knuckles white, as he glared at the white ceiling and clenched his teeth until the muscles in his jaws stood out in garish relief against his skin.

She was speaking now. He had missed something but at least she wasn't mad. She sounded relieved, not at all tired.

"...sometimes. I get like that after the audits. It's just part of life, I guess."

"Yeah," he said, trying to cover the fact that he had missed part of what she said. "But I'm sorry anyway. Everything was so nice, the dinner and the music and everything. How about...."

Before he could say *tomorrow night*, the receiver screeched. A fire-burst of static drilled through his head. With a yelp, he jerked the receiver away. Even after the sound stopped, his ear whistled and buzzed like a manic power saw. Beneath the ringing he felt twinges of real pain, physical pain that bore inward toward his brain. He gingerly put the receiver next to his other ear. Holding it was awkward, but at least he could hear clearly.

"...did you say?" she was saying. "I didn't hear you. Some kind of interference on the line."

"Are you okay?" he asked.

"Sure. Why wouldn't I be?"

"There was some static here, really loud. My ear is still ringing."

"Nothing like that on this end, but it serves you right for behaving like you did. Even Ma Bell thinks you were a cad." She laughed and it took any sting out of her words.

He laughed with her. It felt right.

"I guess it does, at that. I behaved like a real jerk and my telephone is trying to let me know." He whistled that idiotic *doo-di-doo-doo* theme from *Twilight Zone* and they both laughed again.

"Anyway, how about"—he hesitated, moving the receiver an inch or so away from his ear—"tomorrow night?"

"I'd love to." The softness of velvet.

"I'll cook up something special for dinner, I owe you that much. We'll watch a film or something, and then...."

"And then…whatever. Sounds good. See you then."

"See you, Cathy. Good night."

When he hung up the receiver, he stood for a few moments with hand still on the receiver. He grinned boyishly at the sterile white wall.

He felt good.

He stretched, twisting his torso at the hips in a cross between a toe-touch and a stationary jumping-jack. He reached out with his right hand, fingers extended and straight, tendons knotted and strong beneath the skin. His ear stopped ringing.

He felt good, all right. Damn good!

He slept deeply that night, so deeply that he did not remember dreaming. Even though he tossed on his bed and wrapped himself in the light covers and was drenched with sweat for most of the night, he did not wake until the alarm rang in the morning. He didn't remember dreaming at all.

CHAPTER TWENTY-THREE

Cathy arrived at the house on Greensward just before five. She was half surprised to see Payne waiting for her at the open door, looking native Californian in tennis shorts and striped polo shirt. She almost laughed at his boyish eagerness—he was down the steps and at the sidewalk before she had pulled her car to a stop. He dashed around the car and opened her door, bowing low and sweeping grandly with his arm.

"Milady," he said his face tight with mock seriousness. She stepped out of the car and surprised herself by dropping into an impromptu curtsy, holding out the hem of her light summer dress as if it were ten pounds of brocade and pearl-encrusted silk.

"My Lord."

They laughed. Payne gave her a quick hug and steered her up the sidewalk to the house.

The place seemed subtly different as she entered, not quite as glaring as it had been the first time she had visited. Today, the white walls seemed muted, and the TV screens were dead, unreflective gray squares against off-tone walls. It was pleasing, she decided, whatever the difference was.

Payne, on the other hand, was more demonstrably vital, more vibrant. Seated in the kitchen, she watched him bustle through the final preparations for dinner, her interest and her own arousal growing as he reached and stretched, pulling glasses from high cupboards and in the process emphasizing the smooth line of his arm, back, thighs, and calves.

"Let me help," she had offered almost as soon as he had escorted her to a chair in the kitchen.

"Nothing doing. Tonight it's my turn to do for you. And you've never lived until you've lived through...that is, *enjoyed* one of my home-cooked...uh, experiences."

"Uh-oh. Now I'm scared." But she knew that the sparkle in her eyes belied her words and that Payne knew it as well. Instead of helping, she watched.

It wasn't an unpleasant task. Payne was handsome enough, but she had known that from the first time she saw him on the beach south of Zuma. He was also self-assured tonight, less nervous, less upset than on the night before. He moved with a quiet strength she found particularly appealing. She liked the way he smiled and the way he dressed—the pale blue of his shirt and the startling white of his shorts set off his tan and emphasized the muscles of his arms and legs. In spite of a nagging hunger that reminded her that she had eaten nothing since gulping down an English muffin at breakfast, she wished heartily for the meal to be over.

For his part, Payne was thoroughly enjoying himself. He knew Cathy was watching him; he knew because he surreptitiously watched her watch him. Her attention made him feel stronger and more masculine, more desirable, even *sexier*, though he had rarely consciously thought of himself in those terms before. Her feelings for him resonated through the air whenever he passed her, even when he stood across the room and chopped and sliced and poured and stirred, stealing quick glances as often as he dared. Once he crossed to get a cube of butter from the refrigerator and inadvertently—*but oh, how very* advertently *it was*—allowed his forearm to brush against her sleeve. The fleeting touch jarred him more than he would have imagined, and he quickly returned to his chopping and slicing.

As it turned out, dinner was wonderful in spite of Payne's half-serious warning about his culinary expertise. The food was pleasant—but that was not the source of the pleasure. Payne was thoroughly enchanted with Cathy, and she, in turn, felt easily comfortable with this Payne, who was more like the man she had met at the beach than the fellow who had run out on her the night before. That rather distant, slightly frightening, unaccountably cold stranger seemed permanently banished. *This* Payne was, instead, warm and gentle, funny at times, always concerned. She felt special.

After dinner, they washed the dishes together.

Payne didn't have a dishwasher even though he had thought once or twice about buying one. Basically, he wasn't sure he needed one and he wasn't sure the provisions of the will would allow for one. He had almost called about it one day, had the telephone in his hand and had dialed the first four numbers of the lawyer's seven, when he had to...well, he couldn't quite remember now what had distracted him, but he had remembered something and felt compelled to put the phone down and check on it. Something to do with the television in the living room, he thought. At any rate, he had never completed the call. He disliked doing dishes by hand, but there were so few of them with him living there alone that it didn't matter that much.

But at first he didn't want Cathy to help.

He took the plates over to the sink. While he was standing there, she blew out the two candles that were flickering away their last inch and switched on the overhead light. He was scraping the remnants of dinner into the garbage disposal, his back to her. She rubbed her fingers lightly against his shoulders and said, "Okay, now it's my turn. I'll clean up."

"No," he said, rather too sharply as it turned out, because she dropped her hands and he heard her step away from him.

He turned, smiling broadly as if it had all been a joke, planned from the beginning. It might well have been, because he knew no reason for her *not* to help.

"Let them wait, I mean. I'll take care of everything tomorrow."

"No, really, please. I don't mind. I'd enjoy it. And you went through so much work to get dinner ready. It's the least I can do."

He smiled at her last phrase.

"Okay," he agreed. "But only if we work together. I think I must've dirtied every utensil in the place, and it wouldn't be fair for you to have to face that stack alone."

So they worked together, passing dishes, silverware, pots and pans back and forth between them. Things were right again. The momentary sharpness was forgotten as they worked, stacking old-fashioned, translucently white china cups and plates, dropping equally old-fashioned heavy silver-plate knives and spoons and forks and serving pieces into little velvet-lined slotted segments in the drawers. Payne even decided to scrub the bottoms of the copper-clad pots and skillets, something he had neglected for the weeks. He sprinkled the white cleanser across the bottoms of the pots, noting with pleasure the brightly glowing copper emerging as he rinsed the cleanser off. It gave him a feeling of accomplishment, of finishing something. When he got to the last skillet, the thirteen incher that was crusted with burned-on guck from who knew how many spills while he was cooking breakfast, he shifted the pan to his left hand, stretching his right, curling and uncurling fingers that were becoming stiffer and stiffer as they worked.

He rinsed the pan and balanced it on the stack in the drainer, then turned to see if there was anything left on the table.

"Not there!" he shouted abruptly as Cathy started to put a bottle of steak sauce on the top shelf of the refrigerator. "On the middle shelf."

She looked up startled. "But what dif—"

"On the middle shelf," Payne repeated. "Please."

Some of the earlier sharpness trembled, barely discernible beneath the layering of his voice.

"Well, all right," Cathy said, allowing her own voice to take on overtones of irritation and huffiness. "But really, Payne," she turned as she spoke, letting her smile suffuse her face, "you are such a real *pain*. Such an old woman about your kitchen."

For a second he stared at her, his eyes veiled and—for a flickering breath—frightening. Then his eyes cleared and he laughed.

"We'll see who's an old woman," he said suddenly, leaping across the kitchen and enclosing her in his arms and planting a kiss on her lips.

The kiss lingered longer than he had intended.

"Well," Cathy said finally. "I take it back. Certainly no old woman."

Payne looked embarrassed and a bit confused.

"Hey, I'm sorry. I didn't mean to...."

"So, now you're going to make it worse by taking back the best dessert I've had in longer than I can remember. Well!"

She turned away in a mock-fury, then burst into a fit of giggles. Payne looked startled, then joined in. After a long while, they calmed down enough to breath normally.

"That's it," Payne said, glancing around the spotless kitchen. "What now?"

Cathy smiled. "Your choice."

"How about...a game or something." His voice trailed off into silence. Her smile deepened at his words, as if to say *poor fellow, he doesn't dare ask for what he wants. If he choose to play a game, I'll take him up on it, and I can play* that *game better than he can.* She smiled more broadly.

"Chess?" he finally managed to suggest.

She threw her head back and laughed out loud, a long vibrant laugh that bounced off the white walls. "Sure, why not. Chess it is."

She linked her arm through his and steered him from the kitchen, down the hall, and into the living room. He palmed the light switch as they crossed into the room. Whiteness glared from all sides. She sat on the sofa; he squatted on the carpet, his chest level with the board, with her knees directly across from him.

"Black or white?" he said.

"You choose. It's your night." She smiled again, putting more into her answer than Payne might be expecting or used to. But if he wasn't going to make a move, she would.

"You take white."

She reached out and slid a pawn forward—a conventional opening. Cathy was an indifferent player, Payne discovered, but neither was she a novice. Her moves showed potential skill but she seemed disinterested—perhaps even *uninterested*—in the game. He put on the pressure a bit, capturing two pieces in consecutive moves.

"How about some crackers or something?" she said suddenly.

"Huh?"

"Snacks? Got anything?"

"Sure." He pulled himself up and walked into the hall, stretching out his cramped leg muscles.

She watched him carefully until he disappeared into the darkness, nothing with tingling pleasure the subtle movement of muscle in his back, his shoulders, his buttocks. It was time for some major strategy, she decided, since he was apparently willing to sit here and do nothing but play chess all night. Not that she had anything against chess. *It beat going to the dentist or having red-hot pokers punched through your skull, but not by much. At least, not tonight.*

"Can I help?" she called down the hallway.

"No. Everything's under control in here," he answered.

It will be in here, too. Soon. Cathy shifted her position slightly.

Payne reappeared moments later carrying a tray with Wheat Thins, a small half-round of Gouda, and a knife. He had folded a white dish towel into a narrow strip and laid it precisely across his bare arm, *maître d'*-fashion. Without a tuxedo it looked pretty ridiculous, but the gesture was cute. Cathy liked that about Payne. He was *cute*, innocent and yet desirable in so many ways.

"This okay?" he said, repeating his grand-lord gesture with his free hand.

"Looks great."

She took the tray and balanced it on the edge of the chess table, sliding the board over an inch or two to make room. Payne dropped back down onto the carpet and resumed his careful assessment of the game.

Casually—with studied casualness that almost embarrassed her, that would certainly have embarrassed her if she hadn't felt so passionately drawn to Payne—Cathy cut a thin slice of cheese, laid it on top of a cracker and brought slowly it toward her mouth. At the last moment, hand hovering in midair, she stopped.

"Ever play strip chess?" Her voice as was as flat and unemotional as if she had commented on the weather or on the texture of the carpet. She bit down on the cracker.

Payne looked as if he had swallowed a cracker just like it... whole.

"What?" He half choked.

"Strip chess," she repeated, this time smiling that same inviting smile replete with suggestions that never quite became words. "Every time you lose a piece—anything over a pawn, that is—you lose a piece of clothing. It makes checkmate more... interesting."

Payne flushed furiously.

"You just took two of my pieces," she continued, finishing off the bit of cracker between words, "so I owe you two." She slid her feet out of her sandals and held them up by the straps. "Will these do?"

Payne stammered, not sure what to say. He had obviously wanted to make love to her that night; she knew intuitively that he had thought again and again during the day how he should approach her, but to have her take the initiative obviously startled and flustered him. She liked that.

She waited for him to answer.

Finally he nodded. "Yeah, fine."

She handed the sandals across the board. He took possession of them gingerly, as if they were hot. She watched him set them carefully by his side on the carpet, then she reached down and moved her bishop, capturing Payne's knight.

"Your loss...your turn," she said.

He sat back heavily on the carpet and fumbled under the chess table. He held up a shoe, dangling it from the lace like it was a prize-winning trophy fish. He grinned, but there was an element of discomfort in his expression.

They played silently for the next few minutes. Cathy was increasingly aggressive; Payne played more conservatively than usual, losing fewer pieces but making no real gain in the game. In the next several interchanges, Cathy lost her necklace and her blouse. Payne gave up his other shoe, both socks, and his shirt. They lay in a tidy pile on the sofa, almost touching Cathy's thigh.

Payne, for his part, was having increasing difficulty concentrating on chess. As the game progressed, it seemed to him that the room was growing warmer. The white walls glared their own incandescent heat. Twice he shook his head, as if to clear his thoughts. The black pieces lined up along Cathy's side of the board twice began to blur and expand, black boulders in a sea of white. His ears rang; he felt sweat beading on his forehead and lips. *All right, all right,* he thought, angry at himself for reacting so badly *so this is a little different than I figured, a little more direct, but the result is going to be the same isn't it, so why the sweats—why the nervous but horny teenager routine.* The sensations passed. He forced his attention back to the game.

He took a bishop. She stood and slipped her pants down, exposing the long line of her thighs. She now wore only panties and bra, her tanned skin startlingly brown next to their lacy whiteness. She sat down, still smiling, and moved. She captured *his* bishop.

"Check," she said smoothly. "And now you owe me."

He swallowed hard. He wasn't overly modest. And he had certainly worn less in the presence of a woman before. But this seemed...seemed fundamentally wrong, almost like a gentle rape, like when he had pulled the bushes away from the house and exposed it to everyone's eyes, its shadows painfully expunged by unwonted sunlight. It felt as if she were stripping him instead of them removing their clothing as part of a mutual act of closeness and love. He felt an overwhelming impulse to sweep the board clear of black and white pieces and start the evening again, with himself more firmly in control.

He wanted Cathy, that was true—but not like this, not with her taking over so completely. His hand curled around a captured pawn as he stared at her.

"Come on, don't be shy," she whispered. "You owe me."

Right. That was the game. So now it was his turn to stand and loosen the fastenings at the waistband of his shorts and slide the zipper down. The sound echoed from the empty walls, warningly and disapprovingly. He bent and slipped his shorts to his feet. His white bikini briefs were damp at the waistband, tight around the hips.

"Nice," Cathy said. His ears burned as she continued, just a fraction of a second too late for it to have been what she really meant to say. "Nice legs."

He sat down as quickly as he could, almost losing his balance. Cathy laughed as he stared at the board, struggling to return to the game. As much as he wanted her, the sight of her frustrated him. He shifted his weight; he must have strained that hip again when he squatted down. And damn now his hand hurt too, like he had sprained it playing tennis or something.

He studied the pieces carefully. He was going to play serious chess now, regardless of what game Cathy had in mind. He only had one ransom left. He wasn't going to lose it easily. If she won, she was going to have to work damned hard for it.

He studied the board. She watched him.

There. There it was. An opening he would have had to be a blind fool to miss.. His hand darted out and moved a piece

"Check," he said, glancing up at her from beneath a furrowed brow. "And mate."

Cathy dropped her eyes from him to the board. "You're right," she said after a few seconds. She sighed melodramatically, and in doing so somehow restored the sense of fun that Payne had gradually lost.

He felt embarrassed now, not at his state of dress but at what he had been thinking about Cathy. She wasn't that kind. She wasn't manipulative and hard. She was warm and loving and kind and fun and he wanted to love her.

"I lose the game," she said softly. She twisted her arm around her back, loosening her bra. It dropped onto the sofa. All the time she watched Payne, stared at him, pinned him with her eyes as he sat on the carpet. Her breasts were white.

"I forgot to mention," she continued, "that the loser has to forfeit everything left on. I lost so here goes."

She rose, stepped out of her panties, and knelt down beside Payne.

A few minutes later, she whispered, "why don't you turn out the lights."

He stood, his nakedness silhouetted by the surrounding glare. When he returned to her, the living room was heavily shadowed, lit only by reflected light from the kitchen.

CHAPTER TWENTY-FOUR

"Want to watch a film or something?" Payne asked nearly an hour later. "To relax?"

"No, I don't think so. I really have to get going."

He raised himself up on one elbow as she slipped away from him and walked over to the couch.

"But I thought...weren't you going to stay here tonight?"

"Oh, Payne, I want to, but I just can't. I've got to be in to work early tomorrow, and it's just too far from here for me to...."

"I can set the alarm early, make sure you get there in time."

"Thanks, but I better not. Anyway," she laughed, a short happy sound, "Where would I sleep? That cot in your room certainly isn't big enough. And much as I've enjoyed this evening, I can't imagine bunking out on your carpet. No, I have to be going."

She slipped into her pants, then pulled her blouse on, not bothering with her underwear. Payne stood, aware of his nakedness but helpless to hide it. He couldn't spot his clothes at the moment. More importantly, Cathy was getting ready to leave. He didn't want her to.

"Are you sure," he said, breathless. "Can't I...?"

"No. Look, just let me say good night now and go. That will be easier. And I really do have to get up early tomorrow. Okay?"

"Well, okay. But how about tomorrow night."

"Great. I'll call you." She kissed him, then broke away and walked toward the door. "Thanks for a wonderful evening. See you tomorrow."

He stood there as the heavy door swung closed. And for a long time afterward.

He was stunned, unable to think. She had loved him, had virtually seduced him. And then simply walked out. He shook, a sudden chill fingering along his spine.

* * * * * * *

Outside the house, Cathy looked over the top of her car at the darkened windows, the spot of blackness where Payne's front door hung closed. Her hand rested on the car door handle, ready to open it but as yet exerting no pressure. From out here, the house looked deserted. There wasn't a glimmer of light, even though she knew that the living room was vibrantly ablaze.

It was odd, discomforting.

So was what she had just done. For a moment, she had imagined she was giving him a taste of what he had given her last night—then she realized that that simply was not true. She cared deeply for Payne. Making love to him had not been a cheap way to get revenge. It had been meaningful and terrifyingly moving. She had never gone to such lengths before. Her face burned in the darkness when she remembered how she had maneuvered and manipulated him, losing pieces in subtly blundering moves until he was convinced that he could win.

Let him chase her until she catches him.

No, in spite of the way it happened, their making love was not a petty act of revenge. She liked him, maybe even loved him. She wanted to stay with him.

But she couldn't stay there. True, she had to get to work early, but that wasn't the real reason. For a moment there, lying with her head cradled in his arms, the warmth of his body next to hers, she felt vulnerable, exposed watched. She had raised her head, but of course there was nothing there, just plain white walls, white ceiling, white carpet, and the blank gray screen that seemed slightly iridescent in the reflected light from the kitchen.

Still, she had felt uneasy, and as soon as she remembered her early morning appointment, the conscious part of her mind had fastened on it, embroidered it, and finally used it as a means of... escape

Escape.

The idea was ridiculous.

Escape from what? From a wonderful man who obviously loved her?

She would drop her fingers from the handle and walk around the car and up the steps and through the door and drop her clothing on that damnable white carpet and start all over, again and again, as long as either of them remained conscious. And that would prove that....

Her fingers tightened on the handle and lifted up and she felt her body sliding onto the cool seats and her fingers thrusting the keys into the ignition and turning. Slowly, her headlights not yet on, she steered the car away from the sidewalk and disappeared into the darkness. Half a block later, her taillights blinked on like twin red eyes, glowing evilly in the night.

* * * * * * *

When the sound of Cathy's car engine died into the distance, Payne wandered naked through the living room, finally spotting his briefs where they had been kicked behind the sofa. He picked them up, staring at them as if they were an alien creature that had landed in his living room.

They didn't belong to him.

They *couldn't* belong to him.

He would never have bought shorts so abbreviated that they could barely contain him. And he would certainly never have worn them on a dinner-date, as if advertising to anyone who cared that he was a sexy swinger and that all along he had assumed he and Cathy would end up in bed.

No, he wore boxers, like those in his drawer, a dozen pair, all alike.

He strode into the bedroom and dropped the briefs onto his dresser. He pulled the top drawer open, then yanked it all the way out and dumped its contents onto the bed.

Bikini briefs in every color imaginable.

For a moment, Payne felt disoriented, then something snapped like static and he smiled. What a dumb thing to do, dumping his things like that all over the bed. He scooped them into the drawer and replaced it, then pulled on the pair he had worn earlier.

He felt flushed and sweaty. He padded into the kitchen barefoot, grabbed a cold drink from the fridge, and sipped at it while he returned to his room. He took a long pull at the soda and dropped onto the bed. It *was* awfully narrow, certainly uncomfortable for two people to sleep, to say nothing of any other kinds of activities.

Aunt Emilia had never invited anyone in here, he thought, that was sure. For a horrible moment, his mind flashed to the old woman, trying to imagine her naked and in bed with a man—someone young, probably, like the men in those pictures. He choked, remembering the vicious gouges in the photographs. His mind shuddered to a stop. Not her, not here. Never.

He closed his eyes, holding the icy Coke can against his forehead, feeling his muscles release as the coolness penetrated. He shivered, shook his head to clear the after-image from his imagination, tried to replace it with images of Cathy: Cathy smiling at him through dinner, touching him as they worked together in the kitchen, her long fingers reaching out to wrap around a chess piece, her flesh warm and smooth against his.

Something clicked.

He sat up and looked around the room.

Everything was in its place. Everything was silent. Everything was still. The sound was his just his imagination.

Then why was his heart thumping and his blood racing.

Sweat trickled down his sides. He set the half-empty can onto the night table and, clicking off the lamp, lay back down and tried to relax. After relaxation would come sleep. And after tomorrow sleep, and seeing Cathy again.

The darkness in his room lightened as the television screen flickered on, first gray, then silvery, then pearly white, and finally silver banded with rainbows of color.

"What the hell...," he began, pushing himself onto his elbows.

The screen darkened again, then cleared to show a skyline, a river, and a tug moving across the screen. There was no sound, just static.

"How...," he began again, suddenly aware of his voice against the back-swell of static.

For a moment, his vision blurred and the tug became something dark and threatening against the blue. He tried to sit up, but he felt as if someone—some*thing* heavy and hot and dank—had straddled his chest and was holding him down. His muscles locked. His hip froze, the joint unbearably painful and immobile. His hand bit like a claw into the mattress. He broke into a sweat again, forehead and lips and armpits and groin moist and salty. He could smell his own fear. And that frightened him even more.

Still there was no sound except the rushing static that matched the buzzing in his ears. No change of scene, either. Just water and skyline and tugboat.

Then a man elbowed his way through a battered door on the tug and scanned the water, finally pointing at something. Close up. An object in the water, bobbing and swirling. It was dark, almost black, long and smooth like a water-worn rock, like a chess pawn worn against sand. It floated closer and he could finally put a name to the object.

A dismembered human arm.

Rotting and swollen and broken and black and fetid.

Payne could smell the stench of decay. It backed up against his throat and he almost gagged. *What the hell is happening*!

He tried to move, forced muscle against muscle, but he stayed immobile on the narrow bed. His eyes were fixed on the screen by a fascination that he could not refuse. A morgue now. Pieces of bodies cluttering a table. Sound. Voices. Discussing murders.

Payne pushed again, his upper lip curling on one side like it did when he used to work out in gym classes, like when he tried to lift weights too heavy for him. His body was slick and acrid with sweat. His hip and hand hurt too much for him to keep struggling.

He let go *release release release* and fell heavily against his pillow. It folded around his neck and cushioned him, propped his head at just the right angle to see the screen, as if it were acting on its own volition and from years of practice. He forced his body to relax, to give in.

The pain lessened.

Someone else was on the screen now. Someone dark, haunting.

It looked like Pacino. Yes, it was. The image tugged at a distant memory. Where had he heard about a film Pacino...and murders, grisly murders....

He must have missed the credits—but if this was just a nightmare *what else could it be* maybe there hadn't been any. That was it, a nightmare, a bad dream. Too much pressure, too much Cathy, too much....

A name flashed through his mind like a knife, a long and cruel knife, bloody and sharp.

Cruising.

Gays.

Murders.

Pacino undercover as one of them, one of the S&M underground.

Payne giggled, the sound suggesting how close he had come to hysteria in the past few seconds. From nowhere, he remembered a ridiculous joke about M&Ms that he had not understood for years. Then the giggle cut off and his jaw tensed again.

He tried to get up, to turn the set off. He struggled to reach the soda can, to throw it through the monitor or short out the electrical circuit with the rapidly warming residue of soda—to do anything to remove the images flickering across the screen, through his eyes, boring inexorably and perversely into his mind.

He couldn't, wouldn't, didn't want to.

Paralysis sliced like pain through his back. Fiery hands held him down this time, beginning at his hip and surging up his spine, along his shoulders and down his arm, like the numbness he used to get after typing too long on a term paper in school, only this time it was not a numbness but a fire that burned itself out in his fingertips. It was as if he were an electrical conductor, carrying a charge through his body and dispersing it into the fabric of his bed.

He screamed, once and loudly, just as the monitor's volume surged, drowning his voice with a black wave of city sounds.

I give up, he panted to himself, to the monitor, to no one in particular. *Do what you want!*

The tendons in his neck retracted as he fell against the pillow.

He drew a deep breath, quivering with pain and receding tension, sobbing as he stared at the screen.

Pacino penetrating the underground.

The murders began—not so much graphic as suggested but hideous nonetheless.

Twice more he tried to move, tried to wrench himself from the bed as Pacino tried to wrench himself out of that world of darkness and regain the light. Each time the pain returned. The second time brought a tingling pain that focused behind his eyes and turned the room bright with lights. His body seemed to glow, a blue electrical glow that distorted the outlines of his chest and groin and legs until they seemed alien, withered, foreshortened and incomplete. Payne didn't dare resist anymore, didn't dare even look closer at the hollowness where his legs joined. He simply stopped struggling, gave in, watched the images as they flickered through their shadow lives, feeling himself like a character in another film, the guy who was pinioned by machines, his eyelids clamped open as he was forced to watch unspeakable violence to the accompaniment of Beethoven's *Ninth*.

When he fell back to the pillow for the last time, he could barely focus on the screen. He didn't even try to turn away, didn't try to raise a hand or shift his weight on the sweat-soaked sheets. He lay back and watched, grateful that the blue nimbus was receding, too tired for anything but shallow respirations through his half-opened mouth.

Peripherally, without moving his eyes even fractionally downward and away from the screen, he could see his chest, the bulge of fabric at his groin, the swells of muscle that were his thighs and legs. But somewhere, deep inside, he felt gouged, defaced, emasculated and sliced into tiny pieces of bloody flesh, like the victims of the deranged killers in the film.

Like the pictures in the attic.

The film ground inexorably on. Men touched men, kissed men, killed men—he swallowed bile, nearly vomited on himself but choked it down.

At the end of the film, the tug returned, along with the skyline and the water, now only faintly rippled and peaceful. Credits began to roll, then faded out....

And the film began again.

Payne bit back a scream. He couldn't take it again, couldn't lie here, invisibly restrained, forced to watch filth and perversion and....

Then he did scream.

This time the black object was no dismembered arm. It was a body. Bloated and scored with wounds. But he recognized it. He recognized Cathy.

* * * * * * *

When he woke, his body felt hideously stiff, used and abused. He woke suddenly, his eyes flying open and his head snapping up to glance around the room as if he were expecting something. His heart thumped and his muscles twitched. He couldn't remember why.

There had been a dream, he remembered that much. A bad one, from the way he felt.

All he could recall of it was vague and shadowy. Something

unpleasant had happened. To someone.

He couldn't remember, but his body knew. He tried not to move. Only his eyes shifted as he surveyed the room.

The monitor.

His skin ran cold and curdled into gooseflesh when his eyes passed over the empty gray square.

There was nothing there now. Only the dead gray of an unused television screen. He breathed deeply, trying to stretch cramped muscles. It felt as if he hadn't moved all night. He was more tired now than when he went to bed, after Cathy....

He stretched. He stretched again, this time languidly and liquidly, and smiled.

Everything about last night had been odd, but in the light of morning he remembered the chess game as unusually exciting. There was something about Cathy in the residue of his dream, but he nudged it aside, remembering instead their moments in the darkness, on the white carpet. He smiled and stretched again. He felt good. Damn good. It felt good.

He wasn't even particularly surprised to find the front of his briefs faintly stained and stiff.

CHAPTER TWENTY-FIVE

The next time Nick saw Payne was early on a Friday afternoon. It had been even hotter than usual a scorcher for Southern California. The air was still and oppressive, boring heavily into lungs and skin even before the sun rose.

For Nick, it was like a nightmarish repeat of his first day at UCLA years before. The sun had barely risen when he left Chuck's to drive into school, but his car radio had reported over 80° by 5:30 a.m. By 2:00 that afternoon, the thermometer had topped 118° in the shade. Temperatures never soared quite that high in Tamarind Valley, probably because of the mountain breezes at night.

No, it wasn't record-breaking, 100-degrees-plus sizzling, but it was hot, nevertheless, on that Friday afternoon.

Nick had walked down to the twenty-four-hour store a couple of blocks away, a more expensive place than the big chain markets that lay embedded like fossils in each of the malls along the main streets leading to the freeways. But the place was conveniently close *that's why they call 'em convenience stores dumbo* and anyway he only needed a few things. It would be a good walk, he thought, a little exercise for legs cramped from too much sitting.

By the time he returned, though, he was soaked through with sweat, panting and enervated. He set the grocery bag on the kitchen table, stopping only long enough to slide the milk into the fridge. The carton already felt warm. Nick had to have his milk ice-cold, otherwise he would have probably opened the carton and drunk the whole two quarts in one gulp. Ice-cold milk was his weakness, especially on hot days.

But he had to be content with the left-over two inches in a glass of soda he had slid onto the empty top shelf of the fridge that morning. The stuff tasted flat and overly sweet but at least it was cold.

He was still nursing it along when the doorbell rang. He got up. The vinyl of the chair stuck to his back and legs. He felt sticky and gritty himself and wished that he had showered as soon as he got home. By the time he opened the door, he was irritated, almost angry—at himself, at the day, at the heat, at whoever the hell was interrupting him in his eager pursuit of absolute indolence.

It was Payne.

For a moment, Nick was puzzled. Payne seemed oddly out of focus, paler than Nick had last seen him; then Nick blinked to clear his eyes of a sweaty film and Payne shifted into focus again.

Later, Nick wished that he had paid more attention, but life is made up of wishful re-livings of critical moments that somehow escaped our attention the first time.

Even had he thought twice, it might not have changed anything, even at that.

It might already have gone too far.

"Hi," Payne said, rather listlessly Nick thought.

"Come on in," Nick said, opening the door and letting in a burst of hot dry air that somehow seemed appropriate, as if it were intimately associated with Payne's presence.

Payne shook his head. "No, just wanted to let you know that I'm going to be out of town again for a couple of days."

He paused briefly, no more than the space of a single breath, but enough to make Nick feel uncomfortable. "Cathy and me," he continued. The tone was hurried, rather peremptory and brusque. "I'll bring her over sometime and let you meet her," he said, gesturing absently with his right hand, as if that made his lapse in introducing his girl to his friend somehow all right.

"Right now, we're in too much of a hurry. She's waiting for me in the car," he added, again rather oddly, as if he wanted to be sure that Nick kept this one datum firmly in the front of his mind.

Nick glanced over Payne's shoulder toward the car parked along the front sidewalk. He could see a couple of suitcases jumbled in the back seat and what might have been a head and shoulders outlined in the front. He couldn't make out any details.

Just then Payne shifted his weight and inadvertently blocked Nick's view. Nick looked back to his face—but even that was shadowed by the bright sunlight behind him.

Payne rushed on. "Sorry to wait so long, but it just slipped my mind. Could you watch the place for a couple of days? Here's the key. Nothing to do, really, just make sure no moving vans pull up and cart everything off." He laughed but there seemed little humor in the sound.

Nick felt worse and worse about taking the key, but Payne just stood there, hand outstretched, the little brass key glinting.

"By the way," he finished, "feel free to go over and watch a film any time you want."

It was almost the old Payne, but there was an undercurrent of force in his voice. It was as if he knew Nick wouldn't—couldn't refuse him. Payne's tone, his attitude, even the way he held the key out in his cupped palm, the fingers curved and tight so that tendons highlighted along the back of his hand, it all reminded Nick fleetingly of The Greer and the aura she radiated through the black slit of an opening when she thrust her hand out for the rent envelope. She knew that Nick had it. He had no choice.

That was how it felt standing in front of Payne and watching the little brass key glittering in the sunlight.

So Nick laughed and said "Sure, any time. Don't mention it. And have a good weekend."

Payne turned and started toward the car. Then he stopped and looked back at Nick. "Thanks, Nick. Have a good time." He smiled.

The skin on Nick's back crawled—from a sudden chill as

the afternoon breeze, hot as it was, played along his spine. He nodded and Payne left.

For the rest of the afternoon, Nick couldn't concentrate on anything. He tried reading Spenser in the back yard, stretched out on an old recliner in the shadow of a sycamore decades older than he was, sipping lemonade and trying desultorily to make sense out of Una and the Red Cross Knight. It didn't work.

Finally, feeling extraordinarily virtuous for having made the valiant effort, he shuffled back into the house—more a hothouse than anything now that the late afternoon heat had settled with a devilish vengeance—stuffed Spenser back into his niche on the shelf and pulled out something lighter.

Christine. Stephen King's haunted car. The machine that killed. And loved it.

The book seemed the right choice. Nick hefted it in his hand.

Even the weight seemed right, the pressure of the pages against his palm and fingers. Almost immediately he began reading…re-reading, really, for the fifth or sixth time.

The afternoon cooled down from Inferno to merely unbearable torture. Nick noticed the occasional honk or screech of tires at an intersection, usually at entirely appropriate places in the text. He hadn't read the novel for a some years, and in between had seen Carpenter's film version. But even that had been a long while before. Most of his recollections of visual details were vague and at times he couldn't tell whether the text had just lost some of its force or whether he was remembering something from the film that detracted from his concentration.

The idea came gradually.

Why not see if Payne has a copy.

There was a better than good chance that the film was there, given the extent of his collection.

Okay, then, that was the plan. Light supper, maybe a short nap. Then cap the evening off with *Christine*. He would even take his copy of the novel along, work through it while watching the film and make some notes on the changes. He might even pretend that he was doing some kind of literary study on the relationship between verbal and visual in contemporary popular imagination. That should justify the expenditure of time to good ol' Spenser the next time Nick took him down for another try.

It was a good enough plan. It just didn't work out the way Nick anticipated.

By early afternoon he was logy and hot, and for some reason—heat and inactivity and boredom all combining, probably—he felt far drowsier than he should have. He had given the house a desultory cleaning, a task he normally disliked but that seemed surprisingly fulfilling this time.

One room led to another and finally there was nothing left except to straighten a few books, put away a pile of clean socks, and wash three water-speckled glasses huddling on the Formica counter under the shade of the kitchen cabinets.

Five minutes later, even those chore were finished.

Nick felt gritty. *I could probably smell myself a mile away with a cross-wind blowing straight from the factories in Hershey, Pennsylvania,* he thought, so he stripped and showered, reveling in the coolness of water pelting his skin. After the heat the coolness was invigorating.

He finally stepped out of the shower, toweled down, and went into the bedroom. He fully intended to dress but flopped down on the bed instead.

Just for a second.

Just to rest his eyes.

The next thing he knew he was waking up. It was twilight outside, a hot stifling twilight, the smog catching fire at the south-western rim of the basin and spreading its flaming orange eastward to collide with the cooler-tones of darkening blue.

He felt sick. His head pounded and it was hard to breathe.

Damn it, I should have known better sleeping during a hot afternoon always does that to me.

He got up and pulled on clean shorts, slipped a T-shirt over his sleep-rumpled hair, and padded into the kitchen. His stomach grumbled but dinner was the last thing he wanted to face, so he settled for a slice of bread and some cold milk. By now it was icy, just right. He poured a glass, spread a thin layer of raspberry jam on the bread—the slice was already dried out in the minute or so it had sat on the plate while he got the jam bottle from the fridge—and took a bite. He chewed once, twice, three times, then stopped, the lump of bread settling at the back of his throat like a sodden gag. He swallowed hard and gulped some milk to get rid of the bad taste the bread had left.

For a long time, he sat there by the table, staring at nothing in particular, feeling lonely and tired and depressed. He thought of calling someone to come over then realized that there was really no one he wanted to call, or could call. Most of his friends from school were gone for the summer...and they weren't really friends, just acquaintances.

I don't have any friends, he thought suddenly and felt stark tears welling at the corners of his eyes.

The guys at school were gone for the summer. Payne was gone for the weekend. With Cathy.

Nick envied Payne and Cathy, away somewhere together.

Payne.

Nick had forgotten all about his earlier intention to go next door and watch a film. That would help kill an otherwise hideous evening.

He jumped up, nearly spilling the last inch of milk in the glass. He gulped it down, even though it was verging on tepid by now, and slid the carton back into the fridge, slammed the door, and raced through the house, pausing only long enough to grab his copy of *Christine* and Payne's key.

He was halfway across the lawn before he realized that he was still barefoot. But for a change, the normally rough-edged Bermuda grass that flourished in Tamarind Valley's worn out soil felt soft and cool beneath his feet.

As soon as he cut through the pyracantha hedge, though, he was wishing for sandals or thongs. Payne's lawn was harsher than his, rougher, prickly against his soles. Payne hadn't mowed it for several weeks and the grass was tough and uneven. It was turning brown, too—Nick hadn't noticed any water on for over a month. He reminded himself to check with Payne and see if he should take care of it. After all, it was only a matter of opening a couple of valves beside the back porch.

He was still considering making the offer when he stopped, midway between his house and Payne's, his shirt and thin shorts already sticking to his damp skin, the cover of *Christine* lurid red and black in the fading sunset.

He stopped.

Dead still.

It was hard to breathe.

The house was threatening him.

That sounded stupid, he knew. Months later, as he wrote about that afternoon, trying to make some fragmentary sense of what had happened to them all, the statement looked stupid as he typed the words on paper, sitting in the bright light of a winter afternoon. Over the mountains, thunderheads were piling up for a storm. The air was like crystal. And he looked at what he had just written and wondered about himself and his sanity.

The house was threatening him.

It was insane. But it was also true.

The house glowered, threatened. The front porch receded almost visibly into deeper shadow. The thick oak-paneled front door lay hidden within the darkness. So did the glider, although Nick thought that he heard a faint squeal from its rusted chain— it was patently impossible in that thick twilight stillness, but he thought so anyway.

The cyclopean eye that was the attic window caught the final gleam of sunset and fractured the light into scarlet shards, throwing them back at Nick. They seemed baleful and malevolent. Sentient. Evil.

Unblinking, the house watched Nick, its canting shutters transforming in his imagination into cancerous lesions on the mottled flesh of its wreath-red siding. Even the ragged line of shingles jutting over the eaves seemed alert, patient, preposterously alive.

He stood barefoot in the dying grass, armed only with a book, already having to consciously suppress an irrational but compelling urge to fling the book through that upper window as hard as possible, if only to watch the glaring redness shatter, fall inward into the dust of the dead attic, and be replaced by blackness, blankness, and night. Even dark, staring blindness would be preferable to the glow that seemed focused on him.

Something further down the street caught his attention. From the corner of his eye he saw an old couple walking in the dusk. She was supporting him. He seemed frail and fragile, his face almost transparent in the increasing gloom. His arm wrapped around hers, his shoulder rested on hers. She was the pillar, he the vine.

They were watching Nick from where they stood motionless on the sidewalk across the street.

He realized with a shock how odd he must look—wild-eyed no doubt, half naked, hunching near the shadows of the hedge, clutching a book and staring like an idiot at the sagging roofline of an old house.

The couple shifted slightly but made no move to continue their walk. They just stared.

Finally, Nick moved. Turning around and retreating to his own house might have seemed suspicious, so he continued on to Payne's, striding up the steps with a force and confidence he really didn't feel. Keep up the image, you know.

When he reached the door, he glanced surreptitiously over his shoulder.

They were gone—or at least going. They had already shuffled past the driveway of the house opposite and were staring ahead. Most likely they had already forgotten that they had seen him.

He could turn back now, slip across the lawn and back into his own....

That was stupid! Letting a trick of the light scare him. He had Payne's key, Payne's permission, even his blessing. And he had nothing better to do—no, to be honest, he had nothing *else* to do that night.

So he slid the key into the lock and swung the door open.

It was cool, just this side of cold inside. There must have been some kind of air conditioning, although Nick had never seen a unit on the roof or out back. Thinking back, he realized at that instant that Payne's place had usually seemed cooler than his own, but only marginally. Nothing like this. Unless it was just the differential between the house's normal temperature and the oven outside.

But tonight, the air felt downright cold. Especially against Nick's thin T-shirt. His skin prickled. For a moment, again, he considered going back to his place. Just to put on something warmer, a pair of jeans and a sweatshirt, he told himself. But he closed the door instead and stepped through the entry into the living room.

It was pitch black inside. He didn't know what else he should have expected. With those curtains, it would have been dark even in the middle of the day. And at dusk....

But he did know where the light switch was.

Shifting *Christine* to his other hand, he felt along the wall.

And touched something cold and damp and....

The wall.

The plaster seemed super-chilled, clammy, almost resilient, like newly dead flesh.

But it was only the wall.

He touched the light switch plate and flicked the power on.

The light was blinding. It glared against white walls, white drapes, white furniture, white carpet. Everything reflected light except the black chess pieces gleaming like ebony in the center of the room.

He hurried through the room, feeling out of place in his grubby shorts and old T-shirt, once blue but now a decaying gray, so faded that the writing—"SMILE: It Increases Your Face Value"—had almost faded into the background. This room demanded crispness, sharpness, creases in trousers, spit-polished shoes, and shining brass belt buckles.

The hall seemed more inviting—or perhaps merely less overtly intimidating. It was shadowed, with only an angle of light piercing it from the living room. He went into the kitchen first, flicking on that light as he walked through the doorway.

Whiteness here, too. Payne had apparently put everything away. There was nothing on the work counter, no stray bottles or solitary glasses left over from a quick drink before the trip. But at least there were shadows here, angles and patches from the tables and chairs, from the handles on the cabinets. There were enough, at least, to make the place seem less unapproachable. Even the television monitor, hanging dead and silent from its bracket, seemed neutral.

Nick crossed to the refrigerator, opened the door, and rummaged through the shelves. Payne wouldn't mind. Besides, there was almost nothing there except some milk, half a carton of eggs, a couple of slices of bacon next to invisible underneath the coating of fat on the plastic packaging, and a few cans of beer.

He grabbed one of the latter and left the kitchen, leaving the light on and letting the fridge door swing shut by itself. He was in the hall before he heard the soft *whump* of door meeting insulated rubber. He shivered.

That had been the first, the only sound in the place since he had entered. It rang unnaturally loud in his ears, suddenly as threatening as the attic window had seemed. He shuddered away a temptation to turn. Instead, he continued on to the Control Room.

Inside the room, the walls seemed wonderfully alive with colors and shapes, especially after the sterility of the other rooms. DVD cases and video machines, filing boxes, swirls of color everywhere blurred in the sudden light as he flipped the switch on.

He popped the tab on the beer can and tilted it up. The coolness was startling against his lips, even in the chilly air. For some reason, all of his senses seemed different—either blunted or preternaturally sharpened, he couldn't decide which. His skin crawled with the chill, his lips with the biting cold of the beer. His throat hurt from the cold.

His ears hummed—it was the sound of the refrigerator in the next room as the motor kicked in. He swallowed hard, gulping the beer, emptying the can in a single breath. He tossed it into a small wastebasket in the corner, wiping his lips afterward with the bottom of his T-shirt.

Payne kept his files on a narrow shelf on the opposite side of the room. He had managed to check through most of the films and had given Nick a rough orientation as to where to find what. Nick pulled the master list down and checked through entries until he located *Christine*. After that, it took a full ten minutes to find the DVD. Payne's system—or The Greer's, more likely, since he probably hadn't changed it much—was not easy. Nick might have had as much luck if he had simply gone from shelf to shelf reading out titles. But he finally found it, slipped it into the unit Payne most often had him use (*not* the one that acted up that first time), and left the room, closing the door gently behind him. Nick didn't want to let it slam.

He made his way to the viewing room. It felt empty without Payne. Instead of settling into the armchair that had become tacitly his, he stretched out on the sofa, relaxing, enjoying the sensation of the rough texture against his bare legs and through his T-shirt.

He crossed his hands behind him, pillowing his head on them. The angle was perfect.

He closed his eyes for a moment, breathing deeply and enjoying the quiet, the coolness, the stillness. *What's to worry? Stupid to let yourself get jittery.*

The monitor crackled and faded from black to gray and finally to silver. Colors rose and separated into shapes. The film began.

Nick had dropped his copy of *Christine* on the floor. He thought about picking it up, but it seemed too much effort at the time. Later, when he noticed any major divergences, he could always lean over and retrieve it. Not now. He relaxed, waiting for the action to begin.

Only much later did he realize that he had not touched the monitor. Somehow, it knew which room he was in. It had turned itself on.

The film was both a pleasure and a disappointment. There was much of the movement and direction of the novel—transporting it to California weakened it, though. The haunting narrative needed the snow, the coldness, the darkness of King's original vision.

Still, Carpenter's version moved well. Nick gradually forgot his first intention—to compare the film with the text—and just laid back and enjoyed watching it. By the time the film was halfway over, he was almost drowsing. The room was just cool enough to keep him minimally awake. More than once he considered rummaging through Payne's closets to find a blanket or robe or something but the chill never quite penetrated enough to make him move.

Even so, he must have drifted off at least once, because suddenly, characters were standing in a junk yard, a hunk of crushed metal crouched in front of them. One piece squeaked to its original position and the film ended.

He closed his eyes, wishing he could just stay there for the rest of the night. He had done that often enough at home—fallen asleep in his recliner late at night and awakened stiff and unrested the next morning. But Payne's sofa was so comfortable, and Nick felt so heavy, so tired....

A flutter of cold air washed across his face.

At first, half asleep, he thought that he must have left a window open, *probably the bedroom window, I always sleep with it open and in the winter the draught through the house can get bitter.*

Then with a suddenness that unaccountably made his pound and his breath tighten, he remembered where he was. There was no open window here. Nick didn't even know for sure whether windows *could* open in The Greer's house—he had never seen one open, and besides, with the sensitivity of the equipment, stray dust would have been unthinkable.

The flutter returned, more insistent. Nick shivered. On the screen the credits were still running.

He shivered again, feeling the chill bite into flesh and bone through the thin material of his clothes. Chafing one arm with his hand, he sat up, stretched...and froze.

The credits had finished.

For a second the screen was blank, just a flickering pattern of black and silver.

Then the second film began. He stared without thought for several minutes, unable to move, unable to think. The cold intensified, raising goose bumps on his arms and legs, then running in lightning flashes up and down his spine. He felt like someone—something—was watching him with as icy an intensity as he felt toward the screen. He would have turned to look behind him except that he couldn't force his eyes from the screen.

The film was grainy. The colors were so flat and washed out that they suggested one of those persistent films from the late sixties that continually made it onto the Saturday afternoon movie programs in spite of their faded, untrue colors—but even the sixties had never produced anything like this, Nick was certain. The lighting was bad as well, casting shadows so stark as to become abstracted. A quick glance at the screen might almost have left a casual viewer with the impression of an art film, consciously (if not self-consciously) distorting reality for the sake of image. But this was no art film. Texture, color and lighting were serving an altogether different master this time. There was no missing what the film was about. Limbs, naked limbs and torsos entwined like vines grown mad and rank, curling and twisting and swirling in an open sensuality that imparted more agony than ecstasy. Nick couldn't tell how many figures were involved—men and women writhing and coiling like so many maddened serpents. It was morally repulsive, openly sexist, horrifyingly exploitative...and repellently, undeniably fascinating. He watched.

The cold increased. He felt as if at any instant he would see his next breath outlined like a cotton puff in the chill of the room—yet the actions on the screen increased, heated, became feverish and frantic. He could barely breathe. He felt his own flesh, his own body responding, heating, increasing the differential between it and the surrounding air.

One of the men thrust. For an instant the camera focused on the angular planes of his back where muscles suddenly tightened to outline the row of spinal nodules that rippled beneath his damp flesh. There was a moment of relaxation, followed by an even greater tightening, then an abrupt shift in camera angle— at first Nick could not figure out quite what he was seeing—and the entire screen exploded into scarlet as blood ruptured from the man s chest and belly even as he rode to his climax.

It must have been some kind of hideous signal. Within seconds all of the intertwined bodies were sheathed in blood, sliding in death agonies onto thin sheets of blood that glistened like oil and glinted evilly in the angular lighting of the screen.

Nick screamed.

Inside him something tore, ripped through layers of muscle and tissue, like an alien struggling for freedom. He felt sick. He tried to vomit but nothing came. Instead, he doubled up in an agony that burned through sexuality, burned through pulse and breath. Through it all, the house swirled chilling air around him, playing in perverse whorls and arabesques along his back, his arms and legs.

He woke.

He was lying stretched on the sofa, facing away from the monitor. For a second he stared at the intricately woven white fabric inches from his eyes, tracing patterns of light and shadow as something behind him flickered light and dark. A button set deeply into the fabric expanded until it filled the limits of his vision. It became his universe. A world of intricately woven white flickered with reflected shadows—*but no red thank god no red* he intoned mindlessly.

He expelled his breath, shuddering, only then realizing that he had been holding it pent inside. He was bathed in sweat, his clothing damp and clammy. The night air felt chilly but no longer cold.

There was no sound.

Slowly Nick turned to face the opposite wall.

The screen was blank except for the flat gray luminance that usually marked the end of a film.

Nick leaped up and ran from the room, covering the length of the hall in two strides. He flung open the door to the control room and entered, crossed, and jabbed viciously at the eject button on the DVD player. Next to his finger, a red light glowed balefully.

He pulled the disc out. It was *Christine*.

He jammed it back in, punched "play," and watched the monitor over his shoulder. It showed nothing but black and silver. He pressed "play" again.

For a moment the screen remained blank, then *Christine* played again, but backwards this time. The credits rolled from top to bottom. There was no sound.

Nick stood there, transfixed, until the hulk of crushed metal appeared, one piece collapsing back into the ruin.

He reached out to try fast forward.

The machine shorted out. Blue sparks arced from the metal, bit into his wrist, curled around his hand.

Once, years before, Nick had worked at a scout camp. During one campfire ceremony, a brainless idiot cunningly disguised as a staff member spilled a can of gasoline that he had smuggled into the campfire bowl to avoid the embarrassment of not being able to start a fire with three hundred kids watching. The spilled fuel ignited and flickered like a hungry serpent along dry leaves and browning needles. Ten or so of the senior staff members—not one of them over seventeen—had scrambled to the fire, kicking dust and dirt to suffocate the flames. In his haste, the same feckless idiot had kicked the can again. What little gasoline remained in it had swirled out at Nick's feet. In seconds flames licked at his legs, played along the stiff ribbing of his knee-length hiking socks. He could remember looking down, seeing the flames, not being able to move, to think. He could only wait for the pain.

It never came. The flames were fume-fed. They rose to his knees, but only insubstantially. They were mere wisps of color and light devoid of heat. When the fire finally died, Nick was standing there staring down at his legs.

It was the same here.

The blue fire swirled around his hand but did not touch it. He stared, hypnotized by the patterns and the threat.

When he moved, when he jerked his hand away, the pain came.

He yelped and jumped backward and almost tripped. Somehow he stayed on his feet and ran through the hallway, the living room, out the front door and onto the lawn, now a stretch of blackness in the night.

Behind him, he heard something.

Whirling, he saw the door close. He heard metal on metal, locking mechanism tumblers closing on each other, and he knew that if he were to climb those stairs again and put his hand to the cold metal knob and turn, nothing would happen. The door was locked. The house was dark. The fire in the attic eye had long since died.

Nick ran across the lawn, his feet rasped by harsh grass and weeds. He pushed through the hedge, feeling spines of dead growth plucking at his shorts and abrading his legs. At the back door, he paused and looked back across into Payne's yard. In the single window at the back of Payne's place, a sliver of silver light played across dying leaves.

CHAPTER TWENTY-SIX

When Nick woke the next morning, his heart was racing like he had had a nightmare. He was panting. When he sat up, he saw that he was lying on top of the bedspread. The thin cloth was stained with dirt. His feet were tender, almost painful.

He was naked. In a pile beside him, his T-shirt and shorts lay like the discarded skins of molting snakes, coiled in and around and through each other. He stared, frightened and fascinated, trying to remember another kind of swirling and entwining that lay just beneath the surface of memory.

For a second, it seemed that the memories would flood back.

He jumped up, wincing as his feet hit the floor, and dressed hurriedly in jeans and a pair of comfortable old sandals. By the time he had finished, he was calmer.

It had only been a dream; what else could it be, after all. This wasn't the movies, where machines came to life and tried to get people in viciously inventive ways.

This wasn't *Maximum Overdrive* or anything.

This was Tamarind Valley, Southern California, here and now.

He had only had an unusually vivid dream brought on by watching a film about a haunted car. It was only a step further, after all, to a haunted television, like in *Poltergeist*.

He decided that he really shouldn't have invited a double-whammy like that—reading the novel and watching the film in one day. Especially when it was so hot and sleep would be difficult anyway. He should have shut the book and....

The book!

He had left it at Payne's, lying cover up on the floor.

At least that's where he thought it would be.

He pulled on a shirt and started to leave. At the door, he stopped—he needed the key. He slapped instinctively at his jeans pockets and panicked momentarily when his fingers felt only muscle rather than the hard, sharp outline of the brass key. Then he remembered that the key would be in his shorts.

He returned to the pile of clothing in his bedroom and leaned over it. For a second, it was as if the material moved, fluttered like a ribcage rising and falling. He blinked. There was nothing. Just a pair of filthy shorts wrapped around a T-shirt, both of them spotted and stained with sweat and dirt.

He dug gingerly into the pile—it might be his own sweat and dirt but that didn't make it any more, palatable, and the clothes were disgustingly clammy and stuck together. He pulled the key from the pocket.

And nothing happened.

No savage creature lunged at him, no spontaneous fire burst out to consume him on the spot, no flickering of blue flame curled around his fingers.

Flames.

He almost remembered something again. Not knowing why, he stared at his hand. The flesh was whole, tanned and smooth as always. He recognized the white scar from a cut when he was nineteen, then the pink tissue of a healing scrape from a rose thorn not more than a week ago.

Otherwise, nothing else. Nothing new.

There had been no fire, no sparks, no blue energy wrapping around the hand like an insane, insubstantial neon boa. It had been a dream.

He left the room and walked outside. For some reason, he skirted Payne's lawn and followed the sidewalk up to the porch. The front door stood slightly ajar, opening onto a crack of darkness. It looked as if Nick had simply forgotten to close it the night before.

Another clue. What he thought he remembered was an illusion, a dream. The door had not locked itself. It had not happened.

Nick felt a moment of panic. If someone had gotten in and stolen any of the equipment while he was in charge....

He took the steps in a bound, pushed the door open, and turned on the lights.

The living room seemed less glaring than it had the night before. The white was subdued. He walked into the hall, then on to the viewing room. He turned on the light and looked down at the floor.

The book was not there.

He checked in the kitchen, although he knew that he hadn't left it there. Then he tried the Control Room. His palms were sweaty when he pushed the door open; they left damp spots on the polished surface. But the room was quiet, neutral. Everything was in place. He glanced at the shelf. There was not even a gap where the DVD for *Christine* should be. He could see the title printed boldly along the back of the box.

He crossed to the opposite wall and punched the eject button on the player. The slot was empty. He returned to the living room and stood there for a while, searching every corner of the room.

Then he saw something.

The chess set was not quite the same as it had been before. It was still black on white, but the black no longer glistened. It seemed dull. He touched one of the pieces. A gray stain smudged his fingertips. He sniffed it.

Ash. And the acrid smell of burnt paper.

CHAPTER TWENTY-SEVEN

Payne returned unexpectedly later that night.

Nick was still awake even though it was well past midnight. He was lying on his bed in the darkened room, staring up at the ceiling, his head cradled in his arms. If it had been a scene in a film—a *film noir*, no doubt—he would have been smoking, the thin cigarette smoke curling serpentine around his head as he breathed out, no more than a sigh. Half an inch of ash would hang tenuously but undisturbed from the end of the cigarette smoldering between his angular, masculine fingers.

But Nick did not smoke so there was no cigarette, no atmospheric effects from dim light filtering through smoke. Instead there was simply a young man lying motionless on a narrow bed, his profile outlined by moonlight through a single window.

This was no film.

He was afraid to go to sleep. There were, after all, dreams.

Instead, he stared at the splotchy tiles, finding figures in the patterns of light and shadow as they intersected an ancient dark patch caused by a leaky roof years before. Then he stopped doing even that. The figures began to seem too real.

This time he tried to blank everything out, numb his senses, close himself off from anything out there and withdraw. Even that was impossible.

He may have heard the car pull up and a single door slam shut, metal against metal and loud in the stillness. If he did, he made no movement to sit up and look out the window.

Unseen and unheard, Payne crossed the sidewalk, mounted

the porch, and entered the waiting house. He turned on the living room light. In one hand he held his suitcase. Cathy was not with him.

After a few moments, the door closed and Payne's house was as dark as Nick's.

For a long while, both houses remained quiet, silent, dark.

Finally, Nick slept, although fitfully, tossing on his bed as if in pain. Several times, he pressed his hands between his legs as if to still a sharp, sudden pain, and when he did sweat beaded on his forehead and lips.

Each time, the glider on Payne's porch whispered into the night.

Crash!

Nick sat bolt upright, both hands cradling his throbbing temples.

Crash!

Except it wasn't a crash at all. Someone was knocking on the front door. Not even knocking. Barely rapping *gently tapping nevermore nevermore.*

Crash!

"In a minute," he yelled, wincing at the violence his own voice stirred up inside his head. His vision reeled. He wanted to vomit. When he finally stood up, he was so dizzy that the bed spun like an out-of-control Scrambler at a country carnival midway.

Crash!

"Minute!"

He hadn't drunk anything the night before or he might have expected a hangover, might have been at least partially prepared for the rocking pain. And this didn't feel like a drunk headache, either. Mingled with the pain was a pulsing, sickening sense of threat, dream mingled with reality in doses that he could not understand. But he knew that he had slept badly and that he felt sick. Unspeakably sick.

Crash!

"Okay, dammit! I'm coming."

He threw a robe on and stumbled to the living room. Half awake, more than half furious at whoever continued to bang at the front door at this ungodly hour, he worked the sticky lock with the tenacity of a drunk trying manfully to walk a straight line. Finally the door swung open.

"Hi," said Payne. He was blindingly outlined by the sunlight.

Nick pulled back and threw his hands over his eyes, looking for all the world like Dracula being exposed to the rising sun.

Payne stepped in. His smile died, replaced by concern.

Nick stared at him, wondering why he was here, what happened to the romantic weekend Payne and Cathy had planned, whether Cathy was standing behind him on the porch. He moved to tighten his robe tie. Wouldn't do to have it fall open and have Ca thy....

"Hey," Payne said, "You all right? You look like death warmed over, man."

Nick tried to answer but a hot-acid welling in his gut warned him not to open his mouth—something other than words would probably gush out.

"Mmmph," he gulped, throwing his hand over his mouth as he bolted for the bathroom.

Payne followed him, even entering the tiny room and shutting the door.

Nick stood bent over the sink, his eyes hollow and dark-rimmed, his cheeks white.

"You look like hell," Payne said quietly.

As if in answer, Nick dropped to his knees by the toilet and heaved. Once, twice, three times dry heaves that tore through him and made every muscle in his body tremble. For an awful moment he felt as if he were ripping his guts out by the roots as the spasms hit his stomach and throat. Then, with a sense of something like relief that rapidly transmuted into agonizing pain, he vomited great clots of dark and greenish matter, followed by a stinking, acrid bile that burned in his gullet. He was sweating heavily, panting for breath between heaves.

Payne had moved behind him. One hand, one gloriously cool,

dry hand reached around to hold Nick's forehead. The other rested lightly on the sick man's shoulder. For several moments, Payne crouched next to Nick and spoke, although neither of them were aware of particular words—just sounds, low and soft and soothing.

"I'm sorry," Nick mumbled over and over between heaves, his voice an anguished counterpoint to Payne's quiet whisperings. "I'm sorry, I'm sorry."

Finally the siege was over. Nick stayed on his knees for a long while afterward, though. He was shaking now and felt too weak to try to stand. The guck in the toilet bowl smelled horribly; for a moment, he was afraid that he would throw up again, then Payne pressed the gleaming silver handle and, with a thick sucking sound that grated against Nick's ears, the stuff swirled down and around and out of sight. Nick screwed his eyes tight; the movement of the water made him dizzy again, and his stomach rumbled.

Payne still leaned behind him, bent over his shoulder, supporting him and whispering encouragement.

"Okay?" Payne said at last, his voice more normal. "Can you stand up?"

"Yeah," Nick answered shakily, then proved himself a liar by nearly falling back into Payne's arms.

"Let me give you a hand." Payne slipped an arm under Nick's and helped him back to the bedroom.

"What a mess," Payne said instinctively when he saw the bedding wadded on the mattress, the sheets damp and matted. "You have a fight in here last night?"

"Don't know," Nick said. "Didn't sleep well. Sick, I guess. Didn't know it till just now." He tried to make the last sentence into a joke, but the attempt failed. It merely sounded pathetic.

"Sit here for a minute." Payne helped Nick into a chair, then turned his attention to the bed. He tossed the linen onto the floor and rummaged in the open closet for fresh sheets. There were only two sets; Payne pulled the top one off and briskly set about remaking the bed. His hand seemed to be bothering him, his fingers stiffening so that it must have been hard for him to tuck the edges beneath the mattress, but soon the bed was at least passible.

"Let's get you down on here," he said, grinning at Nick. Nick stared back at him. His cheeks had more color now, and his eyes had lost some of their fevered glare. He stared intently at Payne. Payne shifted his weight back and forth as if uneasy.

"What's the matter, my fly open?" Payne said jokingly, as if hoping to break whatever spell held Nick.

Nick blinked.

"Uh, no. Uh, for a moment there, I thought.... I, I don't know."

"Come on, let's get you over to the bed," Payne said.

He pulled Nick up, supporting most of Nick's weight as they crossed the room. Nick's muscles trembled in wrenching waves as he stumbled against Payne. Whatever was wrong, it was obviously pretty severe.

Nick collapsed onto the bed. For a long while he lay there, sweating and panting, staring straight up. Payne laid a hand on his shoulder. It felt cool and comforting; for an instant, Nick half-believed that it was his mother's hand, rough and worn but comforting.

"Be right back," Payne's voice said, and the sensation disappeared. Nick opened his eyes in time to see Payne step into the hall.

A moment later Nick dimly heard the sound of water running.

"This might help," Payne said when he returned. He draped a damp cloth over Nick's forehead and eyes. He sat on the bed next to Nick.

"Do you have any idea what's wrong? You eat something bad? Should I call someone?"

Nick shook his head. "Don't know...what happened. Not food poisoning. Haven't been drinking. Nothing like that. Just...just sick."

There was a long silence.

"It's better now, though," Nick said. His voice was stronger, without the panicky quaver it had had before.

Payne studied his face. The color was returning even more. Nick's breathing was deeper, more regular.

"Okay, but you stay put for a minute." Payne disappeared again. This time Nick heard subdued sounds from the kitchen: cabinets opening and closing, the fridge door whooshing shut, the clattering of china and silverware. Maybe five minutes passed before Payne reappeared carrying a tray with a pot of something that smelled like herb tea.

For a second, Nick's stomach heaved and tried to register a complaint, then the aroma sank all the way in and he felt his nerves unknotting.

"Try some."

"Thanks." He sipped.

The warm tea soothed as he swallowed, cutting through the awful aftertaste that coated his tongue and teeth and leaving him feeling cleansed and warm. He sipped again.

"Thanks, that was just right."

"Lucky you had some in the cupboards, or I would've had to run home for my own. Mom always poured mint tea down me when I got sick. She claimed there was something in the mint oils that settled stomachs. Maybe there is. It sure works for me."

"Me too, apparently." Nick handed Payne the cup and raised himself on his elbows. "I think everything's okay now." He sat up, leaning against the headboard and rearranging his robe.

"You sure?"

"Yeah, I think so." Nick took a deep breath and was surprised to find that his stomach felt calmer. His throat was looser and no longer burned where the hot vomit had scoured through. His teeth still felt gritty, though, and his breath stank.

He sipped the mint tea again, as much for the smell as for the warmth. He set the cup down on the night table, relieved to notice that his hand did not shake. There was no telltale clattering of china against wood, just a single solid thump.

He leaned against the headboard and closed his eyes and breathed deeply. He felt a hand on his leg.

"Well," Payne said, "gotta go now."

"Wait," Nick answered quickly. "What…why did you come over this morning? I thought you and"—he swallowed heavily and forced a sudden resurgence of bile down—"and Cathy were...." He couldn't finish.

Payne laughed lightly. "Oh, that. Well…hey, you don't look so good any more. Should I help you into the...."

"No." Nick waved a hand weakly. "I'm all right here."

"Okay. Well, what I wanted was to let you know that I…we would probably be gone until Tuesday or Wednesday. Can you still keep an eye out on things?"

Nick shook his head. "No sweat. There was a…problem, though. Last night."

"What?" Payne's voice was sharp enough that Nick opened his eyes and looked over at him.

"Not much. Static. A…maybe a cross circuit between the DVD player and the TV. I saw a…sort of a double exposure. I think. I was pretty sleepy."

"Damn," Payne said, softly but full of emotion.

"It wasn't much," Nick said, raising himself on his elbow. He felt pretty good again. Whatever it was, it was passing. Probably getting that stuff off his stomach was all he needed. He swallowed and noticed that his teeth felt cleaner, smoother.

"Probably as much in my dreams as in the machine."

"Just the same," Payne said, "I don't like it. They said they fixed it last time. I'm gonna call that fu…that place and give them a piece of my mind."

He glanced at his watch.

"Can I use your phone?"

Nick nodded.

Payne crossed to the desk and dropped into the office chair and pulled the phone toward him and dialed a number, punching each one as if he were punching someone in the jaw. He seemed full of repressed anger. Nick felt like calling across the room, *Hey, it's okay. No need to kill the guy over a short. Probably just a wire or something.*

"Hello, Tasco," Payne said suddenly. There was a short pause.

"Gunnison. Look, what's with my DVD player. I thought you said that you fixed it...."

Another pause. Nick could hear a squeaky sound, like long-distance mice. Tasco's voice no doubt.

"You bet you will. When?"

After a second or two, he covered the mouthpiece with his hand and looked over at Nick.

"Would you be able to let them in Monday?"

"Sure, but...."

"Monday. By two o'clock. The key's next door. Yeah. Wheeler. Right."

He slammed the receiver down.

"Sorry," he said, with a lopsided grin. "Hope I didn't break your phone. It just pisses me off when they don't do a job right the first time. Waste of their time and mine."

He settled into the chair, leaning back and crossing his legs at the knees.

"I hope it doesn't put you out, having to go over and open up," he said.

"No. I didn't have anything much planned. I was just going to...."

"Well," Payne said, standing abruptly, so abruptly that the chair clicked forward on its casters. "Gotta go. Take care, buddy."

He leaned down and clapped Nick on the shoulder.

"Sure." Payne started to leave. At the doorway, he turned around. "I really appreciate you keeping an eye out on the place. Maybe one day these endless meetings with lawyers will be over and I can start living a normal life."

"Meetings? I thought that you and Cathy were...."

It hit again. Violently, without warning, the spasm hit *it's Old Faithful time, folks, gather round and watch the greatest show on earth! Thar she blows!*

Nick spewed green vomit over himself, drenching his robe and his sheets. The stuff burned like hot bacon grease where gobbets splashed on the backs of his hands and spattered onto his bare chest where the robe had fallen partially open.

"Shit!" he started to say, and the second wave hit, more violently than the first. The smell was horrendous. The pain ripped through his stomach. He almost passed out.

CHAPTER TWENTY-EIGHT

This time it took Payne much longer to help Nick recover. He nearly had to carry the prostrate man into the bathroom and strip the soiled, stinking robe from his trembling shoulders. Payne tossed the robe into a corner and then helped Nick lay down on a couple of towels spread in the tub, his head propped on a folded towel. Payne dampened a face cloth and dabbed away the worst of the stuff from Nick's lips and chin and chest. There were some splotches on his shorts, but that would have to wait. If he didn't get that stuff off the bed, it might seep into the mattress and then they would never get the stench out. He would have to leave Nick there for a while, Payne decided. It was the only place where Nick could lay down, and maybe the coolness of the porcelain might help.

It must have, because even before Payne left to clean up the bedroom, Nick seemed to be breathing more easily. There were no further threats of vomiting. It took longer to change the bed this time, and it was a distinctly more distasteful task than it had been before. Payne wadded the fetid sheets up and threw them into the hallway, then checked the mattress for any seepage. He didn't see any. He opened the window wide and turned on the fan, setting it in the doorway and hoping that the cross current would to blow the lingering stench outside. He stopped at the bathroom just long enough to ask if Nick had any air freshener.

"Kitchen," Nick said weakly, not moving more than his lips. One hand hung over the edge of the tub like a corpse's. It was as pale as a corpse's, too. The fingertips were bluish gray.

"'Neath sink."

"Gotcha."

Payne rummaged under the sink and pulled out a can and went back into the bedroom. The air was already a bit better but it was still pretty rank. He sprayed the room, the corners, the mattress and pillow. The artificial pine fragrance was heavy and cloying but better than the other mess. Maybe when the freshener faded, the room would smell okay.

He stepped into the hall again and picked up the bedding, careful to fold it so that the damp parts were tucked well inside. He went to the bathroom and retrieved Nick's robe as well. It smelled worse than the sheets.

"Where's your washer?" he asked as he balanced the two lumps of sodden material as far from his body as he could.

"Back porch." The last sound was little more than a sigh.

Payne looked over at Nick. The color was coming back again. His cheeks were something less than parchment white. The hand hanging over the edge of the tub twitched, and the nails were pink rather than blue-white.

"Feeling better?"

"Yeah. A little. Stink, though."

He was right.

Payne tossed the robe and sheets into the hall and knelt by the edge of the tub. Nick still didn't move. His eyes were closed, his lips barely open. Payne shuddered at the heavy, rancid breath each time Nick exhaled. Suddenly his own stomach seemed less than stable. He opened the window over the tub and drew in a deep breath of untainted air.

"Let's get you cleaned up now. The wash can wait."

He filled the sink with warm water and soaked another face cloth in it. Carefully he washed Nick's face and arms and hands and chest, rinsing and wringing the cloth, draining the sink three times and re-filling it with fresh warm water. Whatever the stuff Nick vomited was, it was thick and sticky, more like mucous than anything Payne could think of...except maybe for lumpy, greenish, stinking library paste that had begun to separate into clots and a gluey scum. Whatever it was, it wouldn't come off easily. Finally, though, Payne was finished.

"Can you stand up?"

"Think so."

Nick tried, propping one arm on the tub and trying to lever himself up. He couldn't.

"Let me help."

Payne grabbed under Nick's arm and pulled him up.

"Okay?" Payne asked.

"Yeah."

"Let's get you out of those," Payne said.

"Huh?" Nick sounded drunk or drugged. His voice slurred. His throat must hurt like hell, too, Payne thought, and that made the sounds even more ragged.

"Your shorts. They're stained."

Nick looked down. There were three big splotches of vomit, venomously dark against the startling white. For a moment he tensed and looked like he would throw up again. He swallowed carefully.

"'Kay."

Payne helped him strip, holding his arm and waist while Nick balanced first on one leg, then the other, his muscles quivering and the towels beneath his feet shifting on the smooth porcelain. Payne reached across to the towel cabinet, still holding onto Nick's arm—*thank god his bathroom's as small as mine and everything's in easy reach*—and pulled out another towel, the last one on the stack, and wrapped it around Nick's waist.

"Can you walk?"

Nick nodded mutely.

With Payne's help, Nick made his way down the hall and into the living room. He sank gratefully onto the old couch, not minding for once the lumps and bent springs and uphol-stery stiff with decades of spilled drinks and ground-in cookies and crushed potato chips and who knew what else before Nick finally rescued it from the clutches of a yard sale.

"Be right back." Payne disappeared into the hall, stopping

at the bathroom and the bedroom. He continued on to the back porch. He must have been holding the stack of filthy clothing stiffly in front of him, Nick noted vaguely, because he walked with a stoop, one foot scuffing against the floor.

A few minutes later, Nick heard the *thunk* of the washer lid as it dropped against the machine, then the asthmatic *whirr* of the motor.

Payne reappeared a few moments later.

"Everything's in. Towels, sheets, clothes. It's a big load but the washer looked like it could handle it."

"Yeah, it's got an oversized tub."

Nick suddenly giggled.

Here he was, shaking like a newborn colt after having puked his guts all over himself, and his landlord was running up and down the place cleaning up after him, and now he has to dither on about the washing machine! The giggle took on a slightly hysterical edge.

Payne looked confused. He put his hand against Nick's forehead.

"No, no fever."

"I'm okay," Nick said, his voice still uneven. "It's just...it just struck me funny...that...look, I'm sorry. I...it must be gross to...."

Payne shook his head. "Not a word. As long as you feel better."

He crossed the living room and sat next to Nick.

"You hurt yourself?" Nick asked suddenly.

"No, why?"

"It looked like you were limping for a minute."

"No," Payne said. "Just tired all of a sudden."

"Can't figure why," Nick said, then laughed again.

"You must be a whole lot better."

"As a matter of fact," Nick said, "I am. Little shaky, but otherwise...otherwise okay. Look, thanks a lot. I don't know what I would have done...."

"I said, not a word. That goes for mushy 'Thank-you' scenes, too. I'm just glad that I was here. Something like that hits and you're no good for shit. I had the flu once, and I couldn't stand up for days. Lived on 7-Up and lost fifteen pounds. Vicious stuff."

"I don't think this is the flu," Nick said. "It just came, and now it's gone. Not that I'll miss it." He glanced down at himself. "Better get dressed now."

He started to get up.

Payne's hand rested warm on his shoulder, the fingers strong and curved around his shoulder joint, pushing him gently down.

"Rest a while. Don't overdo."

Nick relaxed into the couch. "Okay, Doc. Whatever you say."

"Right. Whatever I say." Payne's hand rested for a little longer, then the fingers suddenly pressed tightly into Nick's muscles, as if they had cramped.

Payne stood up and walked to the front door.

"I wish I could stay here and keep an eye on you," he said, his hand on the door knob.

"I'll be okay. If it gets worse, I'll call my cousin. He only lives half an hour or so away. He can come if I really need anything."

"Still, I wish I didn't have to fly back East. It's not as if I haven't seen my folks in years or anything, but they insist. You know how it is. Take care."

And he was gone. Nick leaned against the uneven cushions and closed his eyes. The day was warm but he felt cold. In a minute, when he felt a little steadier, he would get up and put on a robe, maybe even dress in his sweats and see if he couldn't get rid of the bone-cold that he always felt after a bout with vomiting. Always, but never this much, this deep.

He shivered.

And after that, some more hot tea, maybe a slice of toast. His stomach stayed steady while he visualized the toast, so he figured that the worst must be over.

He stood up, supporting himself with the arm of the couch, then straightening. His stomach hurt, felt like he had pulled the muscles or something, but otherwise he was all right. No head-ache. No nausea. No cramps.

He walked slowly into his bedroom to change.

He didn't think about the fact that at least twice that morning—maybe three times—Payne had bluntly lied to him.

CHAPTER TWENTY-NINE

By Monday, Nick was feeling fine, almost as if his one-day bout with stomach flu or food poisoning or whatever had never happened. Saturday he had slept most of the day, exhausted physically and mentally by the explosively violent outbursts that morning. He didn't see Payne again that day. He slept well enough Saturday night; he didn't remember dreaming and his bed was still pretty much in order when he woke the next morning. Sunday he stayed down again, mostly resting. He had a couple of brief dizzy spells in the early afternoon when he dragged an old *chaise longue* around to the back yard so he could lay on it and read, but they seemed to pass without any further repercussions than a nagging headache that dissipated by nightfall. By and large, the day was quiet, even boring.

Nick did not go over next door to watch any films.

Monday morning, he rose early and got to work, reading steadily until eleven, in spite of another brief moment of dizziness and a slight fever—just over 100° by 10:30. But he didn't feel particularly ill, and by the time he took a break for a sandwich at noon, even that small fever had disappeared. He went back to the reading list. He was still going strong when someone knocked on the door just after one o'clock.

The repairman.

In spite of the problems on Saturday, for a change he had actually remembered that someone was coming by. He already had Payne's key in his pocket when he answered the door. The kid he had seen before in the shop was standing there, still sullenly arrogant to Nick's way of thinking, hip cocked out and thumb through his belt loop as if daring the world to do its worst.

"Wheeler?" It was not quite a question, not quite a statement.

"Yes."

"I'm from Tasco's. Here about the guy's set." He nodded toward Payne's house.

"Right."

Nick stepped onto the porch and closed his door behind him, for some reason making a show of locking up. He didn't usually, but today this kid made him nervous.

"This way." He led the kid across the lawn and up the porch, unlocking Payne's front door with something less of a production, reaching in to turn on the living room light, and standing aside to let the kid go in front of him.

"Some place," the kid said in a low, wispy voice.

"Yeah. The stuff is back here."

Nick went first down the hall, noticing with relief that all of the doors were closed tightly. The hall was nearly black, except for slivers of light under the doors, but Nick knew his way without any problem.

"Here." He opened the door and, again, waited for the kid to go in.

"Nice." Obviously the kid was into monosyllabic communication. Nick nodded toward the DVD player.

"That's the one. It shorts out sometimes."

The kid pulled a rumpled paper from his jeans pocket and unfolded it. He squinted, as if he were having trouble reading the print. He held it at another angle to get more light. He squatted to read something off the machine, then double-checked the paper before he stood again.

"Mr. Tasco fixed it last time it was in the shop. Says so right here." He stabbed at the paper with a long finger. The knuckles and nails were dark with ground-in dirt, like the kid had just come off a shift at the local Texaco station.

Nick crossed next to him and read the work order over the kid's shoulder. The kid smelled of sweat and light machine oil.

"I don't care what that says," Nick said finally, flicking the paper with his finger, "the set doesn't work. I know. I was here when it went bad."

Something passed through the kid's eyes, an unreadable expression that Nick didn't like. He moved away and settled himself in the black chair in the middle of the room. The kid made him nervous.

"What's your name," he asked the kid's back.

"Ric," came the muffled reply. The kid was leaning over the set, probing with some unnamable tool into the dark recesses behind it.

"Well, Ric, how long have you been at this? A-V repair, I mean?"

"Not long. Mostly been a stock boy. This is my first solo." He still hadn't turned around.

Nick sat straighter in the chair. He was suddenly and inexplicably worried—that the kid might not know what he was doing and make things worse. That the kid might, might...well, he wasn't sure that he liked the kid mucking around with Payne's stuff, and he sure as hell didn't like talking to a pair of worn Levi's back pockets. He fell silent and watched.

The kid might not have much experience, but he handled the tools with ease, reaching for one, fiddling behind the cabinets, replacing the first tool in exactly the same place in his folding kit and reaching for another. He seemed to know what he was doing, too, working rapidly and removing the DVD player's cover, then checking a number of places as if he knew just where to look to find the problem.

Of course, Nick reminded himself, it could all be bullshit and Nick wouldn't know any different.

"Can't see anything here," Ric said finally. "I'll have to take it out of the cabinet."

He reached behind and jiggled a wire.

"Fuck!" he yelped and twisted around to face Nick. "Fu...sucker shocked me," he said, rubbing his fingertips together.

Nick struggled to keep a straight face.

"I know. It happened to me, too. That was *before* you fixed it, of course."

Ric's face darkened. "That was Tasco. The old man don't know shit."

Now it was Nick's turn to flush.

"Maybe I should just call him and let him know what your opinion of him is. I'm sure he'd be delighted."

Ric glared. Nick knew at once that he had pushed too hard. This kid was scary, like he had a dozen and a half chips on his shoulder and was daring Nick, or anyone else for that matter, to take a swing at them.

The kid didn't say anything. Instead he returned to his work, reaching gingerly behind the DVD console to work on the wiring again.

Nick leaned back in the black chair and forced himself to relax. *It's okay,* he said to himself, trying not to watch the kid working, *he's not going to brain you with a wrench or break your legs or rape you or anything relax just keep an eye open and your mouth shut.*

He swiveled in the chair, concentrating on the subtle inter-plays of color and design that the rows of DVD cases made—almost artistic, he decided, at times abstract.

That foot or so of case spines over there—the way they fade from blue to black, that has aesthetic possibilities. And that bunch over there.

All the time, he heard the kid's low voice muttering as he worked over the set.

On an impulse, Nick swung his head around to glance at the kid...and sat straight up in the chair. He stared through the doorway into the darkened hall.

It was no longer dark.

"What the...?" he began.

Ric didn't seem to notice.

Slowly Nick rose from the chair, forced his feet forward, first one, then the other, gradually approaching the dark opening into the hall where something—a glimmer, a glow, a sparkle—

reflected from the white walls where there should not have been anything except unbroken darkness.

One step. Another.

"Shit," Ric mumbled from the bank of players as he reached for a different screwdriver.

Nick almost said something to the kid but decided against it. Maybe he was embarrassed; it would seem like calling for help before he knew if he was in trouble.

He ventured another step. Now he could see several feet of hallway wall between the open door to the control room and the living room. The kitchen door and bathroom door on the far side were still closed. He stopped and listened.

He could hear nothing except the kid's occasional swearing.

Nothing...except that, and a subtle crackling like electricity through a low wire on a humid day. Nick's hair prickled along the back of his neck. His breathing suddenly grew shallower and he could feel the stickiness of sweat under his arms. He wanted to go back, to slump into the deep black upholstery and swivel the chair around so that it faced the windows, so that he would not see the open door and the faint flush of flickering light on the wall opposite.

He took another step. Now he could see most of the wall opposite, including the framed diplomas hung with painfully meticulous care. The non-glare glass caught the flickering light and focused it, but still not enough for Nick to tell what was causing it.

It's probably nothing, just shadows in the leaves, or a passing truck, or a car parked next door and the sun shining off its hood, something like that. Nothing to worry about.

A final step, and he could see the opening into the living room.

He screamed.

To hell with embarrassment.

He screamed and didn't care that the kid spun around to stare at him.

"Shit, man...," the kid began.

"Shut up," Nick hissed. He had not moved an inch but now he let his eyes flick from the hall to where the kid stood battle-ready, shoulders hunched forward, legs bent, one hand closed into a fist, the other clenched around a thin Phillips-head screwdriver like it was a foot-long switchblade. Street punk ready to rumble. Maybe the image should have reassured Nick but it didn't.

He looked back down the hallway into the living room.

There was nothing there.

By now the kid was next to him, screwdriver still up. This close, he smelled musky; his arm grazed Nick's and Nick could sense the tautness of muscle in the thick wrist.

"What is it?" Ric asked softly.

"There...it was...it's gone now," Nick said, his voice dropping off limply at the end. He felt shaky and his temples throbbed. The fever seemed to be setting in again. At least there was no nausea. Not yet.

Ric stepped into the hall, still wary and alert. He stalked down the length of the darkness, opening doors as he went, letting in floods of brightness. He got to the living room opening and flattened against one wall. Without making a sound, he spun around, ready to slice and gouge. He twisted to where he could see the rest of the room. He straightened and disgustedly slipped the screwdriver into a small leather pouch on his belt.

When he stomped back down the hall, he did not look happy.

"What's that all about?" he yelled, "screaming like some freakin' fairy at a gang-bang! Your idea of a helluva good time?"

He pushed past Nick, not trying particularly hard to miss him, and returned to the console.

"But it...." Nick stopped. He couldn't describe what he had seen. It would sound stupid, crazy, insane. *There was this figure, see, and it was round-shouldered and stooped and stood like it had hurt its hip and when it walked it would limp, and its hand was gnarled with arthritis when it pointed to me and it was* her *it was The Greer, it was a dead woman only she was alive again and twisted and blue and gray and sparkling like she was all made of electricity and then I turned away and she was gone and when you went out there there was nothing at all.*

"It what," Ric said, hostility oozing from his voice.

"I thought one of the screens in the other rooms might have shorted out. I...I thought I saw, like, static or something."

"Shit," Ric said again.

He thrust the screwdriver behind the machine one more time.

This time there was more than just a shock. Even Nick saw the flurry of violent purple sparks that exploded from behind the cabinet the same instant that the house exhaled a loud crackle and the living room went dark and the overhead light in the control room flicked off with a loud *pop!*

"Blew the whole circuit," the kid said, disgusted now that he was over his original startlement. "Shit."

He obviously had a wide vocabulary and believed in building it, Nick decided, not sure whether to be frightened or relieved.

"Where's the fuse box?" the kid demanded.

"I...outside, probably, on the back porch, I think. That's where mine is," he added irrelevantly.

The kid pushed past him again and disappeared into the kitchen. A moment later, there was another staticky *click* and the lights were on again. Nick glanced over to the console. A shadow of red sparks still played behind it, but they disappeared before Ric returned.

The kid glanced behind the DVD and swore again.

"Whole thing's blown. Have to take it to the shop now. Nothing I can do here."

"What do you mean!" Nick yelped. "Payne didn't give me any authorization to let you take it anywhere. I can't believe it. You come in here and muck around with the circuits until you blow the thing than then tell me with a straight face that it's got to be repaired. Well, I won't let Payne pay for this one, you'll fix what you wrecked or you haven't heard the last of this...."

Ric was right in front of Nick now, looking down at the shorter man.

For the first time Nick really paid attention the play of muscle in the kid's arms, the strength in his shoulders, the tightness of cloth across his chest.

"Listen, you creep," Ric said tightly. "I told you that it has to go into the shop. I got a slip from Gunnison giving Tasco's permission to do whatever is necessary, that's his words, *whatever is necessary*, to get this set working. It's been on file with his signature since the old lady died. So don't give me any shit about what I can and can't do."

He turned away before Nick could say anything and pulled the set from the cabinet. The empty space was a litter of charred cords. The wall was scorched in three places. Nick could smell it from where he stood. The gap looked like some insane dentist had gone at someone's front teeth, ripping one out just for the hell of it.

"But...," Nick tried again.

Ric glared. Before Nick could finish speaking, the kid was in the hall, the console tucked under one arm, its burned cables trailing by his legs like figments of tails. Nick followed, remembering to flick off the lights in the control room, remembering to close the doors into the other rooms. The hall was dark again.

By the time Nick got to the front door the kid was halfway across the lawn, heading toward a battered truck with *Tasco's* scrawled across the side.

"Hey," Nick said in a last-ditch attempt at salvaging his self-respect. "You gotta give me a receipt for that."

"Sure," the kid said. He slid the console into the rear of the truck and slammed the doors, checking to make sure they locked. He walked around to the passenger door—Nick noted again the arrogance of his movements, the almost sexual shifting of weight from hip to hip. He disliked the kid even more. And distrusted him.

The kid pulled out a clipboard and scribbled something on it. He ripped off a sheet of paper and held it out to Nick. Nick took it and examined it closely. Everything was correct. The kid had even written in the serial number—or at least *a* serial number. Nick started to ask to compare the paper with what was actually incised in the casing of the DVD player then thought better of it.

"Okay," he said finally. "I'll have to let Mr. Gunnison know when it's going to be done."

"Tasco'll call. Let's say at least a week." The kid grinned insolently, Nick thought, as if he knew he had won a critical battle. But then why not? He *had* won. The kid sauntered around the truck and pulled open the door on the driver's side. He slid onto the seat and slammed the door.

From inside, he stared out at Nick, who was still standing on the sidewalk, his hand outstretched, the slip of paper that was supposed to be a receipt fluttering in the breeze. Nick felt like a grade-A, class-one, honest-to-God idiot, and he knew that he looked like one, too. *What went wrong?* he wondered, trying to figure out just where he had lost control and the kid had taken over.

"Shit," he said under his breath, then looked up to see if the kid had noticed.

The kid was writing something, probably entering the visit into the log.

Nick went across the yard to his own place and, not without a little relief, went inside. His face burned. He didn't know whether to call Tasco and complain—*but maybe the kid is the old man's nephew or something and he won't believe me and the kid will just get madder and come back some time and....or* just forget the whole thing and get something cold to drink.

It wasn't like him, he decided finally, after two and a half cold beers had disappeared from his refrigerator, to let some snot-faced asshole get him so uptight that he imagined things. He was usually more under control than that. Maybe the whole thing was just a final reminder of his siege of flu on Saturday. After all, there really *couldn't* have been anything in the house except himself and the kid. And the kid hadn't seen anything.

After the third beer, Nick was sure that he had only imagined whatever it was that he thought he had seen. After the fourth, he couldn't quite remember what it was that he had imagined.

CHAPTER THIRTY

Ric watched Wheeler out of the rear-view mirror.

"Freakin' queer," he muttered the guy disappeared into the house next door. "Scared of his own shadow. Shit."

He grinned a distinctly distasteful grin.

He glanced down at the sheet he had just filled out. Everything on it was correct, he had made sure of that. Even the serial number. Tasco had a record of every piece of equipment in this house, along with detailed repair and maintenance records going back at least fifteen years. The old man wouldn't say much about old lady Greer. He probably wouldn't even have let Ric make this run if he hadn't been doubled over with the shits this morning and was afraid to go back on his promise to this Gunnison guy. But there was too much money in continuing business at stake to let this house call slide.

Anyway, Ric had come, he had done his best, and he had filled out the form correctly and completely. He slipped his copy into a manila folder with *Gunniso*n written in capital letters on the tab. It wasn't worth trying to pull something on Tasco. The old man was probably shitting nails right now—*along with everything else in his gut*—waiting for Ric to get back. Hell, this one address accounted for a good hunk of Tasco's total business. Ric couldn't figure out why the old lady had insisted on doing business in a rat hole like Tasco's.

He dug into his jeans pocket and pulled out a keychain. Not the one for the truck. No, that one hung limply from the ignition. He held up the keychain to the light, twisting it so that a shaft of sunlight struck a glistening new brass key. A door key. The key to *this* house.

But he would wait to use it. Now that he had been inside, now that he had seen for himself what the stuff looked like and where it was and how hard it would be—how *simple it would be, freakin' child's play*—to strip the place, he would be back again. Late some night. Long after Tasco's delivery truck had come and gone and no one would ever suspect. He might be a thief, but he wasn't a fool.

He glanced into the rearview mirror again, twisting it until he could see the front door of the house next door.

He might even bring along some friends and they would have a party. Mr. Fairy next door could be the guest of honor.

Then again, maybe Ric would take care of that little job by himself.

He laughed and wrenched the ignition key and pulled away from the curb, interrupting his laughter long enough to curse the ancient truck for its lack of pick-up.

CHAPTER THIRTY-ONE

When Nick heard the crunch of tires on Payne's driveway late Tuesday afternoon he wasted little time in getting outside. He was standing by the car door when Payne switched off the engine and climbed out.

"Nick", Payne said, his voice sounding almost surprised. "How ya doin'?"

"Okay, I guess. Look, there's been...."

"No more tossing your cookies or anything?"

"No, not since Saturday, but...."

Payne opened the back door and pulled out a suitcase out of the car and began carrying it toward the house. "Great trip. But it's good to be back." He started to slip his key into the back door lock when Nick placed his hand on Payne's and stopped him. Nick pulled Payne's hand back, and with it the key.

"What's the matter?" Payne asked.

"That's what I've been trying to tell you. There was an...an accident while you were gone."

Payne's face went white—Nick noticed that it was easier to tell than it would have been a few weeks, even a few days before. Payne's tan, so even and deep not so long ago, seemed paler now. The skin stretched tautly over his cheekbones was suddenly parchment white and ancient-looking.

"It wasn't that bad," Nick hurried on. "The repairman must have touched the wrong wires when he was removing the DVD...."

"Removing?" It was less a question than a muted cry.

268 | MICHAEL R. COLLINGS

"Well, he wasn't going to at first, but after the fire...."

Payne thrust the key back into the lock and twisted it so hard that Nick was afraid the key would either bend or shatter. Neither happened. Payne slammed the door open and dropped the suitcase onto the back porch. The beat-up Samsonite hardside wobbled for a couple of moments before toppling over. By then Payne was already on his way to the control room.

The inside of the house was dark and stale-smelling, but Nick couldn't catch even the faintest hint of the acrid smell of an electrical fire. The kitchen seemed undisturbed as Payne rushed through without even bothering to flick on the overhead light. He pushed open the door to the control room.

Nick hung behind, anticipating the barrage of Payne's fury.

It didn't come. There was only heavy silence in the control room.

Shit, he's probably so mad he can't speak. There goes everything. If I'm lucky he won't toss me out on my ear when my lease is up.

Nick shuffled through the kitchen and across the hall, his shoulders slumped. He was ready to take his medicine.

Payne stood just inside the door, hands on his hips, staring around the room. Nick couldn't tell from the set of his arms whether his anger was red-hot or white-cold—either way, he wished he was in Topeka right at that moment.

Payne must have heard him because he turned suddenly and faced his renter.

"What burned? You said there was a fire."

"Not a big one, Payne," Nick said, more apologetically than he liked. The words came out as almost a whine and Nick immediately felt foolish and childish.

"What burned?" Payne repeated.

Nick slipped through the door, brushing against Payne's shoulder as he did so. The other man did not move.

"There," Nick said, pointing to the gap where the DVD console had been. It was deeply shadowed, no doubt hiding the scorch marks in darkness.

Payne reached behind him and turned on the light. Nick squinted against the sudden brightness—he hadn't realized how close to dark it was, or how dim the inside of the house was. The day had died away so gradually that his eyes had adjusted without his knowing. The sudden flush of light from the three 100-watt bulbs in the overhead fixture was blinding by comparison.

Still blinking and wiping a tear from one eye, Nick turned toward the shelf.

"Look, Payne," he began, "that guy Tasco sent was pretty weird. I'm not sure he really knew what he was...."

He stopped.

There was the empty space on the shelf, still looking like an empty socket where a tooth had been removed, a front tooth maybe, or incisor, but whichever it was one of the most noticeable, whose removal made the resulting smile lopsided, distorted, and eerily wrong.

There was the tangle of wires, looking like exposed nerves jutting from the tooth socket. Nick winced inwardly at the image. He had a deep personal aversion to dentists and wondered why in the hell he had let himself think about the machinery in such painful images. His teeth ached and his ears buzzed, the shrilly insistent buzz of a dentist's drill set on high. *They had found him, after all, found him crouched beneath the heavy coats in the cloak room—a six-year-old kid with a mortal fear of dentists curled beneath the other patients' dripping parkas and fake-fur coats. Flecks of Montana snow, not yet melted in the coolness of the coat room, filtered down on him as he waited, then again as his mother pulled the coats aside and took him from his hiding place and dragged him through the halls and set him in the chair and tilted it back until he thought he would fall out onto his head and crush his skull and his brains would leak out the cracks and dribble all over the dusty green carpeting like lumpy pancake batter. But nobody seemed to care and his mother left the room even when he called for her again and again and again. His eyes tingled through closed lids as trans-*

lucently red as a stained-glass window in a church. The bright-ness hurt even more when Dr. Sutro adjusted the lamp and focused its intensity right at him. He smelled the medicinal air, smelled Dr. Sutro's sweat and heavy breath, felt a rough finger tugging at the tender corner of his mouth. Any second now he would feel the shattering vibrations of steel against enamel, the jolt of liquid pain when the tip touched one of those exposed nerves. The scream he knew had to come eventually scraped insistently at the back of his throat as it built force, ready to burst through....

"Nick, you all right?" Payne's voice cut through the shadow of Nick's remembered terror.

"Yeah, I'm okay I guess," Nick said, shaking his head to clear his mind of the painful images and staring at the empty...at the empty *place* on the shelf, he thought, choosing the most neutral word he could.

The wall behind it was dead white. The wires were covered with plastic protective sheathing, blue and red and white and black. Where the metal was exposed, it glistened in the light with the bright red-gold glow of new copper.

"Where was the fire?" Payne repeated.

"It was there." Nick pointed at the empty space.

Payne went toward the shelf and stooped and ran his finger over the shelf and sniffed the air. "I don't see anything. Did you fix it up?"

Nick shook his head. In the back of his mind he saw the black streaks disfiguring the white wall, saw the wires charred and coiled like dead snakes. He could still smell the acrid-ozone smell of an electrical burst.

Suddenly Payne was standing at his side, holding on to him.

"Look, you don't look good," Payne said. "How have you been since you were...since Saturday. Any repeats?"

Nick shook his head again.

"Dizziness? Headache? Anything like that."

Nick started to shake his head again, then stopped. "A little. Some dizziness on Monday, just before...."

"Before you came over with the repairman." Payne finished the thought for him.

Nick nodded mutely. "Hey, don't worry. The way you were feeling Saturday, I'm surprised you didn't end up in the hospital. I'm sure you saw something. Some sparks, maybe. Only your mind interpreted it as more dangerous than it really was. You can see that there's no problem here."

"But I saw it," Nick insisted. The sparks, the flames, the smell. "I remember everything. And the...."

He hesitated, unable to force himself to mention the phantom Greer he had glimpsed *thought he had glimpsed* for that single awful moment. "And that kid was so rude," he continued finally, "swearing and cursing all the time. Shit, Payne, he even threatened to stab me with a screwdriver! I couldn't just *imagine* something like that!"

"He what?" The words were the right ones, but the tone was not. Payne was laughing at him. Well, maybe not laughing, but certainly not taking him absolutely seriously.

Nick's face assumed a little-boy stubbornness and his lips squeezed tightly closed, as if they had made a decision on their own: *If nobody believes me I won't say anything at all. So there!*

"Come on," Payne said. "Don't be like that. Think it through logically. You've been sick, really sick, and you still felt pretty punk. And someone comes out, someone whose business depends on how well he deals with people. And you claim that he was abusive and profane and physically assaulted you."

"No," Nick interrupted, trying to put things back into the right perspective. But it was so hard. "He only...."

"Physically *threatened* you, then. How long do you think Tasco would stay in business if he did that to his customers? Just once, and the word would get out. Then where would he be?"

"But it wasn't Tasco. It was this kid, Ric was his name, I think."

Nick heard the little-boy whine in his voice and hated it. It was as if his mother had caught him in the cookie jar—*wrong image* (his mind broke in) *she didn't have a cookie jar, try again with another simile, one that works* th*is time*—as if his mother had caught him snitching the last of the chocolate chips hiding in the crumpled plastic package and was scolding him. Payne's voice had that old woman's *I know better than you young man and you'd better listen to me carefully before you get into more trouble* timbre that Nick hated, too.

"Okay, so it wasn't Tasco himself," Payne continued. "It was one of his employees, though, and you can bet that he would take any complaints seriously, especially from me, considering how much business I've given him over the...."

"Come on, Nick, you can't really believe what you are saying. There's nothing here. No smoke, no burned insulation, no ashes. Nothing. Isn't it easier to believe that you saw something that wasn't here, that you were more feverish than you realized and imagined a problem that just didn't exist."

Payne's voice was calm. His words were reasonable. Nick tried to hold on to what he knew—*believed*—were his memories, but he couldn't do it, not as strongly as before. He walked to the shelf and ran a finger over the wall, even flicked a fingertip against the exposed copper wiring, half expecting to feel the nip of a shock. Nothing. The wall was smooth and white. The wires were dead.

He didn't want to accept Payne's explanation, but unfortunately it did make sense. More sense than his own story did now. Maybe he did remember the kid as being more abrasive than he really was. Maybe he just held the screwdriver oddly and Nick thought he was being threatened. Maybe the phantom-figure had been only that, a phantom stirred up by sickness and dizziness and overwrought nerves. Maybe.... Maybe.

"See you tomorrow," Nick said abruptly. "Sorry if I worried you. I'm...I better get on home."

He dug into his pocket.

"The repairman left this for you. The pick-up receipt for the set."

He held out a neatly folded paper. Payne took it and read it.

"This proves that I'm right, doesn't it. Look, everything is in order, down to the serial number. Neat and orderly and precise, even if the handwriting is messy. It doesn't look like the work of someone who tells long-standing paying customers to fuck off."

Nick shivered. The last words sounded terrible coming from Payne—too harsh, too coldly obscene for him. For an instant, Nick felt as if he were going to vomit again, then the moment passed and he just felt tired, exhausted, drained.

"Okay, I guess you're right." *There it was, the admission of defeat, just like his mother was always able to wring from him even when it was an admission that he would have sold his soul to keep from her she always knew how to get it out.* "Sorry." He wasn't sure what he was sorry about, but he was definitely sorry.

"Hey, don't worry," Payne said broadly. "No problem. You just get home and take care of yourself. Get some rest."

He walked Nick to the back door and held the screen open for him, like Nick was a cripple or a little kid whose arms were too puny to put enough pressure against the door to keep it open.

"And thanks for keeping an eye out," Payne called as Nick crossed through the hedge into his own yard.

Nick didn't answer. He waved one hand half-heartedly, as if to say *yeah don't mention it anytime boss*, and disappeared into his own house.

CHAPTER THIRTY-TWO

Payne stepped back inside. He was more worried than he had let on. He was almost angry and not sure quite what to believe. He had never known Nick to lie. He wasn't himself sure about the theory that Nick's illness had led him to some sort of hallucination, but there was nothing to suggest anything else.

He returned to the control room and examined the wall. There was no evidence that it had been painted over, no streaks to suggest that it had been washed down. He picked up one of the lead wires. The plastic sheathing was untouched, with a feathering of dust along one surface that implied that it had lain undisturbed in one position for quite a while. Not a hint of scorching or fire. The copper wire inside was still bent in a half circle, as if it had fit around an electronic lead and had been removed when someone unscrewed the lead; the wire had not even been pulled loose.

He passed his hand over the shelf, but even before he did, he could see the slight discoloration where the set had sat for so many years without being moved.

No evidence at all of anything wrong.

But Payne frowned anyway. Something was not right. Maybe he *should* call Tasco and check it out. He went into the kitchen and was reaching for the wall phone when two things happened simultaneously.

First, he remembered that it was after nine o'clock; surely Tasco's would be closed by this time, and leaving a message on the answer machine did not seem like the best approach. If

Nick was right and the guy working there—what was the name, Ric?—was unreliable, then there was a chance that he would get to the tape first, maybe he got there early and unlocked or something, and he could easily erase it. Payne's hand hesitated, not six inches from the receiver.

And at the same instant, the phone rang.

His hand pulled back, the only physical indication of how startled he was. For a second he considered not answering, then he pulled the receiver off the wall hook.

"Gunnison."

"Payne, is that you?"

"Cathy? Sure it's me. Who else would it be?"

She laughed. "I don't know. It's just been so long since we talked, and every time I've tried to call for the past few days the phone has rung once or twice and then gone dead. I thought maybe you were having trouble with the lines."

Payne frowned again. "No, no trouble. That is, I don't know of any trouble."

Actually, now that she had brought the subject up, he became aware of a high-pitched buzz in the earpiece. He held the phone an inch or so away. That helped.

"I've been...out of town for a while. Up to San Francisco to check on some property there."

"I wondered. I thought maybe you decided not to see me anymore."

"No," he said with a laugh. "Nothing like that. Just business. Boring business."

There was a brief moment of silence from both ends of the line. The circuit was still buzzing, Payne noticed.

"Well—" Cathy said.

"Say—" Payne began at the same moment.

They both laughed, but the sounds echoed hollowly through the telephone.

"Go on," Cathy said.

"No," Payne said, "Ladies first."

"Well, I was wondering if you wanted to come over tonight.

You know, drinks, a little music. My roommate's out of town again." There was an unspoken invitation in her words: *And we can be alone here, for as long as we want.*

"Thanks, but I'm awfully tired right now. Just got home, not more than half an hour ago."

There was another silence.

"But maybe tomorrow," he added hurriedly.

"Yeah, tomorrow. Here? I can fix dinner and everything."

This time the pause was barely long enough to be noticeable but it was there nevertheless.

"I'm not sure...okay, tomorrow."

She waited for a second, then, "Payne? Are you still there?"

"Sure. Why?"

"I thought the line went dead again. I couldn't hear anything at all."

"There is some interference tonight. Your voice is crackling. Look, I'll call you in the morning and set things up for tomorrow night. And I'll have the phone company come out and check the line. Okay."

"Okay."

Over the static, her voice sounded unsure, fragmented.

"Gotta go now. See you tomorrow." He waited for a sound that might have been Cathy saying something like "see you later" and then he hung up.

He thought about calling the telephone company and reporting a problem with the line, then decided that the call had to wait a minute. His bladder was full from the trip and he felt suddenly that if he didn't empty it he would burst.

When he came out of the bathroom, he went right into his bedroom. He hadn't been lying when he said that he was tired. He was more than that, he was exhausted. He couldn't remember ever being so bone-tired before. All he wanted to do was drop down on the bed and watch something mindless and entertaining and drift off to sleep.

He pulled off his wrinkled suit coat and tie and shirt and stepped out of his pants, letting them drop to the floor. He fully intended to hang the suit on the back of a chair and let most of the worst wrinkles pull out. But he didn't. Instead he put on an old pair of jeans that had shrunk until they were tighter than he liked, and a T-shirt that his high-school girlfriend had given him on his eighteenth birthday. It was at least two sizes too small but he had kept it for sentimental reasons, folded neatly and tucked in the back of his sock drawer. He pulled it over his head. The material stretched across his chest, cinched around his arms.

It felt right.

Outside, the night air was so warm that the T-shirt was enough. He didn't bring a jacket. He started the car and backed out of the driveway and headed down Greensward to the junction with Kennedy Avenue and then turned right—south—and followed Kennedy through the business center of Tamarind Valley and onto the freeway heading south. By the time he noticed where he was, he had left the freeway and followed one of the main arteries—he didn't know which one—eastward, toward the foothills of the Santa Monica Mountains. He was almost directly beneath the *HOLLYWOOD* sign and could see it glowing against the blackness of the hillsides.

At the first intersection he turned right, onto a street ablaze with lights and store fronts. It was busy. Even though it was past ten o'clock, some of the places were wide open and doing business. He saw a couple of restaurants, half a dozen bars. Motels with glaring neon lights sat interspersed among them. Vaguely he wondered where he was. He crooked his neck and looked out through the side passenger window to see if he could spot a street sign at the next intersection.

There was a sign on a steel post—white letters on a blue background and easily readable in the garish light coming from around the painted-over windows of an all-night bookstore on the corner, but he didn't read the letters.

Instead, he stared at the woman.

She had white spiky hair, not blonde but white, dead-fish white that accentuated her make-up—black mascara so dark that it made her eyes look like empty wells into nothingness, lipstick so dark that it looked black, might even have been black where she opened her lips to smile at him and licked them with a flickering tongue. Her dress was short and slit almost to the thigh. The top was tight and short as well. From where he sat in his car, he could see enough of her breasts that his breath caught. She leaned toward him and smiled again.

The light changed from red to green and he floored the accelerator and the car shot out into the intersection, barely missing a low-slung sporty model that had tried to make the yellow from the other street and was still halfway in Payne's lane. He swerved around it and lifted his foot to slow the car. Fortunately there was little traffic and the incident had caused no more than the turning of a couple of heads. The guy in the sports car hadn't even noticed, probably.

Payne checked in his rear-view mirror.

She was still at the corner, her hand raised toward him, one finger protruding stiffly upward.

The next light was red when he got there. He stopped, staring straight ahead, his foot poised over the accelerator and ready to go. He would turn here, onto a darkened residential street that would lead back to the freeway and from there back to Tamarind Valley—eventually—and he would go to bed and get some rest and be ready for work tomorrow.

The light flickered to green.

He pulled straight ahead, passing more of the same kinds of businesses, all open, all brightly lit with flickering red or yellow or orange lights, all brightly painted in garish colors. There were fewer bars, more bookstores and arcades with *ADULT* spelled out in flashing lights. More women standing on corners and by doors and along curbs.

He felt his face flushing.

At the next corner, he stopped again. This time, he looked out the window instead of straight ahead, his curiosity getting the better of him. After all, back home they hadn't had a *real* "Red-light District," just one waitress at the Stop-n-Snak who was rumored to be unusually friendly to men after hours, if you caught her in the right mood and left a big enough tip. Payne didn't know about that; he had never tried, never felt the need to try.

So now that the initial shock of surprise was over and he knew where he was and what to expect—*this is California, after all, wild California where you can find anything you want*—he decided to look things over. Purely out of curiosity.

He glanced through the window on the passenger side.

A man stared back. A boy, really. His hair was not as spiky or as obviously bleached as the woman's had been. It was modish and long, blond but more like sun-bleaching than bottle bleaching. His jeans were tight, with horizontal rips at both knees, smooth enough at the edges to let everyone know that they were there to be stylish not because the jeans were old. He wore no shirt, just a dark denim vest that hung open to reveal his chest, tanned and lean and gleaming in the light as if he were sweating from hours of hard work. He smiled and stepped forward, hips thrust forward provocatively. He was about to rest one hand on the car door.

The light was still red—*how long are the lights around here don't they know that people might need to get somewhere shit why doesn't it change*—and the man's hand was only inches away when Payne jerked the car to the right and spun around the corner, missing the man by only inches but he was safe and the street was dark and lined with trees and apartment buildings with shades down or no lights at all and the night air whistling through his open window cooled his face and he gradually slowed down and shifted his hips in the seat to a more comfortable position and stretched his legs out to relax them.

He must have pulled too hard on the wheel, too, because his hand hurt, from the knuckles through to the palm, like a spike had been driven through the central web of nerves. He pulled over.

In the rear-view mirror he could not even see a glimmer of lights from the street, whatever one it had been. There must be a hill between it and where he was parked. He breathed heavily and deeply, massaging his hand until the shard of pain disappeared and he could move the fingers easily again, grip the wheel and angle out into the lane and move toward the freeway again.

Pulling into the westbound lane, he drove on into the night.

He was almost at the Kennedy exit before he felt totally calm again. He signaled and made the transition from the fast inside lane to the center lane, then again to the outside lane, just in time to glide smoothly into the exit lane without braking or touching the accelerator.

He slowed gradually, timing his progress so that the red light at the base of the freeway exit flicked to green just as he arrived and he could pull out across two lanes of Kennedy and head east without even pausing.

He was okay.

He was in control again.

Halfway between the freeway and Greensward, he decided to stop for something to drink. His throat was dry and tight, and he knew that he didn't have anything at home. A soda would be right.

He cruised slowly until he saw the red and green sign that identified an all-night 7-Eleven®, probably the only place open between the freeway and his place. He turned into the parking lot, stopping in the empty slot right in front of the doors.

The place was empty. The only person there was the guy behind the counter, youngish, about Payne's age. A surfer-type from the looks of it, working nights so he would have his days free to spend at the beach. Payne walked through the store to the back and followed the line of glass doors until he found the sodas. He pulled out a single can with his right hand. The metal was so cold that it hurt against his palm, reminding him of the stab of pain earlier. He shifted the can to the other hand. It was less sensitive, and the can didn't seem as icy. As an afterthought, he grabbed a six pack as well, careful to hold it by the plastic handle.

He walked slowly back to the checkout stand.

The man watched him. Payne could feel eyes boring into him as he approached the counter. He wished suddenly and feverishly that he hadn't worn *that* pair of jeans, *that* T-shirt. He felt naked and exposed.

"This be all?" the man asked as Payne set the soft drinks on the counter.

"Yeah."

"Sale on the six-packs, you know. Two-forty-nine each. Singles are sixty-five. Almost cheaper in the long run to get another six-pack."

"That's okay. This'll do." The clerk nodded and began punching buttons on the register. "Three thirty-five."

Payne pulled out his wallet and withdrew three singles.

"Just a minute," he said, dropping the crumpled bills on the counter. "I've got the change in my pocket." He started to reach into his pocket, then realized with embarrassment that the material was stretched so tight that his hand wouldn't slip in. He knew he had some change in there. He looked down and could see the coins outlined against the denim; but he simply couldn't get to them.

He glanced up.

The man was still watching him. He reached into the wallet again and pulled out another bill.

"Sorry. No change."

The man rang up the payment, counted out change and handed it to Payne. He stuffed the coins as far as he could into his pocket, aware that the serrated edge of one quarter stuck out half an inch.

The man bagged the drinks. Payne picked up the bag and started out.

"Hey, man," the clerk called as Payne reached for the door. He turned.

"Yeah?"

"You didn't slip or anything out there in the parking lot, did you?"

"What?"

"Well, you're limping pretty bad, like you're in real pain, and I wouldn't want the store to get sued because you fell in the parking lot or anything."

"No. I didn't fall. Polio. When I was a kid."

"What?" For an instant, the clerk's eyes widened.

"Pulled the muscle. Bad break when I was a kid."

"That's not...."

"It doesn't really hurt," Payne said quickly. "Just looks that way when it acts up."

"Look, I'm sorry. I didn't mean.... I was just worried...."

"It's all right. It wasn't that bad"—*like hell it wasn't, the pain, the twisting, the hours of therapy, and the uncertainty of not knowing whether the legs would ever bear weight again or whether the disease would turn really nasty and stuff her into an iron lung for the rest of her life but she beat it by god just like she could beat everything even death itself*—"and it was a long time ago."

He started through the door.

"Polio. Shit, I thought they licked that one fifty years ago," the counter man said, more to himself than to Payne.

They did, Payne thought as he unlocked his door and tossed the package onto the passenger seat. They did. *And I never had polio.*

CHAPTER THIRTY-THREE

Payne was badly shaken when he finally angled into his own driveway and up against the closed garage door, so much so that he left the bag of sodas on the front seat of the car when he bolted from it and crossed the back lawn in three long steps that were almost a run, and slammed through the door and escaped into the silence of his house.

What was I doing?
Why was I thinking about polio?
Why do I hurt so much, my hips and my wrist?
Where was I tonight?
Why did I drive out there?
What was I afraid of?
Why am I afraid?
Afraid. Afraid. Afraid.
Too many questions.

No answers. He kicked his shoes off, not caring that they flew across the back porch like canvas and white leather missiles and thumped hollowly against the inside wall, leaving faintly green stains on the white paint.

He stripped his jeans off. He pulled the T-shirt over his head and wadded it up with the pants—both legs inside out so the white-blue threads showed, pale and wraith-like—and threw them into a darkened corner of the porch.

Exhausted, he went into his bedroom and threw himself down on the bed, sweating and panting and more frightened than he had ever been in his life. He still didn't know exactly why he was frightened or what he was frightened of.

He lay for a long time, his arm crooked over his eyes to shut out the filtered light. He listened to his breathing and his heart-beat, noting how both gradually subsided, how his pulse thinned and his body quit spewing sweat from every pore.

Finally, he opened his eyes and dropped his arm to his side. He was breathing normally. He was all right now.

He sat up and thought about a shower or a cold drink. He even remembered the sodas sitting on the seat of the car. They were no doubt tepid now, probably as warm as the night air.

But instead of taking a shower or getting the drinks, he went down the hall to the Control Room and walked in, flicking the light switch on. The sudden brightness hurt his eyes. He squinted and almost raised one hand to shade his eyes but stopped before completing the motion. His eyes adjusted quickly. Without moving, he scanned the room, the shelves of cases stacked neatly on every wall, the equipment on his left, all of it bright and spotless and perfect except for the hole where the missing DVD unit should be. But there were still the other two, and he could rig them in tandem and they would play two films sequentially. That should get him through most of the night.

He crossed to the other side of the room, to the comedy section of the library, and grabbed a disc at random. He glanced at the cover.

Hold That Ghost. Abbott and Costello. Not a bad film, as he remembered. Some funny moments.

I keep my money in my head...in my head...in my head.

He walked down a few more steps to the science-fiction section and repeated his previous action, reaching up and taking out a case without looking at the title.

Forbidden planet. A moldy oldie. Still, not a bad film. It had held up pretty well over the years.

He put one of the discs into each of the DVD units, switching on the small auxiliary unit that allowed for continuous play between the two. He had never seen a set up quite like it before; this one looked homemade, probably something Aunt Emilia had cooked up.

He set the timer-delay for five minutes. That gave him enough time to slip out the back door and grab the sack of sodas, pull an ice cube tray from the refrigerator and a glass from the shelf on the way through the kitchen, and set them all on his night table. He glanced up at the monitor. Nothing yet. He checked his watch. A minute or two left before they went on.

He hurried into the bathroom and grabbed a wash cloth and soaked it in cool water and passed it over his forehead and down his face, under his arms, along his shoulders and chest. Then patted dry with a clean towel. Not a shower, but enough for now.

From the other room, he heard the hiss of static.

The films were beginning.

He returned to his bedroom and dropped onto the bed, pouring himself a drink of soda and plopping three ice cubes into the half-full glass. The soda fizzed and bubbled and threatened to spillover the top of the glass. He sipped at the froth, nearly choking when he breathed some of it up his nose.

He settled back to watch the films.

Hold That Ghost was first. He got all of ten minutes into it, sipping at the soda now and then, before he settled back onto the pillow and fell asleep.

He roused a couple of times during the film, opened one eye and closed it again and drifted back into dreamless sleep. The only time he noticed enough to place the plot of the film was when the little fat guy—*Abbott or Costello, damn, can't ever remember which is which*—reached into the moose's stuffed head and pulled out roll after roll of illicit money (*in my head in my head in my head in my head*) that nobody expected to find there.

The image triggered something in Payne's mind, and for a moment he struggled to figure out what. But finally the struggle was too difficult and he was too tired. He closed his eyes.

When he opened them again, the monitor showed a scene in full color. *The Abbott and Costello thing is off, then, and the other one, what was it? Yeah,* Forbidden Planet, *that one's on. I like it, should try to watch it.*

He wanted to, he tried to, but the exhaustion that had filled his body like a drug was still too strong, too heavy. He roused several times, almost often enough to keep track of what was on. But well before the final scene, he was sleeping again. Another phrase rolled over and over itself in his mind now. *The monster from the Id* repeated again and again until it sounded like a litany. In the wilderness of his dreams he saw himself

walking down the long aisle of a church, between rows and rows of silent watchers who turned their heads away from him when he moved past their pews. His legs rustled against something soft and filmy but he didn't dare look down, didn't dare look anywhere except straight ahead, into the wooden Christ hanging from a dead-white cross and staring at him *with dead-white eyes. The Christ was naked, with great gouts of white blood oozing from every inch of its body. He tried to turn and run but something spoke in Walter Pidgeon's voice and said* monster from the Id monster from the Id *and terrified Payne until he screwed his eyes closed and saw no more but only felt the silkiness brushing against his naked legs and dropping like a veil over his naked shoulders and back. He reached the end of the cathedral aisle, stood squarely beneath a gigantic dome made of pink translucent glass, and listened to the bass murmurings of the worshippers, whispers that rose and fell like waves and crashed against his ears. For a long time, he could only* listen. *He didn't want to open his eyes,* couldn't *open his eyes because he knew that the dead-white Christ was staring down at him with dead-white eyes and that the shadows behind the image were black as black and rustled with hidden sounds. The whispering grew, deeper and darker and more rumbling, voices edged with pain and horror. The silkiness grew sticky where it touched the tops of his thighs and he felt a scream growing from within, surging through his gullet to press against his teeth where he clamped them shut. He breathed through his nose and smelled the acrid smell of vomit and the churning smell of oceans at low tide, the fishy smell of oceans where the waves*

*have rolled back and exposed the naked shoals. And he opened
his eyes and he*

screamed but didn't really. No sounds came out, even though
the air exploded from his lungs in painful gulps that hurt his
throat as they strained outward. He was sitting upright on
his bed, his body bathed in sweat and his hands held out in a
warding gesture that seemed both necessary and ridiculous. He
was staring at the monitor.

Forbidden Planet had apparently finished some time before
because another film was playing, a third film that he hadn't put
into the machine, couldn't have put into a machine because the
third unit was out being fixed. He didn't recognize what this
film was. He could see the characters clearly enough, but he just
couldn't identify any of them. There was a woman, youngish
and attractive but at the same time hard and harsh. Payne didn't
like her from the first image. There was a youngish man as well,
quiet and studious, but there was something effeminate about
him—nothing obvious or vulgar, just a matter of the hand held
so or the shoulders swung in just that way. Payne felt the same
instant distrust of him.

And there was a third character, a man, listening to the others
as the other two talked around him as if he didn't exist. The
sound was bad, gritty and raw, and the voices muffled the words
until he couldn't understand a bit of the dialogue, but there was
apparently a love triangle of some sort that he could not quite
understand. The sets were more impressionistic than he liked,
with broad swatches of white and black in quasi-geometrical
patterns that denied any illusion of perspective and forced the
three characters—in living color—*off* the screen and into his
room. He had never seen anything like that, but he didn't like
the effect. Without thinking, he inched himself along the bed,
away from the monitor, until his back pressed against the headboard.

The white enameled wood rubbed coolly against his skin.

He stared at the monitor.

He knew that he should recognize the characters, but the

names just wouldn't come. He struggled to attach a name, a date, anything, to the film, but it was impossible. Nothing fit anything he remembered, but he felt as if he had seen the film an infinite number of times (*remember those people who watched* Star Wars *five hundred times or more, standing in interminable lines for hour after house just to watch it again*)—he felt as if he knew before each line was spoken what it would be, what intonation the character would use, how the hand or lip or shoulder would move to add depths of meaning to the words.

It terrified him.

And then, suddenly, with the clarity of a frosted window suddenly drenched with heated air, the characters came startlingly to life and he saw that the central character, the one listening and watching to the other two—the central character was *himself.*

"No!" The sound was as much moan as cry. It could have carried on the night air until it slipped through the cracks in night-veiled windows all along Greensward. It could have nipped at sleeping ears and twisted and brought dreamers out of their dreams with vague memories of pain and fear and insistent feelings of evil.

But it didn't. Instead, the sound hung against the walls and drooped to the floor and lay like heavy oil against the polished wood floor.

"Nooo!"

Payne thrust himself from the bed, his feet barely touching the floor as he ran through the door and down the hall. The other doors were closed, except for the entry into the living room. Something blue and silver tinged with red flickered in the living room, reflected from the white carpet and furniture. He ran into the room, standing in the center, his chest heaving and his breath heavy. He stared around the room; his eyes were white against the darkness and looked more like the eyes of a hunted creature than of a human.

He glanced up at the inner wall where that monitor—like every other one in the house—was playing the same scene.

Himself.

With a single fluid motion he scooped up the black king from the chess board and threw it against the monitor. The piece *ping*-ed and rebounded and landed silently on the carpet.

"Noooo!" Payne screamed again, feeling more than hearing the sound as it echoed and echoed through the room. He grabbed an edge of the chess board and flung the board through the air. The leather-sheathed cardboard spun three times before smashing into the monitor as well. The screen shivered. It cracked in a single jagged lightning-bolt that ran from corner to corner. The chess board dropped to the ground.

He ran from the room, ran like a frightened rabbit back to the light and the security of his bedroom. He threw himself onto the bed and covered his head with the pillow, pulled the sheets up around his ears.

Still he could hear it, the *hiss-hissss* of static.

Then it stopped.

For a long time Payne did not move. Then he turned just enough to look over his shoulder at the monitor.

A single figure dominated the dark center of the screen. It was old and bent, draped heavily with black cloth that disguised features and height and weight and sex. When it moved, it moved with painful, anguished slowness. One foot dragged behind the other, scraping arhythmically against the concrete of a night-shaded walkway. The figure held one hand curled tightly against its side.

It was shuffling away from the camera while remaining in the center of the screen. Just as it reached an invisible but critical place on the sidewalk, it stopped and began to turn.

Payne watched, a knot of terror growing in his stomach.

Before he saw the figure's face, he twisted away, so violently that he felt a spasm of pain through his hip, as if he had sprained it. He buried his face in the pillow and wept silently into the white pillowcase, biting down on the cloth until it was sodden and sticky and he breathed the fluid stench of his fear and horror.

CHAPTER THIRTY-FOUR

Payne sounded different when he called Cathy the next morning to talk about dinner that night. His voice was strained and hoarse, as if he had yelled too long and too loud at a home-club championship basketball game that had gone into over-time. Their conversation had been short, almost curt at times, but she was relieved to hear him.

"Seven okay?" he asked.

"Great, can I bring anything?"

"Nope. This one's on me."

"Shall I dress...formally?"

That melted his stiffness a bit. Payne made a small sound that might have been a stifled laugh or a chuckle.

"No, nothing like that. Just don't put on too many layers. We might end up...playing chess or something."

She wanted to respond, and was wondering how much overt sexiness she could get away with talking to him over the telephone without offending him or coming on too strong, when he made the issue moot by hurrying on. The stiffness was in his voice again.

"Gotta go. Lots of things to do today. See you tonight." And then he was gone.

Cathy stood listening to the distant buzz of the lines and wondering.

By evening, she felt better about the situation. Payne was a little odd at times, but who wasn't. And most of the time he was a gentleman, the stablest, most considerate man she had known in…in a long time, she started to think, then amended it to *ever*. He was the most considerate man she had *ever* known. She suspected more than a little that she was falling in love with him. Tonight could be more important than just a dinner among friends, no matter how good the friendship was. It could be the start of something deep and wonderful.

So watch it. Don't come on too strong. Let him take the lead.

It wasn't that Cathy was particularly manipulative; it was merely that she felt strongly about Payne.

The feeling intensified as soon as she saw him that night. He didn't come out to the car this time. In fact, she had her finger stretched out to push the bell before the door opened and Payne stood before her. In the shadows, he seemed paler than usual, worried, thinner almost, except that not enough time had passed since they were together for him to have changed that much physically. It was just a trick of the light.

"Hi," she said, her voice rich with as much sensuality as she dared project.

Even in the dim light, she could see him flushing. Her smile broadened. That was one of the things she liked so much about him. He was boyish, innocent, naively modest about so many things. A refreshing change from most of the men she had dated, who probably never blushed in their entire lives and would probably have been willing to strip naked in front of a capacity crowd at the Rose Bowl if it would ensure their getting laid after dinner.

Not Payne. Of course, that didn't preclude the possibility of his getting…no, she refused to use the phrase and instead substituted *of their making love after this dinner.*

"Come on in," he said at last, starting as if he were coming out of a mild trance. "Come in," and he reached out and took her hand, and his was warm and felt strong and masculine. Cathy wondered again at the levels of the man, sensitivity and strength, masculinity and innocence.

She smiled and let him lead her into the living room. For a second she stood there, not quite a foot from Payne, looking over his shoulder into the room. The drapes were closed and the inside lights were on, so there was an odd texture to the lighting that she found mildly unappealing. And more. Something was wrong in the room itself.

Instinctively, she glanced around. It took several seconds before she noticed it: a thin crack in the television monitor. If the light hadn't struck the screen just so, highlighting the smooth line of the fracture, she probably would not have seen it at all.

And there was something more.

One of the chess pieces was missing. It seemed a minute thing, one piece after all. But in a room as sparse as this one, any change, no matter how small, affected the sense of balance.

"Payne," she said, "what happened?"

He glanced at the monitor. The movement seemed studied, as if he were waiting for her to ask, as if he had rehearsed his reaction to her question. She felt a tingling along her spine.

"Oh, that," he said, suddenly off-hand and casual. "Damnedest thing. I had this weird dream last night. Really off-beat. I don't remember any of it now—you know how it is, especially with the strange ones. Anyway, all I remember is that I dreamed I was standing in the middle of the room, still dressed in my pajamas, and I had apparently just chucked one of the chess pieces at the monitor. Must've thought it was a monster from outer space or something, the Crawling Eye coming to get me out of the depths of Dreamland." He laughed. "Anyway, when I got up this morning and came out, there it was, a crack down the face of the set. And the chess piece is missing. It must have rolled under the couch or something."

He turned to face her and shrugged, a little-boy shrug that warmed her and drew her closer to him.

"You okay now?" she asked.

"Sure." This time there was a shrug in the voice as well. "What's a dream, anyway. Yeah, everything's great."

And for a while, she believed it.

Dinner was not as complicated as the first time she had come to his house. The food was good but simpler—steak and salad and ice cream for dessert. This time, there was no argument about her helping to clean up, and afterward they found their way easily into his bedroom and from there onto the bed, and they discovered that the bed might be narrow but it was not too narrow for two people to make love on. It was lingering and gentle and wonderfully fulfilling for her, and when she fell asleep with Payne's head resting on her shoulder and his arm around her waist she could not imagine ever feeling as complete or as happy.

CHAPTER THIRTY-FIVE

Payne woke to the shrillness of Cathy's voice. For a moment, it sounded as if a harpy or a banshee had infiltrated his home and was intent on destroying his peace.

"Payne, damn you, how could you? How *could* you!" She repeated the phrase, not as a question but as an inquisition.

Payne was groggy, still half asleep. He was naked, cramped against the wall on the narrow bed, his body welded to hers. He was partially aroused and felt the tension of her flesh against his. His arm lay across her waist, not really holding her down, he decided, but holding her closer to him.

"Payne!" She threw his arm back and sat up, pulling away from him.

He rolled back toward the wall and braced up on his elbow.

"What? What's wrong. What did I do?"

The sleepiness was passing, leaving in its place a deep confusion.

What was wrong with her?

"That!"

She pointed an accusatory arm toward the wall. He twisted around until he could see clearly. The monitor was on. It had not been on when they had made love, nor when they had drifted happily to sleep. He had not had it on all day, for all he knew there wasn't even a disc in either machine, not since he had replaced *Hold That Ghost* and *Forbidden Planet* that morning, just after he had noticed the crack in the living room monitor and had looked around for the missing chess piece.

The screen couldn't be live. It was that simple.

But it was.

And it was playing a film that he had never seen before, a kind of film that he had never seen, never even consciously wanted to see. Sure, there was a lot of skin in the discs the old lady had stockpiled in the Control Room, even some with pretty extended episodes of nudity. He thought fleetingly of *Equus*, of flashes of bodies in teen-rebellion films like *All the Right Mov*es, with Tom Cruise and what-was-her-name tenderly discovering themselves for the first time after the crude and violent episodes of back-seat groping. He had seen a few, but he had never sat down and consciously looked for any.

He had for sure never looked for anything like this.

In the first instant, staring through sleep-bleared eyes, the only thing he saw was pink—flesh pink that moved and pulsated and writhed. It resolved into sharper focus, an inverted dome of pink that suddenly became a woman's breast, filmed obscenely close and graphic.

"Hey. I....," he began, and the scene changed. The camera shifted to the male, fully aroused and penetrating. Payne swallowed. It almost seemed as if the monitor were showing him what they had done the night before, he and Cathy, in the privacy of his own room, his own bed. Only there was no love here. The woman was bleeding, the man vicious in his barely restrained violence masquerading as love. He struck her brutally across the breast

The film became even more graphic, more perverted.

"How could you!" Cathy was up now, her back to the monitor. She held a corner of the sheet in front of her as if to protect her from the violation of Payne's eyes. With a quick movement that was itself violent and angry, she twisted the sheet from the bed, leaving Payne naked, and wrapped it around her.

"But I...I....," Payne said, even more confused. "Did you put that on?"

She stared at him, her eyes monstrous and white. "How could you think that," she said in a voice that was frighteningly cold.

"That...that filth."

She refused even to glance over her shoulder. She knelt down and retrieved her panties and bra, struggling to put them on without dropping the shield that the sheet provided.

"But I didn't, I *couldn't* have," Payne protested. "Hey, I was right here, asleep, the whole time. I couldn't have gotten out of bed without you knowing it, could I?"

"I don't know how you arranged it, but I won't stay here and watch something like that."

Payne allowed his eyes to focus on the monitor. It showed more of the same waves of flesh and undulating movements.

He swallowed. His body was reacting to the visual images, even as his mind warned him that he shouldn't, that he mustn't.

Too late.

"You like that, don't you," Cathy said, and again it was an accusation, not a question. "You like watching that kind of thing and you like making me watch it. Maybe you have some other ideas, maybe you want me to do *that* to you."

She jerked her thumb violently over her shoulder and riveted his attention back to the screen.

"No," he said, but the denial was an instant too late, an instant too hesitant.

She didn't speak again. Suddenly she was dressed—or nearly—and rushing through the door, her shoes in one hand. She disappeared into the hallway.

"Wait! Cathy!"

Payne grabbed the sheet, still warm from her body, and threw it around his waist, feeling ridiculously like someone in a toga-party movie that had somehow gone fatally awry. Fully half the sheeting trailed behind him on the floor.

"Wait! I swear, I don' know how that got there. I didn't...I wouldn't try anything like that on you."

She was at the door. Her back was toward him, her hand on the knob.

The living room monitor showed the same scene. There was no sound except a thick static gurgling, which was just as well because the woman was obviously screaming in pain and the man was equally obviously reveling in her terror.

Cathy stopped, her shoulders stiff and her hand still touching the knob. But she didn't turn it. She didn't step through the door. Not yet.

He still had a chance.

"God's truth, Cathy. I didn't set this up. I don't know what happened. A cross-circuit, maybe. Maybe one of the sets shorted into an adults-only channel. I've been having some trouble with them lately."

He paused and watched her shoulders for some sign. They were still stiff. But she hadn't turned the knob.

"I wouldn't...I mean, I like...*love* you too much to do anything like this. Please. Please."

The final sounds hissed through the room, mingling with the static.

"I'll call you tomorrow," Cathy said finally. "We'll talk."

Her shoulders dropped—fractionally, it was true, but they dropped and he breathed a deep sigh.

"Okay. Tomorrow."

He didn't dare say more. Maybe this was enough to salvage things.

She turned the knob and was through the door before he could move. By the time he had crossed the living room and stood on the darkened porch, she was at her car. He watched her unlock the door and swing it open.

"I didn't do it," he called. "I swear."

"I'll call you tomorrow."

Then she was inside the car and the engine roared and the lights blinked on and she was gone. Payne stood on the porch. After a long while, his fingers loosened their grip and the sheet dropped to his feet. Then, after another long while, he noticed that he was cold and he went inside and closed the door and locked it.

The monitors were still playing, but even as he stood there, they flicked off. All at once, as if someone had thrown a switch, the living room was thrust into darkness. The bands of light beneath the doors in the hall died as well. The only light came from the bedroom.

He went down the hall, almost turning into the bedroom. At the last instant, he kept going. He opened the door to the Control Room. Everything was dark and still. The two players were off. Even the idiot lights were black.

He crossed the room and laid his hand on the machines. They were cold. They hadn't been running since the night before. The other equipment was cool as well.

"What the hell happened, then?" he asked no one in particular. The words hung on the air. There was no answer. "What the *hell* is going on?"

He returned to his room. The bed was a shambles. The covers were on the floor. The top sheet was missing and the bottom one was pulled out all around the mattress and lumped in the center of the bed. Even the mattress was twisted a couple of inches off the box springs at the head of the bed. The clothing he had worn that night was scattered everywhere, as if the room had been hit by a tornado, but he didn't remember their lovemaking as being that violent, that breathlessly rushed.

He glanced at the monitor.

Silvery blackness reflected only his shoulders and his face staring upward.

He turned out the light and threw himself onto the bed. Tomorrow he would call Tasco. He would get the guy out her to go over every inch of wiring in the damned house if necessary, but he would find out what the hell was happening and make sure it would never happen again. He would call Cathy and explain that…well, explain that he would make sure that she would never be subjected to anything like that again. That he loved her. That he wanted her to be with him.

The bed was uncomfortable and he was chilled but he did not move to rearrange the covers. He fell asleep.

CHAPTER THIRTY-SIX

As Payne slept, a subtle light fell across his body, outlining the line of muscle in his arm where it crossed his chest, of leg where it stretched toward the bottom of the bed. At first the light was silvery and Payne's body seemed etched in silverpoint, as if it were an anatomy study by Leonardo or Michelangelo come suddenly and gloriously to life. Then the light mutated into something else, assuming a reddish tone that made the blood rise to the surface of Payne's flesh and suffused him with a glow that was in some unutterable fashion more pornographic than the overt activities he and Cathy had glimpsed on the monitor minutes hours…a lifetime ago.

The monitor watched Payne, watched him sleep. He lay on his side, his knees drawn partway up as it to surround and protect. One hand lay half open near his mouth. It would take little imagination to believe that he was an infant, suckling his own thumb. The monitor patiently watched Payne's arms and legs as they moved slightly. It watched his eyelids flicker and twitch with the rhythmical movements of REM and deep sleep.

After a while, Payne rolled onto his back. His face was still averted from the light, as if even in sleep he were aware that it was shining down on him. With one movement he flung his arms away from his body, his hands fisted so tightly that his knuckles bled white. His legs stretched until he was nearly cruciform on the bed—a blood-red Christ against a shadow of blood-black shadows.

On the screen, the film flickered back into life. The man

knelt there, tumid and frightening and demanding. The woman returned too, and now beneath the blood her face shifted and altered. The cheekbones dropped fractionally, the eyebrows thinned, the lips curved just that much more. The changes were subtle and gradual. Even had he been awake Payne might not have noticed them.

But the changes were there nonetheless, definite and irreversible.

Beneath the blood and the terror and the pain, Cathy Litton stared mutely at the camera, her mouth open in voiceless agony, the transformation completed at the very moment that the woman in the movie choked and screamed and choked again and died.

CHAPTER THIRTY-SEVEN

A little after 8:30 the next morning, Payne made two telephone calls, both from Nick's.

"My phone's on the blink," he explained tersely as he walked through the front door past Nick and entered the living room. Nick had been awake for a while; that much was obvious by the half-eaten piece of toast he had in his hand when he opened the door to Payne's knock.

"You don't mind if I make a couple of calls from your phone, do you," Payne continued. "Local, of course."

"No problem," Nick answered just as curtly, leading the way into his bedroom-study and the only phone extension in the house.

"Help yourself." With that, he left the room.

Payne listened to the footsteps as Nick re-entered the kitchen. When he heard the scuffing sounds of a chair being slid across the linoleum—presumably Nick resuming his interrupted breakfast—he picked up the receiver and dialed the first number.

"Cathy?"

There was a long pause.

"Look, Cathy, don't be mad. I promise that I didn't have anything to do with that...with what happened. The set must have crossed wires or something, picked up a film from some porn channel or something. I don't know." The words came out in a rush, with no pauses for her to answer. He finally stopped speaking and listened to the sound of light breathing at the other end.

"Cathy?"

He heard nothing but the faint hissing of breath.

"Cathy, are you there?"

"Yes." This time he heard the relief in her voice as well as the words, flooding through him and felt a similar relief

"Look, what can I say? I'm sorry it ever happened. How about coming over tonight and letting me show you how sorry I really am. Dinner and...."

"Okay," she said quickly, "but at *my* house."

Payne hesitated for a second, then: "Sounds good. About seven all right?"

"Yes. And Payne," she added after an equal moment of hesitation, "don't wear too many layers. I might pick up a chess set in town this afternoon."

"Sure," he said, grinning as if she could see him through the wires. "See you tonight."

He braced the receiver against his shoulder as he pressed his finger on the set and cut the line. He lifted his finger, waited for the tone, then dialed the second number. He did not know this one by heart, so halfway through he had to dig a card out of his shirt pocket and refresh his memory.

"Tasco's Audio," the voice said. It sounded like the old man himself.

"Mr. Tasco?"

"Yes, sir."

"This is Payne Gunnison."

"Ah, Mr. Gunnison. We've gone over your DVD player carefully but I'm afraid that we can't...."

"I'm not calling about that right now. Something else happened last night, a cross-circuit between the tandem consoles and one of the satellite channels, I think."

"I'm sorry, Mr. Gunnison, but I don't think that such a thing is possible...."

"Well, maybe not. But something happened and I want the whole setup checked out as soon as possible. Today, if you can get to it."

After a few seconds of silence, Tasco answered. "That would be very difficult today, Mr. Gunnison. I am leaving at noon for my daughter's wedding in San Diego, and I won't be back until next Monday. I just came in this morning to take care of a few last minute...."

"I want it done today," Payne said, his voice abruptly harsh and grating. "Today, Mr. Tasco. Or I'll have to take my business to a shop I can depend on."

"No, Mr. Gunnison, that won't be necessary. I could send someone out...this evening perhaps? After we close at seven?"

Payne smiled. Good. The old man wasn't about to let *this* account slide, that much was obvious. Offering house calls and after-hours checks. Damned good.

"That will be fine," Payne began, then remembered that he would not be at home that evening. He would be with Cathy. For an instant, he felt a strong pull to call Cathy and cancel; he almost said something about it to Tasco when he shook off the impulse. What the hell, he thought, Tasco's been in the house often enough. He should be trustworthy if anyone is. "That will be fine," he repeated, "but I won't be home this evening."

"It would be much better if you could be there, to point out what was wrong."

"I *won't* be there," Payne said, suddenly and irrationally angry at Tasco's interfering tone. "I just told you that. And I'll tell you right now what is wrong. I hadn't set the players up at all. No discs, power off. In the middle of the night the monitor came on and showed a...."

"But that's impossible. There's no way that...."

"The monitor came on," Payne repeated forcefully, "and showed a...a pornographic film, I suppose from the After-21 channel or something."

"But your system isn't connected to any of those. They require special decoders that...."

"*I know that*," Payne said, his voice rising to a hollow screech as he yelled into the receiver. "*But the damned thing played a skin flick anyway. I want you to get your ass over here and fix it. Understood?"*

"Yes, Mr. Gunnison. I'll have to send my assistant...."

"I don't care who the hell you send. Just fix the damned thing!"

He stopped and forced his voice back down into its normal ranges. When he spoke again, he sounded like Payne Gunnison rather than like a harridan-voiced shrew. "I'll leave the key next door with Mr. Wheeler."

"All right." Tasco sounded emphatically less enthusiastic and more rigidly courteous than he had. "Tonight, Mr. Gunnison."

Good, Payne thought, *time to remind him who's boss, never let him forget that I pay him, not the other way around. Keep him on a short leash and make sure he gets the work done.*

"Tonight, then." Payne dropped the receiver into the cradle and turned around.

Nick was standing in the door way, staring at Payne.

"'I'll leave the key next door with Mr. Wheeler,'" Nick repeated sullenly. "What key? When?"

"The key to my place," Payne said. "Tasco's man is coming over here tonight to check out a problem with the system. He'll pick up the key from you."

"No," Nick said abruptly, turning away and disappearing into the kitchen.

Payne followed him. "What do you mean, 'No,'" Payne demanded.

"Just what I said. I don't want to have anything to do with Tasco or that...that psycho he has working for him."

"Come on, Nick, all you have to do is hand the man a key."

"No, I don't want to. And I resent the fact that I seem to be turning into your secretary. Pick up this, Nick. Deliver that, Nick. Wait around for something else, Nick. Stay at home to be at my beck and call, Nick. Did you think to check to see if I was even going to be home tonight?"

"Are you?" Payne's voice was cold.

"Well...yes, I guess so. But I wish you had asked me first,

anyway. I don't like that guy. I don't want to be anywhere *near* him."

For a moment, Payne felt like forcing the issue. *I own this house, I can kick you out on your ass whenever I want to, send you packing with all of your precious books. You better do what I say or else I'll....* Then he realized that this was Nick he was talking to, Nick Wheeler, the guy who was still his best friend in LA, probably the only friend he had right at this point. Instead of threatening, he nodded his head.

"Okay," he said. "You're right. I was out of line. I don't know why I didn't check first. Maybe it was just because I was on the phone and you were in the other room. I'll put the key in an envelope under the mat on the porch and leave a note for Tasco's man on the door. Would you mind keeping an eye out for him, though? You don't have to say anything, just make sure no strangers wander onto the porch and find the key. Tasco said he'd send him over some time after seven."

Nick nodded. "Okay. That much I can do."

"Good." Payne glanced at his watch. "Hey, it's getting late. I've got to get going. Thanks for the help. See you later."

With that he left the kitchen. Nick didn't follow. He didn't even see Payne to the door.

That's all right Payne told himself as he closed the front door. *He'll settle down later.* I'll have to invite *him over, maybe tomorrow night. Have some dinner. Watch a film or two. Play a little game of chess.*

Whistling a low tune, Payne crossed the lawn to his house.

CHAPTER THIRTY-EIGHT

By six-thirty, Payne's house appeared empty of all life. It was still bright daylight outside, California summer-daylight, golden and warm. But the house looked dark and cold, Nick thought as he glanced up from his desk at the shadowed porch. Even squinting he could only barely make out a small blot of white fluttering next to the door. It was probably the envelope with the note for Tasco.

Or Tasco's psycho helper.

Nick still didn't feel comfortable with the arrangements, not even with just having to watch for the guy. As far as Nick was concerned, the bastard could take a long walk off a short pier; he could stick his head in a bucket of water three times and bring it up twice; he could take a flying leap from any bell-tower on any campus in the glorious state of California. Nick thought of a couple more possibilities, feeling better with each one, until finally his mood broke and the house next door seemed less threatening and less shadowy.

He turned his attention to his books and read steadily for nearly forty-five minutes. He was just turning the page when the squeal of brakes sounded through the open window. He looked up. Along the edge of the window he could just make out the front bumper and tire of a van the same color and make as Tasco's.

It probably *was* Tasco's, he thought dispiritedly.

Until that moment, he had half hoped that no one would show. He dropped his hand and the page fluttered down as well. He sat back in his chair, watching to make sure the guy found the note.

No one appeared on the sidewalk.

He must be checking a work roster or something, Nick decided. He leaned forward, just enough to see the passenger window. Sunlight reflected from the glass, turning it opaque. And the angle was wrong anyway, so he could not tell for certain whether or not anyone was still in the van. He leaned further forward, letting his hands support his weight.

The front door rattled. Nick straightened and spun around, scattering his book and note cards onto the floor. His heart thumped unaccountably and his hand shook. Someone thumped insistently and impatiently on the door again.

"Just a minute," Nick yelled and half-ran out of the room.

He was breathing heavily by the time he pulled the door open.

"Tasco's," Ric said, his mouth twisted into what Nick could only think of as an evil grin.

Nick stared.

"The key, man. For next door. You got the key, right."

Nick stared. He shifted his weight until his body was mostly hidden by the door.

"Look, man, I got a job to do. I need the freakin' key!"

"I don't have it," Nick blurted out. "Payne...Mr. Gunnison left it under the mat. On his porch."

He slammed the door and leaned heavily against it. *That creep was one scary bastard!* Nick didn't know how or why, but Ric seemed threatening just standing in the doorway. Nick listened but did not hear any movement on the porch. In a cold sweat, he ran through the living room and into his bedroom and leaned over the desk and looked out the window.

Ric was just stepping up onto Payne's porch, one foot mashing down with what seemed unreasonable violence against the rough concrete. Nick watched intently to make sure that the man found the key. He didn't want anyone from Tasco's coming back to knock at his door.

At that moment, the man turned his head and looked into Nick's window. Their eyes caught for an instant—an infinitely horrifying instant for Nick, who felt all of his pent-up dread and horror concentrating in that single unwanted interchange before breaking and flooding through him. He drew back, then leaned forward only long enough to slam the window closed and shut the curtains.

By that time Ric was in the shadows of Payne's porch.

Nick stood numbly in the middle of his room for a long while. His hands trembled but otherwise he did not move. Finally, he stared around him, looking for all the world like someone just coming out of a coma, a Johnny Smith suddenly impelled back into this time and this place.

He glanced toward the closed and draped window.

Even though the material was translucent enough that the streetlights sometimes bothered him at night, he could see nothing of the house next door, not even a dark form penetrating vaguely through the curtains.

He breathed deeply and realized that his hands were shaking and that his heart was pumping wildly.

Forget Payne, he decided suddenly. I'm getting the hell out of here! He grabbed his wallet and checked on his money—three twenties and his credit cards. That would be plenty. The way he felt right now, two nickels and a plastic spoon would have been enough.

He rummaged up a pair of pants, an extra shirt, a pair of underwear, and a blue windbreaker with UCLA stamped in cracking white letters on the front and ran with them into the kitchen. Fortunately, he had parked his car on the side driveway for a change; usually he just left it out front where it was easier to get in and out. His driveway was barely single-car width, and the house on the other side—the non-Payne side—was bordered by ancient hibiscus plants that overhung Nick's driveway like the shadow of doom. He had meant to say something to the owners, but he had only seen someone in the house once or twice in the past year. Apparently they (if it was *them* and not just *him* or *her*) rose early, worked late, and spent most of their free time somewhere else.

For whatever the reason, he had never spoken to them about the bushes, had barely spoken to them at all in the time he had lived there. And besides, as he would have been the first to admit, the bright reds and yellows and pinks during the summer months created a beautiful view from his kitchen and through the side living-room window. So, finally, it was just easier and more convenient for him to park along the front curb. This once, though, because the last time he had driven it he had done his monthly shopping and didn't want to carry the heavy bags any farther than necessary, his car was parked between the two houses, with the bulk of his own place between him and the man at Payne's.

Nick slid into the front seat and started the engine. He backed up, reversing his usual direction and angling the rear of his car in front of his own house so that he could head down Greensward and away from Payne's. In the rear-view mirror, he saw the back of Tasco's truck. He couldn't see any of Payne's house.

Without knowing where he was going, except that he didn't plan on returning until late, late that night, maybe not even until well into the next day, Nick eased the car into first and drove slowly, quietly down Greensward, making as little noise as possible, like a nervous bridegroom trying to elope with an equally nervous bride under the nose of an irreconcilably angry future father-in-law.

CHAPTER THIRTY-NINE

Ric didn't even try to keep the smirk from wrinkling his face as he stomped up the sidewalk toward Gunnison's. He had known all along.

The little pansy, coming on to me like that, like I was a queer or something. I was right about that one, and I'm not gonna let him get away with it.

As he started up the steps to the house, he felt someone watching him. The back of his neck prickled and his skin grew warm along his neck. He turned in time to see Wheeler staring at him through the window, leaning so far forward that his goddam nose almost touched the glass, like he couldn't get enough of watching Ric, watching his shoulders and arms in the sleeveless T-shirt Ric had worn on purpose, watching his ass in his tight jeans. Ric shot a look that should have blistered his pervo eyes right out of the sockets, but Wheeler just kept looking so Ric turned and climbed the steps. He had plans for Wheeler but they would have to keep. Someone might see him if he went back now. It was still daylight. If he got inside Gunnison's place and puttered around in there until it was dark and no one could see him, he could slip across the bit of grass and teach that little rosebud a lesson, teach him that some people don't appreciate....
Later later later later, Ric promised himself. He grinned at the prospect.

In the meantime, there was an envelope flapping like a surrender flag from a tack in the door frame. He ripped it down and opened it, dropping the envelope at his feet. A gust of wind picked it up and swirled it around the porch until it finally landed smack in the seat of an old rusted swing.

Ric barely noticed. He studied the letter for a while before dropping to one knee and turning up the corner of the woven fiber mat. There he found another envelope, smaller than the first. A shape that felt like a key slid to one corner when he grabbed the envelope. He ripped it open, too, shook the key into his palm, and dropped the torn scraps of paper. This time there was no breeze. The paper lay where it fell.

He held the key up and examined it. He dug in his pocket and pulled out a Playboy Bunny keychain. A single key dangled from it. The two keys were identical.

"Damn," Ric said, "blew a buck-fifty on making that copy, and now Gunnison leaves me his own key, opens up the house for me. What a waste. Damn!"

He worked the copy loose from the key chain, hefted it in his hand, and then threw it into the bushes that lined the edge of the porch.

The other key fit smoothly—*sometimes they didn't and you had to jiggle and twist but this one fit smoothly just like slipping it into a chick*—and Ric turned it easily. The door swung opened. The house was surprisingly dark inside, almost pitch black, even though the sun was still a long way from setting. Ric walked on in, closing the door behind him and locking it from the inside. He slipped Gunnison's key onto the Bunny keychain and dropped the whole thing into his hip pocket.

He knew where the electronics systems were. He had been there before, of course, but this time he was alone. This time he was as interested in the rest of the house as he was in what waited in the back room. He felt for a light switch and turned the light on.

The living room gleamed so brightly that he had to close his eyes for a couple of moments. His eyes must have gotten adjusted to the shady porch, and now all this light reflecting from the white nearly blinded him.

The first thing he did was cross the room to check out the

monitor on the wall. *Not bad. New. Good condition.* He reached up to the mounting screws that held the bracket to the plaster. His fingers examined the smooth paint that covered the screws. *Philips head. Three. No problem.* This monitor alone should bring a couple hundred bucks or so. And there were more of them in the other rooms.

He glanced around. Four video cameras pointed toward the center of the room from brackets in each corner. He stood in front of one of them. The lens was wide enough that he could see himself in it as a dark blot against a white background. His body was distorted and his head foreshortened by the angle of the lens. On a quick guess, he figured he could get maybe two hundred each for the cameras.

Shit, nearly a thousand bucks, maybe more, just in this room!

There was nothing else, though. Nothing worth stealing.

He went down the hall, checking the rooms as he came to them, turning on the lights and stepping inside to survey the possibilities. There were monitors and cameras everywhere, at least one of each in every room. He could see his money roll growing thicker with each room.

Except for the video stuff, the place offered pretty slim pickings. A chair and a couch in one room. Nothing much in the bathroom except another monitor and camera.

"What does the guy do in here, anyway?" Ric asked himself aloud.

The echo from white plaster walls and white porcelain fixtures sounded spooky. He didn't say anything out loud for a long time after that. Still, he had asked what he figured to be an interesting question, and he began to imagine some equally interesting and arousing answers.

The room across from the bathroom was apparently Gunnison's bedroom. It looked too fussily prissy for Ric's taste. Effeminate, although he didn't consciously frame the word; in fact, he did not even *know* the word. He was content to look his contempt at the dinky little bed that just needed ruffles on the covers to make it look like it belonged to a Sweet Sixteen And

Never Been Screwed. Otherwise there was only a dresser and a closet.

He opened the closet and rummaged through the clothes. There was nothing there of interest. Gunnison had shitty taste in clothes, Ric decided. Everything was too small for him anyway.

He crossed to the dresser and opened the top drawer. Same here. Boring and bland. He saw neat rows of neat white crew socks with neat white heels and soles—Ric's own socks tended toward shades of gray and brown, depending on how long he went before finding some chick who would kill to do his washing for him. Next to them were rows of black dress socks folded not rolled, elastic tops facing outward. Ric tugged one top experimentally and ended up with a pair of dress socks hanging from his fingers. He flung them back into the drawer and slammed it shut.

He tried the next drawer. It was full of white T-shirts. Along the edge there was a stack of hankies ironed and folded like Ric's grandma used to do with his grandpa's when Ric was a kid. He snorted his growing scorn.

The next drawer afforded the first surprise of his visit. It was stuffed full of underwear. If he had thought about it, Ric would have expected Gunnison to stock up on plain white boxer shorts, probably starched and ironed and stacked exactly one on top of the other, just like everything else. At the very worst, there would be Jockeys, whiter and crisper than Ric was used to pulling on (when he bothered with underwear at all, which was rarely).

The riot of colors startled him. He pulled a pair out, holding them at a distance between his finger and thumb. He glowered at the skimpy briefs that were barely more than a band of elastic around the top and a pouch in front.

Shit, this guy's as wimpy as Wheeler, he thought. Maybe they get it on together over here, watch some fag movies and get it on in the bathroom or the kitchen.

He dropped the briefs like they were contaminated and pushed the drawer closed with his hip. He didn't open the rest of the drawers. He left the bedroom almost immediately.

The kitchen was a zero, too. He could locate no toaster, no Mr. Coffee, no microwave, nothing that he could pass on for a few more bucks.

So...it was just the electronics stuff. And the rest of that was all stored in the back room.

Before he opened the door, his mind had already begun toting up the street value of what he knew was there. Two more DVD players, pretty new and in top condition, with yards of top quality wiring connecting them. A couple of stereo systems— turntables, amplifiers, tuners. Three different radios, one with police bands, the other two not quite so sophisticated but all three worth at least a hundred more each.

And the records and tapes and cassettes and discs. All totally untraceable, especially the discs.

He ran his fingers over the film cases, noting titles, deciding which ones he would get rid of, which ones he would keep for himself. Gunnison had a good collection, including some pretty sexy things. Ric smiled.

But first....

He crossed over to the DVD consoles and began unplugging jacks, disconnecting wires, unscrewing screws. He lifted the first player out of its place on the shelf and carried it into the kitchen. He set it on the table near the door. He figured on getting most of the stuff in here, then backing the truck up to the door and moving it all after dark, when the truck would keep anyone from seeing what he was up to.

Except maybe the squirrel next door, but by then he won't be in any condition to say anything to anyone.

Ric smiled. It promised to be a good evening.

Oh, he would have to kiss the job with Tasco goodbye. No way he could pretend that he didn't have anything to do with this rip off. But by the time anyone found out that the stuff was gone, he would be gone with the stuff and Tasco's truck. He knew some guys out in the Valley that could handle this much loot easily. Then he would disappear for a couple months, take a vacation, maybe to Acapulco or somewhere before he came back and got into the stream again.

He returned to the back room for the second load.

He walked in. And stopped.

Something was wrong.

He listened. His ears were ringing fiercely, like he was standing under a high-tension wire on a scorching hot day. He shook his head and yawned to pop his ears. That helped a little, but not much. The ringing continued, as irritating as hell.

He looked around the room. Maybe something was running that he hadn't noticed.

Something was.

The monitor on the far wall glared at him.

Tough as he was—and Ric *was* tough, in spite of his obsessive, narcissistic posturing—he was startled.

There was more involved here than just a television screen playing to an empty room.

Enclosed in the gunmetal-gray rim that surrounded the screen, he saw an image of himself staring into a television screen.

He spun his head to stare into each corner of the room.

In the round lenses of four cameras he saw himself replicated.

"What the hell!" he shouted, breaking the silence.

No matter how he twisted or turned, the monitor continually showed the same thing: *him*, up close, his face distorted like he was seeing it through a fish-eye lens.

He slapped the on-off switch on the remaining console two or three times, but the monitor kept repeating his image through bands of snowy static that broke up the picture at eerily regular intervals.

"Shit!"

He was out the doorway and halfway down the hall before the thought of running clarified enough for him to know that he *was* running.

The living room was dark except for the light spilling from

that monitor. Without looking at the screen, he circled until he was standing in the middle of the room. He took a deep breath and raised his eyes.

He saw himself frozen in a facial close up so detailed that he could see pores in his skin. The white carpet he stood on, the white walls and the white furniture that surrounded him echoed reflections of colors from his dark hair, his dark eyes, his deep skin tones that stained the whiteness like clotting blood.

Ric was scared.

For the first time in his life, he was scared spitless.

And that fact scared him more than anything—that he could be so afraid when there was nothing in the place but a bunch of TV sets and cameras. It shouldn't bother him, but it did.

As he watched his own image on the screen, it changed. The camera angle drew back until his shoulders appeared, then his chest, encased in a black sleeveless T-shirt. The black material swallowed up most of the screen and the room suddenly grew darker.

At that instant, Ric bolted for the front door.

The second his fingers touched the brass knob, the room lightened briefly. There was a thin crackling, a suffocating ozone smell, and a piercing shriek from Ric that was swallowed whole by the white walls and white draperies as electrical current tore through his fingertips and up his arm, paralyzing it to the shoulder.

Before the sound died, he grabbed his injured arm and hugged it tightly against his chest as if that would bring back feeling, any feeling, even the shooting pain of the current. He swore, deeply and venomously and vehemently, and threw his weight against the locked door, almost numbing his good shoulder from the impact. His paralyzed arm dropped loose, flopping uselessly like a shirttail in a high wind.

Through his fear rose another complex of emotions, even more distressing for someone like Ric.

Embarrassment. Humiliation. Shame. Helplessness.

He grabbed his dead hand and tucked the fingers between his

belt and his waistband, tightening the worn leather around his fingers until they couldn't slip out. Then he turned back to face the house.

The front door was out as an escape route. That was obvious even to him. But there were windows he could crash through. The back door was part glass and therefore vulnerable. He forced himself to calm down and think things through. He closed his eyes and pulled gasps of air into his lungs. His muscles tingled with the effort. He focused his attention on his injured hand and arm. He slapped his forearm as hard as he could.

Yes! There was a tingle. The fingers wobbled when he tried to move them. He slapped himself again, and once again. The tingling increased to a low pain.

At this rate, he would be all right in a few minutes. There had been no permanent damage. Nothing he couldn't handle if he....

The lighting changed.

He glared at the monitor, as much in anger now as in fear.

It showed him full-figure, his arm limp at his side, his hand tucked ridiculously into his belt. He was staring at himself, and the expression on his face startled him.

Suddenly the monitor showed a different room and a different figure. He stared at it, trying to identify the figure that floated like a gray shadow through a static-fogged background. It seemed hunched, dark, twisted, but it was moving.

There was someone else in the house with him.

Ric straightened and smiled. This was something he could handle. Whoever figured on mind-fucking him was in for the shock of his lifetime.

"Who's here?" he yelled, his voice loud and steady. "Who the hell's in here?"

The only answer he received was a dead silence relieved by the electronic buzzing from the monitor.

"Come on out, the game's over," he called. "I know you're here. Wheeler, you bitch, is that you?"

He raced down the hall, slamming doors open and scanning each room in turn. As he went, he continued yelling obscenities, describing in graphic detail what he was about to inflict on Wheeler's body when he found him.

There was no one in any of the rooms.

When Ric reached the back room, he stopped in the doorway. From there he could see the screen. It was still playing the image of the crippled figure. Now it was closer to the camera, but still shadowed so deeply that Ric could make out no details. Except that it seemed threatening.

He backed out of the doorway and backed down the hall, closing each door as he came to it and locking out the sight of the monitors that repeated the same image as if it were a short loop running incessantly over and over.

Without knowing it, he found himself backing into the living room, watching the hallway for any signs of intruders.

Something struck his leg.

He spun, and in doing so tipped a small table over and spilled chess pieces across the room.

He regained his balanced and tried to take stock of what was happening.

His arm was tingling more now, and the fingers moved enough that he could pull them from the belt. He still couldn't lift the arm but at least it wasn't flopping around and getting in his way.

It was his right arm, too. His fighting arm. He had to reach across with his left and dig awkwardly in his hip pocket for the knife he always carried after working hours.

When he finally worked it out, it felt odd and foreign in his grasp. But he had fought left-handed in a pinch more than once. He didn't like to, but he could do it now.

He crouched in a fighting stance, the knife weaving in front of him as if he expected attack from any quarter.

"It's no use."

The voice came from nowhere and everywhere, as if the walls themselves had spoken. Ric was so startled that he nearly dropped the knife.

"Who's out there?" he yelped, and this time his voice broke

into high ranges he hadn't heard in years, not since he became a man and stuck it into his first woman.

"You can't fight me." The voice had an odd timbre to it, as if it were coming from a machine rather than a human.

Ric couldn't tell whether it was male or female, probably because it was distorted somehow to make the game more exciting for the prick who was dumping all of this shit on him.

"Yeah? That so? Get your ass out here and we'll see. Stop hiding, Wheeler, come on out and face me!"

"You want to see me? Very well."

The figure in the screen was more distinct now. The reception was still lousy, though, Ric noted even though his rising panic.

The picture suddenly broke up into static lines. The faint hints of color died into stark black-and-white. He couldn't even tell which room was being filmed.

"I got a knife," he yelled, brandishing the four-inch blade into the air in front of him. As he moved, he caught a movement out of the corner of his eye.

He whirled.

One of the cameras had swiveled in its bracket to focus on him. A small red light just below the lens blinked slowly on and off with hypnotic regularity. Ric checked the other three cameras. Each was tilted directly toward him, and each showed the same red light.

He backed up until his legs struck the edge of the couch. The cameras followed him. They moved when he moved and stopped when he stopped.

His eyes darted to the middle of the inner wall where the monitor glowed like a demon's eye.

The figure had disappeared.

In its place, the screen now displayed something that sent chills in a rapid tattoo up and down Ric's spine.

It showed *him* again.

But this time the image was not simply Ric the way he was standing in the living room.

In this new apparition, his arms were raised over his head as if he was trying to surrender—*come out with your hands up—come in and get me, you dirty copper!* The face on this other Ric was twisted like he was screaming his throat raw, but no sounds came out of the screen.

He stared at the picture.

He didn't even notice when the knife dropped from his hand because at that moment the picture died, then the screen readjusted itself to show him again.

He was naked, trying to cover himself with one hand while the other flopped helplessly at his side. This Ric *this chicken-shit coward, that wasn't him at all, never him, never*—was crying openly. Tears streaked his face. Yellow-green tendrils of snot dribbled from his nose. The lips quivered like a baby's.

"No. *Noo!*" he screamed. He tore his eyes away long enough to look at the cameras.

The red lights were blinking more rapidly, almost in sequence with each other.

When he turned back, his image had disappeared from the screen and the figure had reappeared, closer to the camera now and blocking out most of the background. The picture was clearer, but Ric still couldn't see who or what it was other than just a dark form that seemed shrouded in blackness but that reached out toward him with something that sparkled and glistened and shot a tremor of terror through him even before he recognized it.

When he did, he screamed again.

It was his own knife. Locked into an image on a TV screen.

He looked down at his feet where the knife had fallen.

It was gone. In its place he saw a knot of fluorescence that became a sparkle of blue like an electrical spark thrown from an overloaded transformer in a dark room.

He looked up at the monitor.

His image was back, still naked, still struggling as if against invisible bonds, still trying to cover himself with his hand and in the background some music played, something that he had heard before—that was it, "Satin Blue," the music from that flick he had seen last year, the one with the creep who tortured and murdered, the film where this woman finds a man in her closet and comes at him with a knife and makes him strip while she kneels in front of him with the knife and *something flashed across the screen, something blue and quick and threatening and there was a spurt of blood from the groin and his image screamed* and Ric screamed as the blade sliced through his groin, severing the worn threads of his jeans as if they did not exist and cutting deeply into his flesh.

But the real pain, the pain that he felt in the instant before realization and shock set in, was not that of a knife.

It was an electrical current, a blue-white flash of power that slit him from groin to throat, that snapped along his spine like a high power line in a hurricane. It tore his breath from his throat, the air from his lungs so that he could not scream. It wrapped his testicles and his bleeding sex in living pain and twisted and tore and at the last instant he saw himself in the monitor, bleeding and dying and falling, and he saw the figure in front of him now, no longer encased in metal and plastic but *it can't be but there it is, shit there it* is standing not a yard from him, hunched and shadowed, the bloody blade of his own knife gripped in one twisted hand.

"Who...?" Ric tried to say, but all that came out was a liquid gurgle.

The knife moved again, swiftly and unerringly. This time it was aimed higher and penetrated his stomach.

The figure thrust once, and Ric could feel its hand against his gut when the knife pressed into his stomach. The skin was hot and sticky and felt like a Fourth-of-July sparkler pressing against Ric's flesh.

Then the sparkle burst into an explosion of pain as the knife twisted upward, gutting him.

He might have died then. By all the laws of nature he probably should have died then, either from shock or from trauma or from loss of blood. But he didn't.

Instead, the red lights beneath each of the cameras began blinking so rapidly that they became a blur, and in the instant that the knife penetrated Ric's heart, they flashed into fingers of blood-red flame that whipped across the room and encircled him from four directions.

The figure reached out and became part of the flame and in joining it transformed hot red into cold blue. He didn't die, much as he desperately wanted to, not even when the real pain started. Nor did he die when layer after layer of skin was stripped from his body and disintegrated and then sucked away to become part of the blue flame that grew stronger second by second. Nor even when the muscles and sinews and tissues of his body sloughed off and the flame consumed them as well. Not until the bones began to disappear, first the small bones of the fingers and toes, then the larger bones in the legs and arms and ribs—only then, perhaps, did Ric finally die, although it would have been impossible to name the precise instant when life ceased to be enclosed by what remained of a human husk.

When finally what did remain was no longer recognizable as human, the blue lights flashed once in concert, blindingly bright, and then there was darkness throughout the house.

Almost.

First in one room, then the next, finally in each room, the screens came alive.

Each showed variations on the same image. Ric helpless. Ric emasculated. Ric subjugated and submitting. Ric screaming for release while the phantom-figure toyed with him as cruelly as a satiated cat played with a terrified mouse.

The episodes all ended the same way. Ric died. Then there would be a moment of blackness and quiet (*let's all stand and observe a moment of silence in memory of....*) before the sequence began again, the loop repeating over and over.

If the images had been merely films, they would have been perverted and inhuman.

But they were not films.

And throughout each agonizingly infinite second, Ric finally understood that this cruelty would never come to an end, that he would never truly die.

CHAPTER FORTY

Payne arrived home just after three o'clock. He had planned on staying the night at Cathy's. She had apparently planned on it, too, and in spite of the passionate intensity of their love-making (or perhaps because of it), she was obviously angry when he woke suddenly and got out of her bed and began pulling on his clothes.

"What's wrong?" she asked.

There was no light on in the room except the diffuse glow of LA at night from outside the window. He didn't answer. Cathy sat up and turned on the light.

"What are you doing?" This time it was more a demand than a question.

"Got to get home," he said.

"Why? Can't you...."

"No! I've got to get home." He grabbed his shoes and socks and opened the bedroom door.

"I can't explain it," he said in an attempt at placating her. "I've just got to get home."

And with that he was gone.

As soon as he pulled up in front of his place an hour later, he knew that his feelings had been right. Something was wrong. There was a van parked by the curb. Tasco's van. It should have left long before.

He killed his engine, jumped from the car, and ran up the steps.

The front door was locked. He rattled it but it felt secure. No one had broken in, at least not this way.

He glanced around and saw the remains of the two envelopes scattered on the porch. He fished out his own key and opened the door.

It was dark inside, pitch black, and the air was heavy with an unfamiliar odor, oily and coppery and ashy all combined into something that made Payne's stomach lurch. He rushed in, hitting the light switch as he did so.

Just inside the door, he stopped.

He was a fool, he realized, for running in like that. If there was a thief and he was still in the house, Payne had just set himself up as a perfect target. He could get killed.

He backed into the entryway and listened.

Nothing. Not a sound.

"Hey, anyone in there?" he called.

Still nothing. No footsteps, no slamming of the back door.

"I'm armed and I'm coming in," he called again, his voice echoing through the house. He looked around the edge of the entryway into the living room. Everything seemed in order. He crossed the living room, went down the hall, opening doors as he went. Everything seemed to be as he had left it.

Except the kitchen.

One of the DVD consoles sat on the kitchen table. Payne hurried into the control room and breathed a sigh of relief. Everything else was there except the unit Tasco was repairing and the one on the table. For an instant, he considered forgetting the whole thing, then he realized that even though there had been no robbery, something strange must have happened. The damned truck was still parked out front. His equipment had been moved. And there was that lingering odor and the greasy feeling in the air as he breathed.

He went straight to the telephone and called the police.

They arrived within fifteen minutes. He explained everything as best he could. They snooped through the house, opening doors and cabinets and drawers. They even called Cathy to check Payne's own statement that he had come directly from her place.

"Just routine," one of the officers assured him, but after a while it almost seemed as if they suspected Payne of doing something, maybe wiping out Tasco's man for the sadistic fun of it. Finally they came to a decision.

"There's really nothing we can do, Mr. Gunnison," the officer said as he stood under the porch light and slipped a notebook back into his pocket. "There's no sign of forced entry. You admit that you left a key under the mat."

"Stupid move," the other cop muttered, but Payne elected to ignore him.

"And nothing is missing," the first continued, also choosing to ignore his partner's remark.

"Except, of course, one TV repairman," Payne said.

"Yes, there is that. But there's no evidence that he was here long, or that he left under duress. We'll contact Mr. Tasco about the truck

"No good," Payne said impatiently. "He's out of town for the week. I don't know where exactly. Someplace near San Diego."

"We'll see what we can do to locate him," the officer said, "and in the meantime we'll get the truck towed away."

To impound it, Payne thought, but he didn't care about that.

He was tired and confused and frustrated. As he stood on the porch watching the cops leave and realized that dawn was breaking and that his shoulder and hip and knuckles hurt so badly that he would have to take at least three or four Excedrin this time to knock the pain down, he didn't care about anything.

He went inside and dropped onto his bed.

He fell asleep almost immediately, so he missed the moment when the screen over his head flickered on to replay again and again and again the agonies and the intimacies of Ric's death.

Payne woke several hours later feeling unusually refreshed.

He stretched and was relieved to find that all his joints moved easily, without any hint of pain.

CHAPTER FORTY-ONE

When Payne woke at 8:30, he wanted to talk to someone but there was no one. Nick was gone, had apparently been gone all night, certainly since before Payne himself got home. Nick's car was not in the drive, the house was locked up and had that indefinable air of an empty place, even if the emptiness has lasted only an hour or so. Payne had no idea where Nick might have gone.

That left Cathy but he was afraid to call her at all. After the fiasco with the film two nights before, and his running out on her last night—*this morning*, he corrected himself—any hopes he might have had of a deepening, even a continuing relation- ship with her seemed dim at best. He still wasn't entirely certain why he had rushed away. All he could remember was that he had been lying half asleep next to her when the flash had come, so quickly and fragmentary that he could not tell precisely what it was. But it had impelled him to leave. Not even Cathy would be willing to take that explanation as excuse for the way he had behaved.

Other than Nick and Cathy, there were only the lawyers, a mercenary lot who had apparently cared little for Aunt Emilia and now cared less for Payne. As a person. As a client, of course, he was number one on their hit parade and would remain until the last hint of legal complexity concerning the will was resolved. Sometime around the year 2020, Payne thought bitterly. But to call one of them at 8:30 in the morning and ask for help, even for a listening ear—that was patently impossible.

For a long time, he moped around, sitting in a chair, slouching on the sofa, wandering into the kitchen for a drink, stopping to fix toast and eggs and wash up afterward and discover to his amazement that it was not yet nine and he only had most of the day stretching endlessly before him instead of all of it.

He thought about working in the yard but could not bring himself to go out and drag the mower from its final resting place.

He even thought about watching a film or two. But today he could not. The towering shelves of cases had no draw for him; or, rather, they seemed vaguely repellant, as if part of him were interested, part of him were not.

The slack-eyed monitors made him nervous.

He finally decided on finishing his laundry. He loaded soiled clothing into the washer, then watched it whish and swirl with the intensity of a mother hen whose chicks are about to leave the nest. He hung his things out on the line in the back yard, pinning the wooden clothes pins onto the material with a savagery that surprised and frightened him. He was glad when the chore was over and his clothes fluttered in the breeze like a neat line of ghosts waving poignant farewell to the living. White T-shirts, white socks, white sheets and pillowcases, white towels—hand and kitchen varieties.

It wouldn't be hard to learn to hate white, he thought. He remembered his mother's clothesline as a riot of color even when she did whites, what with the pastel bands and prints on nearly everything. His eyes ached from that memory and from the glare of sunlight reflecting from his own wash.

He went back into the kitchen and took two Excedrin. He swallowed them with a glass of water, remembering with shuddering horror and an acid flavor at the back of his throat the story Nick mentioned once about some guy who dry-swallowed them. Sure way to go crazy, Payne thought, grimacing from the bitter after-taste of the two pills.

Another glance at the clock. 11:53. Almost half the day dead.

He sat at the table in the kitchen, thinking about nothing in particular and drawing invisible arabesques with his forefinger on the flat white surface.

12:15.

He stood and walked over to the telephone and lifted the receiver and, before his better sense and his pride got in the way of simple decency, dialed Cathy's number.

Before it rang through, he set the receiver back on the hook and stepped away.

After what seemed a long while, he lifted it again and dialed and dropped it back down with a clatter that echoed through the room.

On the third try, he finally allowed the circuit to ring through. He listened through five rings, six, seven. At ten he would hang up.

Eight.

Nine.

"Hello?" It was her voice. "This is Cathy Litton. Hello?"

"Don't hang up, Cathy," he said, although that was not what he intended to say.

She didn't answer him but she didn't hang up, either.

"I'm sorry about last...this morning. I just got a feeling that... that something was wrong here at home. I couldn't explain it and I didn't want to say anything for fear that you would think I was crazy. But that was all. Really."

He waited for the passage of three heartbeats, then:

"Cathy?"

"Yes, Payne, I'm still here."

He took a deep breath. "Well, there was something wrong."

"I know. The cops called me, remember? Making sure you had been with me."

He heard a brittleness in her voice that bothered him.

"I'm really sorry. Things have gotten out of hand. But believe me, I'm trying to take care of it. Really." He heard a sharp intake of breath.

"Are you all right," she asked quickly.

"Yeah, I'm fine. The robbery, or attempted robbery at least, was nothing. Some of the audio stuff was moved around.

Nothing missing, though. I don't quite know what happened. The police checked everything out and left and..."

"Payne," Cathy said, her voice soft and low. "Are you sure you're all right. Are you telling me everything? You sound... strained. Tired."

"Tired," he said with a curt laugh that punctuated the word. And then he realized that it was true. "Yeah. I'm tired. I haven't had much sleep since I left your place. And"—*come on let her know how you feel about her don't keep it in any more she has a right to know*—"I sure didn't get much sleep there. Thanks to you. I…uh...I love you, Cathy."

His ears burned and his cheeks felt like flames. After all, she was beautiful and talented and clever and loving and probably had more boyfriends than she knew how to handle and he was only a stumbling idiot from back East who seemed to know how to get into more trouble with her than any single individual might be expected to manage.

Well, if worse comes to worse and she laughs at me, I can always stay away from her part of Southern California. Keep most of LA's millions between us.

He waited for her answer.

"Payne," she began, and he knew how she would continue: "You're a nice enough boy but....," followed by a hundred and one reasons why he should never have been born. He felt like he did when he asked the most popular girl in his high school class to a movie: "No thanks. You're a nice enough but...." He had been crushed but at least it had been good practice for what was to come this time. He braced himself.

"Payne, I think I'm in love with you too. It's just that you can be...well, that there are some things we need to talk about. Seriously. Can you come over tonight."

Can I come over—watch out for my dust! Watch me fly!

"Sure. And Cathy...."

"Yes?"

"Thanks."

She laughed. She didn't even ask him what he was thanking

her for—maybe he didn't know for sure himself, but her response broke something and he laughed.

They spoke for a few more minutes, then he hung up, slowly, almost sadly. The interlude has been wonderful, perfect. She had given him more and forgiven him more than he had a right to expect. Much more. He looked around the kitchen, at the white cabinets and refrigerator and walls.

Out of the corner of his eye he saw the wash flapping on the line, wraith-like and insubstantial. The fluttering quickened and expanded until it seemed as if all he could see was white. He had driven through a snowstorm in Minnesota once during a Christmas vacation with a couple of cousins. They had been caught in a whiteout. Even that did not compare with the barren absoluteness that seemed crowding in on him at that moment.

Suddenly he couldn't stand not to take a physical action that would match the elation he felt inside, *not* to break through the veil of white that surrounded him and froze him and suffocated him, *not* to see color in the wilderness of white.

Let there be color!

He wrenched the refrigerator open and, after a glance up and down the shelves, grabbed the plastic squeeze bottle of catsup jammed securely behind the little silver railing on the inside of the door. He pulled the bottle out, up-ended it until the catsup had drained into the narrow neck and backed up against the lid, then opened the lid and shut the refrigerator door with a kick of his heel.

He stood in the middle of the room and closed his eyes. Suddenly he flailed his arms in wide manic circles, laughing as his fingers squeezed the plastic bottle. Coldness and dampness splattered his face and he laughed again. He felt more coldness and dampness on his neck and arms. Then there was no more and the bottle made an empty sucking sound when he relaxed his grip.

He stood for a moment, breathing so heavily that he was almost sobbing, inexplicably afraid to look. Finally he opened his eyes.

The kitchen looked like a slaughterhouse. Every surface was stained with drops or blobs or masses of deep crimson where the catsup had been flung around. He had expected to see...well, to see life and energy, color and vitality. Instead, he saw only blood and death and the charnel house.

He looked down. He was covered, head to foot with the stuff.

Images from countless splatter films forced their way into his imagination. *Friday the Thirteenth* carried to the nth degree. *Halloween* ad infinitum. *Slaughter This* and *Massacre That.*

He shuddered.

He stripped out of his stained clothes and tossed them into the sink and filled the sink with cool water. He remembered from somewhere that hot water would lock the stains in. He squirted a capful of Ivory dish detergent into the water—*even the bottle is white*—and swirled it around with his fingertips until a scum of foam formed. The water was tinged with red and the tiny soap bubbles were frothy and pink, like a visible, last gasping breath of a man dying of tuberculosis. He shivered again but not from coldness.

Leaving his clothes to soak, he looked around at the mess. He would have to clean it all up soon, before the catsup had a chance to dry. He remembered all too well how hard it could be to scrape catsup off plates that had sat overnight after hot-dog bashes during the summers at home.

He sighed and started in.

There were some old rags on the back porch. He wadded them up and used them to scrub the cabinets and the walls and the floor and the windows. He sponged the table clean, leaving pink soapy foam wherever the sponge passed. It must have taken him well over an hour before he was even close to finished.

Most of the stuff was off the walls and floors when he ran out of rags. Everyone he could find was already sodden and red-stained. They lay lumped together on the concrete floor of the back porch, looking like a gigantic suppurating wound swollen with hot pus. The sight made him slightly nauseous.

Only the windows were left to clean, though. He wrung the

last rag as dry as he could, hoping that it would be absorbent enough to clean the red scum from the glass, but all it did was smear it and make the window look even filthier. The sunlight glared through the glass, bright and red-tinged.

What he needed, he realized, was newspapers. That was a trick he remembered from home. The best way to get a window spotless was to finish drying it off with newsprint. The first time he heard about it he was skeptical, but when he saw the results he was convinced. Something in the ink pulled the dirt off, something like that. He wasn't sure how it worked, but he knew that it did. It left neither streaks nor a light powdering of tissue filaments.

The only problem was that he didn't have any newsprint.

He did have something else, though. Plenty of it. Something that he wanted to get rid of anyway.

He went into the bathroom and took a quick shower, rinsing off the thin layer of sticky catsup-and-soap that had settled on his skin while he cleaned. He toweled dry and pulled on a pair of cut-offs. He pulled a kitchen chair into the hall and stood on it to open the access into the attic.

The box sat there, right where he had put it days before. He didn't bother to climb into the attic—trying that from the chair would have been too precarious, since his shoulders barely cleared the opening and he had no desire to pull himself by brute force over the dust-caked rafters and up into the attic.

Instead he balanced on his tiptoes long enough to pull open the box flaps and grab the top half dozen or so magazines. He dropped them at his feet without looking at where they fell and closed the flaps. He slid the access cover closed and stepped down from the chair. His bare foot slipped on one of the glossy surfaces and threw him off balance. He tumbled backwards, ending up on his side amidst a flurry of full-color photographs. For an instant he froze, seeing in one of the photographs a pose that must have been, for the photographer at least, identical to the one he had inadvertently taken. Except that he was clothed.

He scrambled to his feet and stuffed the magazines into a

disorderly pile and carried them, still without looking at them, into the kitchen. He dumped them unceremoniously onto the counter next to the sink and ripped a handful of pages from the first and crumpled them up and began rubbing away at the catsup-stained glass.

Magazine paper didn't work as well as newsprint. The glossy surface seemed to smudge and smear more than it cleaned. He tossed the sodden wad of paper into the trash can underneath the sink and ripped out another handful of pages.

The same. They made only a marginal difference on the windows.

He pressed harder, drawing the paper across the glass. The twisted curve of a leg protruded between his fingers. He dropped the paper and shrank back as if he had been burned. He grabbed the wad and threw it into the trash can after the first. Then the rest of the magazines, still in their disorderly heap.

He heard them thud on the bottom of the can, a strangely hollow, echoing sound. His headache was back.

He looked at the clock.

A little after five.

He couldn't finish the job right now, that was sure. Tomorrow. After he had a chance to talk everything through with Cathy.

He started from the kitchen. Still barefoot, he skidded on a damp spot just under the door. He didn't fall but the change in balance was enough to throw him against the doorjamb.

His hip struck the wood, then his shoulder. His fingers wrenched as he tried to stabilize himself. And then the danger was over. He was fully balanced again. But the side of his body ached as if it were on fire.

He took another shower, a lingering warm one, then dressed in slacks and sport shirt and lay down on his bed. Just for a moment.

Just to relax.

CHAPTER FORTY-TWO

Payne woke with a start. The hands on the electric clock in the bedroom said 7:23.

He jerked himself out of bed and almost stumbled when he put his weight full on his right side. The shoulder felt inflamed, the hip joint so bruised that he had trouble standing straight. And he was late. He wasn't sure if Cathy would put up with one more piece of strange behavior from him. He would have to hurry.

He limped to his dresser and opened two drawers, pulling out clean white socks and a pair of undershorts—noting absently that one pair was lying haphazardly on top of the others rather than being neatly folded and stacked as was his wont. He opened his T-shirt drawer and took out one that had faded from pristine white to ivory over the years. There was a tear along the right arm, but he pulled it on anyway, wincing when his shoulder registered pain.

His old jeans were hanging in the closet where he had put them after washing them. He struggled into them, hampered both by the tightness of the denim and by the pain in his leg. When he finally got them on, his limp was accentuated by the tautness of the material on his hips. He experimented walking up and down the hall a few times, trying to eliminate the lurching imbalance as much as possible. The pain had lessened. He ambled into the kitchen to swallow a couple more Excedrin.

He was standing at the front door, his hand just touching the brass knob and his body reflected distortedly in its smooth surface, when he realized that he had forgotten where he was going. He thought for a moment. Stupid, of course he knew, it was important, he was going to...to....

His ears buzzed lightly but enough to distract him from his thinking.

Hold on, concentrate, I'm going to see...see...see *her*.

He breathed his relief.

Her.

He was going to see her and talk to her and they would understand each other perfectly and they would become one and live forever after....

Her.

Cathy Litton. The woman he loved.

He gripped the knob with his hand. His head ached again, suddenly and insistently. He opened the door and stepped out. He was on his way to see....

Who?

He thought about taking another couple of Excedrin but decided against it. The cool evening air should help. He would open the windows of the car and let the cool air rush over his face. He would close his eyes to receive its gentle touch on his cheeks, breath in its fragile fragrance through his nostrils.

And then he was in the car, the engine roaring as he depressed the accelerator and pulled away from the house. The setting sun reflected in a quick, solitary wink from the attic window.

The evening traffic was light. At least lighter than he had expected.

He decided to avoid the freeway. After all there must be hundreds of other ways to get there. He might see some place new and different and enjoyable.

He settled into the seat and drove, barely noticing street signs and angles and directions. His mind settled into a numbing rhythm.

Shift, clutch, shift, brake, shift, clutch. Mechanical. Mindless. unthinking.

A dim part of himself, almost buried beneath the rubble of

collapsing consciousness cried out a single word: *Cathy*!

Payne sat up straight, startled to see his car hurtling through a red light on a street he did not recognize. For an instant he considered pulling over to the curb and getting his bearings. The meeting with Cathy was too important to take any chances on getting lost. He twisted in his seat, trying to get more comfortable, then it registered with a shock like an electrical current that he was not wearing his slacks and sport shirt. The jeans were the tight ones that he had intended to throw out; the T-shirt, a hopeless wreck that was more holes and thin patches than shirt and was only waiting for one more good rip before it found its way into the rag bin. His feet were snug inside tennis shoes instead of the roomier polished loafers he had set out at the side of his bed earlier that evening.

"What...?" he began.

He pulled the steering wheel sharply to the right, barely bothering to check in the rear view mirror for on-coming traffic. The car swerved into the parking lane of a three-lane boulevard, bouncing off the low concrete curb with a wrench that sent a lance of pain up his arm. He twisted the wheel back to the left, not even bothering to check this time, but luck was with him and there were no cars following so closely that they couldn't swerve and miss him.

He steadied into the middle lane, heading up toward the foothills just beneath the *HOLLYWOOD* sign. As soon as he pulled away from the curb, the pain subsided.

He kept driving, aimlessly following street after street.

Maybe ten minutes later, his shoulder knotted up suddenly from tension and from the wrong angle of the seat. He fingered the lever at the side of the seat and the back gave an inch or two. That felt better. He lowered the seat another inch. *Ahhh, much better*. He settled into the depths of the seat, letting his free hand rest lightly on his thigh.

As the car began climbing the first steep hills, his fingers tightened and curled until they touched his palms.

By now it was dark. The streets were unrecognizable. Most of them were lined with dark apartments characterized by drawn shades and closed doors. Only the intersections were lit, with a flurry of stoplights and pedestrian-crossing lights and overflow lights from businesses on the busier cross-streets. He passed three such streets, not bothering to check the names, then on the fourth he veered right and turned.

This part of L.A. looked familiar. Not in specifics—he still didn't know what street he was on; but in general it felt familiar. Right.

He kept driving.

CHAPTER FORTY-THREE

Leigh pushed raggedly long blond hair out of eyes that seemed as hollow as tombs, spectral as well as sepulchral beneath the harsh glare of the neon lights overhead. It was twilight; the evening was just beginning and the traffic on Sunset was picking up like it always did. Cars rolled by, slowly the first time, even slower the second; by the third time, the drivers made little pretense of wanting to get anywhere. They cruised more or less openly, twisting their heads to see through the windows, squinting against the glare. Most of the time, especially when they leaned forward to talk with the drivers, Leigh and the others were reduced to little more than silhouettes.

The evening breeze rose slightly, drifting up from the valley floor to nuzzle the foothills. Even at that, though, it was warm, hot almost beneath the lights, and Leigh hoped that the right one would come along soon. The new boots that had been in a Kirby's window front only four hours before pinched—nothing serious, just enough to let the owner know that they were new and to make standing around like meat on a rack that much more miserable.

But what else was there to do?

Leigh needed money; the drivers needed...companionship.

Two needs satisfied with one simple exchange.

A couple of cars drifted past, but Leigh didn't try to catch the drivers' attention. Two were middle-aged men, too old for Leigh's taste, and for a while yet Leigh could allow taste to dictate over necessity. Last night's work had been good; the economic crunch was not critical yet.

Leigh yawned hugely, and then surreptitiously (as if surreptitiousness were necessary) undid the top two buttons on a vividly printed top that would have been more at home amid the bikinis and beach towels at Zuma. Deeply tanned flesh glinted in the neon light.

Leigh imagined the effect and leaned back, satisfied.

A red light blinked to green a block away. In a few seconds the next shift of drivers rolled past. Leigh watched closely without seeming to—eyes narrowed against the light but not enough to crease at the corners or furrow the brow. That would eventually be fatal. Leigh was still young in a city and in a market that placed its highest premium on youth—or at least the illusion of youth. But there was no use taking stupid risks.

Three cars passed without slowing down. One was filled with kids, hubby driving and wifey nagging him as they went. They were lost or something. Leigh heard enough to know that she was yammering at him for misreading the map. The kids watched the passing lights with eyes that glittered as brilliantly as did the neon lights that attracted them. One of the kids— Leigh couldn't tell if it was a boy or a girl but it had longish hair and an androgynously round face and smiled sweetly—waved as they passed. Leigh raised a hand and waved back. Mums must have seen the gesture because she whirled around and slapped the kid's hand. The car disappeared before Leigh heard the kid crying.

By then, the clock on the bank building across the block had announced that it was fifteen minutes into prime time. Leigh leaned against the peeling wooden frame of a garishly lit window and undid another button. More tanned skin glowed. More provocative shadows curved beneath the neon lights.

For a moment, there was an unusual pause in traffic, then… *wait, isn't that the same car that went by just a couple of minutes ago—long enough for it to turn at the next intersection, follow the block around, and pass by right here, right now.* Leigh knew to the millisecond the time it would take. There was no mistake.

Yeah, the car was a repeat all right.

From what Leigh could see of him, the driver looked okay, although Leigh was experienced to know that looks meant nothing in this business. Mr. Clean could be carrying any number of foul diseases, and Mr. Hot-to-Trot could have a blade in his pocket that would cool anyone's action. Still, this guy *seemed* a likely prospect.

Leigh settled down for the waiting game. By the clock on the bank, three minutes and forty-seven seconds elapsed before the car passed again. The time was a bit faster than usual but still possible, assuming that the driver took the alley half a block south of Sunset and drove faster than was strictly safe.

The car began slowing nearly a block before it approached Leigh's spot; by the time the license was visible, it couldn't have been going over five miles an hour.

Okay, this is it, Leigh decided in a breath and stepped to the edge of the curb.

The car slowed to a quiet stop. Leigh waited. After a long pause, the driver leaned over and rolled the passenger window down.

"Hi," he said. He sounded nervous.

"Got the time?" Leigh said, twisting a naked wrist up to prove that there was no watch there and to create the illusion that there was a good and proper reason for this particular car being at this particular spot.

"Yeah." The driver glanced at his arm, turning his watch face until it caught the light.

As he read the time, Leigh glanced over the top of the car at the bank. The guy's watch was three minutes slow but Leigh didn't feel it necessary to let him in on that little secret.

"Thanks," Leigh said when the guy finished and dropped his hand back onto the steering wheel.

"Late for an appointment?" the guy asked. His voice was higher pitched than Leigh might have expected, but rough, harsh, as if he had a touch of laryngitis.

"Naw," Leigh said slowly. "Just wondering. Nice night, isn't it?"

The bait was out. Now it was time to play the fish and see if it bit.

Careful not to move too quickly, not to say too much.

The guy had to make the first move. Leigh knew enough about police entrapment to stick by that cardinal rule of the trade.

"Nice." The guy was sweating. Either he was just a driver who happened to slow down at the wrong time or he was new to the area. Leigh decided to give him a little more line—enough to set the hook if the fish wanted to be reeled in, but not enough to rebound and give the angler a sharp crack across the cheek.

"New car?" Leigh slid one hand along the door, careful to keep it in sight of the driver. The fingers were long and sensuous, the movement provocative without being explicit. It had worked often enough. It worked this time, too.

"Yeah, got it a couple of weeks ago," the guy said, still almost whispering in that eerie high-pitched voice. Leigh thought for a second about cutting bait and running, but the guy continued. "Like to try 'er out? Take a spin?"

"Sure." The words had barely died away before Leigh was settled in the passenger side of the car—it wasn't anything special, just a fairly inexpensive foreign job, but what the hell. A guy's car was usually his pride and his weakness, no matter how much of a clunker it might be. This buggy was okay. Nothing special, just okay.

The driver pulled away from the curb, being ostentatiously careful to check the rear-view mirror for on-coming traffic. Leigh smiled. They were like that a lot of the time, so intent on what they were going to do (or fantasized that they were going to do) that they drove extra carefully—no use taking chances and having to explain someone like Leigh to cops or, worse, to wives.

They followed Sunset for at least a mile without the guy saying a word.

"Smooth ride," Leigh said finally, continuing the pretense

that the car was the focus of attention. "Good shocks."

The driver still wouldn't say anything. The car turned just before Sunset crossed over the Hollywood Freeway. They paralleled the freeway for half a dozen blocks. The guy hadn't said a word.

"Look...," Leigh began.

"I'm not very good at this," the guy said abruptly.

Still Leigh glanced over. The bright light of a pedestrian crossing revealed that the guy was wearing a worn T-shirt that stretched tightly across a nicely muscled chest. His pants were tight, too, and his legs were as well defined as his arms and shoulders. Not body-building bulging biceps or anything that obvious, just good and solid body tone. Leigh liked them that way.

But the light also revealed that the guy was trembling. His shoulders twitched and his chest heaved as if he were drowning and struggling for breath. Beneath the roar of the engine, Leigh heard the man's breath, ragged and shallow.

"Hey," Leigh said, "it's okay. Nothing to worry about."

Leigh's fingers pressed reassuringly against the back of the guy's hand.

But only for a second.

The guy's hand felt like a claw. The fingers were knotted and twisted and tight and curved. They felt deformed. The skin was icy as well. Leigh didn't like the feeling that transmitted itself through that single touch. Now the guy was trembling even more, like he was going to throw an epileptic fit.

One of Leigh's friends had pitched a fit right in the middle of the locker room after gym class in high school. It had looked just like this.

"Hey, are you all right. Not sick or anything?" Leigh asked but at the same time shifted nearer the door just in case. The lock-pin was up and in this slow traffic it would be safe enough to bolt if things got really weird. Sometimes business could edge into danger. Not often, though. Leigh was pretty careful. But this pick-up looked like it might turn into one of those few times.

The guy didn't answer. He gripped the wheel so hard with his left hand that the knuckles gleamed like polished bone; his other hand began rubbing up and down the taut jeans, his elbow almost touching Leigh's as it moved.

"Come on," Leigh insisted, "are you okay or what?"

"Yeah," the voice came out unconvincing, even higher pitched, almost like an old woman's. "I'm fine. Relax."

They cut over the freeway and drove for ten or fifteen minutes into the northern-western portions of the L.A. basin. Leigh wasn't that familiar with the area, especially when the guy began following unlit residential streets that blended into each other like long, dark dreams. Leigh tried to catch a glimpse of at least one street sign, maybe one that named the town as well as the street, but they were too dark and too high.

With one hand on the door handle just in case, Leigh settled back and watched the driver. He was good-looking enough, fairly young. But the more Leigh studied him, the less there was to feel comfortable with. The guy was too stiff. It felt to Leigh like more than just normal nervousness, even if this was the guy's first time. But he seemed too much in control for it to be the first. The set of the neck, the angle of shoulders, and above all the incessant, irritating *scrape* of nails against denim felt all wrong.

Leigh was about to ask for the guy to pullover—and failing that to catapult from the car the next time it slowed for a stop sign or light—when the guy suddenly pulled toward the curb and stopped. He killed the engine.

"This is it," he said, twisting in his seat and pointing across Leigh's chest toward an old house set well back from the street. But Leigh paid more attention to the claw-like hand than to the shadowy house. The tendons and ligaments strained and bulged against the backdrop of muscle and bone; the knuckles were so swollen that the skin was as tight as a bladder and ready to burst.

It was an old man's hand, gnarled and twisted with decades

of arthritic damage.

But this guy was young.

The hand rose and one of the fingers ran down the line of Leigh's jaw. Leigh shivered. Teeth clamped convulsively and painfully down on teeth. It was a feeling that Leigh was not used to.

"Smooth," the voice murmured in the darkness.

Leigh felt a chill that spread along each vertebra and then penetrated every nerve and descended into the core and froze the blood.

"Smooth and young," the voice said.

The finger rose and fell, rose and fell.

Leigh tried to reach up and push the hand away but could do nothing, not even speak. The finger threaded through Leigh's hair, pulling it away from the neck and then letting it fall slowly back into place. The finger paused at the back of Leigh's neck before following the line of shoulder and arm downward. Leigh's nerves broke.

It might be fifty miles back to Sunset and it might take all night to hitch or hike back there, but enough of this shit was enough. This guy *couldn't* have enough money to make a night with him anything but a nightmare.

The passenger door flew open and, before the driver could tighten his grip on Leigh's arm, the passenger seat was empty and Leigh was running down the sidewalk toward a brightly lit intersection maybe three streets away. The sound of feet thudding against pavement, stumbling where the pavement was cracked by roots and years, re-capturing the rhythm and thudding on—the sound would mask the subtle whine of the car engine following closely behind that Leigh expected at any moment.

Only at the end of the first block did it seem safe to steal a glance backward.

The guy was still parked in front of the same house. The car was dark. No lights showed. The window was a black mask reflecting the sparse streetlights. The guy was standing on the sidewalk, halfway up to the house. With the streetlight falling on him, he was clearly visible to Leigh. He stood stiffly, almost like he had a killer headache and was afraid to move for fear his head would fall right off. Or like he did not quite know where he was or how he had gotten there but did not like what he was seeing. He raised his head and stared in Leigh's direction.

"Up yours," Leigh yelled down the deserted street. The appropriate gesture followed almost immediately.

The man shook his head hard, as if he were just waking.

"Weird," Leigh said and turned and kept walking as quickly as possible, checking with every other breath to make sure the weirdo wasn't following, but there was no movement, not a sign that there was any life at all along the street. At the corner a sign identified the street as *Greensward* and beneath that, in smaller letters, Leigh read the city name: *Tamarind Valley.*

Shit, Leigh thought, even farther than I thought.

Breathing a deep sigh, Leigh walked the rest of the way to the stop-light. On one corner stood a Mobil station; on another, an all-night store with a brightly lit pay phone booth just outside the glass front doors.

A couple of minutes later, leaning against the booth and panting from the exertion of the three-block sprint, Leigh decided that Kerry was the one most likely be home and in anything like a reasonable condition to drive.

With a shudder and a sigh, Leigh dug into the change pocket of the worn jeans and pulled out a quarter.

Kerry better the hell be home, he thought, glancing over his shoulder to where Greensward disappeared into the darkness.

He just better be.

CHAPTER FORTY-FOUR

For almost a week after a police detective came by the house to question him about Payne Gunnison, about the still unresolved and increasingly frustrating disappearance of Tasco's repairman, about the death of The Greer, even about the neighborhood on Greensward in general, Nick knew that Payne was home even though he never saw the other man.

On the one hand, the general sense of disarray that had characterized the house while The Greer was alive had returned like the first dying leaves of autumn. The lawns hadn't been trimmed since that first time. The Bermuda grass had begun fringing the sidewalks again, spreading like moth-eaten lace across the crumbling edges of mildewed concrete. Here and there dandelions and broad-leaved plantains and sickly green, prickly stemmed weeds of varying sorts took up solitary stands amid the lower grass.

From his window, Nick watched a foot-high dandelion just below one of Payne's living room windows progress from bud to full head of sunny yellow to wispy gray and finally disperse its seed across the lawn. Payne did nothing to stop it.

In addition, most of the shrubbery around the house was rapidly reasserting the jungle-like density that originally hid the place. The vine along the front again screened much of the porch and crawled along the eaves until it shadowed the single window, making it look more and more like a monstrous eye smudged around the edges with badly applied mascara.

On the other hand, there were subtle and not-so-subtle signs around the house that Payne was very much present. Nick never saw an open door or window, never saw a thick white drapery rustle or a hand twist around the hem, but the positions of the lids on the garbage cans lining the alley shifted slightly from day to day. On trash pick-up day, one of the gleaming tin lids was tilted against the can and reflected the sun's light into Nick's back window. The next day, all three cans were tightly closed. When Nick surreptitiously examined the cans later that afternoon, a freshly filled white garbage bag lay curled like a reverse shadow at the bottom of one.

Worse, though, was what happened at night. Nick was increasingly concerned about and simultaneously wary of Payne. Payne's abruptness about the key, coupled with Nick's deep-felt discomfort about Tasco's repairman that Payne had taken so lightly, made Nick less than excited about being with Payne. In spite of the initial warmth of their friendship, now the thought of sitting in the front viewing room with the man, in the near darkness watching a film, nearly made Nick break out in a cold sweat.

All in all, the more Nick thought about Payne Gunnison, the less comfortable he felt. It almost was enough to make him wish for The Greer instead.

Almost.

At night, that *almost* dwindled to a virtual certainty. During each interminable night following his spontaneous vacation in a dust-ridden and cockroach-infested cabin along the Crest Highway to Big Bear, he had split his time between worrying whether that psycho Ric would suddenly pop up and beat the living tar out of him for some reason Nick could never quite define, and watching the silver flickering reflecting from the leaves behind Payne's place—the same eerie lights as before when the Greet was alive, only more constant and consistent now.

The sounds returned also. They began well past midnight and continued until just before dawn. The *screee, screee, screee* of rusted hinges set Nick's teeth on edge and made him irritable and nervous from lack of sleep. Once, during the second night, he had the impulse to get up, dress, and go next door with a can of oil and do a number on the porch glider, whether Payne was sitting in it or not. He got as far as fumbling beneath the kitchen sink for the Three-in-One machine oil that he kept there, when he suddenly pulled his hand back only inches from the can.

He straightened and stood in the middle of the kitchen, wondering what had brought him out there. The next thing he knew, he went back into the bedroom and gathered up his covers and made a surrogate bed on the living room couch. It was lumpy and scratchy, and the *screee, screee, screee* was only deadened by the intervening walls, not silenced. But the difference proved to be enough to allow him a few scattered snatches of sleep during the night.

By the evening of the fourth day, he was not sure how he would make it through one more night without committing mayhem or murder. As events turned out, he didn't have to.

* * * * * * *

Less than half an hour before twilight edged into purple darkness, Payne's front door swung open and Payne stepped out. If Nick had chanced to look up at that instance and seen him, the sight would have helped calm Nick's nerves.

This was the old Payne. You could see it in his step, in the way his arms swung loosely at his side, in the tan arms and legs set off by a light blue polo shirt and dark blue cargo shorts and white tennis shoes.

Payne looked healthy enough, even if he did not look particularly happy. In fact, he looked as if he had just come to a difficult decision. His forehead was deeply furrowed and his lips were set in a determined line. His feet slapped hard against the sidewalk as he strode up Greensward to the telephone booth by the all-night store at the intersection. He stepped into the booth but did not dial right away. He hesitated for a long time and then finally picked up the receiver. He held the receiver to his ear until he heard a dial tone. He dropped two dimes in the machine and punched a number. Before it rang through, he hung up and retrieved his dimes.

He repeated the process. He was more definitely ill at east now. He was sweating even though the evening was not especially warm. His shirt clung stickily to his back. His breath rasped shallowly through the closed space of the booth and the black plastic telephone receiver felt slippery and pliant against his palm.

This time he let the phone ring through.

"Hello."

"Cathy?"

"Yes. Payne? Is that you? What happened? You never...."

"We've got to meet. Tonight. As soon as possible."

"I can be over in just a few...."

"No," he almost yelled through the mouthpiece. "Not here. Somewhere...else. How about the...."

His voice dropped and faded.

"Payne? Payne, are you still there?"

At the sound of her question the angular squareness of his shoulders dissolved into a rounded hump that distorted the outline of his arms and back. Through the thin weave of his polo shirt, it was as if firm muscle had degenerated in a heart-beat into stringy sinews and flabby tissue. He seemed to lose half a dozen inches in height. His hand tightened into a claw that hitched nervously at his leg just below the hem of his shorts.

"Cathy." He consciously tried to straighten his shoulders. He laid his palm against the scratched glass of the phone booth and pressed against it, struggling to force the fingers straight, to make the knuckles smooth and round instead of knotted. Pain cut through him like a knife blade, sharp and biting. His breath hissed through pinched lips.

"Payne," Cathy said tensely. "What's wrong?"

He almost told her, God help him, he almost broke down the barriers and let the words rush out to enflesh the pain and the deep-set fear. For a second his shoulders struggled to recover their strength.

Then they sagged even lower. His hip pained so much that he could barely breathe. He slumped against the wall of the phone booth. He wasn't sweating any more.

"I don't want to see you any more, Cathy," he said clearly and distinctly. There, it was out. Flat and cold and stiff, delivered in a high-pitched monotone she had never heard from him.

"Oh," she said. Just that one sound was all that she could make, as if the entirety of her shock and surprise and disappointment and anger could be compressed into a single exhalation that passed for a word even though it was less than that... and far more. "Oh."

"It wouldn't *work* between us."

"Is there someone else?"

"No," he answered quickly, so quickly that she must have understood him to mean the opposite because she cut him off without waiting for further clarification.

"Fine, then. Just don't bother to call me again. Ever."

She hung up. From the sound of it, she had slammed the receiver into its cradle. The persistent *buzzz* of the tone rumbled through his ear as he held the receiver close to his head, pressing his temple into the earpiece as if to assuage a headache.

For a moment, his eyes misted and he straightened. His lips moved as if he were speaking, but no sounds emerged. When he stepped out of the phone booth into the full blackness of night, he hurt in the same familiar old places—pains like unwelcome spirits that haunted this body in the darkness of each night. The searing pain spiked through his joints until he nearly sobbed.

The walk back down Greensward was a prolonged exercise in physical agony. His hip felt as if the bare bone were scraping against a metal blade. His flesh was afire with sluggish blood that pounded feverishly through constricted veins and joints clotted with calcium deposits. Moving his feet was harder than wading through knee-deep molasses on a frosty winter morning. His shoulder and hand pained as well, and he clenched his fingers into a fist and hunched the hand close to his side as if to protect it.

By the time he passed the house where the Harrisons had once lived—*old busybodies deserved everything they got and more shit on them*—the sharpness had retreated a little, leaving behind only the biting memory of pain. He was barely limping when he slowly mounted the porch steps. His footsteps rang on the wooden planks.

Less than fifteen minutes later he emerged again. The polo shirt and cargo shorts had disappeared. In their place he wore faded jeans that were frayed at the cuffs and in horizontal slits across both knees, and a T-shirt that sculpted the arcs and curves of his torso. He glanced toward Nick's place and then hurriedly away when he saw no lights through the window.

CHAPTER FORTY-FIVE

Driving.

He hadn't known what a rush it could be. He had never experienced anything like it before, certainly not back home in Pennsylvania where the only roads were winding two-lane relics from forty years before that were constantly torn up and fracturing and disintegrating beneath winter snows until the safest speed was barely more exciting than a snail's crawl. A crippled snail, at that. No, back home offered nothing like the freeways here. Nothing like the vast serpents of concrete and steel that arced the city and bisected it and anatomized it, pulling pieces away from the center and keeping them tenuously connected to the living network by stretching the thin arteries of roadway like fragile skin.

Driving.

Tonight he didn't bother with the air conditioning even though the air was muggy. He kept the windows open and the hot acrid breeze from the freeways blew into his face. He breathed the exhaust fumes like they were a whore's perfume. His head felt lighter and lighter. He kept the windows down even when he angled off the freeway and headed northward into the tangled maze of boulevards and streets that defined Hollywood by night.

Cruising was easier with the windows already down, he discovered. His hand felt better but the knuckles still twinged when he twisted them. With both front windows open he didn't have to lean over and struggle with the knob when the hustler sauntered over at the stop light and stuck his head inside and struck up a conversation that concluded with him sidling in next to Payne and slamming the door behind him.

"Nice wheels," the punk said conversationally. Payne recognized the conventionality of the opening as well. Pawn forward two squares.

The next thing Payne had noticed about the kid was that in spite of his age—certainly not over twenty, maybe only eighteen or so—he was trying to come over as at least a minimal punk, with tight black jeans, a silver chain that dangled from hip to hip, no more than the requisite piercings, and a leather jacket slashed diagonally down the front. But his hair was within reason, and there was no more beard than could legitimately be expected by the end of a long day, and the eyes seemed intelligent, if overly cold and calculating.

What the hell what do you expect anyway true love compassion and sensitivity for a couple of twenties, the eyes seemed to challenge.

Payne didn't answer the gambit. Already the situation seemed too much like a repetition of what little he remembered about that other night. He didn't want to think about that night. He didn't want to think about it at all because thinking made him see staticky flashes and images of things he had never done, people he had never....

Instead he turned to stare at the clock on the bank building a block away. It read not quite 10:00. Still early.

The punk must have caught the movement and interpreted it correctly, because he grinned tightly and said, "Long night ahead, huh?"

"Yeah."

"Alone?"

"Yeah."

"Not much for talking?" the punk said. He settled back into the seat and stretched his long legs in front of him and stretched his arms over his head and into the back of the car.

When he relaxed again, one knee rested lightly against Payne's leg and one hand draped lazily, with studied casualness, over the headrest of Payne's seat. Payne felt the hairs on the back of his neck prickle.

"Name's Alan," the hustler said quietly. His voice was a surprise; somehow it didn't fit his appearance. Too quiet. For an instant, Payne almost felt like he wanted to like the kid.

Alan waited for a long while, long enough for Payne to pull away from the curb and into traffic, long enough for the car to successfully maneuver minor traffic jams at two intersections before he seemed to understand that the man at the wheel was not going to answer.

"What's yours?" he asked finally.

"Huh?"

The car veered sharply as his hands twitched on the wheel.

"Your name, man, what's your name?" There was an edge of irritation in Alan's voice.

"Uh, P—Peter." Payne stumbled over the sounds. He spit them out as if they were bitter poison, aware even as he did so that the hustler no more believed him than he believed the hustler.

Alan. How grand!

But for the night—for the next hour or less, maybe—they would become Alan and Peter.

So be it.

The rest of the trip passed in virtual silence. Every now and then, Alan would speak but Payne rarely answered with more than a monosyllabic "yeah" or "no," often with only an indecipherable grunt. Alan's comments grew more acerbic and biting as the car roared through the darkness. Twice Payne felt hot pressure on his leg, and twice he shifted gears even though the engine complained. He stomped on the clutch with his left foot and on the accelerator with his right, just enough to move his leg away from the heat of the hustler's knee. Twice he shook his head and breathed sharply through his teeth, *Not yet. Not now. Not here.*

By the time they reached the house on Greensward, Payne was tense and sweating. He could smell his own stench and was revolted by it. His T-shirt felt sodden under the arms and around the neck and waistband. His jeans had become a hothouse, capturing his own heat like a furnace in the warm night air. He wished faintly for the cargo shorts and the feel of cooling air through the sprinkling of hair on his bare legs. The image faded and disappeared and there was only heat and pressure and confinement. His hand curled along the seam, the fingers claw-like and rigid. His knuckles grazed the hustler's. His fingers retracted into a tight fist.

He swerved the car into the driveway and killed the engine.

"This it?" Alan said sullenly, craning his neck around to get a better view of the house. In the darkness there was little visible except white window frames caught between the moonlight and the harsh shadows from the eaves.

"Yeah," Payne answered in the same harsh tones he had used during the entire drive.

"Figures," Alan grunted.

Payne swung his door open and stepped onto the driveway. He closed the car door quietly and started toward the back porch, his shoes crunching lightly on the thin layer of gravel that led to the back door. Behind him, Alan had gotten out as well. Payne heard a muffled *thump* as the door closed.

"Quiet," he said.

Alan looked over at him, then glanced around as if he were afraid that the two of them were being watched.

The neighborhood was dark. Not yet 10:45 and already almost all of the lights were out.

Halfway to the back porch, Payne changed his mind.

"This way," he said, his voice barely more than a whisper. His foot caught in the ankle-high grass as he walked around to the front, giving a curious *swisssh* sound to his passing. Alan walked without making any sound.

They mounted the porch. Alan waited patiently while Payne dug in his pocket for the key and rattled it twice against the lock before managing to insert it. The *click* of metal against metal rang loudly in the quiet as the lock mechanism slipped and the brass knob turned with a low squeal.

Payne stepped in without a word. Alan followed, waiting just inside the entryway for Payne to turn the lights on.

As soon as they were on, Payne motioned Alan ahead. He lingered for a moment to lock the front door and draw the curtains that separated the living room from the shallow entryway. He snapped them shut with a practiced flick of his wrist, yet realized with a distant shock that he was closing them for the first time since great-Aunt Emilia had left the house for the final time.

"Weird," Alan said almost immediately, then looked challengingly at Payne. "The color and all. Drab."

"I like it," Payne said curtly.

"Yeah," Alan said.

Again the silence lengthened uncomfortably before either of them moved.

"Take your jacket?" Payne said suddenly.

"Sure," Alan said, shrugging out of the split leather jacket and handing it over by its collar. Payne disappeared into the hall, opened a door and after a few seconds closed it again. He reappeared in the living room without the jacket.

Alan was stalking around the room, staring at the monitors. As Payne watched him, watched carefully molded muscles move beneath tight layerings of cloth, Alan suddenly seemed more bestial than human, a raving, ravishing beast only partially trained and needing desperately to be caged.

And tamed.

And broken.

And used.

Ric would like him flickered through Payne's mind, along with a hazy image of a human form splayed against a static-riven blue-silver screen, screaming silently into an electronic night. Payne shook his head and the image disappeared. For an instant, he felt a cold shock as he saw a stranger standing in the middle of his living room, dressed like a....

Alan reached out his hand to touch the smooth surface of the wall.

"Don't!" Payne said sharply, his voice strained and high pitched.

The hustler flicked back his finger as if he had burned it. He looked at Payne. There was a question in his eyes, as well as smoldering anger, as if Payne had no right to speak to him like that. As if he were determined to make Payne pay for arrogating that right.

"Special paint," Payne said hurriedly. "Has to be kept clean. Spotless. For the video set-up." His voice sounded apologetic and he hated himself for that. The hustler looked around at the cameras staring down from the four corners and at the blank monitor on the back wall.

"Never seen anything like this," he breathed, his purpose for coming with Payne momentarily forgotten, or at least ignored.

Payne knew that Alan was mentally calculating the value of the equipment hanging so easily within reach on the walls. *Let him. It'll get him as far as it did the other one.*

Again the flash of an image and Payne's stomach rippled.

"Pretty wild," Alan finally said.

"There's more," Payne said. "Come on."

He took Alan on a quick tour of the house an abbreviated version of the same tour he had given Nick not so many weeks ago, when everything was still new and intriguing to Payne himself. This time, the whole experience seemed flat and uninteresting in spite of Alan's obvious interest in the complexity— and expense—of the sound and visual systems. They ended up in the control room.

"Go ahead," Payne said. "Pick out a film. We can watch it before we...."

Alan seemed almost ready to laugh when Payne's voice choked off. Insultingly he turned away from Payne and scanned the rows of films. Before long, though, his face took on a rapt expression, like a child-in-the–candy-shop sort of thing but touched with hints of experience and perhaps even cruelty that made his face uniquely unsettling.

Payne watched him skim through the comedies and dramas. He scarcely bothered to look at the musicals. After a few moments, he turned back to Payne.

"Don't you have anything...*hot*."

He winked and hooked his thumbs in his belt loops and tugged on his jeans, just enough to show a thin line of skin between his T-shirt and his pants. The skin was smooth and hairless and tanned.

Payne swallowed and nodded toward the far corner, the one that was hidden most of the time behind the door when it was open. Alan fingered the backs of the cases at shoulder height, then followed them down and finally bent over ostentatiously to examine titles on the shelves nearest the floor. The movement revealed a wider line of skin along his back. He leaned forward and the line widened provocatively. Alan seemed to be studying the titles, to all appearances unaware of the effect his movements had on the state of his clothing.

When he pulled a case out, he did so quickly and decisively, as if he had found just what he wanted and nothing else would do. Payne didn't see the title, but he caught a glimpse of the cassette box, garish and highlighted by flesh-toned forms, before Alan pulled the disc out and shoved it into the DVD player.

"How does this thing work?" he asked Payne abruptly. He left little question as to who was ultimately in charge of this evening.

"Here, let me," Payne said quickly. "You go on back into the living room. I'll set the timer for ten, no, fifteen minutes, that should give us time to...get acquainted."

"Sure," Alan said. He grinned and disappeared into the hallway. Payne shoved the disc in and twisted the timer switch on and left, turning out the light as he closed the door.

"Hey, man, uh, where's the john?" Alan demanded as soon as Payne entered the living room.

"Second door on the right," Payne said, dropping heavily onto the white sofa in the middle of the room. He pointed down the hall. Alan followed the line of Payne's finger and left.

"This one?"

"Yeah," Payne nodded.

Alan opened the door and went in.

"Light's on the wall. Right hand side," Payne called after him.

A second later a shaft of light split the hallway, then disappeared as the door closed.

CHAPTER FORTY-SIX

Payne leaned into the softness of the couch and closed his eyes, feeling the material surrounding and encompassing him. For what seemed a long, long while, he relaxed and let the couch enfold him. Suddenly, enfolding and nurturing transformed into smothering. He choked. He struggled to pull out of the half-dream he had become and back into himself.

He felt the blackness he had felt so often before pushing irresistibly against his brain—it would push until it punched through and then there would be a blank spot, a place where he would do things and not remember them except for frustratingly imprecise and rapid static-filled images that would haunt his waking hours and torture him in dreams.

Not this time! Not ever again!

His back teeth ground together from the strain of his decision, catching the tender inner tissue of his cheeks and shredding the flesh. He tasted the salty warmth of blood but his jaws tightened even more, as if he were fighting an enormous battle. The veins in his neck became swollen with blood and his hands clenched and unclenched in his lap. In spite of the struggle going on inside him and the chaos of remembered sound that pummeled him, for the moment the rest of the house was deathly still.

Then, through his inner turmoil, he heard something out there.

He opened his eyes at an unexpected hissing crackle.

It was too soon for the film to begin. There had to be six, seven minutes left. Maybe ten.

The crackle intensified, sizzling through the air.

He stared at the monitor hanging on the wall directly opposite him.

The screen showed nothing but snow at first. Then so quickly that there was no perceptible transition between haze and clarity, it resolved into a startlingly precise picture, mostly black and white in the background but with a single vivid splay of color at the center.

The scene was playing in Payne's bathroom. The hustler was obviously unaware that he was being watched.

The veins throbbed in Payne's temples again and he struggled to close his eyes to the temptation of the image on the monitor—but to do so was to encourage the blackness to come closer, to press harder. He grabbed his right hand with his left and wrenched the fingers open, twisting so hard and so violently that the pain stabbed more intensely than if he had broken them. He reveled in his decision to endure the pain because for an instant the blackness retreated. He shifted on the couch, contorting his torso and hip in an invitation to pain.

He moaned, his voice barely loud enough to make itself heard as Alan's voice sounded through the monitor. The hustler was humming as he washed himself.

Payne's head tossed back and forth. He wrenched his eyes open and stared at the monitor and what it revealed, then screwed them shut and turned his head away. But even then it was simply the act of an instant to open his eyes again and watch the monitor before he bit his lips so hard he drew blood and deliberately forced himself not to watch again.

And again.

And again.

All the while wondering how long Alan would take, why he didn't come out, what he was doing in there, then opening his eyes long enough to see and then closing them again and wishing that Alan were gone, that he were in the room next to Payne and touching him, that Payne were alone and far from here, that Payne were next to Alan and could feel the body heat radiating from him.

The front door rattled.

Payne sat straight up. His forehead was bathed in sweat and his eyes started from their sockets as if he had just seen a ghost. He glanced frantically around the room, for the moment unable to place the sound. Then he recognized it.

Someone was knocking on the door.

Slowly he worked his way out of the couch and limped toward the door. He passed through the curtains and drew them behind him before he turned on the porch light and opened the door slightly, no more than a crack.

To anyone outside, he would be at best a faint silhouette, at worst a thin darkness against the backlit curtains.

Nick stood on the porch, his hand poised to knock on again.

"Sorry to bother you so late," he began, "but I...I haven't seen you around much lately and I was worried about you. Is everything...?"

"Everything is fine," Payne said curtly.

"Well, like I said, sorry it's so late. I saw a light in back so I figured you might be up. I just wanted to let you know that...."

"Thanks." Payne closed the door until all that Nick could probably see would be a shadow and the white tips of his fingers where they grasped the thick oak door. "Good night."

He shut the door.

Quietly but firmly.

Good-bye.

He limped back into the living room.

The monitor chittered softly as it relayed the sounds of sink taps running and skin rasped dry by a rough white towel. Payne tried not to watch, but his hip threw him off balance and as he twisted to regain balance, his eyes locked onto the monitor. Without watching where he was walking, he limped to the sofa and was about to drop back onto it, exhausted and hurting but at the same time excited and nearly breathless.

The bathroom door opened.

At the same instant, the monitor fell silent and dark.

Alan came into the room.

Payne stared at him.

He had removed his shirt and his shoes and socks. His toes sank into the carpet pile, dusky tan consumed by white. But Payne's attention was on the man's wide shoulders and deep chest and flat belly, all ridged muscle and tan and strength. The top snap on his jeans lay open. The head of his brass zipper glinted coldly.

Payne's throat was suddenly dry. His heart thrummed inside his chest as if it were trying to force an escape from some threatening, debilitating prison of its own making.

From deep inside, from places he didn't know existed, he felt the first stirrings of...of anger, of fury.

The shock rattled him. He stared at Alan without seeing him.

Anger.

Fury.

Rage.

He felt sick, physically sick—he remembered suddenly Nick's siege of vomiting a few days before and felt as if he were going to be just as sick. Or worse. He swallowed hard against the rising heat and forced his stomach to hold onto its contents, forced his throat to constrict against the nauseating bile that tried to burn its way out. Tried to force the blackness back into secret places of horror he had not consciously known existed until that moment.

Anger.

Fury.

Rage.

He concentrated on them. Images rose and beat at the wall of his concentration and withered away in futility.

He *could win. He was winning!*

Alan seemed not to notice anything wrong with Payne. He twisted his lips into something that was half grin, half contempt—just the thing he figured would turn this guy on. In an unknowing perversion of Cathy's actions in that very room, perhaps on that very spot, he began removing the last of his clothing. His actions were studied, teasing, and taunting. Physical action transformed into overt sexuality designed to arouse.

In spite of himself, Payne was chained to where he stood by the couch. He could not move, could not blink, could not shut out the sight that he wanted/despised *watch Alex watch Beethoven's glorious ninth all ultra-violence o my droogs* and still the rage and fury beat at him, trying to force its way out.

It is possible! I can win!

The hustler dropped his hand to his zipper.

"Come on, relax, man," Alan's voice said, even though it barely pierced the roaring in Payne's ears. He stepped toward Payne.

"Let's get going."

Nooooo!

The cry started somewhere deep inside but died before it could force its way through Payne's throat. It was strangled by another complex of rage and envy and confined fury that had plotted and planned and waited for years.

Yesssss.

Alan paused, his hand outstretched until it almost touched Payne's shoulder. Something that might have been fear surfaced in his face.

Nooooo.

Payne struggled with everything that was himself and this time the sound emerged, faint and frail, barely a breath. But it was enough.

Alan stepped hesitantly backward. His expression changed as well, unalloyed and unmistakable fear appearing, disappearing, then surfacing and remaining as he looked at Payne.

All around them, the walls crackled to life, sputtering and popping like Fourth of July fireworks.

Alan shot a quick glance at the monitor, as if expecting to see the opening credits of the film he had selected. Instead, there was nothing on the screen.

Nothing except blankness gradually replaced by a dim

figure, a blue nimbus that pulsed on the screen and grew larger and larger.

An inarticulate burst of sound ripped through Payne's throat, escaped the imprisonment of the swirling blackness that sought to restrain it, and exploded into the room. Alan heard it and wrenched his attention back to the other man and then screamed himself.

Agony tore through Payne, an agony so intense that every cell in his body must be ripping apart, every nerve simultaneously exposed to excruciating stimulation. His body burned from head to foot. He held his hands helplessly in front of him, as if pleading with the hustler, as if he needed something only the other man could give.

His hands glowed. The flesh trembled and quivered and vibrated with every breath, with every thudding heartbeat.

He felt a rush of fury that was scarcely less unbearable than the agony, and his hands flared with a blue glow that formed hands superimposed over his own but not his own. He watched in stricken horror as the pseudo-hands tore themselves away from him. The movement generated another wave of pain that nearly forced him into unconsciousness. He didn't know how he could withstand such pain and live.

He felt a second wave, a contractive ripping even more agonizing than the first, as legs burst through his legs, shrunken and rounded shoulders shattered his shoulders, as pendulous breasts penetrated the smooth surface of his flesh from within.

A human figure—vague and ill-defined and insubstantial and incomplete—vibrated between him and the hustler, but Payne barely noticed. All he knew was that the rending pain was suddenly, blessedly over. His tissues were intact, his muscles and bone whole and unencumbered. He suddenly felt...*good*, healthy and young and stridently male and potent, fully himself. The whorl of blackness was gone, totally gone, and with it the threat he had suffered under since...since he first entered this damned house, he realized with a shock.

He also felt unutterably weak. His arms trembled. His legs

quivered as if he had just finished a marathon obstacle course. He pulled air into exhausted lungs with great sobbing gasps even as he struggled to keep his eyes open and watch as the phantom figure transformed before him.

There was another loud crackling sound that would have panicked him if he had not been so close to unconsciousness. Red lights flashed beneath the lenses on each of the four cameras, and from the blank expanse of each lens a thick darkness that was almost solid, almost fluid spewed out. It shot across the living room from each corner simultaneously and struck the figure squarely in the chest.

The figure and the darkness coalesced into something horrid and solid and ancient, something twisted and diseased that Payne had never seen in the living flesh yet instinctively recognized.

He recoiled, holding his hand in front of his closed eyes and concentrating on his own fury at what had almost been taken from him.

The figure moved toward him, then hesitated.

The monitor crackled to life, showing an identical image on the screen: Payne sprawled on the floor, hand raised in a gesture of defiance and warding, the figure hovering only a few feet from him. Then the figure backed away. The movement was paralleled in the monitor, as if the figure were rehearsing on the screen what it was performing in actuality in the middle of the room.

Payne caught a glimpse of the screen. Now the camera angle had reversed. Payne no longer lay at the center. Instead the screen focused on Alan, caught the hustler in the act of backing slowly away. His image was suddenly and inexplicably naked.

The figure approached him. This time, in reality, it was Alan's turn to scream and cringe in horror. Dimly, Payne heard the slap of bare flesh against the wall as Alan fell back and pressed against the wall as if he were trying to become invisible. And now, in reality, Alan was naked, as naked as the terrified image of himself that played on the monitor.

Through some trick of nerves, even through his increasing exhaustion, Payne felt the cold wall slap against his own back, saw the horrifying figure approaching him as if he were huddled against the wall, then coupled those sensations with gushing memories of the sickeningly mutilated magazines in the attic.

Nooo!

This time Payne's cry was for Alan, not for himself—and he was himself at that instant, although he could only guess how long he might survive intact. Perhaps it would be long enough.

The figure was almost touching the hustler. Alan slid further down the wall until his knees buckled in front of him. His hands covered his groin and his head shook back and forth, back and forth, as if the futile act of negating the apparition would somehow destroy it. His throat was working frantically but no sounds were coming out. Tears glistened on his cheeks and dropped onto his chest and shoulders.

Payne forced himself to move, but it was like struggling against the incoming tide. His muscles worked, his joints worked, every one—but to little effect. He reached out with a hand that was neither crippled nor deformed.

But slowly.

So slowly.

Too slowly.

The simple effort was almost too much. Black spots swam before his eyes, obscuring the figure.

And already the figure had changed again. The vague blue electrical nimbus had absorbed the darkness that shot from the cameras until even from behind, even though his exhaustion, Payne recognized the outlines of a woman he had never seen but knew as intimately as if she had been part of him.

And she had been.

He felt sickened at the realization, but tried with renewed efforts to move quickly enough.

The phantom woman reached a twisted finger toward the boy cowering at her feet. There was something contemptuous in the way she ignored Payne and his agonizing but increasingly ineffectual struggle to reach her. There was something even more threatening—contempt joined with equal parts of seething hatred and a thirst for revenge—as she bent and reached down past the boy's staring eyes, past his face twisted beyond fear, past his heaving chest and trembling shoulders, and touched, oh so gently barely skimmed the soft pliant surface flesh of the hustler's masculinity.

Blue electrical nimbus touched solid flesh.

For an infinite instant, nothing changed.

Payne seemed frozen, his hand stretching out but lacking yards of touching the figure's hunched over shoulder. The figure was a statue, equally frozen, a counter-image of the figure that glowed from the monitor. The boy huddled against the wall, his head now thrown back until his throat seemed stretched to the point that it would shatter if he tried to breath.

She touched him again.

With a speed that shattered Payne's consciousness, the blue fire engulfed the boy.

Payne saw no more.

CHAPTER FORTY-SEVEN

The hustler's mouth dropped open in a stupefying scream that never came. He breathed in to form the scream, and the fire plunged into his mouth and down his throat and it felt as if it were in his own lungs, burning and searing tender vital tissue.

The hustler twisted once, convulsively, and toppled.

The monitor hissed like a thousand serpents and the screen replayed the instant again and again, the man's death flickering across the screen while the image broke and re-formed, broke and re-formed, like momentary interruptions of transmission during a thunderstorm.

Dying. Dead. Dying. Dead. Again and again.

And now the scene was interspersed with similar scenes in which the man at the center was not the boy.

First there was one man, dark and young and once arrogant but now broken in spirit and body. Then another man joined the first; this one was not so young, not so arrogant. This man had suffered more than any of them. Something about him suggested years, decades of torturous non-existence imprisoned through the perverted will of one brilliantly insane woman.

The episodes wound around each other, cutting back and forth among the three with a dizzying speed. Each time Alan appeared, his image was sharper, crisper, more defined—and the other two watched his agonies as if through them they could find even minimal ease from their own. The three drew closer and closer to the center of the screen, the figure circling them exactly the way the phantom was circling Alan's now lifeless body.

Finally the three men blended into one, and the shadows that filled the room swirled and spun and the air reeked the acrid tang of burning flesh; and the ghastly remnants of Alan's body were engulfed in flickering blue and the figure swept through the flames with her hands and pulled the fire into her, onto her, laving her arms and breasts and shoulders with the living flame that reveled in the essence of death.

She turned toward where Payne lay unconscious on the floor. Her lips—even more substantial now, thin and cruel and tight—curled in a parody of a smile. She moved toward him, gliding more than walking.

She bent over to touch him, to re-enter him permanently and forever.

Or at least until that body grew old and withered and diseased and it was time to find yet another.

The screen crackled.

She looked up at it.

It showed a new scene. Someone—*that damned busybody woman that didn't know when to leave well enough alone*—was on the porch, reaching out to ring the bell.

Time froze for an instant, then the figure faded visibly.

Streams of electrical fire tore from her flesh and were pulled back into the lenses of the cameras; the rest of her body dissipated into insubstantiality like a fog bank on a bright, hot morning and was absorbed silently by the dead-white walls.

On the screen, the woman's outstretched finger came closer to the black button staring out from the monk's cowl of the doorbell.

When the bell buzzed, the living room suddenly flared with light and then the lights died completely.

CHAPTER FORTY-EIGHT

For the first few seconds, Nick simply though his eyes were finally rebelling. It was late, after all. He had been working all day. Now he was tired. The single interruption in his reading—that frustrating walk over to Payne's a little after dark—had resulted in an uneasy mixture of embarrassment and humiliation and concern but had done little to relax him.

When the lights seemed to dim the first time, he naturally assumed that it was just his body's way of telling him to pack it in for the night and get some rest. The first diminution in power was too slight for him to think that it was anything but psychological in origin.

When the lights dimmed the second time, he glanced up at the lamp in time to see the subtle brightening of the bulb through the shade as the power returned to normal.

When the power dropped for the third time, he thought he heard something as well. He laid the book down and concentrated. Distantly, he could distinguish a moaning sough like a strong wind rustling through dry cattails in the swamps back home in Montana. Or perhaps it was more like the hollow, echoing cry of a scavenger bird circling above the desert floor. He couldn't be sure.

But the images that surfaced in his imagination startled him, so much so that for the moment he nearly forgot the sound itself. And it was not repeated.

At least not for a while.

After the fourth wave-like dimming of the lights within

five minutes, Nick thought he had identified the effect. Had the phenomenon occurred in the middle of the day, he would have called it a brown-out, one of those recurrent rolling power-outages that afflicted the L.A. area during times of peak power usage, especially on hot summer afternoons when air conditioners and humidifiers are coupled to the normal load demanded by millions of refrigerators and washers and driers and vacuums and dish washers and televisions and DVD players. The power lines simply couldn't support the demand, and the result was a series of vacillations in the power flow.

Not a full-fledged black-out, although they did occasionally happen. Instead, much of Southern California would get a dose of a brown-out.

But, Nick reminded himself, they usually happened during the day. As far as he knew, they never happened at night when the power demand had peaked and most of the consumers had tapered off on their use. And so far that summer, there had not even been any brown-outs.

He waited a while to see if the drop would repeat again, but it did not. He considered going to bed since it was, after all, nearing midnight. He went so far as to close up his books and take a few seconds to straighten the desk so he could begin fresh tomorrow. He turned off the desk lamp, then crossed over to the floor light and turned it off as well and stood in the darkness.

But he didn't go to bed.

Instead he walked through the house and onto the front porch. It was still hot, although not oppressively so. He sniffed. Beneath the scent of roses and jasmine and damp grass he could detect an odd undercurrent, an unusual smell that reminded him of hot wiring or ozone or burnt insulation.

He sniffed the air more carefully, turning his head in different directions in an attempt at pinpointing the source but the faint odor did not increase. He shrugged and decided to ignore it. It was probably just a car with an overheating engine somewhere down the block.

He leaned against one of the porch supports and allowed

himself to get lost in his thoughts. Mostly he thought about Payne Gunnison. Nick tried not to look at the house next door. In fact, after a few minutes he moved to end of the porch furthest from Payne's place and next to Nick's own driveway. From there all he could see was the edge of his house, the sleeping fronts of the houses across the street, and the shadowy masses of hibiscus that overhung like threatening storm clouds over the driveway. Too bad they don't have any fragrance, he thought as he watched the subtle movement of blossoms highlighted by the bright moonlight.

From his new position, he resumed his train of thought.

Something was wrong with Payne. He didn't sound…well, he didn't sound natural. Like himself. Nick remembered jokes about funerals—*doesn't he look like himself, doesn't he just look so natural, just like himself*—but for once the punch lines seemed strained and hollow and unnatural.

This was no joke, he knew. Payne didn't look like himself. He didn't look natural. He didn't sound natural. He didn't act natural.

Thinking about Payne and the way he had opened the door and then dismissed Nick like the lowliest of peons made Nick shiver. He hugged himself and leaned his shoulder against the porch pillar. It was almost like….

He straightened, his heart beating a frantic tattoo inside his ribcage. The whole experience had been almost like handing The Greer her rent check on the first of every month.

No, that wasn't right. Not almost.

It had been exactly *like it.*

The same dark silhouette, the same gnarled fingers clutching at the door as if the body attached had expected him to burst in physically and rape her in her own living room.

Nick swallowed hard.

What the hell was going on over there?

He listened hard but could hear nothing beyond the whispering of breezes in the hibiscus and the faint hum and crackle of the power lines as they crossed a corner of his yard and disappeared into Payne's. The night was normal, a typical summer's evening on Greensward. Nothing to worry about. Nothing to be concerned about.

Except that Nick was increasingly convinced that it had not been Payne Gunnison who answered his knock next door.

Not really.

Maybe physically it was, but Nick realized with a rush of fear that Payne—the Payne who came over that first morning and asked for help digging out oleander roots, the Payne who had shared laughter over films and had done more than anyone to move Nick closer to becoming part of the human race again—that Payne had disappeared long ago, gradually to be sure, but inexorably.

And someone...some*thing* else had taken his place.

Nick stared into the night and tried to convince himself that everything he had thought was really as absurd as it sounded.

Demon possession.

Transformations.

Evil souls taking over righteous ones.

Shit, what insane nightmare would he come up with next?

Werewolves in the bushes? Vampires in the attic? Frankenstein's monster creaking around in the run-down garage?

He shook his head, trying to shake loose the tendrils of worry and replace them with a firmer grip on clear-sighted reality.

A noise distracted him.

A car roared down Greensward, cut around sharply in front of Nick's place, and stopping at Payne's, its brakes screeching painfully. Whoever was behind the wheel was in a hurry, on drugs, or just naturally the world's worst driver because the front passenger tire hopped the curb and spun, cutting deeply into the scraggly grass.

Someone got out and started running up the sidewalk.

In the half-light that spilled out of the car when she opened the door, Nick realized that at this hour it could only be one person.

"Cathy," he yelled, straightening away from the pillar and leaning over the balustrade. "Cathy Litton?"

She paused on the sidewalk and turned toward his voice.

"Who's that?" she said softly.

He stepped off the porch.

The stars were out and the moon, where it hung just over the tops of the trees, was nearly full. There was enough light to distinguish shapes and forms. She could probably see him.

"I'm Nick. Nick Wheeler."

She hesitated. Obviously part of her wanted to rush up the sidewalk to Payne's front door, and just as obviously another part wanted to do anything in the world except that.

The second part won.

She turned away from Payne's house and approached Nick.

"How is he?" she asked without any preface, indicating Payne's house with a quick nod of her head.

"I...I'm not sure," Nick said, taken by surprise. Her question suggested that her fears paralleled his own. Something was wrong with Payne. They both knew that. But what?

"He called me tonight," she said. "He was...he...he sounded cruel. Abusive. I hated him and never wanted to see him again. And then after he hung up I remembered his face and his smile and his touch. He couldn't be the kind of person who would say those things to someone he...someone he loved," she finished weakly.

Nick felt distinctly uncomfortable. He really hadn't expected to find himself neck-deep in dialogue that sounded like it was straight out of a bad soap opera. He didn't know what to say in return, which was all right, because Cathy wasn't expecting anything from him.

"At first I swore I wouldn't even call," she continued, as if oblivious to Nick's presence. Her eyes glinted darkly in the dim light but her face seemed as expressionless as her voice. "Then I decided I couldn't let it end that way. I had to see him, make him say...make him tell me to my face. I started to drive over here, then couldn't. But here I am."

She looked directly at Nick. Now there was open pleading in her eyes. "Maybe you could come over with me, just to...."

He shook his head.

"No," she said after a moment of silence, "you're right. This is between him and me. Nick," she said, caressing the name in such a way that he felt as if they had known each other for decades, "he talks a lot about you. He appreciates your friendship. He respects you. I hope that he hasn't turned on you as well."

Nick's silence was answer enough.

She squared her shoulders and turned away. Nick watched her until she disappeared into the darkness of Payne's porch.

He turned to go into his own house. He was exhausted. Sleep would come easily tonight.

He had not even reached his front door when she screamed.

He spun around in time to see a hideous blue glare illuminate Cathy's body. The unearthly glare threw the entire porch into a harsh brilliance that was terrifying in the clarity of the details it showed.

In an instant Nick could see that Cathy had rung the doorbell. From the way her body arched away from the house, yet her arm stretched stiffly toward a spot by the door jamb, Nick realized that her fingers must still be touching the old-fashioned round button Nick knew so well from delivering so many rent checks on the first day of so many months. He remembered the distant *buzzz* of the bell, the hollow silence as it died, the haunting sounds of The Greer as she opened the door.

Cathy never got that far.

The *buzzz* rose to a high-pitched crackling whine that Nick could hear even across the two front yards separating them. He saw the electricity flooding out of the buzzer and into Cathy, saw her body go suddenly limp, then twitch and jerk as if it had a life of its own. He saw her and knew that she must surely be dead and then the front door opened and someone—Payne, it seemed, although the figure was somehow wrong—nearly fell through it from inside and in the process knocked against Cathy and broke her contact with the buzzer.

Both bodies fell to the porch with a hollow thud. They rolled together in an excruciating echo of passion until they lay silent and still beneath the rusted porch glider. Nick could see no more movement.

By that time, he was halfway across the lawn. In another three seconds, he was on the top step of the porch, looking down at where Cathy and Payne lay intertwined in each other, arm twisting across leg, head resting on stomach in an obscene parody of love-making—obscene because this was a mingling of death, not a mingling of life.

The door-bell button glowed with a threatening iridescence.

Nick knelt beside the two bodies. The smell of scorched flesh hung heavily in the air. He could see that Cathy's hand was badly burned. Her fingers were twisted and blackened. The palm was already a mass of blisters swelling with body fluids rushing to repair the damaged tissues.

Something moved within the tangle of singed clothing and scorched flesh.

A hand that was unburnt. The fingers flexed, curled, and straightened.

It was Payne's hand.

Nick knelt and felt at Cathy's neck, shakily relieved to feel a pounding pulse. She was unconscious but alive.

By that time, Payne's eyes had fluttered open. His eyes were dull, his stare vacant, but his lips moved meaningfully.

"Tried to…," he said in a voice so feeble that Nick could barely distinguish the sounds. "Make her…stay away…couldn't control…save her…Cathy!"

The last sound rose into an anguished cry as Payne raised his head enough to see Cathy lying across him. He seemed to recognize Nick at the same instant, because his eyes suddenly brimmed with tears and he moved his hands as if he were struggling to raise Cathy but could not find the strength to do anything.

"Take it easy," Nick said. He carefully lifted Cathy's body

up, surprised at how heavy she felt even though she was inches smaller and pounds lighter than himself. Half-dragging her, he pulled her off Payne until she lay stretched out and silent on the porch.

By that time, Payne had raised himself onto his elbows and watched Cathy with anguished eyes.

"Is she...?" he began, then broke off as if he could not bear to hear the answer to his unspoken question.

"She's alive," Nick said, glancing over his shoulder along the visible portions of Greensward. No one moved. Not a single window showed even a glimmer of a light.

"I've got to get help," he said a moment later. "You stay here, I'll call the cops."

He stood and took a single step toward Payne's still open front door. He did not want to go in *there*—he would rather stick his naked arm into a pit full of furious cobras than walk beneath the thick oak lintel and into the black pit of the house... but lives might depend on him getting help as soon as possible. For once he tried not to think of himself. There was Payne to think of first, and Cathy.

He took another step.

"No!" Payne said, his voice tinged with terror and barely repressed fury. "Don't go in there. She'll.... It will…!"

Nick took one more step. He had made his resolve; he would keep it come hell or high water.

Payne struggled to his knees, his arms outstretched toward Nick. "For God's sake, Nick, *don't go in there*!"

"But I…."

Payne gestured with his hand. "Call from your place. I'm okay. I'll watch out for her."

Nick hesitated. After all, Payne's phone was tantalizingly close. It would only take a second and....

"Go, please. Believe me."

"Okay," Nick said, already pounding down the step and across the lawn. Less than two minutes later, he was running back, breathing heavily as he stood at the bottom of the porch steps.

"Ambulance should be here soon," he panted. "How is she?"

"Okay, I think," Payne said. He seemed to have recovered quickly. He was kneeling by Cathy, cradling her head with his arm, his hand against her neck as if to reassure himself that there was still a pulse.

"Let's get her down from here."

"But shouldn't we leave her where...?"

"Help me!" Payne said, and suddenly Nick was on the porch and helping to support Cathy's body as they carried her down the steps.

"This is far enough," Payne said after glancing over his shoulder. "I hope."

They laid her on the sidewalk halfway to the street. Payne pulled off his shirt and rolled it up and put it beneath her head.

She moaned faintly at the movement. Nick chose to believe that it was a good sign, a sign that she might be coming out of it. That she might survive.

Payne stood slowly and turned to face the house.

Nick listened for sounds of the ambulance, the fire truck that always accompanied it, the police cars that might even now be on the way. He heard nothing except the faint crackle of the power lines.

He looked up.

The line cut across the lawn not ten feet from them and disappeared into the corner of Payne's house. At that moment, he thought he saw a faint blue pulse at the juncture of house and wire.

He rubbed his eyes.

There was nothing there.

He turned to say something about it to Payne, but Payne was already moving up the sidewalk toward the house, slowly, stiffly, as if he did not want to go there but had no choice.

"Payne," Nick called. Payne said nothing.

"Wait here." Nick ran up to him and put his hand on the other man's shoulder. He felt muscles stiffen but Payne did not hesitate in his solemn stride toward the house.

"Come on, man. Cathy's hurt. She…."

"Leave me alone," Payne said quietly. "Leave me alone."

He shook Nick's hand loose and continued on his way.

Nick looked back at Cathy. She seemed little more than a light blur against the sidewalk. In the seconds it took for him to focus on her, Payne had mounted the porch steps and approached the front door.

For the second time in ten minutes, Nick made a conscious choice that went against everything he would have expected himself to do. Nick followed Payne onto the porch of The Greer's house.

Even before Nick was fully in the shadow of the porch, Payne had stepped inside the house.

Immediately, the texture of light spilling through door altered. It was as if all light had been simultaneously extinguished, replaced an instant later by the staticky blue-silver glow of the television screen.

Nick was across the porch and into the house before he had a chance to think any further about what he was doing. He had made his decision.

Inside, the air stank. He breathed a lungful of the foul stiff and almost retched, but then he saw Payne and forced his stomach to quiet. Payne stood in the center of the room, his attention fixed on the monitor. Nick glance at the screen. It was on. A picture flickered across the glassy surface. From where he stood, he could see the picture clearly.

It showed Cathy, her face distorted as though viewed through a fish-eye lens, her eyes slanted painfully tight, her mouth distended and her teeth curved like a vampire's. Blue fire flickered around her head, and even though there was no sound other than the static crackling of electrical pulses, Nick knew that she was screaming. The picture flickered and steadied, flickered and steadied, repeating like a tape replaying a loop, endlessly crucifying Cathy and then beginning again.

Then Payne cried out.

"No! I refuse!"

Nick wanted to ask what Payne was yelling about but didn't trust himself to speak because now through the darkened hallway he saw a ghostly outline. His stomach tightened and for an instant the blue-silver whiteness of the living room swam and Nick thought he might faint. Payne, however, stood straighter and taller than before and turned until he faced the figure straight on.

"Go ahead, old woman, try," he said, not raising his voice this time but instead speaking in an icy tone that frightened Nick more than theatrics and histrionics would have. The figure paused halfway down the hall, then continued its slow, inexorable forward progress. Nick backed away until his shoulders struck the door jamb but Payne remained where he was, standing in the center of the room later, Nick would have bet that it was the exact, mathematical center of the room. Payne glared at the apparition that was now only a few inches from the entry into the living room.

"Do your worst," Payne said again, his lips twisting into a sneer. "I know what you are now. I understand everything. And I won't let you get away with it."

At the sound of his voice, the figure paused again. One part separated from the rest, became identifiable to Nick as a hazy hand shape that passed in front of what gradually resolved into a head. Nick blinked. The figure looked like something one would see on a badly focused television, vaguely human but without any distinguishable features. Payne, however, seemed certain of who or what he was addressing.

"Get out of here," he said, letting his voice to rise until he was yelling. "I refuse to believe you. Get out!"

The figure lowered its hand and stepped into the living room. The light from the monitor struck it, suddenly endowing the form with weight and solidity and strength. Nick swallowed hard and tried to yell to Payne but no sounds would come.

The figure stared at Payne for a second. Nick half believed that he recognized the form, the twist of shoulder, the dragging foot he had glimpsed in the instant that the form left the hall shadows and entered the open light. Then the figure raised its hand again, but not to pass it in front of its own head like someone trying to clear his vision. Instead it pointed to each of the four cameras in turn. As the hand passed over Nick, he shuddered. His flesh prickled and the hairs on his arms and hands stood on end, like he remembered once when he was a kid, just before the great-granddaddy of all electrical storms hit. He didn't have time to remember anything else.

At the instant that the figure pointed to the last camera, the voice resonated through the room. For the first and only time, Nick Wheeler heard the voice of Death, and it chilled him beyond anything he could have imagined.

"You are mine," the voice intoned, gesturing directly at Payne. "You are me."

From each corner, a bolt of darkness flashed and converged on Payne. At the same instant, the figure flung a fifth bolt that struck Payne dead in the chest. His mouth opened in a cry of torment, but the sound was swallowed by the static crackle that rose and strengthened until it consumed everything and Nick could hear nothing else, not even the pulse-beat of his own heart as his blood throbbed through his temples. He saw nothing, heard nothing but Payne's agony and Payne's silent scream.

The beams of blue focused and tightened around Payne. Nick saw Payne's hand curl tightly against his leg, the fingers becoming claw-like, twisted, arthritic. *The fingers of an old woman filled with hatred and fear.*

"No!" Nick screamed, and then a wild pulse of electricity hit him and spun him out the door.

As soon as he was in the darkness, the power abandoned him. He rose shakily to his knees. Through the door, he saw the figure approach Payne and reach out to touch him. Nick could see the form within the nimbus more clearly. And even though he had never seen that face clearly before, he knew it in an instant.

Nick looked around wildly, searching for some way to save

Payne. In two frantic steps he was at the edge of the porch, kicking at the ancient timbers of the glider, feeling the wood give way beneath his feet, hearing the ripping sounds of half rotten fibers separating, and suddenly the glider crashed to the planking. He stepped on one of the seat timbers, bracing it beneath his feet, and pulled on another. The glider fell to pieces beneath his hands, leaving him with a yard-long length of jagged two-by-four that he hefted in his hand like it was a club.

He started toward the house, then stopped.

On an impulse, he grabbed the rusty chain that hung from the rafters and jerked. The chain had supported more weight than his for more years than he had been alive. But never all at once. Always before, both chains had held up their end of the glider and distributed the weight evenly. And never before had the weight come as a single sharp jerk. And maybe, just maybe, Nick yanked with more force than he would have guessed he had.

For whatever reason, the chain gave an anguished *screeee* and the eye-bolt holding it pulled from the rafter and the chain dropped with a crash onto the porch. One end flashed up and struck Nick on the shin but he didn't notice it, not even when the warm blood seeped through the gash. Dimly, as if part of him were merely an observer, he heard a distant sound that his brain identified as a siren. That same observer-part reassured him that probably less than two minutes had passed since he had called the police. But the intellectual assurance did little good.

Because Payne might already be dead.

Nick grabbed the chain and raced into the house, fully expecting to be met head on with a blast of current that would fry him in his shoes.

But he wasn't. Instead, he saw that the figure stood only inches from Payne's face. Payne still writhed in the twining force of the fields billowing through the camera lenses. His mouth was twisted in a horrifyingly silent scream, his eyes tightly shut as if by closing off vision he could close out the reality of what stood before him. His arms and shoulders were masses of muscle bunched against the effort of trying to break free and for an instant Nick was afraid that the figure—The Greer—would simply lash out and destroy Payne.

Then he understood in an intuitive flash that she would not. She *needed* him. *Needed* his body. Physically, at least, Payne Gunnison was safe.

The ghostly hand rose closer. The fingers were parodies of the twisted claw that hung uselessly at Payne's side. In another instant it would touch.

Adam and the finger of God In the Sistine Chapel Nick thought madly and then he lunged.

"Payne!" he yelled, hoping to break Payne out of the stasis that controlled him.

He hit Payne full in the shoulder and felt a ripping current tear through his own shoulder and chest, but at the same time, to Nick's immense surprise, Payne toppled over beneath him. The ghostly hand swept the air just over Nick's scalp. His skin crawled and he rolled away from the figure and onto his knees.

He swung at the figure with the board. It passed through unharmed, flames flickering along the splinters at the end. The figure shook with silent laughter and the four cords of current focused again on Payne where he lay groaning on the carpet.

Without thinking, Nick spun the glider-board like a javelin toward one of the cameras. The splintered end shattered the glass lens and the apparatus behind it exploded in a shower of sparks. One of the lines of light died.

But even before he saw the effect of his first attempt, Nick had spun to face another corner. He whirled the rusty chain once over his head. It passed through the figure, just as the board had done, but this time there was a difference. The chain did not emerge blackened and smoking. Instead, the figure seemed to part—temporarily, to be sure, *but it parted*—as the chain passed through.

He swept it around in a second full circle. This time the figure pulled back just enough for the end links to miss and hum uselessly through the air. The figure seemed to draw into itself, as if the touch of the metal had hurt it. Nick felt a flurry of exaltation.

It could be hurt!

He spun the chain, feeling it gain in speed and momentum until the three links he held in his palm pulled at the skin. There was a pinch and a sharp pain and he knew that a rough edge had sliced his palm—the rational observer-part wondered briefly about when Nick last had a tetanus shot but he whipped the chain around for a third time and let it fly.

Like a rattlesnake striking, the chain flew straight to the corner and in an instant disintegrated the second camera. The lens exploded, sending glass and sparks into the room. Part of the chain hung limply from the camera, the links vibrating and shivering, and then suddenly whipping back and forth in a shower of sparks that chittered and crackled and fell in a torrent of fire onto the carpeting and drapes, smouldering where the sparks landed, then setting the material aflame.

The figure twisted and howled in agony and writhed into the darkened hallway as the flames surged up and began licking at the white walls, at the paint, and at the internal wiring that had been so critical to The Greer's experiments.

But Nick didn't notice any of that.

As soon as the chain left his bleeding hand, he plunged sideways and grabbed Payne, who was struggling to stand. Behind them, in the third corner, the camera blew, spitting shards of glass that sliced through the bare skin on Nick's unprotected hands and arms. He was bleeding and so was Payne, but both men were functional.

Together, they crossed the room, ducking through the open doorway as the fourth camera burst, scattered even more sparks across the carpeting. Nick looked over his shoulder into the room, in time to see the television monitor explode in a snowstorm of glass shards and fractured tubes and melting wires. The explosion carried such force that it scorched the upholstery of the white sofa and fused the plastic table. One by one, the chess pieces—white as well as black—melted and slipped into the flames. The room burst into flame with a soft *whuumph* more frightening than a more violent explosion would have been.

They stumbled onto the porch and down the steps. A gust from the house caught the front door and slammed it behind them.

At the base of the steps, they stopped.

Lights bathed Greensward. Red lights and blue lights and white lights, stationary lights and lights that spun wildly into the night. The first of the lights pulled up in front of the house and dark forms disengaged themselves from trucks and cars.

For an instant, both men were blinded. They threw their arms in front of their eyes and felt the warmth of blood as it flowed across their foreheads and into their eyes.

"Cathy!" Payne cried.

He stumbled forward, almost falling, but reaching her at the same moment the first of the paramedics knelt at her side. Another caught Payne as he fell. Someone else—a fireman, maybe—grabbed Nick under the arm and propelled him away from the house just as the front windows blew out and showered the porch with glitters of pulverized glass.

Flames licked along the wooden rafters, and the leaves of the vines that had almost recovered the wildness that The Greer had fostered withered beneath the heat. The blast struck Nick full in the back and, in spite of the arm that tried to support him, knocked him to the ground. He struck his head against something hard.

CHAPTER FORTY-NINE

Nick woke to sensations of heat and a cacophony of sound.

Even before he struggled to lift the iron weights that hung over his eyes, he felt the heat on his face, on his arms and neck.

He heard voices as well, but could not distinguish any words.

He opened his eyes.

At first, he could not understand what he was seeing. There was only an indeterminate glare of red-orange framed in the middle of universal blackness. The glare seemed both immediate and distant. Since there was nothing else visible, he didn't know whether it was close or miles away.

He could feel its heat on his skin. It must be close.

A shadow blocked part of the glare and where the shadow fell on his skin, Nick felt a delicious coolness.

"He's okay. Not too bad," a voice said. Something touched Nick's wrist. A finger and a thumb. Someone checking his pulse.

With that perception, events pulled together and Nick tried to sit up.

"Take it easy," the voice said. "You got no breaks or deep cuts, mostly scratches and bruises, but don't try to move too fast."

Nick nodded numbly but continued moving until he was standing—a bit wobbly to be sure, but standing. His back rested against the side of the paramedics' truck. A man in a dark uniform hovered beside him, as if afraid that Nick would suddenly topple over and damage himself further.

Nick waved his hand, meaning the gesture to say *hey, I'm*

okay now, no problem.

The man in the uniform shrugged and moved away.

Nick closed his eyes for a moment. He felt all right. Stings from cuts, sure, and places where he felt like his ribs and arms and back had been hit with sledge hammers. His leg burned. There was an awkward bulkiness there. He looked down and saw the bandages that swathed him from ankle to knee. But other than that he was fundamentally okay.

He raised his eyes and looked around. Payne's house was engulfed in flames. The roof had fallen in and flames hurtled skyward through the emptiness where the attic had been. The cyclopean eye was gone; that part of the front wall must have toppled inward because the porch was burning but unlittered by debris.

Dark silhouettes flitted in the night between Nick and the fire, and he knew from their frantic attempts to fight the fire that he could not have been unconscious for very long.

He stood away from the truck and took a few steps. He was a little dizzy. Nothing that time and a long rest wouldn't cure.

At the edge of the street, a clot of dark figures huddled around something. They parted long enough for Nick to see two men standing on each side of a slim form sitting in the open doors of the ambulance. Someone else was standing in front of her, his back to Nick and his attention riveted on the woman being cared for my one of the paramedics. Nick recognized the woman.

Cathy!

He stumbled toward the ambulance.

"Cathy!" he yelled, oblivious to the fact that he barely knew the woman, that he had spoken to her only once.

At the sound of his voice, she looked up and started to call to him. He tripped on a fire hose and pitched forward. Someone grabbed him by the arm—careful to avoid the bandages plastered here and there on his skin like military badges of valor—and propelled him around one of the trucks into the relative calmness and quiet of the street. When his eyes got used to the dark, Nick looked around.

The street was clogged with fire trucks and police vehicles and news crews in—and in two cases *on*—vans. Beyond a fragile barrier of wooden barricades connected by yellow plastic ribbon, neighbors and strangers stared, some at Nick, others at the fire raging beyond him.

"Hey, man, you okay?" the man holding onto Nick's arm asked.

"Where's Payne? Mr. Gunnison?"

The man looked blankly and shrugged.

"The owner. It's his house that's burning."

Comprehension dawned and the man pointed back toward the knot of people standing where the ambulance had been only seconds before.

Nick studied the group. Yes, there was Payne standing next to Cathy. From this distance, and from what little Nick could see of him, he looked unharmed, other than a bandage across his forehead. Nick started across to him, then slowed and stopped. Payne looked well.

Too well.

Nick remembered seeing Payne in agony in the living room, remembered the flashes of current scouring Payne's body and whipping him around. Nick remembered the thing inside as it reached out to touch....

"Payne!" he yelled. Payne jerked his head up as if startled and stared for a moment.

Nick felt a chill begin at the base of his neck and ripple down his spine.

The clump of forms parted. Payne said something to Cathy and touched her on the shoulder and then turned away and walked toward Nick. He walked slowly, painfully, as if he hurt in every joint. But he didn't limp. He didn't shuffle or drag one leg behind him. His shoulders slumped, but it was the slump of utter, bone-breaking fatigue not of age or disease, and when Payne grabbed Nick's shoulders both hands were strong and steady, with fingers that were young and slender and strong.

"You all right?" Payne asked.

"Yeah. How's Cathy?"

Payne grinned suddenly—it was so unexpected that for a moment Nick's exhausted brain interpreted the movement as a grimace, a threat.

"She's going to be fine. Burns are mostly superficial. No concussion, they think. They're bandaging her hands now."

Nick wanted to say something but suddenly his well of words failed. So did Payne's, apparently, because they both turned as if with one motion and watched the firemen scurrying around the house.

Sometime during the fire, sparks had landed on the roof of the garage because it was burning strongly now as well. A line of hoses protected Nick's place on one side and the Harrisons' on the other.

Payne's house would be a total loss. That much was obvious to everyone. The sense of frantic effort diminished. The best the fire companies could hope for would be containment to only the two structures.

The two men crossed through the darkness and stood near where Cathy sat on a chair that neither of them recognized. One of the neighbors must have brought it out for her. It was a white aluminum chair with white webbing touched with blue. In the reflected glare from the fire, Cathy seemed sitting on cold flames.

Nick shivered and turned away. The three of them watched the fire for a long time. None spoke.

Gradually the flames died down. Gusts of sparks exploded as interior walls fell or rafters gave way, but the worst was over. Some of the spectators filtered away, enervated by the dying fire or exhausted by the late hour. One by one the camera crews departed, and several of the fire trucks.

Officials stood by Payne for long moments at a time asking questions in low voices. Payne answered curtly, with one- or two-word responses, often only shaking his head or nodding.

Several times, firemen or paramedics tried to persuade Cathy to go to the hospital and have the burns on her hand treated further. She held up her hand. The gauze wrappings glowed redly against the firelight. She shook her head resolutely. She refused to leave the yard on Greensward. Her eyes never left Payne, except when she allowed them to stray to the fire for a few seconds at a time.

Through it all, Payne watched the house as it died. Nick watched it, too. Neither Payne nor Nick nor Cathy grieved at the loss.

CHAPTER FIFTY

By dawn, the fire was dead. The first streaks of daybreak burning through the spiky fronds of palms further down Greensward revealed only charred remnants of the house and the garage. The lawn had burned for several feet from the house, and the rest of the yard was a mass of trampled grass mixed with ashes and water into a filthy quagmire. Deep tire marks scarred the ground.

Payne and Nick and Cathy had not moved all night.

With the coming of the dawn and the final last burst from the fire, there was time for more questions about how the conflagration might have started.

"Probably electrical," Payne said quietly to one of the questioners. "I'd been having some trouble with...with the wiring."

Then later, sometime around nine or ten, came a moment when Nick saw Payne grow tense. The three of them had moved over to Nick's porch. They had picked at a quick breakfast Nick threw together, sitting where they could see most of the house next door.

Payne stiffened when several official-looking people entered the rubble and began prodding at the water-soaked ruin. Payne got up from the porch and walked around the shattered walls, keeping the investigators in sight. Nick could tell that Payne expected them to find something at any moment.

The prospect obviously frightened Payne. He stood for more than an hour more, waiting and watching.

By that time, Payne was pale and trembling, on the verge of

collapse. The stress of the night, of whatever had happened to him inside that house, had finally caught up with him.

"Be right back," Nick said to Cathy. She nodded. She too was pale. Her hand hurt but she still refused to leave until Payne could come with her.

Nick went across the devastated yard and put his hand on Payne's shoulder; Payne jumped at the touch. Nick left his hand there and for a long time afterward, he felt a trembling that seemed to come from deep inside Payne.

"Hey," Nick said finally, "come on back to my place."

Payne didn't answer. He watched the investigators intently, waiting.

"Come on," Nick said again. "How about a cup of coffee or something."

Payne started to answer, but at that moment several figures emerged from the rubble. Their clothing was sodden with ash-blackened water. They conferred with other official-looking types on the ruin of Payne's lawn, then disappeared into vans and cars. One of the official-types separated himself from the others and came over to Payne.

"Sorry that we couldn't save anything, Mr. Gunnison," he said. He shook his head slowly. "The fire was too hot. There's nothing inside, nothing salvageable. Sorry."

Payne nodded. "We'll need to contact you later today...," the man began.

"He'll be next door. At my place," Nick said.

"Okay," the man said. And again, "Sorry."

He left.

"Let's go," Nick said, walking toward his place. Payne looked up, as if he were coming out of a trance, and stared at the ruin.

"He must have gotten out," he said softly.

"What?" Nick asked. "Who?"

"Uh, nothing," Payne said, turning away from the rubble.

He sat down on the wooden planks of Nick's porch and leaned his head against Cathy's legs. She ran the fingers of her uninjured hand through his hair. To Nick, it looked like a heartbreakingly tender moment for both of them. Neither spoke. Neither needed to.

Nick had plenty of questions to ask Payne, of course. And Cathy probably did also. Most likely Payne wouldn't be able to answer many of them. He had already suggested that there were great gaps in his memory over the past weeks, blank spaces filled only with fleeting, staticky images that he preferred not to think about.

But there would be time later on to dig deeper and discover as much of the truth as they could.

Time.

Nick glanced at his watch and noted with a mild sense of dismay that the calendar window read *August 1*.

What happened to the summer, he wondered to himself, shaking his own head as if he, too, were coming out of a trance. So much time had passed; he had so few memories of it.

Most of his reading lay untouched in his bedroom. But somehow he couldn't feel disappointed. The important thing was that Payne and Cathy were sitting together on his front porch, that they touched each other in ways that made Nick feel as if any previous suffering would be fully and fairly repaid by the happiness they felt at this moment.

Payne looked over at the ruins of the house, and for a second his face took on an expression of pain and loss and fear. He looked away, and in a moment or two, Nick heard him whisper something to Cathy: "I'm back to stay. I'll never leave you again. Ever."

Cathy leaned over and kissed him. This time it was Nick's time to look away.

But only for a little while.

ABOUT THE AUTHOR

MICHAEL R. COLLINGS is a Professor Emeritus at Seaver College, Pepperdine University, where he directed the Creative Writing Program for over two decades. He has published over 120 volumes of poetry, novels, short fiction, and scholarly studies of such contemporary writers as Stephen King, Orson Scott Card, Dean R. Koontz, and Piers Anthony. Recent works include *The Art and Craft of Poetry* (1996, 2009); *Toward Other Worlds: Perspectives on John Milton, C. S. Lewis, Stephen King, Orson Scott Card, and Others* (2010); *In Endless Morn of Light: Moral Agency in Milton's Universe* (2010); *In the Void: Poems of Science Fiction, Myth and Fantasy, and Horror* (2009); *Matrix: Growing Up West—Autobiographical Poems* (2010); and a Book of Mormon epic, *The Nephiad: An Epic Poem in XII Books* (1996, 2010)

He has been a frequent participant at literary, science fiction, fantasy, and horror conferences and symposia over the past quarter-century, and has served as Academic Guest of Honor at the World Horror Convention (2008); Special Guest of Honor at ConDuit (2008); Guest Scholar at EnderCon (2002); Academic Guest of Honor at MythCon XXVI (1994); Author Guest of Honor at HorrorCon '89 (1989); Poetry Guest at LosCon XXVII (1989); and Guest of Honor, Poetry Guest of Honor, Academic Guest of Honor, and Special Guest at various meetings of the Life, the Universe & Everything Marion K. "Doc" Smith Symposium on Science Fiction and Fantasy (1992-2010).

His fiction, also published through Wildside Press, includes:

The House Beyond the Hill: A Novel of Fear (2007); *Wordsmith, Volume One: The Thousand Eyes of Flame* (2009) and *Wordsmith, Volume Two: The Veil of Heaven* (2009); *Singer of Lies: A Science-Fantasy Novel* (2009); Wer *Means* Man, *and Other Tales of Wonder and Terror* (2010); *Three Tales of Omne: A Companion to* Wordsmith (2010); *Devil's Plague: A Mystery Novel* (2011); *The Slab* (2010), the story of a haunted tract house in Southern California…that consumes people; and *A Pound of Chocolates on St. Valentine's Day* (2011). His fiction is available in both print and e-book editions.

With his wife Judith, he has also published *Whole Wheat for Food Storage: Recipes for Unground Wheat* (2011).

He is now retired and lives in his native state of Idaho.

www.ingramcontent.com/pod-product-compliance
Lightning Source LLC
Chambersburg PA
CBHW022206030726
47494CB00021B/1582